Ordinary People

Part XV

Phil Boast

ISBN: 978-1-916732-24-7

Copyright 2023

All rights reserved. No part of this publication may be reproduced, stored in a retrieval system, or transmitted in any form or by any means, electronic, mechanical, photocopy, recording or otherwise, without prior written consent of the copyright owner. Nor can it be circulated in any form of binding or cover other than that in which it is published and without similar condition including this condition being imposed on a subsequent purchaser. The right of Phil Boast to be identified as the author of this work has been asserted in accordance with the Copyright Designs and Patents Act 1988. A copy of this book is deposited with the British Library.

i2i Publishing. Manchester.

www.i2ipublishing.co.uk

Contents

Chapter 1. Times of Uncertainty 5

Chapter 2. The Importance of Coffee and Biscuits 23

Chapter 3. The Rescue 45

Chapter 4. The Feminist Principle 65

Chapter 5. A Visitor, a Journey, and a Homecoming 87

Chapter 6. Concerning a Party, and the Buying of Olives 105

Chapter 7. Concerning the Manor House, and a Continuing Journey 135

Chapter 8. A Breakfast of Fried Rice 155

Chapter 9. A Witches Coven, and The Trials and Triumphs of Ross Farrier 177

Chapter 10. More than a Kiss 199

Chapter 11. The White House 219

Chapter 12. One More Secret 241

Chapter 13. A Homecoming, a Guilty Secret, and an Uncertain Future 259

Chapter 14. Of Idiocy and Irony 277

Chapter 15. Sex and Furniture 299

Chapter 16. A Possible Future 319

Chapter 17. A History Rewritten 349

Chapter 18. Singing in the Shower 371

Chapter 19. Unexpected Visitations 391

Chapter 20. Upon a Certain Day at Glebe House 413

Chapter 21. Life After Death 437

Chapter 22. A Greater History 459

Chapter 1. Times of Uncertainty

She took the key from its place beneath the loose stone in the wall, and opened the door to the old house. There was a musty, unlived-in smell about the place; no one had apparently been here for a while, despite the inner circle of witches having access at all times if it were needed. She opened windows, and set the kettle to boil for tea. There were used cups on the draining board, but otherwise little sign that anyone had been here during her absence. There was much to think about, and much to do, but today her soul and spirit breathed a deep sigh of relief to at least be alive, and to be here, when there had been times during her ordeal when she had wondered whether she ever would be here again. Later she would walk in her beloved woods, but for now she must see to her immediate domestic circumstance, bake bread and inspect the contents of her freezer to see what was there to be eaten. Charlotte on the whole gave little regard to that which she ate, so long as it was fulfilling, tasted well enough and provided sufficient nutrient, and there was as her inspection discovered enough food about the place to sustain her for now, until she next felt able and inclined to leave here, and buy fresh fruit and vegetables.

She showered, and changed her clothes, which in itself was a relief after the last days, and as she was kneading dough she began that which would be a long process of reliving all that had happened, and considering what might happen from here onwards.

Her infiltration into the sect had in fact and in certain ways been easier than she had anticipated; any stranger in the town of Headwater was a matter of consequence, it seemed, and she had been approached, and from there onwards it had taken all of her learned skill in understanding and controlling the minds and thoughts of others to see to it that she had undergone her initiation, and become one of their number. She had worked alone; the others, Maria, Sylvia, Amanda and

Rosalind would in the end have no part in it, and Sophia, who would have gone with her had she asked, she had not asked, and she had quickly become glad that she had made that particular decision. Where they all were now and that which had happened here during her time away was something she must find out, and whether indeed her unilateral actions would see to her replacement as the head of her coven. None of them was ready, or would be able to give sufficient of their time and energy to the task of taking her place, save Rosalind, whom she knew would replace her if she could, but Rosalind had ambition for its own sake, and would she was sure bring the wrong influences to bear on the inner circle, and from thence to the wider coven of witches. There would be a vote, she was certain, or at least all would say their piece and a conclusion and consensual decision would be reached, and she would likely have to fight her corner, and impart bad news as well as good, but still, that was not something for today. As her dough was rising she checked her telephone, which she had deliberately left here, and she had missed better than twenty calls, and had received about the same number of messages, which she would read and deal with in due course, but not today. As her loaves were baking she ate a simple meal; she was hungry, now, and a great weariness had come upon her, but she would not sleep, not yet. When her bread was done she put on her walking shoes and made for the woodland paths, and to the stream wherein lived small fishes, which would have lived out their small lives quite oblivious to all that had gone on since she had last been here, and she needed the thought of such simple and ignorant continuity. Some things were certain; having made her excuses and thus made good her escape, she hoped that she would never again have to return to Headwater; in that regard and in that place she had in all likelihood done all that she could, and the question that she must now address was, had it been enough to justify all that she had done, and all that she had put at risk? Could the mission that she had set herself that which now seemed so long ago be said to have been a success, or abject failure? She began the search for answers to these questions as she walked, and would continue to do so in the coming hours and days, but she was to her so great relief home, at least, and she had not been followed here, so she was safe, at least for now, and that was somewhere from which to start, was it not?

The domestic circumstances of the owner-occupier of number twelve, The Green, had of late undergone a sea-change, which had effectively happened over a single day. Reginald Pratt had hitherto throughout his adult years lived a life of domestic solitude, indeed in all regards had he lived so. He would see his sister on occasion, but otherwise had no surviving family, and had as good as no friends beyond the borders of the village which he had made and now called his home. This solitude, particularly since his retirement from his employment with the Local Council, had seen to it that Mister Reginald Pratt had become that which one may call rather set in his ways, and he had until still quite recently assumed that this would always be his lot in life. He had once tried keeping a dog, but as we have heard this did not work out well, and his attempt to see the point of walking somewhere for the sake of walking there had seen to his discovering a dead body in a stream, which had rather discouraged him from further adventures in this regard, and he had not in any case discovered the point. And so, he had gone back to his old ways, and in truth he had rarely indeed been overly discontented with his state of being, at least not manifestly so, having nothing else within the realm of his own experience with which to compare it. But then, following an episode of uncharacteristic domestic nihilism, which might be said to have made manifest a deeper malcontent, a now significant other had been paid to clean his house, and had thence entered the arena of his emotional being. This occurrence had made him see his life in whole new light, and perhaps ironically had put him in touch with an emotion of which he had barely been aware before, which was one of loneliness. But still, he was married, now, which was something else that he had not envisaged happening until just before it had happened, and she who was of significance and had entered said emotional arena had now entered his house, where from here on she would reside, and from here on, everything in this regard would be different.

Gwendolyn had bought little into her own new life in the material sense. She had during her long tenure in her already furnished, rented accommodation, bought a few items of furniture, which included a table and single chair, but she had not brought these with her; a house only needed one dining table after all, and there were more chairs now, so she was not sorry to leave these symbols of her own solitary life behind her. She had brought clothes, and one half of Reginald's only wardrobe and a chest of drawers had been vacated and set aside for her things, her things also extending to toiletries, so space had been allocated for these on the imitation marble sink-surround in the bathroom. And so, in the physical sense at least, Gwendolyn's few possessions had caused little disruption to a generally orderly household.

However and of course, with the possessions came the possessor, and the lady herself, and both parties to the new circumstance had now to adapt to living with the other, which was a different matter altogether. Gwendolyn was careful during these early days not to invade upon Reginald's private time, where he might sit quietly reading a book, or studying the inhabitants of his tropical fish tank with apparently enwrapped interest. She was ever conscious that it was she who was the invading force, and did not wish to invade any further or more quickly than was appropriate or necessary, given the necessity of her physical and material presence.

That which she did attempt to do, as quickly as she was able, was to acquaint and familiarise herself with others who lived in the village; a process which had begun on her wedding day, and would quite naturally begin with her closest neighbours. Reginald was some help in this regard, but there were apparent gaps in his knowledge, which Gwendolyn set about the business of filling as best she could. On one side of number twelve lived the Baxter family. Esmeralda Baxter was, as far as Gwendolyn had seen, a large and somewhat overbearing and rather coarse character, whereas her husband, Norman, was a slight and far more withdrawn individual, who displayed a far higher yet understated intellect and refinement than did his wife. Their son, Benjamin, was still at school, and his elder sister, Isabella, was about to begin her attendance at Cambridge University, but she had as yet had no interaction with either offspring. On the other side lived Alice Turner, mother to twin girls, whose father, Peter, lived at number eight, and they apparently shared the care of the children between them, the two girls living in either household at any given time. She would see Peter out on the village Green from time to time, teaching the girls ball games and such, and all seemed content enough with this somewhat unconventional arrangement.

The person with whom Gwendolyn was best acquainted was Meadow, and she determined to patronise the village delicatessen regularly, and to get to know her better. Meadow seemed to Gwendolyn to be little short of a beautiful, blonde-haired angel, who she knew had been instrumental in the practical matters pertaining to her marriage, and had in her quiet and understated way been the prime-mover in the wedding reception on the village Green on the day of her marriage to Reginald. Keith she had also come to know a little, the other witness to her marriage, and he who was currently in charge of the internal conversion of the old village church, at the behest of a rock musician, a gentleman called Ashley Spears, who had also attended the reception for a short time. Keith, it seemed to Gwendolyn, was beneath a somewhat rough and unkempt exterior another gentle and intelligent soul, and Gwendolyn had come to like him, also. So she was by degrees coming to better know the residents of the small and beautiful village in which she now lived, and that which she did not yet know about them she would come to know, in time, and the day that she had by her employer and quite by chance been given instruction to clean a certain house on Middlewapping village Green, now looked to her to be perhaps the most significant day of her life.

'What are you smiling at?'

Gwendolyn was seated at the lounge table, and Reginald was on the settee about the business of solving a cryptic crossword puzzle when he had glanced up and made his enquiry.

'Was I smiling? I didn't realise it.'

'Were you thinking about something?'

'Yes, I suppose I must have been.'

'Anything in particular..?'

'No, my dear, nothing in particular, just thoughts, you know?'

'Yes, I see. Would you like me to make some scrambled eggs for tea? I suddenly rather fancy scrambled eggs...'

'Yes, alright, only let me make them, you carry on with your crossword.'

'Oh, well, if you're sure...'

'Quite sure...'

She stood up and made for the kitchen, and the pan cupboard. Such a small, shared moment, the like of which would be the stuff of her life from now onwards, and which were a part of much bigger things, saw to it that Gwendolyn was still smiling as she broke eggs, and lit the gas on the cooker.

Two other people to whom Gwendolyn had yet to be formally introduced were Will Tucker and Emily Cleves, who no longer resided beside the village Green, or in the housing estate into which they had both been born, but now passed their days at Jacob's Field, a smallholding, which was for the most part run by Emily, and which was situated just outside the village bounds. At this point in our tale, however, Will and Emily are on vacation in the country of Turkey, a country which Emily in particular had long held ambition to visit. Prior to their departure, they had decided that they would stay in accommodation which Emily would describe as 'posh' somewhere in central Istanbul, the hot, bustling city in the north western most part of the country. They had not made any reservation, on the basis that this holiday was to be an 'adventure', and as much would be left to chance as possible. Their much-delayed flight had at last landed in the late evening, and they had taken a taxi from the airport, and asked the driver to find them a good hotel. This had proved more difficult than they had anticipated, however, since the driver spoke virtually no English, and the conversation had gone along the lines of;

'Hotel, please...'

'Hotel what...?'

'Don't know, no reserve...Expensive...Hotel good....Good location...'

The driver, who was large and of somewhat surly countenance, had sort of nodded and shaken his head at the same time, and proceeded to take them on that which seemed to them to be a tortuous and serpentine route through the city, pointing out places of interest along the way, such as *'City Wall'*, and *'Sultan Ahmed Mosque.'* This was all very well, but both passengers were tired, and keen to see the end of their journey, and the entrance to a hotel, and in any case they were paying for the taxi. Will decided that something must be said, and for now it had better be said in hushed tones.

'He's taking the piss, Em, we're going miles in all different directions…'

'Yes, we do seem to be…'

Emily had been spokesperson thus far, but now Will leaned forward and intervened.

'Hotel…..'

'Yes, hotel…'

Which appeared to make little or no difference to the situation, and Will became worried.

'What's going on, is this guy okay do you think?'

'I don't know…'

At this juncture, the driver pulled over at the roadside; they were by now in a barely lit backstreet, with no hotel in evidence, and little evidence of anything else which would give them encouragement. The driver left the vehicle and walked to a group of equally surly-looking men, who were seated in conversation and playing a card game around a table, and all attention was now on the taxi, and the two passengers therein.

'Oh great, now we're going to get turned over.'

'What do we do…?'

'Well we can't exactly run, our bags are in the boot…Shit, this is a bad situation, Em…Welcome to Turkey.'

After a few moments, during which time talk around the table was very evidently about them, the driver walked back to his taxi. He carried something in both hands, and rapped with a hard object as best he could on the rear window next to Emily.

'What should I do, Will?'

'Open it, I suppose, my door's not locked so if it turns nasty I'll punch him on the nose and we'll leave that way.'

'Okay...'

Emily opened her window, and the driver leaned in, and handed each of them a small glass of steaming liquid.

'Tea....'

'Tea....?'

'Tea....'

The driver now smiled for the first time, a large, beaming smile, and returned to his friends, who Will and Emily now surmised were probably other taxi drivers. A sense of relief now permeated the back seat of the taxi, the tea was sweet, and refreshing to tired minds and pallets, and Will was the first to speak.

'Well that was...Interesting...'

'Do you know what I think he's been doing?'

'Do tell...'

'Taking us on a city tour...'

'What...? It's pitch-black and nearly midnight.'

'Even so, I reckon that's what he's been doing.'

'We had him all wrong, didn't we?'

'Looks that way....'

The quite delicious tea having been drunk and the glasses returned, the journey continued, and within minutes they pulled up on the frontage of a quite fine-looking hotel. The fare was moderate, and perhaps out of relief that his fears had proved unfounded, and the fact that the journey had taken somewhat over an hour, Will offered a large tip, which was returned by the driver with a shake of his head. Bags were removed from the boot, the driver spoke to the hotel porter, the taxi departed, and with some relief Will and Emily walked through the cool and airy hotel reception to the desk, where smart receptionists awaited them, who were one male and one female.

'Hello, do you speak English...?'

'Of course...'

'Do you have a double room available?'

'Of course, how many nights will you be staying with us?'

'Ummm…We're not sure, yet, probably two.'

The formalities taken care of, Will and Emily were shown to their third-floor room and their bags duly delivered, whilst Will set the kettle to boil for coffee. It was by now well after midnight, and the bed invited, but both needed a little time to process their first experience of Turkish hospitality, which had begun with a taxi driver.

'Well, lover-boy, we're here then. I'm going to take a shower.'

'Yeah, me too…Em, what's the hotel called?'

'What…?'

'You know, the hotel we've just booked into, what's it called?'

'I don't know, I'm so tired I forgot to look…'

'Yeah, me too in all the excitement of actually getting somewhere…'

'Well, it's a nice room, anyway, and it's a bed for the night.'

'Sure, we'll take care of the details in the morning, then, like where on earth we are, that kind of thing.'

'Yes, let's do that…Anyway I need a drink, what's in the mini-bar?'

Will opened the refrigerator and unscrewed two bottles of Scotch. They touched bottles.

'Well, here's to adventures, then, William, my love.'

'Yeah, looks like that part's already started.'

Whatever the hotel may be called, which would be ascertained the following morning after a good night's sleep, it had four stars after its name, and their room enjoyed partial views over the city to the Bosphorus, the busy, always turbulent and oft-times controversial waterway which separates the continents of Europe and Asia. Emily had rather pushed the agenda of this vacation, on the basis that Hebe, their occasional and now trusted help, would only be available to take charge of their smallholding and goat farm during the summer school recess. Will had quite easily obtained unofficial leave of absence from Keith for two weeks from the contract at Glebe House, on the basis that much of the work was for now in the hands of specialist subcontractors, and so here they were. The plan was to spend two or so days in the city, acclimatising and seeing whatever sites may be there to see, before heading out in a hired car on a road trip, which would see them headed to and along the south coast, returning to Istanbul via central Turkey. They could not guarantee the quality of their accommodation from here on, and nothing was booked, since they had no idea where they might be on any given day, so Emily had decided that they should live in comfort at either end of their adventure, and the taxi driver had in the end understood them well enough.

As we now join them on the first full day of their vacation, they are drinking tea at a small café outside a spice bazaar, having spent the morning visiting two Mosques and a palace, and both had needed the refreshing beverage.

'There's a lot to see, Em....'

'I know, we'll never pack it all in....I think the Blue Mosque is my favourite so far, I mean I know it's been reconstituted and it's a museum now, and it's not the biggest, but I thought it was more beautiful than the other one.'

'I think you mean deconsecrated, and that's a shame, in a way, it's kind of lost its spirit, but that's progress, I guess. It was a Christian church originally.'

'Yes, I know, and I bet that wasn't a peaceful handover.'

'No, probably not...'

'Anyway, I'd like to go on a boat-trip.'

'Sure, if we've got time.'

'Still, whatever, I think it's wonderful just being here, don't you, just kind of soaking in the atmosphere of the place, it doesn't really matter what we do.'

'So, it's agreed, we leave the day after tomorrow, yes?'
'Yes, let's stick to the plan, as far as it goes.'
'Sure…Anyway, you hungry..?'
'Starving…'
'Okay, let's find some street food, do a couple more mosques or whatever, then head back to the hotel. We can sort out a hire-car from there.'

Percival was safe. Her powers of influence and persuasion had as good as certain seen to that, at least, whereas prior to her involvement with the sect he had in any final reckoning been a marked man. Now, however, the blame for all that had occurred rested firmly on the shoulders of Rebecca, and over that she could have no influence, and in this at least she had failed, and if Rebecca were to be protected henceforth then this matter rested with the witches, and with her coven. They had rendered Percival unconscious, and he was to be driven to and abandoned somewhere; she could not see to his avoidance of that punishment for his prior actions, as far as they were known, but that would be an end to it, and she had seen to it that he would awaken to water and painkillers, whereas had things been different, and had she not been there to intervene, he may not have awoken at all. He had done all that she had instructed or advised by means of her covert and cryptic notes, and by some means he had come to know that she was there at his abduction, and this she hoped would have been some comfort to him. In any case he had taken the tranquilizer with no resistance, one final act of absolute trust in her, so in this at least she had succeeded, although his condition and state of mind on awakening would have been far from tranquil, she was sure. Percival had found his way to the white house in search of her, and his visit had been the catalyst for all that had occurred since. Her heart had gone out to him for all that he had endured since his involvement with Rebecca, and he it was who had unconsciously and finally persuaded her that something must be done; that she must somehow try to better understand all that had happened, and bring such influence as she could to bear on that which would happen from here on. To this end she had put herself in great danger, she saw this with absolute clarity, now, but she could see no other way, and as she sat now beside the stream and watched the small fishes as they went about their innocent business, she hoped that Percival's ordeal had not been too harsh, and that he had found his way quickly back to safety. She would look for him, when the time was right, but not yet, and at least he too could go home now and live his life, and of this Charlotte was glad.

After their third night in Istanbul, and following two days of quite intensive discovery of this so historically significant city, Will and Emily checked out of their hotel, the name of which they had by now discovered. They had liked the hotel, which was indeed conveniently located, and had decided that they may as well stay here again on their way home.

'We'll be back in a couple of weeks, we're driving to the south coast and back.'

This statement met with disbelieving expressions from the reception staff, and with no comment, which was not encouraging for the two intrepid travellers. This was quite early morning, and Will and Emily had arranged to pick up their hire-car at the earliest available time, in order to put some long miles behind them by the day's end. Their aim was to arrive in Izmir, a large town on the west coast, by the evening, spend the night there, and from there make the south coast by the end of the following day. Their first challenge in this respect was to make it through the city and out onto the open road, with Will driving and Emily navigating, and this proved challenge enough for their first experience of driving here, where the rules of vehicular engagement were somewhat different from those which they were used to. Stationary queues of traffic waiting at traffic lights were a cacophony of noise and horn-blowing, with every driver seeming to compete for every inch of forward progress for no particular reason that Will and Emily could see; when the lights changed seconds became valuable, and upon this Will saw fit to comment.

'Christ, what's the rush, no one's going to get anywhere any quicker by making a lot of noise about it. I mean look at that guy, he's trying to cut in, what's the point?'

'I don't know, just be all polite and English about it, we'll be fine.'

'Hmmm…Anyway at this rate we'll be lucky to get out of the city today.'

'Don't worry, Will, it doesn't matter how far we get. We're on holiday, and if we don't make it to Izmir we'll find somewhere to stay along the way. Find your Zen-like place…'

'Yeah, I guess…'

In the event the ever-chaotic traffic became lighter as they traversed the outskirts of the city, Emily had found them to the right road, heading south, and from there onwards their progress became quicker, albeit that the road was often in less than perfect condition. After three hours of driving past towns and smaller settlements in otherwise dry and open countryside, they stopped at a somewhat unprepossessing roadside café, where the proprietor made them welcome, and they dined on mezze and more of the sweet tea which seemed to be served everywhere. The food was delicious, and having ascertained where they were, and having consulted their online map on Emily's 'phone, they found that they had in fact made quite good progress.

'You know,' said Will 'we might actually do this, if the road and traffic don't get any worse than this.'

'Well, we'll see, but we're doing okay so far.'

'The car's performing well anyway, I'm glad we upgraded.'

'Yes, that was a good move.'

By the early evening they had reached their intended destination, and by now both were exceeding tired from the long drive.

'Right, well there's the sea, so I guess we're here. Start looking for hotels.'

They stopped outside a small and comfortable-looking establishment.

'This'll do, don't you think?'

They secured their room via a friendly receptionist who spoke sufficient English, and the room was basic but comfortable, and at least had air conditioning. They showered and ate in the small hotel restaurant, which offered only local food, which they ate with relish, as they were both hungry. By mid-evening they had retired to their room, showered again, and were abed before the hour of ten o'clock, their tiredness being met in equal measure by the sense of excitement engendered by this part of their holiday.

'This is fun, Will....'

'Yeah, going okay so far...We'd better get up and at it tomorrow, though, it's about the same distance to the next place.'

'Where is the next place?'

'I don't know, you're the navigator, I'm just the driver.'

'So how do you know how far it is, then?'

'I'm taking a wild guess. We're about mid-way down the country, so, you know...'

'Yes, I know. Well let's just see how far we get, we can decide where to stop when we get there.'

Will yawned.

'I hope we make the south coast by tomorrow evening, the Aegean Sea is calling, or is it the Med?'

'I'm not sure where one starts and the other finishes.'

'Anyway, I'm knackered...'

'Well, go to sleep then, you've had a long day. Whatever sea it is will still be there tomorrow.'

She pressed her body against his, and closed her eyes, but Will was apparently not yet asleep.

'William, what are you doing, I thought you were tired.'

'I was, I am, but I seem to have come over all unnecessary all of a sudden.'

'Hmmm...Well don't keep me up all night, it's you who wants the early start in the morning, if we're to get to where we don't know where we're going yet.'

'Live for the moment, that's what I say.'

'It's not what you said just a minute ago.'

'Yeah, philosophy's a funny old thing...'

So what then of Rebecca? She was living in the town, now, or so Charlotte assumed, and was doing well enough with her child and her ceramic work, but for how long could she keep her location a secret from them? Percival had clearly been lying when he had said that he did not know where she was, and that had been a critical moment of the interview, but the lie had been believed, the moment had passed, and she had not needed to intervene. So she must also see Rebecca, and warn her, and from now on she must keep herself better hidden, else they would find her in the end. Rebecca's past and her past actions were close behind her now, and her desire for a life more ordinary was if anything farther away than ever. The coven had a duty to protect her; such things had been enshrined in the philosophy and doctrine of the coven since now distantly historic times, and Rebecca had a daughter, now, the latest in the line of Jane Mary, who would also come under this protection, regardless of anything that anyone of the inner circle may think or say to the contrary. So this was also a critical time in the deep history of the coven of white witches; that which happened from here on would be of absolute significance as a precedent to the whole of its future, one way or the other, and if the others would not act then she must continue to act alone, and if this were to be so then so far as Charlotte was concerned the coven would cease to have any deeper meaning; it would exist only for the sake of its day to day existence, and nothing more.

So then, there was much to do and to consider, and she must call a meeting, but not yet. She was exhausted after her long ordeal, and above all else needed time for her thought processes to find their way to some sort of conclusion and resolution as to where to go from here, literally as well as metaphorically. How much time this would take she could not yet be certain, and she could not be long about it, but today was for today, and she was home. She stood up, breathed in the warm, woodland air, and made her quiet and contemplative way back to the white house; to bread and to comfort, and from thence to a far less certain future.

Chapter 2. The Importance of Coffee and Biscuits

It was a working morning, and Keith had not long been about his business at Glebe House, organising sub-contractors and deciding on his and Damien's work for the day, when his mobile telephone rang. He did not recognise the number, but answered the call; one of his suppliers, perhaps, but it was not one of his suppliers, and the person who spoke was about the last person of his acquaintance that he would have expected to hear from.

'Yeah, Keith, it's Percival.'
'Hi, what's up, man?'
'Do you have wheels?'
'I've got Will's Land Rover for a couple of weeks whilst he's away, why?'
'I need you to do something for me, a big favour, actually.'
'Sure, whatever…Are you okay, you sound kind of cranky, are you in some sort of trouble?'
'Well, that's relative term, but you might say so.'
'Right, so, how can I help?'

'Hi Batty, it's me…'
Barrington was at home, going about his usual evening affairs, when his telephone rang, and it was his youngest sister.
'Hi Maisy…Everything okay..?'
'Yes, I think so, mega busy as always, but I'm holding it together, I think. Anyway, reason for the call, I might be staying over at yours tomorrow night, if that's okay.'
'Sure, of course, you don't have to ask, and in fact usually you don't.'
'Thought I'd surprise you by not surprising you…So you're not cohabiting with the strange yet lovely Sandra yet then?'

'We haven't quite got to that stage, not weekdays anyway. So any particular reason for the visit..?'

'Yes, well Anna, that's Anna Merchant, our director, has decided it would be a good idea if we all meet at the Manor House, that is at least the main actors and some of the crew, maybe, just to get a feel of the place, you know? I mean everyone's still learning lines and such, so we're quite a way from anything serious happening there, acting-wise, but his Lordship's given the okay, so it looks like it's going to happen.'

'I see, well fine then, I'll see you tomorrow.'

'Okay, no idea what time yet, but you'll be at work anyway, so I'll probably be there when you get home, all being well. I'll cook if there's any food around.'

'Sure, whatever...'

There would be food around, which May would probably not cook, but Barrington looked forward to seeing his sister in any case, as he always did.

That which soon became clear to Percival was that his unconscious form had been unceremoniously deposited at about the most isolated place that southern England had to offer, deliberately so, he was sure, and this indeed assumed that he was in fact in southern England. In any case, as he walked, still somewhat uneasily, downhill from his elevated place of awakening, distant, isolated farmsteads were the only visible form of human habitation. He supposed that he could walk to one of those, but they were some distance away, and probably better to head downwards to a road; there was as good as certain to be a road through the valley, and where there was a road, there would be passing vehicles. It was also the case that water tended to follow gravity, and water was his primary concern, and he was more likely to find it there. He could see no river, but there should at least be a stream, or at the very least standing water.

It occurred to Percival as he walked that his situation was rather like that of a feral animal, and a lost feral animal at that, no longer concerned with the finer points of life, but rather with the business of survival. He had brief visions of his body being found by the wayside by a passing pedestrian, perhaps one month hence, but these visions were fleeting and academic; this would not be the death of him, he was sure, but he must take his present predicament seriously. His head still throbbed, he had only enough water remaining with which to take his next dose of painkillers, and he was far from restored to his full strength after his ordeal. He rested at intervals, during one of which he took tablets and finished his water, but by slow degrees he finally found himself on more level ground at the valley floor, where a brook ran beside a single-track road. He now sat by the brook, refilled his bottle and drank thirstily, and took stock of his situation. He could walk along the road, which was level terrain at least, but he had no sense of which way he should walk, or how far it would be until he came across the first human abode. He was desperately tired, now, the light was fading rapidly with the setting sun, and rainclouds had begun to gather at the valley's head. No, to attempt to walk very much further in his current condition and in darkness would be a mistake, so the only alternative was to find such shelter as he could, rest for the night, and continue his journey in the morning. Reluctantly and with some effort he stood up, walked in a certain, uncertain direction, until after another half an hour or so and to his great relief he saw a building by the roadside. It was a small, mostly derelict stone-built construction, too small to be any kind of a cottage, so perhaps it had once been a shepherd's hut or silo for storing grain, although there were no arable fields hereabouts, this was livestock country. In any case whatever had once been its use it was a building, which upon entering where once would have been a door, he found to be partially roofed in slate, and there was sufficient open floor space upon which a lost and weary traveller might lay his head. The floor was of broken, cracked but adequately sound concrete, and Percival sat down with his back against the stone wall, drank more water from his plastic bottle and smoked his last but one cigarette. This was better. He had not yet found his way back to civilization, or food, or any means of buying food if he came across any, and hunger now gnawed at his stomach, but he had a roof over his head, of sorts, and there was a road; to this degree at least had he improved his circumstances since awakening from whatever he had been given to drink, that which now seemed like a long time ago. There was some clearly old and partially – rotted hessian sacking to one corner of the building, and with this he fashioned some sort of mattress and pillow, upon which to lay his still aching head. He took off his jacket and lay it over him, to afford him some warmth during the cold night ahead, and fell quickly into deep and dreamless sleep, just as the rain began to fall.

'So, at what time do we expect the invasion, then?'

Lady Beatrice had bought herself and his Lordship their morning coffee and digestive biscuits, and returned to the marital bed, a place of some historical significance, since it had witnessed the conception of all three of their children. Nowadays however it was coffee, made with milk, and digestive biscuits, the milk being a concession allowed after negotiation, and the biscuits being limited in their number in the interests of his Lordship's continued health.

'Hmmm…? I'm not certain, sometime this morning I would think.'

'Couldn't they be more specific?'

'Well they said mid-to late-morning, but you know how these things go, trying to get several people together at one place, and most of them being actors at that. I don't think we really need to get involved, Victoria took the day off specifically to be here, and I want her to take over the reins, so to speak. I think it's more of an orientation exercise at this stage, but we'll see.'

'Yes, we will…I still have my severe reservations about all of this, you know.'

'Yes, I know, my dear, and I haven't signed off on it yet, not officially anyway, I can still stop it if you want.'

'Don't be silly, it's far too late for that now, Victoria would never forgive me.'

'Well, there is that…She's been a bit off the last few days, don't you think, even by the standards of our beloved daughter?'

'I don't know, I can't say I've noticed anything in particular.'

'No, well perhaps I've become overly sensitive to her state of being in my old age, but I can usually tell when something's troubling her, which is most of the time, so it's probably nothing out of the ordinary. I'll keep an eye on things.'

'Well, she certainly won't open up to me, she never has. Anyway who's coming today, do we know?'

'Victoria ran through the names with me again last night, there's…'

'I know their names, Michael, I was wondering which of them were coming, that's all.'

She knew their names, of course; she would no doubt have taken time to research them as well, despite her severe reservations.

'Well Anna Merchant, of course, she who instigated the meeting, and she was hoping to get the four main players here, I believe. Whether David Bates will put in an appearance is a moot point, this meeting in particular is more to do with directing than producing I daresay, and I expect May Thomas will attend.'

'She who made the first contact, however that came to be...'

'Apparently she has a brother who lives in the village or some such, Victoria knows the details of it.'

'Well, I've asked Susan to come in early and help Molly do a clean-up.'

'Really...? I wouldn't have bothered, once this starts in earnest I daresay any cleaning up we do will be fairly academic.'

'Nevertheless I want the place to look at its best.'

'Well whatever you say, my dear. Are you going to eat those biscuits?'

'What...?'

'You haven't eaten your biscuits...'

'Oh go on then, you can have them, I suppose.'

'Thank you, I daresay nobody ever died as a result of eating a couple of extra digestives...'

'No, I daresay not.'

Percival awoke in the chill, dim light of the morning, his mouth and throat feeling as though he had not drunk in days. He sat up, drank the remainder of his water, which tasted somewhat organic but it was water, at least, sat against his wall and took stock of the situation. His head at least had more or less ceased to ache, the last effects of whatever he had been given had apparently been dealt whilst he slept, so that was something, and perhaps from now onwards he would be able to think more clearly, once he was fully awake and had regained complete control of his faculties. He urinated in the corner of his shelter, and looked out onto a somewhat overcast morning. It had rained overnight, and the sun had not yet risen over the hilltop; out there in the civilised world where time had meaning it was probably around five or six o'clock; he had slept well, and long. He put on his jacket, sat down on a pile of stacked slates which had once been constituent of the now missing part of the roof, and lit his last cigarette. He noted that his hands were shaking, whether from the cold or lack of food, or reaction to his recent experience he couldn't tell, but it was likely all of these things in combination, with some caffeine withdrawal thrown into the mix; he would at this moment pay quite a lot of money for a double espresso, if he had any money to pay with.

So, what to do from here? He could get more water, and the fact that he was more hungry than he could ever remember being was an inconvenience, for now, and nothing more. After this he was out of cigarettes, and something would have to be done about that, and as soon as was possible. All that he could do, he supposed, was to walk the road in one direction or the other, on the assumption that eventually he would come upon a house, or a farm, and could present himself at someone's front door. Quite how he would explain himself and his condition was something he would have to give thought to, but that was something which he would deal with when he came to it, first he had to come to it, and that was not yet a given.

He stood up, stretched some life back into his unwilling limbs, and walked out into the damp, cold morning. He refilled his water bottle from the stream and set off in the direction that he had been walking when he had found his shelter, looking back once to better commit the place to memory; had he not happened upon the small and now apparently forgotten building, his night would have passed in a very different way. The place had served a purpose which would not have been anticipated during its construction.

He walked for perhaps an hour, seeing nothing alive except grazing cattle and a few frightened deer which ran to the hills upon seeing him, a reaction which he could readily understand, but then he saw her. A woman in her forties, he presumed, walking toward him in distracted manner, a dog which Percival assumed to be a Labrador of advanced years walking quite slowly a few paces ahead of her. She saw him, from a distance of perhaps a hundred metres, and slowed her pace. An early morning dog walker, such a simple, ordinary thing, and a woman, which Percival considered to be unfortunate; her instinctive reaction on seeing a man on that which was probably her regular walk, coming apparently out of nowhere and looking as he must currently look, would likely not be a good one. She was dressed in a light-blue raincoat and green Wellington boots over slacks, and as they approached one another, he could see she also wore an uncertain and suspicious expression, which was something else that Percival could understand well enough, but at least she had not turned back on seeing him. So, smile then, Percival, look harmless, and try to look as though nothing in particular was happening, and see how this encounter would play out from there.

Victoria Tillington was in a self-imposed state of alertness and readiness during this particular morning; she knew that her father wished her to be the main representative of the Manor House from here on, and it was a role which she was more than willing to take on, even if, as she anticipated, it would entail her using her allotted annual leave from the gallery to do so. There was nowhere that she particularly wished to go, and no one in particular to go anywhere with. There were others at the gallery who took vacations together, and she had on occasion received invitation to join them, but she had always thus far declined, and they no longer asked. In any case Rebecca was now living in the village, and her situation would need resolution, little Henry would soon begin the new regime of living sometimes at Glebe House, and the news that Alexander had been bewitched, and that this bewitchment had caused his death was something with which she had not yet come to terms. So Victoria had no plans to travel, and she needed the distraction of this new project more than ever, now, which was in any case something well worth the taking time off from work for, and today was the beginning of that. It was also the case that she and her father had agreed that as far as possible, her mother should be prevented from taking on any kind of significant or dominant role in proceedings, and so it was that Victoria was seated on her step, drinking coffee and smoking a cigarette when the first of the cars drove through the Manor House gates and up the long, gravel driveway. The car stopped in the wide, sweeping parking bay in front of her, and May Thomas emerged and walked towards her, and the two women smiled.

'Hi, Victoria…May I call you Victoria?'

'Well, that's my name…'

'Okay, well I thought I'd better ask.'

'And now you have, and of course you may.'

'Great…I thought I'd better be the first to arrive, you know, since nobody knows anyone else.'

'Indeed…I haven't met anyone yet. So who's coming?'

'Everyone important apart from Graham Dean, who's still filming on location in Switzerland, but he'll be ready when the time comes, so we've got David Blake, Maurine O'Connell and Ursula Franks, and Anna's bringing one of our set people, I think. Everyone should be arriving within the next half an hour.'

'Okay, well, would you like some coffee?'

'I'm fine, thanks, but do you mind if I join you for a cigarette?'

'Please do.'

May sat down beside Victoria.

'I don't usually smoke, but I'm really excited by all of this, and a bit nervous for some reason.'

'Well, it is an exciting project, from both of our perspectives.'

'I'm glad you think so...Oh bloody hell, someone's already here, I think this is Anna. No time to chat, then, sorry...'

The second car now made the journey from the gate, and Anna Merchant and two men now approached the steps as Victoria and May stood up and walked to greet them.

'Hello...'

'Anna, this Victoria, who'll be our main go-to person from now on...'

The two women held hands briefly.

'I'm pleased to meet you, the daughter of the household, I believe.'

'Yes, that's me, and I'm glad to meet you, too.'

'I've brought Clive with me, he's to be our artistic director, and Paul's one of our technicians, so you'll be working quite closely with them initially, before the actors arrive on set.'

The introductions were made, and within the next ten minutes three more cars arrived on the scene, bringing with them Maurine O'Connell, David Blake and Ursula Franks, faces and people who hitherto had been characters on Victoria's television or cinema screen, here now in the flesh, and perhaps for the first time the whole of this venture became something real in Victoria's mind. All were casually dressed, but even so they had a certain presence, and all of them took a few moments to take in the exterior of the Manor House whilst introductions were completed. Last to meet Victoria was Maurine O'Connell, who looked even slimmer and more voluptuous in real life than she appeared on screen, and to Victoria's eyes every bit as beautiful.

'This is a lovely house, I'm sure I will look forward to working here.'

'Thank you, and well, I'm pleased to meet you.'

'Yeah, this looks like the kind of place where scandal and intrigue would go on.'

This was David Blake, a tall man of rugged good looks and obvious charisma.

'We'll be taking the whole thing back a few hundred years, of course, but I bet it's no different now, is it?'

'You'd be surprised, and you probably wouldn't believe me if I told you.'

They smiled; distraction indeed, and so it had begun. Not all of the actors had met before, and for a moment amidst the general noise of conversation Victoria found herself somewhat overwhelmed by so auspicious a gathering.

'Well, I suppose we should all go inside, then, please follow me.'

She was walking to the side of the narrow road which would best face oncoming traffic, if there was any oncoming traffic to face, and Percival had noted that he had not seen or heard a single vehicle pass during waking hours in his refuge. In any case he was careful to stay on the opposite side of the road as they neared one another, and his first encounter was in fact with her dog, which came to greet him and allow him to rough the animal around the neck and head. So, speak then Percival, and keep it light and conversational.

'Good morning...'

She did not speak, and she continued walking, so it fell upon Percival to further his monologue.

'Look, I wonder if you could spare a moment, this isn't how I'm sure it appears, I assure you I'm quite harmless.'

Whether it was his words, or the way that they had been spoken, or perhaps she trusted the instincts of her dog more than she trusted her own, but she slowed her pace almost to a stop, and Percival noted a subtle yet discernible softening of her expression.

'That's what they all say, isn't it?'

So, the lady had a sense of humour, then, which Percival considered to be another positive, and he did his best to smile, although she did not. He also decided that a bit of honesty would be the best policy.

'Truth of the matter is I'm in a spot of bother. I find myself with no telephone, no money, and no way of getting to where I want to be. In fact if I'm quite honest, I've no idea where I am.'

She had stopped by now, but both kept a safe distance between them.

'Oh dear, that is unfortunate.'

She had a pleasant voice, but Percival could not place any particular accent.

'Indeed, and I won't bore you with how I found myself in such a situation, but I could do with some help, to be honest.'

She was clearly undertaking a full assessment of this strange encounter, and of this strange man, which was taking a little time, so Percival continued.

'I've just spent a night in that, whatever it is, along the road there.'

'The storage house...'

'If that's what it is, or was.'

'That's what I call it, anyway, although nobody's used it since I lived here. Anyway, how can I help?'

The assessment was apparently at least partially complete, and the words fell like music on Percival's ears.

'I just need one 'phone call, that's all, and I wonder if I might prevail upon you.'

Further assessment, and the seconds seemed like minutes.

'I see, well I don't have a 'phone with me, so I suppose you'd better come back to the house.'

She turned, her aged dog turned with her, and Percival followed and caught up with her, still keeping his distance. This was not the end of his ordeal, but it felt at least like the beginning of the end. His hunger had not abated, he badly needed a cigarette and caffeine, but here was another milestone in the improvement of his circumstances. She was silent, perhaps still assessing, so Percival spoke.

'I don't suppose you encounter many people on your morning walks.'

It was weak, but it was something.

'You're the first, and I've lived here for five years. So what happened? Don't tell me, you were set on and robbed by highwaymen....'

'The truth's even more bizarre than that, actually.'

'Well, go on then, an explanation for a 'phone call seems like a fair deal.'

'Okay, well, yesterday I was abducted by a religious sect, held captive, then drugged unconscious and dumped up the hill there in the woods.'

'What religious sect?'

'I don't know, one that doesn't like me very much....I mean this all sounds ridiculous, I know, but it's the truth. I mean, thank you, you know, for your help, and for believing me.'

'The jury's out as to whether I believe you or not, but as you say, your story's so ridiculous that I am inclined to think it must be true.'

'Nobody would make it up, right?'

'Something like that...'

'So where are we, actually?'

'On the road between Valedene and Polsden, about midway between the two...'

'Right, and what county would that be in?'

'Dear me, you really are lost, aren't you?'

'I was unconscious for quite a long time.'

'We're in Hampshire, quite near the Sussex border, that's in England, by the way.'

Hampshire....Probably a couple of hours' drive from home; that could have been worse...He could see her house, now, at least he assumed it must be her house; a two-storey cottage set on its own beside the road, the stuff of picture postcards, and in complete isolation. Had he kept walking a little further yesterday evening he would have come across it, but hindsight is a wonderful thing.

'Listen, I can't be long, I have to go to work.'

'Just one 'phone call and I'll be out of your way...I just have one more question, what time is it?'

She consulted her watch.

'It's a quarter past eight. I work at the hospital.'

The latter was unnecessary explanation, especially since he had no idea as to which hospital she referred, but he concluded that she was probably a doctor. It was later than he had thought. He must have slept for a longer time than he had guessed, which surprised him, given the place and circumstances in which he had slept; his nervous system must have needed the time to recover from whatever it was he was recovering from. As they walked, Percival gave consideration as to how best to use his one 'phone call. Normally he would use the contacts directory on his 'phone, but in the absence of that he had something in his favour, at least, which was that he had always been good with figures, and could hold 'phone numbers in his head, often regardless of how few times he had used them. He very much wanted to 'phone Louise, she would be wondering why he hadn't called, but that would not be his best or most practical option on this occasion. No, there was one obvious person that he had better call.

'Well, this is us.'

'Yeah, I was wondering which house was yours.'

She smiled at that, which was the first time, and let herself and her dog into the cottage.

'Wait here a moment…'

'I'm not going anywhere.'

Said moment later she returned with a telephone, which she handed to him, and waited; he tapped in the number, and although he knew who would answer he was relieved to hear a familiar voice, a part of his life more ordinary, and he hoped the way back to it.

'Yeah, Keith, it's Percival.'

As the party ascended the steps, Lady Beatrice appeared at the door of the Manor House, and was all smiles as Anna once again made the introductions, and thanked her Ladyship for allowing the use of her beautiful house.

'Oh, that's quite alright, we're all so much looking forward to having you all here…'

And to David Blake;

'It's so good to meet you, I thought that your portrayal of Jesus in the *'Genesis'* series was quite outstanding, and *'The Trials and Tribulations of Mister Thompson'* is quite one of my favourite films of last year.'

And to Ursula Franks:

'Welcome, Ursula…Might I call you Ursula…? And may I say that you're even more handsome in real life than you are on the screen.'

During the tour of the house, which took the better part of two hours, Lady Beatrice gushed forth in ever enthusiastic manner to her visitors, Molly made tea and coffee for everyone, and his Lordship made a brief appearance to be introduced to everybody whom he had not met. Before his departure back to his study, however, he had a brief aside with his daughter.

'Well, we're seeing a different side to mother regarding all of this than we're accustomed to aren't we?'

'Do I get the sense that you feel as though your thunder has been somewhat stolen..?'

'A bit, yes...'

'Well what did you expect, my dear? Don't be too hard on her, she's the Lady of the house, after all, and her concerns are genuine. Better this than the other reaction, don't you think?'

'Yes, I suppose...'

'Don't worry, you will come into the ascendency once things get going. Anyway, I think I'll leave you to it.'

'Aren't you joining the tour?'

'I believe I've seen it all before, and I'm sure we will become well enough acquainted with everyone before we're very much older.'

The youngest of the three players in attendance was Maurine O'Connell, who was to play the pretty teenaged daughter of the household during the production. She was in fact in her early twenties, but she looked younger, and it was with her that Victoria found the most instant rapport, and the two women fell into easy conversation.

'So, what's your character's name?'

'Haven't you been given a script...? No, I suppose there's no reason why you should have been...I'm Catherine, with a 'C'...Well, they were all Catherine, Elizabeth or Anne in those days weren't they? I suppose I'm going to be playing you in a way, aren't I, only daughter and all...'

'Well, I hope you're going to make a better job of it than I have.'

'Hmmm…I doubt that, I'm about to make a real mess of things, but I won't spoil the plot for you. You only have one brother, is that right?'

'Yes, Michael, recently married and flown the nest, as it were.'

'Is he older or younger…? Sorry, this is none of my business, is it?'

'It's quite alright, he's older….'

'I've got three brothers, in the film, I mean, none in real life, and no sisters in either. They had bigger families in those days, didn't they, loads of them died young I suppose.'

'Yes, I suppose they did….So is this a departure for you, a period drama?'

'Yep, although I don't exactly have a long, varied and illustrious career to depart from…So far the oldest thing I've done was the '60s, when I was working in a café in the East End and had to go cockney, so that was all mini-skirts and tight-fitting tops. This'll be a bit different, I'll have to posh-up my accent a bit for this one, and remember what it was like to be a teenager.'

They smiled, and it occurred to Victoria that anything complimentary said to this actress by her mother had been notable by its absence, which did nothing to lessen her sense of empathy toward her. It also of a sudden occurred to Victoria that her mother's uncharacteristic absence during certain times and most evenings of late could be accounted for by her watching productions which the four leading players had been involved in, which she somewhat grudgingly supposed was fair enough under the circumstances; she would take her father's advice and let her mother have her moment of glory, and listen to her complaints with as much stoicism as she could muster once they had all gone.

In due time the party assembled once more outside the Manor, and the group began to make their departures. Anna, who had developed a strong sense of how things actually were within the household, exchanged telephone numbers with Victoria, and saved her last words for the daughter of the family.

'Well, thanks for letting us do that, I'm sure everyone will be the better for it during the build-up.'

'You're welcome.'

'I daresay the next person you hear from will be David, our producer, but I'm sure I'll be in touch during pre-production.'

'Okay, well I'll speak to you soon then.'

She left, and she was the last to leave, and Victoria sat down on her step and watched as the last car departed. Victoria was also pleased that the meeting had taken place, and that she had taken the day off work to attend. This was exciting, and distracting, and both of these things she needed now, and would need in the weeks ahead. Not only during Elizabethan times did people die young, after all, and she had once had two brothers.

Percival gave Keith the names of the villages, and the county.

'Hampshire…? Man, how did you end up there?'

'It's quite a long story, and I'm on a borrowed 'phone. Suffice to say I've got no money or means of getting any.'

'Okay, so in the Land Rover I'm guessing between two and three hours. I'll look up the villages and find the road, so what about exact location?'

'I'll be outside a house called….'

'Glen Cottage.'

'Glen Cottage, you can't miss it, there aren't that many houses, and I won't miss you.'

'Right…I'll be on my way in ten minutes.'

'Thanks, Keith…'

'Sure…'

The call was ended, and the telephone returned.

'Thank you, I wish I could pay for the call, but under the circumstances...'

'It's okay...You really are in trouble aren't you?'

'Well, I hope my troubles will soon be over, thanks to your kindness.'

'And what you told me, is that really true?'

'Every word...I'll be able to dine out on this one for some time.'

'So will I....Right, so what have you drunk?'

Percival took the plastic bottle from his jacket pocket.

'I've been on stream water.'

'Well, that shouldn't do you any harm, but give me the bottle. Do you have a headache, nausea, anything like that?'

So, a doctor, then...

'Not anymore, and I've actually got tablets for that. I'm fine, really, despite outward appearances.'

'How far away is your friend?'

'We reckon two to three hours.'

'That long...'

'I could have 'phoned for a cab and paid at the other end, but I'd have had to take out a mortgage, first, and anyway the person who's coming to get me is someone I should talk to.'

'Right, well, wait a minute...Christ, I should really stop saying that.'

Now they both smiled; she went back into the house, and returned a few minutes later with the bottle, which he assumed she had filled with tap water. She also handed him a plate, upon which were some shortbread biscuits, and best of all from Percival's perspective, a cup of hot, steaming coffee. Wellington boots had now been exchanged for shoes, and she carried a small bag over her shoulder.

'Here's something to tide you over. Look, I really have to be going, you'll understand why I can't let you in...'

'Of course, this could still all be an elaborate ploy to help myself to the family silver.'

'Something like that...I'd like to cook us breakfast and hear more of your story, actually, but the patients won't wait.'

'Listen, you've done more than enough, and I really do appreciate it. Rover doesn't look as though he could guard very much anymore.'

'His name's Sam.'

'Nice dog...'

'So just for the record, your name's Percival, yes?'

'That's me...May I know your name?'

'I'm Fiona...'

'Well, *"nice to meet you"* doesn't really do it justice, but you know what I mean.'

'Do you mind....?

She raised her telephone.

'Not at all, although I'm probably not looking my best...'

She took a photograph.

'For posterity, and otherwise nobody will believe me...'

'Sure, and if I did take the family silver, they'd know who to look for, right?'

'That too...'

She closed and double-locked the door, walked to the side of the house, and returned wheeling a bicycle, which was not a recent model. She placed her bag in the saddlebag, and mounted at the roadside.

'Well, I suppose this is goodbye, then. I hope your friend gets here quickly.'

'He's on his way, that's the important thing, and at risk of repeating myself, thanks, you know?'

'You're welcome...And try not to get abducted again, I might not be here next time, shift-work, you know?'

'Don't worry, I'll be keeping a keener eye out for religious sects in future.'

'You do that...'

She rode off, and Percival watched as his saviour disappeared around a bend in the road. He had liked her, regardless of how circumstances may have influenced his feelings; she had accepted his story with remarkable readiness, had asked few questions of him, and he had a sense that she had liked him, too. There was a milestone opposite the house, and Percival wondered briefly how many centuries had passed since anyone cared how far they had travelled on this particular road. In any case he took his cup and plate across the lane and sat down on the ancient stone. The biscuits and coffee tasted as manna from heaven; strong and black with no sugar, as he always took his coffee, although she had not asked. Hitherto since his awakening his full concentration had been focussed upon improving his predicament, but now he allowed his emotions some leeway, and wiped gentle tears from his eyes with the sleeve of his jacket; he was not home yet, but it was now only a matter of time, and Keith was coming.

Chapter 3. The Rescue

Meadow had not long opened the delicatessen for the days' trading when the ringtone sounded on her mobile telephone, and the caller was Keith.

'Hi Sweetpea…'

'Yeah, hi, just to say I've had a bit of a change of plan to my day.'

'Oh yes…? Are you in the Land Rover?'

'I'm on a rescue mission. Percival's got himself in a bit of trouble.'

'What kind of trouble?'

'I don't know, but he's stuck with no money or whatever, I'm on my way to pick him up.'

'On your way to where..?'

'Hampshire…'

'Hampshire…? What's he doing in Hampshire?'

'Getting himself into trouble, that can happen in Hampshire.'

'Keith, you're not making any sense.'

'Look, I don't have any details, he was on a borrowed 'phone, but he needs wheels, that's all I know.'

'So is he in any danger, I mean is this a dangerous situation?'

'Doesn't sound like it, although you never know with Hampshire.'

'Well, just be careful, okay?'

'Of course…Anyway, better go, got a Land Rover to drive, I'll talk to you later.'

The call ended, and Meadow continued with her preparations, now with a slight feeling of unease, and uncertainty as to what her man was getting himself involved in. Her thoughts were interrupted, however, by the sense of a presence behind her, and she turned to see Rebecca standing at the back of the store. Rebecca's move to her new accommodation had been a quite easy thing, which had occurred late one evening, after darkness had descended upon the village Green. She had brought with her few possessions, which mainly consisted of clothes for her and Florence, and a few of the books which she had recently bought from the bookstore, where she had encountered another witch, an encounter which had set this chain of events in motion. Rebecca had always travelled light through life, and this appeared still to be the case.

'Oh, hi Rebecca, everything okay?'

'Yes, thank you, Florence is sleeping, and I wondered if I might take up a few moments of your time.'

'Yes, of course, I'm not exactly rushed off my feet at the moment.'

In the quiet of this rural valley, sound travelled a long distance and became entrapped between the hillsides, and Percival heard the vehicle before he saw it. Having drunk the coffee provided he had placed the mug and plate on the doorstep of Glen Cottage, and returned across the road to his milestone; at such times people may find comfort even in such things. He sat down on the rough grass verge, his back against the ancient stone, lay his head back and closed his eyes, and the next indefinite time was spent partly awake, partly in dream-filled sleep, and partly somewhere between the two, and in this state did he hear the unmistakable sound of a Land Rover approaching. He collected his thoughts and emotions, and stood up as the vehicle rounded the bend and pulled up beside him, and Keith spoke through the open window.

'Give you a lift somewhere...?'

Without speaking, for at this moment he could find no words, Percival took his place on the passenger seat.

'Man, you look fucked-up, fuck happened to you?'

'Yeah, I'll tell you all about it, just get me the hell out of here.'

The road was too narrow to easily turn the vehicle around, so they continued onwards.

'You know, Land Rovers are great vehicles, but the steering lock's crap.'

'As I recall there's a farm-track not far away.'

They came to the derelict stone building, next to which Keith found sufficient solid, level ground by the roadside to manoeuvre the vehicle.

'That's where I slept last night.'

'Man, I hope they didn't charge much…How was room-service?'

'Lousy…'

'So, where to..?'

'Home, but first breakfast, I haven't eaten since yesterday morning. Christ, has it only been a day?'

'I think there's a transport café on the main road.'

'That's the place, I'm buying, but I'll have to borrow the money. Sorry, you know, to drag you away from work, I'll cover you for the day as well.'

'No need, I'm sure Mike Tillington can spare me, I'll put it down to admin or whatever, and Damien's overseeing for the day, so it's all cool.'

'If you're sure….So where's Will?'

'Turkey, I believe, some kind of road – trip, Em's idea.'

'Right….You know, you're the first vehicle to pass this way since I found myself here, place is like the land that time forgot, fucking valley of death, you know?'

'Just the one house, then…'

'I was lucky, the lady was walking her dog and let me use her 'phone, otherwise God knows what I'd have done, a few minutes later I'd have missed her.'

'Yeah, that was fortunate…So how did you, you know, find yourself here?'

'I'll tell you over breakfast. I need to buy cigarettes.'
'We'll find a garage or whatever.'

Within another mile, or maybe two, they reached the village of Polsden, which appeared to have no shop, but here was the junction with a main road; Keith turned the way that he had come and they stopped at a garage where Percival borrowed money to buy cigarettes, which he considered to be a major step forward in the furtherance of his return to normality.

A little further down the road was indeed a transport café, which offered a large parking area for heavy-goods vehicles.

'This looks like us...'

They ordered their meals; two full English breakfasts with everything, and two mugs of hot, sweet tea, and took their seat by the window. The place was quite sparsely patronised, aside from them there were two or three lone lorry drivers and a gang of road-maintenance people, the entire clientele being male.

'So, come on then, in your own words and your own time, what's happened in your life in the last twenty-four hours?'

'So, what's to talk about?'

Meadow set the kettle to boil for her morning cup of herbal tea, earlier than was usual, and she and Rebecca sat down at the table at the back of the store.

'Well, it's about the accommodation that you've been so kind as to offer me.'

'Oh yes, are you missing anything? To be honest I haven't had time to do a proper inventory since, well, since my father died, and you're coming here was rather sudden and unexpected. My father had few needs.'

'No, it's not that, everything's fine, and I too have few needs, in fact that's the point, really.'

'What's the point?'

'Well, the point is that Florence has settled in quickly and likes living here, and, well....I'm going to ask you whether you would consider making this a more permanent arrangement.'

'I see....But I thought the point of it is that you're hiding out here, and how long is that sustainable for? Surely you need to be somewhere where you can come and go as you please, and the place really is in need of some renovation, which we were intending to do as soon as possible.'

Rebecca smiled.

'I've lived in far worse places, Meadow, and for a long time, and as far as hiding goes, I'll manage, I'm a witch, after all, and the other thing is that I feel safe here, in the village.'

'But isn't this the first place that whoever is looking for you will look?'

'Possibly, but I won't tell if you won't.'

'Well I won't, of course, but sooner or later people will find out that you're here, and I can't be responsible for what happens then.'

'I know, and I don't expect you to be, of course, but there's only one person looking for me, and I'll know if she comes, and I'm sure you'll tell me anyway if anyone arouses your suspicions. I wouldn't put you or your family in any danger, of that you may be certain.'

'But won't you have to work?'

'Yes, I will, but in that respect this place has advantages as well. I mean to say that anywhere I live will need to have or at least have access to a workplace, and I won't return to the studio now, but the covered area at the back would serve my purposes well enough, at least for the summer. I would need a wheel, but otherwise just some shelving and such, which I could take care of. I could work from here, and there's an area of garden where Florence could be outside.'

'I would hardly call it a garden, that's been rather neglected, too.'

'But I could make it a garden, I'd be happy to do that, and we look out over fields, so in that respect the location is perfect, too, we can walk out through woods and meadows quite unseen and unnoticed. You would provide everything I need from the delicatessen, so I wouldn't even need to go out for food. I have money, Meadow, and I'll pay rent at the going rate. I could even make some small pieces which you could have on display in the shop, so we could both benefit from my working here, if that's the sort of thing you would consider.'

'Well, you've clearly thought it through.'

'Yes, I have. I'm very well aware of your opinion of me, and that's something I quite understand, so if you think better of it then I will understand that, too, but I have to ask.'

'I'm not aware that I've ever expressed opinion about you.'

'No, you haven't, at least not to me, but you know something of my history, and you and I have been through a lot together, have we not, at the Manor House, and at Howard's Bench. You've seen what I can do, and I've seen what you are capable of, and we may not be friends, but I like to think that we have a connection, which may work for me or against me, and that of course is entirely up to you. I know you can't decide now, and that you'll need to speak to Keith, but I'm asking you to give the matter some thought before making a decision, that's all. If it ever became difficult for you then I would leave, I promise you that.'

'Right…I just hadn't quite expected this, that's all.'

'I know, and I've only just moved here, but I at least have made up my mind that I'd like to stay, at least until the weather turns cold.'

'Well, let me sleep on it and talk to my family this evening.'

'Of course, we'll speak again soon…Meantime I think you have a customer.'

The wind chimes sounded a note of caution as Meadow walked to her counter.

'Good morning, is there anything I can help you with?'

The food arrived, and as they ate, Percival began.

'So last morning I got a visit from a hired thug, who drove me somewhere for a meeting with the chicken stranglers, I suppose somewhat over an hour's drive away, things are hard to judge when you're blindfolded.'

'Just one guy..? Wish I'd been around, I'd have punched his lights out and sent him on his way.'

'Yes, you probably would, but anyway, there we were in a hall or some such, I had my hands tied and they were in robes, hoods and whatever.'

'That seems to be the dress code.'

'Anyway they wanted to know about Rebecca, like where she is.'

'So it's her they're after, not you, is that it?'

'Seems that way….Anyway I pleaded ignorance and somehow they believed me, I think, in any case they gave me some kind of liquid sedative which rendered me unconscious, and I woke up in a wood near the place you found me. By now it was evening, I had a blinding headache, so I camped out in the hut or whatever it is, and this morning I came across Doctor Fiona walking her hound.'

'She's a doctor…?'

'That's my assumption, she talked about patients, anyway. Key thing is she let me use her 'phone, and the rest of that part you know.'

'Right…So what don't I know?'

'Quite a lot, actually…'

'I'm all ears…'

'I'm probably biased, under the circumstances, but is this exceptionally good food?'

'Yeah, it's a good breakfast….'

'Anyway, so lately I've been in contact with the head of the white witches, whose name's Charlotte. I took it upon myself to go see her at the white house, that's like the centre of the coven of white witches.'

'You went there…?'

'I didn't know what else to do, Keith, I was completely at a loss, and something had to be done. So Rebecca gave me directions, somewhat grudgingly, and very much against the witches' code of conduct, but anyway, we met, the head witch and I, I told her what had been going on and she decided to help me, or rather if I read it right she decided to help Rebecca, with me as a by-product, but it didn't turn out that way. Then all went quiet, until she started leaving cryptic notes through my letter box at the cottage.'

'What kind of notes?'

'Suffice to say that the last one said that whatever happened I should just go along with it, that I should be at home and that I should trust her.'

'So she knew you were going to be abducted?'

'Yeah, she knew, and that's where we get to the part which I can't get my head around. She was there, Keith, in the hall with the chicken stranglers, she's somehow become one of them. I mean I didn't see any faces, but I've gone over it in my head so many times, now, and it must have been her, it was her, and I still can't imagine how or why that came to be. The point is that she must have been somehow influential in any kind of decision-making process, in the sect, you know? That's the only explanation I can come up with, and it could be the only reason that I'm still alive. Not only that, but the head chicken strangler or at last their spokesperson said that I could go home, that I could…Well, just get on with normal life, and that if I saw Rebecca they wanted to know where she is.'

'And then they drug you and dump you in some valley in Hampshire, that's not normal life.'

'Yeah, well I suppose that was just a demonstration of their power, you know, a sort of *'Look what we can do'* from them to me. And that's the other thing, when I came 'round I had water and painkillers in my jacket pocket, which someone must have put there, and I assume that was our Charlotte, but she's a person I need to speak to before I can know anything for sure. It's all still so unclear to me, but now I'm here eating breakfast, so you know, it could have ended up worse.'

'I suppose so…It just seems so…I don't know, why not just ask, you know? Why bother with the abduction at all, and what about trashing your place and leaving messages on your wall, what was that about?'

'Apparently that was a person or persons from the sect who took it upon themselves to make life difficult for me, rather than being company policy. It's all fucked-up, Keith, but like I say, it could have been worse. There's other stuff you don't know, but I need a cigarette with that, and I wouldn't mind if we continued the journey while I tell you.'

'Sure, of course.'

They spoke of other matters of less import as they finished their repast and left the café, and Percival lit his cigarette as they climbed back into the vehicle. Percival had eaten, which had taken him another important stage along the road to his eventual recovery, but he wanted to be home, now, and at least to be making progress in that direction.

By the time Meadow had served her customer, Rebecca had gone, so she made tea for herself only and gave consideration to their conversation. That which had begun as a temporary refuge for a witch had perhaps turned into something else, and she had to assess her own feelings about that before she spoke to Keith later. Meanwhile Keith was rescuing Percival, and she had no clue as to what that was about, but Keith seemed as matter-of-fact about it as he was about most things, which had always been his way. When the children were growing up, it was she who would worry about the small things, like the usual childhood ailments, or having no money to buy food, Keith taking the attitude that it would all get better in the end, and it always did. So, Rebecca, then, she who had with her sisterhood of witches saved Percival's life at Howard's Bench, and had in a way saved Victoria's child from an ancient witches' curse, so far anyway, so it was hard to see her as a wholly bad person, despite all of the bad things that she had done. And now she was gentleness and politeness personified, and on a practical level the extra rental income with no fuss would be welcome. Having someone that she knew living above and behind the shop also had its advantages, and if Rebecca did indeed tame the wilderness that was currently the garden then that would be all to the good, neither she nor Keith had found the time to look after it properly during her father's tenure. The wind chimes broke her reverie, and she walked to her counter, leaving her thoughts and feelings to for now find their own way to conclusion.

As the journey continued, the environs and the roads became more familiar to Percival, and whilst he could not claim to have a faultless sense of direction, he had a question for the driver.

'Which way are we going home?'

'The scenic route, there's no point in taking this heap out onto major highways, we're just as quick village-hopping I reckon.'
'Fair enough....'
'I've been this way on the bike before.'
'Going where?'
'Nowhere in particular, I do that sometimes, and I tend to stay on the 'B' roads. I'm not decrying Land Rovers, by the way, this fine piece of engineering will still be going long after these shiny new cars have rusted away, but top speed's about fifty, they weren't built for motorways.'
'Sure...'
'Pity I didn't have the bike, we'd have been home by now.'
'This is fine, I don't think I'm up to a fast bike ride at the moment.'
'Anyway, you were about to say....'
'Yeah, well the thing is, a while back I hired a hit-man to get in amongst the sect, and he got a bit carried away with it all and killed a few of them.'
'Well, I suppose that's what hit-men do, right, it's a part of the job description.'
'Sure, but I was expecting a bit more ongoing information before, you know...'
'Before he hit anyone...'
'Exactly, anyway one of them I kept away from it, put him into a kind of enforced sanctuary, which has sort of won me a friend on the inside, or at least he owed me one, and he's the only one who knows it was me, and he's not telling. The rest think it was Rebecca who was behind it.'
'Jesus....'
'Yeah, well back then it was war, you know, and they were coming for me, so it was a kind of pre-emptive strike, you might say, but it's gone a bit sour, now.'
'So why did you let the one guy off?'

'Yeah, that's another story, but let's just say that he and I have some history.'

'So that's why they're after Rebecca…Who the fuck are they, anyway, I mean what do they worship, or whatever.'

'I've still no idea, Keith…It's some kind of secret society, obviously, but as of now I've no sense of what secret they're keeping, and I've not been invited to join. So they're after Rebecca, and I guess Charlotte's influence didn't stretch as far as getting her off the hook. She's another person I'll have to speak to, and at least I do actually know where she is.'

'Actually you don't…'

'What…?'

'She's had some trouble from a different quarter, the black witches are also after her for past sins, and these are real rather than assumed, and she's had to leave her flat in town.'

'So do you know where she is now?'

'She's living above the deli.'

'What…?'

'Yeah, Victoria went to see Meadow, asked if Rebecca could stay there for a while, sort of hide out whilst she sorted her shit out, and Meadow agreed.'

'Christ Keith, that's all a bit near home, isn't it?'

'Well, you know Meadow, always there for a friend in need. Like at Howard's Bench when you were about to be ritually sacrificed to the cause, whatever the cause is.'

'And I've never forgotten that…This all takes a bit of sorting out, doesn't it?'

'It does, and it's supposed to be a secret, you know, that she's there.'

'I won't say a word, of course.'

'Apparently it's only one witch who's after her, now, for stuff she did back in the day, like torching the black coven and killing a couple of them.'

'She's not entirely innocent as regards the sect, either, so this isn't entirely my fault.'

'She burned the temple, right? Seems to be what she does...Fuck it, Percival, how did we ever get involved in all of this?'

'You're not involved, Keith, or at least you weren't until now, and I don't mean today, this is a one-off, but if Meadow's taken her in then it changes things.'

'Yeah, it does...I mean I'm not so concerned about the black witch, Meadow eats witches for breakfast, the evil one won't get past her, but the sect's a different matter.'

'And who's evil anyway, right?'

'Yeah, there's that...I mean the sect could be anything, Secret Society for the Protection of Squirrels, or whatever the fuck...'

'Indeed....'

'Still, at least you're not on the hit-list anymore, that's true, isn't it?'

'Yes, that's true, I think...I believe I can live in peace from now on.'

'Abductions and drugging notwithstanding...'

'If they were going to kill me....'

'You'd already be dead.'

'That about sums it up...Thing I've always had over them is that I know where their temple is, but I think we've gone past that now, and now there's the Charlotte factor. Thing is, and I haven't had the time to get my head around it yet, but I have a sense that what just happened had to happen, if you know what I mean. It was a part of a process, or rite of passage, or some such. I sort of had it coming, and what it amounts to really is one bad night and more inconvenience, and as I keep telling myself it could have ended up much worse, and probably would have done but for Charlotte.'

'Witches are a mixed blessing, you might say, they get you into all kinds of trouble and then get you out of it again. So what now..?'

'I don't know, Keith, like I say I need to talk to some witches, but my immediate future needs a gallon of strong coffee and a hot bath. Whatever they gave me is still in there, and I need to sleep it off.'

'Sure....'

'If you don't mind I'll just zone-out for a while and admire the scenic views, we'll talk everything through when I'm feeling a bit more myself.'

'Yeah, you do that, we're not far from home now anyway.'

Rebecca walked out into the overgrown garden at the back of the store, where a few ornamental shrubs had outgrown their place, and Keith had kept an area of what had once been lawn under some degree of control with occasional use of a strimmer. She had not tended any kind of a garden since childhood, when she would help her father sometimes, and the idea of bringing this chaos back into some kind of order appealed to her. At the back of the store was a quite narrow, covered area with a corrugated plastic roof, with a storeroom beside it, which was used as a repository for old crates and so on, and which could be cleared and made into a working area. So it could be done, on a practical level, but that aside the fact of it was that Rebecca was glad to be living in the village again; from the room above the shop she could look out over the village Green, and had view of the Manor House in the distance; not so far from Victoria. So there was the place, but there was also Meadow herself, whose spirit had a presence here, and who would be here herself during working hours, and in both of these regards Rebecca felt safe here, and had quickly concluded that she would like to stay, at least until she was certain that the danger to her and her daughter had passed. So she had asked the question, and now must wait for an answer, which she very much hoped would be in the affirmative.

There was no turning space at the end of the lane leading to Percival's cottage, so Keith reversed the Land Rover and stopped beside Percival's front door.

'There you go, door to door...'

'Thanks Keith, I owe you a beer for this one. Are you sure I can't at least cover the petrol?'

'Wouldn't hear of it, just the beer's fine, and make it soon, you've been carrying this for too long on your own, and I know the reasons, but Meadow and I are involved, now, so keep us updated, okay?'

'Yes, I will....You want to come in for coffee?'

'I'm good, man, and you need to rest.'

Percival did not however make a move to immediately exit the vehicle.

'What's up?'

'I don't know, just getting my head together, you know? Seems like a long time since I was last here.'

'Yeah, I'm sure...Look, if you need company later come to the bus, okay, I'm sure we can rustle up some extra bean burgers or whatever. You've had a bad experience, and there might be a delayed reaction.'

'Thanks, Keith, I'll bear that in mind, and you know, thanks for today.'

'You're welcome...'

'Anyway, if I don't see you later I might be away for a couple of days, I've got a relationship to rescue.'

'Louise and you holding it together through all of this..?'

'Well, that remains to be seen, but I think I'll head to Brighton, if she'll have me, the sea air might do me good.'

'Well good luck with that...'

Without further words Percival got out and opened his front door, and Keith began the short journey to the bus; he would thereafter go and see Meadow at the deli, tell her of his eventful day and have the rest of the day to himself.

Percival set his coffee machine about its business and checked his 'phone. He had missed three calls from Louise, two last evening and one this morning, and there was one written message.

'Where in hell are you, I've been trying to call.'

Yeah, *'in hell'* was about right. He had to rationalise, and keep a sense of perspective; it had only been one night, and he was okay, and still alive, and things could be better from now on. With the help of Charlotte he had it seemed made some kind of peace with the chicken stranglers, so something had been achieved, but at this moment he felt exhausted, and in no condition to properly rationalise anything. No, leave all of the deeper thoughts of the deeper future for later, and 'phone her this evening, she would be working now anyway, and what he had to say needed her not to be working. *'Hi, sorry I've not been in touch, I've been a bit tied up with something.'*

He poured coffee, sat at his desk and lit a cigarette. So, Rebecca was back in the village, hiding out from the witches, and there was something to be considered, but not now, and instead Percival turned his thoughts to his immediate options. It was just after two in the afternoon, he could clean up, sleep for a while and still make it to Brighton by early evening, but thought better of it; he would go tomorrow, so it would be tomorrow evening before he and Louise could be alone together, but there was no helping it, better put some time for recovery between this moment and that. He had resisted bringing Lulu home, but he very much wanted to see his dog, now, and would need her company tonight, so, to the bus, then, and maybe take Keith up on his offer, then take Lulu for an evening walk. Anyway, first a shower and then to sleep;

everything would seem different and he hoped better having slept; the future, be it deep or otherwise, could wait until then.

During the early evening, Keith gave Meadow account of his day, and she gave him an account of hers; and they had a decision to make as regards Rebecca, which they both agreed would need to be slept on, at least. At a certain point Keith's telephone rang, and he did not immediately identify the caller.
'Hello...'
'Oh, hello, I'm sorry to trouble you, but this number was used earlier by...Am I speaking to Keith?'
'You are...'
'My name's Fiona, from Glen Cottage.'
'Oh, hi, the lady who took care of Percival, is that right?'
'Yes, that's me...I was just wondering what happened, I mean did you two meet up okay?'
'Oh yes, all done, he's safely back home.'
'Oh, good...Well that was it, really, I just wanted to check that he was alright.'
'He's fine, thanks, none the worse for having been to Hampshire...'
'I'm sorry...?'
'Nothing...Look, he might be here later, do you want to talk to him directly?'
'No, that's okay, I was just checking in, really.'
'Well thanks for doing that, and thanks for helping, you know?'
'That's quite alright...Just pass on my best wishes to him when you see him, will you?'
'Sure, I'll do that.'
'Well, bye then....And once again I'm sorry to bother you.'
'No bother at all. Did he tell you, how he found himself in your neck of the woods?'

'He mentioned something about being abducted and drugged by some cult or other. So that was true, then?'

'Yeah, happens to him quite a lot, I'm always telling him to steer clear of cults, but he won't listen...'

She laughed, somewhat uncertainly, the uncertainty arising from whether or not she should be taking this conversation seriously.

'Anyway, thanks again, really, I don't know what he'd have done without you, and nor does he.'

'Tell him he's welcome, and if he's ever out this way I'll invite him in next time.'

'I'll be sure to tell him that...'

The call ended, and Doctor Fiona Graham put on her wellington boots, put Sampson on his lead, and walked out into the quite pleasant evening. As a general rule if she walked in this direction she would leave the road, and take one of two pathways which led either way up the gentle escarpment into the meadows, but this evening she walked as far as the storage house, and for the first time she looked inside the small building. There was hessian sacking on the floor, she saw where he would have lain his head, and there was one cigarette butt beside his sleeping place. So, a story verified, and she now supposed that everything else that he had told her was also true. Doctor Graham had been married, twice, neither marriage having lasted for very long, and at her still quite young age she had settled for a life of solitude with her dog, who had been faithful to her throughout. Otherwise she lived now for her work, and her patients, but she was not entirely immune from the feelings which may be aroused in a woman when a tall, dark, handsome, mysterious and quite charming stranger appears out of nowhere in the quiet of the morning of an ordinary day. She would likely never see him again, but she had an image on her 'phone, and would tell her friends, and with that she must be content. And yet, just for this moment, as she stood in this small, derelict building, on another ordinary day, she allowed herself the thought of how life might have been different.

Chapter 4. The Feminist Principle

Brighton railway station is a terminus; trains which arrive here make no further onward progress, but must return from whence they had come, and all passengers here alight, and so on this late afternoon did Percival. He had had only brief discussion with Louise on the previous evening, saying only that he had been unable to return her calls, or even be aware of them, for reasons which he would explain when they met, and that he would meet her after her day's work in a café which they sometimes frequented near the seafront. She had been short and rather terse with him, and Percival was all too well aware that Louise was becoming increasingly unhappy and dissatisfied with their and her circumstances, and her exile from the cottage, where she had not now been for some considerable time. He had asked her to be patient, and she had been so, but her patience had now it seemed come to its natural end, as he could quite well understand. The previous afternoon he had slept, had not awoken until the early evening, and thereafter had done none of the things which he had intended to do. To have eaten his evening meal in the company of Keith and Meadow had been in some ways a fine thought, but he had no wish to yet recount or relive once again the events of the previous day and night, a subject which would have naturally and inevitably been the dominant constituent of their conversation. Nor did he wish to enter into discussion regarding Rebecca, or witches or cults in general, so he had 'phoned Keith and made his excuses, which had been accepted without question. He very much regretted not seeing his dog, but it would only have been for one night, and he would have had to return Lulu to the bus before coming to Brighton, since he had no idea as to how long he would be here for; no, better to leave her where she was settled, so that their reunion when it came would be a more permanent thing. Instead he took a long bath, drank whatever beer was in his refrigerator, ate such food as he could find out of tins, watched three episodes of a rather average American drama series, and retired at midnight, in the hope that he would awaken refreshed and fully recovered in the morning, which had been this morning. Today he had gone to town to buy cigarettes and provisions, eaten a late breakfast at an in-town café, and taken coffee at Dawson's Coffee House, which had become two coffees, having secured the one table outside in the lane where smoking was tolerated. Here had he finally come to the end of a process, whereby he felt more able to put recent events behind him and look to the future, which would he hoped begin in this seaside town, from whence the trains went no further.

'Hi, everything okay with you?'

Every day, weather permitting, Abigail would bring little Henry and Nathaniel out into the garden for their 'outdoor time', and most days that Ross was working they would meet for conversation. There was still a certain awkwardness about this; they were, both assumed, in a relationship one with the other which went beyond the fact that they had a shared employer, but this was working time, and they were both working, so it was perhaps not a natural situation for two young people who were still in the process of getting to know one another, and finding their way into a relationship which was still in its infancy. As we now encounter them they have just begun such a meeting, and Ross had made enquiry.

'Fine thanks, you?'

'Yeah, still trying to tame the wilderness…I'm sort of in limbo until I find out what's going to be needed for the film, you know? We need to turn the garden into something which looks about five hundred years old, which is doable, sort of, but I'm still not sure which bits of the garden are being filmed. How's it all going to affect you and the wee ones, anyway?'

'I'm not sure yet, either. I think we might all have to decamp to Michael's house when filming starts, so I may be away for some of the time.'

Abi was aware that the imminent onset of filming had made the matter of the children's absence from the Manor easier to excuse for Michael and Victoria, although no firm date had yet been set for their first excursion to Glebe House, but it would be quite soon, she was sure.

'I'll miss our daily conversations.'

He smiled, and the smile was returned.

'So will I....'

'Anyway, how are you fixed for getting away next Saturday?'

'That should be possible, why?'

'It's my birthday, on Sunday, actually, but we're having a bit of a gathering of friends at the house on Saturday night, and well, I'd like you to come, if you can.'

'Oh, well, I'll talk to Victoria, but I can't see any reason why not. So it's a party then, is it?'

'That's the general idea.'

'Okay, well I'll ask the question, but assume I'm coming.'

'Great...'

'I'll look forward to it.'

During such early stages of a young romance, there may come a time when both parties to the romance give consideration to the possibility of its reaching a deeper level of intimacy, but it had better not be spoken of by either party, so here was a further awkwardness, which required delicate negotiation.

'You're welcome to stay over, you know, if you want, and if you can get your docket signed.'

'Oh, okay, I'll see about that, too.'

'You can sleep in my bed, that is to say you can have my bed, I'll sleep on the floor somewhere, or whatever.'

'I wouldn't want to evict you…I mean I wouldn't want to be any bother.'

'It's no bother at all, I mean these things don't really get going until the wee hours of the morning, so, you know….'

Both smiled, neither feeling that they had handled negotiations particularly well, but both assuming that no harm had been done by their collective ineptitude.

'Okay, well, let's see, shall we?'

'Sure….Anyway, I'm glad you're coming.'

'I'm glad you invited me.'

'We'll see how to get you there, I'll write the address down.'

'Or I could give you my 'phone number and you can message me.'

'Good idea…I don't carry my 'phone when I'm working.'

'Nor do I.'

'Tell you what, give me a minute.'

He left, and returned with a piece of paper torn from a notebook which he kept in his shed for noting matters pertaining to the gardens, upon which he had written a number.

'Here's mine, send me a message and we're in business.'

'Okay, I'll do that. Anyway, best get on I suppose.'

'Indeed…See you soon, then.'

She smiled again, collected her charges and continued their walk around the grounds. Abigail could recall well enough the last time that she had been to a party, and it had been a long time ago. Throughout the course of the day and amongst other things her thoughts would turn to what she should wear; perhaps at last she would have reason to resurrect one of the two party-style frocks which she had brought with her which had hung in her wardrobe ever since, she would see to the matter this evening. Then there was the matter of Ross himself, his apparent feelings for her and hers for him, and how she would feel about sharing his bed. To give herself, for the first time, to a young man that she still did not know well was something to consider, but she liked him well enough, so she would see, and anyway, she was going to a party, and that was a good enough thought to be going on with.

Percival knew the streets of Brighton quite well by now, and could select his route to Kemptown. Today he walked through the North Lanes, across The Level, then instead of walking James's Street he turned right to the seafront; he was early for his appointment and so he walked the promenade, where people were enjoying the beach on this quite sunny but blustery day; the sea would still be cold at this time of the year, but a few brave and determined souls had crossed the pebbles into the moderate swell. At just before the appointed time he turned inland and found a table, and ordered his coffee, and at just after the appointed time Louise arrived, having been home to refresh herself and to change her clothes, which were now a summer frock, light jacket and sandals. She ordered coffee and sat opposite him, and as people who know each other well will do, both assessed the state of the other before anyone spoke, and Louise was the first to do so.

'Well, who is she, then?'

'Who's who…?'

'The woman who you spent the night with…'

Percival smiled, ironically.

'I was at home alone last night.'

'I'm not talking about last night…'

'Well if it's the night before, I slept in a derelict store house somewhere in Hampshire, although I'm still not quite sure where. I was alone then as well. I left my 'phone at home, had no choice in the matter, actually.'

Further assessment, and there was no lie here.

'Hampshire....'

'Hampshire, it's nice this time of year, although I hadn't intended to go there. Would you like to know how I've spent the last couple of days?'

She drank from her coffee, and he began, and told her the whole story, sparing no detail, and ending at the time that Keith had dropped him off at the cottage.

'Since then I've been sort of sleeping it off and preparing myself for this conversation.'

'Jesus, Percival....'

'The only woman I've spoken to since my abduction was Doctor Fiona, and we didn't get further than coffee and biscuits.'

'So...Now what..?'

'So now you can come home, and I'm going to ask you to do so, and now perhaps you will understand why you couldn't come back before.'

'But...I mean is it really all over?'

'Well, who knows, really, but yeah, I think so, at least as far as the chicken stranglers are concerned. I believe I am no longer a person of very much interest, except in as much as I may be a way for them to get to Rebecca, who's taken up temporary residence above the deli.'

'What...? She's back in the village?'

'Looks that way, although I haven't seen her yet...Nor have I spoken to Charlotte, which will be an interesting conversation when it happens.'

'Well, what can I say....? I mean I don't know what to make of all of this yet.'

'Nor do I, to be honest.'

'I think I'd rather you'd slept with another woman. I actually began to think that Sally had come back.'

'Nothing like that, although since it's cards on the table I did see Sally, her tenants have mysteriously disappeared and she came back for a night, stayed over at my place, but it was separate bedrooms.'

'Whose idea was that? Separate bedrooms, I mean, not hers I bet.'

'Well, I can't speak for her, but I wasn't in the game, I've been living like a monk.'

'I don't want to hear about your dirty habits. What do you mean, disappeared?'

'In that they aren't there anymore, and nobody's seen them for some time.'

'And Sally stayed at yours....'

'And nothing happened, and she's back in Oslo, or wherever, and we haven't spoken since, she's left it with the agents for now. I want you back, Louise, if you'll come.'

'If I'll come....'

'Well, maybe you like it here, I don't know.'

'Well, it's a separatist house...'

'I know.'

'And I spend my life with high feminists and thoughtful, sensitive and considerate men.'

'Sounds like a breeze...'

'Whereas you are a thoughtless, inconsiderate bastard...'

'Yeah, there's that...'

'Where are you sleeping tonight?'

'I don't know, that was dependent on this.'

'Right...Well you book the hotel, I'll get a change of clothes and meet you back here in half an hour.'

'Which hotel..?'

'Any hotel, we can go posh or sleazy, I don't mind.'

'So will you come back, to the cottage, I mean.'

'That depends....Will you continue to be a thoughtless, inconsiderate bastard?'

'I'll do my best.'

'Okay I'm in, then, at least for tonight, after that we'll see. I believe in the feminist principle, Percival.'

'I know you do.'

'And I do appreciate thoughtful, sensitive and considerate men.'

'I never thought otherwise...'

'Good, well that's straight, then.'

'Sorted, I would say....So where's the downside?'

She stood up

'Ever heard of too much of a good thing?'

He smiled and she left without expression, and the smile continued as he reached for his mobile 'phone, and looked for telephone numbers.

Later on this same day, which was by now evening, Keith and Meadow returned to the delicatessen, this time taking the side passage which led to the door of the accommodation which lay behind and above the retail outlet. They had decided to meet with Rebecca as soon as may be, had decided that this had better be done together, and she was at the door by the time they had reached it.

'Hi...'

'Hi, may we come in?'

'Of course...Tea, everyone...?'

'Yes please.'

That which was now the shop premises would once have been a sitting room, behind which was the kitchen, which also nowadays served as a storage area for products not yet on display, and off the kitchen via a small anteroom was the shower room and toilet. From here, stairs led up to the only bedroom, which was the biggest remaining room in the accommodation, and which also now served as a lounge. Beyond the kitchen was a small brick-built extension, which was also used for storage, and beside this was covered area, which led into the quite small garden. The only dining table and chairs were in the kitchen, and there were only two chairs, the table being only large enough for two people to sit and eat comfortably. Rebecca filled the kettle and cleared space on the table.

'Please, sit down.'

Keith moved a wooden crate, which would serve as a third chair, and all three now sat, the only other person present being Florence, who having assessed the visitors set about the business of playing with a wooden spoon on the old brick floor.

'It's good to see you, Keith. I mean I welcome you both, of course, but you I see less often.'

'Yeah, well we thought we'd better have a word, you know?'

'Of course...'

'Thing is, Meadow tells me you want to stay here for a while, is that still the case?'

'Yes, it is.'

'Well, to be honest and to be quite clear we sort of have our reservations, especially me, actually, and that isn't because of you, it's the circumstances, you know?'

'Yes, well we must be honest, and I do understand.'

'Everyone's safety has to be the first consideration, that's the point, and we have our doubts as to whether this is the safest place for you to live.'

'Yes, well as I say, I understand what you're saying, and it isn't something I haven't considered. The safety of Florence is always uppermost in my mind, regardless of any danger to myself.'

'And yet you still think it's a good idea to live in the village?'

'Yes, I do, and I have my reasons for that. I can look after myself and my daughter, Keith, and expect and hope for nothing from you or Meadow aside from your permission and blessing for us to stay here, something which I will pay for, of course.'

'We get that, but I mean it's hardly the Ritz, is it?'

'It isn't a bus, either, but you're happy enough, are you not?'

'Yeah, there's that...What I mean though is that Meadow's father was happy just to be close to Meadow, and didn't care much about his living conditions, I mean the guy was hanging out in a bomb shelter when we found him, but we were going to give this place a good overhaul before we let it out to strangers.'

'Well that's just it, isn't it, we're not strangers, are we?'

'No, of course not, we're all friends here, and we've been through a lot together, hence our particular concerns about your wellbeing.'

Rebecca now stood and made tea for everyone as she spoke.

'It would be difficult though, would it not, to let this place commercially? I mean there's a certain, let's say, crossover between the shop and here, is there not? Where would you store everything, and Meadow uses the bathroom, and I'd be happy of course for that to continue, but how would that work otherwise?'

'We've discussed that, of course, and we'd find ways. We're not saying that there aren't good things about your living here from our perspective, and we want to help, otherwise you wouldn't be here at all, but we need to talk it through before we all make final decisions. I understand that you'd want to run your business from here, buy a potting wheel or whatever they're called.'

'Yes, I'd need to work, of course, and the wheel I have at the studio isn't mine, and it's seen better days anyway, so yes, I'd buy a new wheel, and I'd need to ask you to make some space in the storeroom, but otherwise I'd create my own workplace, and be very undemanding. I've also lived in bad places, Keith, and here we can be warm, we have a kitchen and bathroom, and well, it's just a place that we'd be happy to live out the summer. It'll get too cold to work here in the autumn, but even then if I'm still here I'd pay to enclose the working area somehow and buy a heater, but that's all for the future. First I have to try to persuade you to let me stay at all.'

'Yeah, well don't go all witchy on us, Meadow's here don't forget.'

All smiled at this.

'Meadow has proven herself to be quite impervious to the influence of witches, so I wouldn't even try.'

'Okay but to be serious, there's another witch looking for you, is there not?'

'Yes, so I believe, but I'd be ready for her if she comes, and she'd have to find me, first. She and I have a complicated history, one might say. We owe one another our lives, and that's something which I'd rather not try to explain, but it's nothing I can't deal with.'

'And what about the sect, the chicken stranglers, they're still baying for your blood, aren't they?'

'Perhaps, but…Well, I don't know, to be honest.'

Keith and Meadow exchanged looks; they had agreed how this should be played if the subject was raised, and the subject was here.

'We might be able to give you an update on that. Yesterday I had to rescue Percival from the back end of nowhere, he'd been abducted by our hooded friends, drugged unconscious and left with no means of contacting or getting back to the world.'

This gave Rebecca pause, and Keith and Meadow waited whilst she gathered her thoughts. For a moment her presently open countenance closed upon itself, and for a moment they caught a glimpse of the very different person that Rebecca could become, and which they had both been witness to.

'Is he okay?'

'He's fine. He reckons he's off the hook now, but he doesn't think you are, and we'll let him tell you all about it.'

'Where is he now?'

'Probably in Brighton, but he's coming back to live in the cottage, and we now get into something which we aren't prepared to talk about, that's between you and him. For now let's just say that you should be aware that you're still a person of interest as far as the sect is concerned.'

There now followed another moment's pause, before;

'It doesn't change anything, I still believe that this is the best place for me to live.'

The words were said with conviction, but something had changed now in Rebecca; a darkness had come upon her thoughts, and even she with all of her wiles and skill in deception could not hide the darkness entirely.

'The thing is,' she continued 'it isn't just the practical matter of my perhaps being able to live and work in one place, which would prove difficult elsewhere, and I know I'm a witch, and that my problems aren't over, but aside from the practicality of living my life…Well, I do have feelings, you know?'

'So you're a sort of human witch, then….'

This made the two women smile, Meadow because she loved Keith, and even Rebecca's countenance now lightened a little.

'I suppose you could call me that, but even coming back here for so short a time has made me realise that…That I don't want to be alone with Florence anymore, I've lived so much of my life alone, and I don't want that again, and even if I don't see people, I'll still know that people are there, that Meadow is in the shop during the day, and you aren't far away. I'm close to the Manor, here, and to Victoria, and I live with the hope that one day we might be reconciled, and be together again as we once were. Perhaps that's a false hope, but the hope remains, and that aside I know that having come here I don't want to leave, not yet, but it's up to you, of course, I don't want to be anywhere that I'm not welcome, and I don't want to make difficulties for you, or impose myself where I'm not wanted. If you tell me to go then I'll go, and that applies at any time.'

Keith and Meadow again exchanged looks, which contained a brief but decisive dialogue, and it was left to Keith to conclude the conversation.

'Well, I suppose if you put it like that….'

'I don't know how else to put it.'

'Sure, and it was well put, so okay, you can stay until we know more about what's going on with the chicken stranglers, which needs Percival's involvement, but once you two have had that conversation, if you still want to stay, then you can stay.'

'Thank you, to both of you.'

'If and when it comes to it I'll clear out the storeroom, it's something we've been meaning to do anyway, and that tap's been dripping for as long as I can remember, so we'll do some running repairs, but is there anything else you'd need, furniture – wise?'

'No, and if there is I'll buy it, but we're quite content with things as they are, and if all goes well with Percival you must let me know how much, and when you would like me to pay the first rental.'

Florence now began hitting the floor with her wooden spoon with somewhat more enthusiasm, which drew the attention of the three adults.

'She's getting hungry, I should make us something.'

'She's a beautiful child, isn't she,' said Meadow 'and so quiet and well-behaved.'

'Better than either of our two girls at that age…' Said Keith

'She has her moments, and she can be a real chatterbox if the mood takes her, but she can be shy in the presence of others, no matter who they are. In my biased opinion she's the best of children, I'm very lucky.'

'Well,' said Keith 'let's hope your luck holds, and this becomes a safe place for you to live.'

'Yes, let's hope for that.'

They finished their tea, and Meadow spoke.

'Well, I suppose there's nothing else to be said for now, so we'll go, shall we, Keith?'

'Sure.'

They stood, and Keith returned the wooden crate to its rightful place.

'So, once again, thank you both, for your understanding.'

'I expect I'll see you tomorrow,' said Meadow 'and we'll try to speak to Percival when he comes back.'

'Is he still with Louise?'

'We think so,' said Keith 'although I don't know if he's sure about that himself.'

'I hope they work things out, it's been a difficult time for all of us.'

'Well, let's hope it gets easier from now on.'

They left, and walked through the now dark evening across the village Green, to the bus, and to their own modest home. Both were thoughtful, and Keith was the first to break the thoughtful silence.

'So, that's that, then, she stays, I suppose.'

'Looks that way...'

'She didn't though, did she? I mean I wasn't bewitched or anything, was I?'

'No Keith, you weren't bewitched, just a sucker for a damsel in distress.'

'But you agree though, don't you, that she can stay?'

'It was I who first told her that she could hide here, so yes, I agree, at least for now. Just don't go looking for sexual favours in return for your gallantry or generosity of spirit.'

'It wouldn't be the first time that had been offered, and I hadn't done anything then, but I'm not really into witches, I'm more of an angel kind of guy.'

'Well, if I see any angels I'll let you know.'

She took his arm, and they walked home with a moon waxing almost to the full above, which sent their shadows across the grass as they made their way.

'Hi Abi...'

'Oh, hi...'

At the time that Keith and Meadow were walking home, Victoria was in search of Abigail, whom she had now found.

'Everything okay..?'

'All fine, they're both asleep...'

'Good....I've been talking to Mike, I understand that he's offered you an extra allowance for buying clothes and such when you make the move to Glebe House.'

'It was mentioned, but it really isn't necessary, I can take clothes from here.'

'Well, that's good of you, but it's Mike's money, I would take advantage of it if I were you, I mean you'll need toiletries at both places and so on. Anyway I said I'd pay and get the money from him later, so....'

Victoria handed over an amount of cash that she and Michael had agreed upon, Victoria having secured a more generous allowance than Michael had first mooted, on the basis that she knew more about the price of women's clothes than did he.

'That's....That's very generous.'

'Are you sure it's enough?'

'Christ yes, I don't spend much on clothes anyway, I can buy loads with that, if you're sure....'

'Quite sure...Look upon it as hush-money, for keeping family secrets.'

'Yes, well that sounds more exciting than a clothes allowance.'

They both smiled.

'So when do you anticipate our having to decamp?'

'Well, we may as well wait until filming starts here, or at least until they start tearing the place apart to make us look authentically historical, and we're not sure when that will be yet, but best be prepared.'

'So you don't know what stage they're at with production, yet.'

'No, and I don't know much about film making, but imagine they're at the rehearsal stage, and maybe auditioning for minor parts and so on.'

'Sure, I suppose....'

'Well, that's done, so I'll leave you in peace.'

'Okay, well, thanks.'

'You're welcome, and thanks again to you for being so accommodating.'

'Actually, there was something else I wanted to ask you.'

'Oh yes?'

'Is it okay if I have time off on Saturday evening?'

'Yes, of course.'

'I was hoping to stay with a friend overnight.'

'Please do, we must owe you quite a lot of days off anyway.'

'Well that doesn't matter, but this Saturday would be good.'

'Tell you what, why don't you take the weekend, I'm not working so I can take over on Saturday morning, that'll give you time to shop for clothes and so on, if you want to.'

'Oh, okay, that would be great, thanks.'

'Good, that's settled, then, see you tomorrow.'

'See you...'

Victoria left, and Abigail remained with her thoughts. She wondered what Victoria would make of her friend being the gardener, who was something more than a friend, but she let that thought be, for now. She had some money, so she would make a rare excursion into town and look around the shops, and perhaps upgrade her wardrobe. Earlier in the day she had pulled out her party frocks, but she was not certain about either of them, so she might even buy a new dress for the upcoming event. In any case, all things considered, and in a relative sense, Abigail's life had of a sudden taken on a new momentum. When nothing much of any great moment happens in a person's life, anything which happens can take on a significance greater perhaps than the event itself, and Abigail was going to a party, and she had met a young Irishman whom she liked very much, and who knew where that particular aspect of her young life might lead.

The next morning Percival awoke before Louise, put the kettle to boil and opened the window of their second-storey hotel room. He leaned out and lit a cigarette, and watched as a few early pedestrians walked the street below him. This was hardly 'The Grand', but it was adequate, and had been close by, and their evening had been spent in increasingly intoxicated conversation in a nearby public house, and their night in certainly intoxicated passion in this adequate hotel. No conclusive conversation had been had regarding Louise's return to the village, but for both in their different ways the night had been necessary as a way back to one another after their partial and sporadic separation, which had begun after their return from India, and Percival had needed to put good experience between himself and the preceding days. For Louise this had been a working day, but before the previous evening had begun she had made a telephone call, and the others would cover for her. And so to a hangover, the mitigation of which Percival now began by making coffee from the two sachets provided by the hotel. He had done this as quietly as he could, but now there came a stirring from the bed, and a head emerged from the covers.

'What's going on…? What are you doing?'
'Making coffee, if you can call it that...'
'God, is it morning already….'
'It was already morning when you went to sleep.'
'Hmmm…This version of morning's got daylight though….I need medication, pass my bag, will you?'

The bag was passed, with coffee, and both took painkillers, this being a very different circumstance from the last time that Percival had needed painkillers.

'I need a pee…'

She stood up and walked in her beautiful nakedness toward the door which led to the corridor.

'Louise, the bathroom's that way….'
'Oh, silly me, and there was I thinking I was awake.'

Percival returned to bed with his coffee, which he placed on the bedside table as he lay his head down on the pillows. Despite the hangover, the inner smile which had begun during their meeting in the café was still there, and if anything it had increased in its intensity, but today was a new day, and one night of passion did not a reunion make.

'So, what now, bastard man..?'

She climbed back into bed and sat up beside him with her coffee cup.

'Long or short term..?'
'Let's start with short….'
'Well, I've paid for breakfast and we forgot to eat last evening, so that goes quite high on my *'to-do'* list. After that we drift into less certain waters.'

'You mean it depends whether I still want to commit to spending the foreseeable future with you or not?'

'Yeah, that could have an influence on the day.'

'Hmmm....'

'That doesn't sound very committal.'

'It depends what you foresee. Do you foresee being abducted by any more weird cults, or being visited by any of your witchy friends?'

'No, I don't foresee any of that, I mean there're a couple of witches that I'll need to speak to, but I think I'm in control of the situation.'

'And do you foresee springing any more end-of-holiday surprises on me, like evicting me from hearth and home?'

'Can't see that happening...Anyway we have to be on holiday for that to happen.'

'I'm owed some leave.'

'Anywhere you fancy going?'

'I can think of a few places.'

'Okay, so here's the deal, I take you on an all-expenses-paid trip to the location of your choice, you come back and live at the cottage.'

'For the foreseeable future...'

'Of course...'

'Hmmm...'

'You're saying that a lot at the moment.'

'I don't know, makes me sound a bit like a kept woman, how do I know you won't use your paying for everything as a way of taking advantage of me in a sexual manner, which would go against my feminist principles?'

'I wouldn't think of doing such a thing.'

'Yes you would.'

'Yeah, you're right, I might do that....'

'Being a male bastard and all...A leopard never changes its spots, after all.'

'That's true....You can pay half if you want, then you could take advantage of me, half the time.'

'I think I preferred the first deal.'

'Okay, well the offer still stands.'

She got out of bed.

'And I will give your offer due consideration. Anyway, short term I'm starving...I need a shower, then breakfast, a woman can't make life-changing decisions on an empty stomach, this woman can't, anyway.'

'Fair enough, and I need a cigarette.'

'It's a non-smoking room.'

'Nature will find a way.'

He smoked, the number of passing pedestrians having by now increased, and after a few moments she emerged from the bathroom, enwrapped in a hotel towel, by which time he was all but fully dressed.

'Aren't you showering?'

'Later, probably, breakfast first, I think we've got the room 'til ten o'clock, or thereabouts. I've got no change of clothes anyway.'

'Not thinking ahead then.'

'Not making assumptions, I could have been on the next train home.'

'True....So anyway, how are we going to get all my stuff from the house?'

'What stuff?'

'You know, stuff, clothes and such, there's more than I can carry in one go.'

'Oh, so....'

'Yes, Percival, I'm coming back, what else did you really think was going to happen?'

'I wasn't, you know....'

'Making any assumptions....'

'Exactly...'

'Well now you can, so stop being an idiot and start being practical.'

She opened her overnight bag and began dressing.

'That's a life-changing decision before breakfast.'

'Well, there you go, just goes to show what can be done, doesn't it?'

'Yeah, I guess...'

'I'm not leaving again, though, whatever happens.'

'I won't ask you to.'

'From now on I'm in control of my life, and if that means living with a thoughtless, sexist, male bastard then that's what I'll do.'

'Is that all a part of the feminist principle as well?'

'Yes...'

'That's confusing, from a male perspective.'

'Yes, I'm sure, so anyway, how do we do it?'

'Keith's got Will's Land Rover, I could probably borrow that after work this evening.'

'Okay, so you go home, I'll sort things out at the house, and you come back for me this evening.'

'Sure...Do you think I'll be allowed in the house to help carry stuff to the car?'

'I'll probably meet you at the front step, separatist is separatist, after all.'

'Fair enough, I won't expect to be invited in for tea, then.'

'I wouldn't bank on it. Anyway, shall we to breakfast?'

'We shall.'

In the event it would not be until the afternoon that Percival would find himself on the train heading away from Brighton. By now the hangover had abated to the extent that it allowed clear thought, and clearly the last day and night had been everything that he had hoped they would be. Near-future travel destinations had been discussed, but no conclusion had been reached, and in truth Percival cared not at all where they might go; after so many weeks of uncertainty, of his living in London and staying in hotel rooms, Louise was coming home, and if it had taken a few hours of unconsciousness and one night sleeping rough in a derelict store house, it had, in Percival's considered view, been worth every moment of it.

Chapter 5. A Visitor, a Journey, and a Homecoming

Upon a certain early evening, a visitor came to the bus. At the time of his arrival, Meadow and Keith were seated outside having eaten their repast, enjoying the last warmth of the sun before the night chill began, and they saw the gentleman coming from a distance as he walked the lane which led to their home. He was smartly but casually dressed, and carried an attaché case and a somewhat circumspect expression, as though he were here for the first time and was seeking something, both of which in fact were the case. Keith and Meadow exchanged looks, Keith put aside his guitar and Meadow put down her sewing, and Keith asked the most obvious question.

'We weren't expecting this, were we?'

'No, of course not, I would have told you. We've only spoken once by 'phone since, well, you know, and all I did was tell him roughly where we lived.'

'Right…Well he's here now.'

'Be nice, Keith, and try to keep an open mind.'

'Always, in both regards.'

The man approached and Meadow stood, for it was surely she that he had come to see.

'Hello Sebastian.'

'Hello Meadow…Keith…'

'Yeah, how you doing..?'

The question received the expected answer, which was no answer, and Meadow spoke.

'This is a pleasant surprise.'

'Is it? I hope so, and I'm sorry to come unannounced, and there's no excuse for that, I just…'

'Well, you're here now, so would you like some tea?'

'Tea would be nice, thanks. So this is where my sister lives, I've so often been curious…'

'Yes, this is us, be it ever so humble.'

Sebastian took a moment to take in the scene; the bus, the trailers wherein the son and daughters to his half-sister had latterly lived their lives, and the beauty and quietude of the location.

'It's….Well, not really as I had expected, although I don't know why that is.'

Meadow made to walk inside, but Keith interrupted her progress.

'I'll make the tea, have a seat, I'm sure you two have got stuff to talk about.'

Keith put a chair which he had made of surplus offcuts of wood from a previous building contract in close proximity to the place where Meadow had sat, and where she now sat again, and Sebastian occupied the seat.

'So, what brings you here, aside from your curiosity?'

'Legal papers, pertaining to your inheritance, ostensibly anyway…Everything's in order, so I just need you to sign, and Keith to witness, then we can do the money transfer.'

'I see…Are you allowed to do that, without a solicitor present, or whatever, and is Keith okay as a witness?'

'Yes, it's all legal, don't worry, the solicitor's a good friend, but let's do that later. I also came to see you, Meadow, although you may as well know that the money's a bit more than we discussed, you'll be receiving just in excess of a hundred and sixty grand.'

Keith, who was by now at the door of the bus, turned briefly and exchanged looks with Meadow before going inside to fill the kettle.

'I see, well….I'm very pleased, of course.'

'And I'm pleased to be the bearer of good news for my sister. Like I said at father's funeral, I'll need your bank details, but after this the transfer should only take a few days.'

'Well, what can I say but thank you, Sebastian.'

'Don't thank me, thank the old man, I'm just the conduit.'

They smiled, and it was a moment when there was so much to say that neither knew how to begin to say it, but now Meadow spoke.

'So, what were you expecting?'

'I'm sorry...?'

'You said that this wasn't what you were expecting.'

'Oh, right....Well you told me you lived on a bus, but....It's just, I don't know, so beautiful here.'

'Well, it's a beautiful evening, and we have to do the winter as well, but we like it.'

'I can absolutely see why. So that's where the children sleep, then, although they aren't children any more, of course.'

'Yes, that's them. They all started life on the bus, but as they grew we sort of extended, although I don't think any of them are home at present.'

'That's a shame.'

'Tara's with Ashley Spears, making music, and I'm not sure where the others are. Rosie will be moving to Brighton soon when she starts at Sussex University, and Basil's eager to become independent as soon as he starts work.'

'Well, they're all doing fine, I'm sure, and I love Tara's music.'

'You played one of her songs at the funeral, that was good of you.'

'It seemed appropriate, and like I say, I'm a fan anyway, she's got a beautiful and very distinctive voice.'

'Yes she has, although I'm not sure where she got that from, certainly not from me.'

They smiled again, just as Keith emerged bearing three mugs of herbal tea, and joined the small ensemble.

'Don't mind me, this is your gig, man, do what you came to do.'

'Well, for a start I feel that I should apologise for Veronica's unfortunate outburst at the...At dad's funeral. There was no call for that.'

'She was upset, obviously, and no harm done.'

'Veronica took the disappearance of our father the hardest, to be honest, and she's never really forgiven him for leaving.'

'The guy was sick, man,' said Keith.

'Yes, of course, but it was all so sudden, there was no warning. One day a successful and respected surgeon, the next a...Well whatever you might describe him as, a tramp, I suppose.'

'We found him living in a bomb shelter,' said Keith 'he'd sunk pretty low.'

'Yes, and it wasn't just any bomb shelter, was it?'

'And Veronica blames me for his coming here to look for me, am I right?' Said Meadow.

'She does rather take that line, unfortunately, but there's another way of looking at it.'

'Which is what?'

'Well, perhaps without you, he would have had nothing to focus his thoughts on, as it were, during that which I suppose we can only describe as his breakdown. I won't bore you with the details of how he and my mother had drifted apart, emotionally, and it was the work, I think, which got to him in the end, but he wasn't happy at home, I see that now. So, having you here perhaps gave him a reason to go somewhere else, like I say, an alternative something to put his mind to, if you understand me, although I'm not putting this well.'

'You're doing fine,' said Keith 'and that makes sense.'

'Yes, it does,' said Meadow.

'And the cricket team must have helped his recovery,' said Keith 'guy was a fine bowler of a cricket ball.'

'Yes, there's that, too, although I didn't inherit his love of the game, I'm afraid. I don't know a lot about his life here, and nowhere near as much as I'd like, but I do understand that this community took him under its wing, so to speak, and I for one can quite see why he wanted to stay here, and why he wanted to help you, Meadow, but our sister can't see it that way. All she sees is a man that she loved leaving us, and she's never really understood why that happened, so please don't think too badly of her.'

'I don't,' said Meadow 'and perhaps I could have done more to try to reconcile him with you both, but he was quite adamant that he wanted to stay here, and that he…Well, that he had done all that he could to try to get close to your mother again, and to you, so there was really nothing else I could have done.'

'I'm sure none of this is your fault.'

'It was never the case that he didn't love you and Veronica, but after his fall, well, let's just say that there were limits, I think, to what he felt capable of doing, and feeling.'

'Sure…And it must have been quite a shock for you, when he revealed himself as your father.'

'You could say that….By that time we'd already opened the delicatessen, so, yes, it was a shock, I never expected to see either of my parents again.'

'Well, speaking for myself, and now that he's no longer with us, I'm glad that he found you. I have another sister, now, and that's something I wasn't expecting, so a lot of good has come out of this, albeit that the way to our sitting here talking together hasn't been an easy one for anybody, and I'm sorry for Veronica. She's a good person, and she and I are quite close, but she lost her father, which has been a hard thing for her to bear.'

'Of course…So does she know you're here?'

'Not specifically, to be honest this was all rather spontaneous on my part, I fancied a drive, you know, and thought I'd drive somewhere where something could be done. She knows I've been sorting out the money, so she's aware that you and I are in touch.'

'So does she mind about that, the money, I mean?'

'No, well a bit, perhaps, but it's not really the money. Veronica's a successful person in her own right, and we'll all do okay in the end. Neither she nor I knew very much about our father's private financial affairs, so it's not money that we'll miss, and this is what dad wanted, so any objection that either of us may have is academic in any case.'

'Yes, I suppose....Anyway, I'm glad you came, and I'm sorry you missed the children.'

'So am I...Neither Veronica nor I have any kids, so I remain hopeful that one day I might get to know them a bit.'

'I'd like that.'

A moment of silence followed, whilst tea was drunk and thoughts were further gathered, and now came a change of subject.

'I was wondering, could you tell me anything about Connie, or Constance, is it, that our father was involved with? I've heard the name mentioned, but that's about the extent of it.'

'Well, there's not much to tell, really, other than I think her family are from the West Country. She's lived here for many years with her sister, Pearl, who moved to India a couple of years ago. She's a lovely, gentle lady, but I can't say I know her well, otherwise. I think she and father found comfort and companionship in each other.'

'So is she in the village presently?'

'Actually no, after the funeral she left for India to stay with Pearl, and I think she'll be away for a few weeks. We're sort of looking after the house whilst she's away.'

'I see...Well, as long as the old man found some sort of happiness in the end...'

'Yes, I believe he did.'

'And this is a truly beautiful village, isn't it, quintessentially old English, he would have liked it here, I can see that. Anyway, I've kept you long enough, so let's get these papers signed and I'll be on my way.'

'Are you sure, I mean have you eaten?'

'Yes, thanks.'

'Well it's a long way to come, so thanks for coming.'

'It's a pleasure, and as it happens I had little else to do this afternoon, so it was a pleasant drive, and I'm glad to have seen where you live at last.'

'You're welcome to stay for longer, I'm sure there's more we could say to one another.'

'Yes, I'm sure there is, but today was for the documents, and just to try to cover some basics, and it's quite a long drive back. I hope we can meet again soon, though.'

'I hope so too.'

Sebastian smiled to himself.

'What's funny?'

'Nothing....I was just going to say that my ultimate wish would be that you and Veronica could be reconciled.'

'Well you'll meet no resistance from me in that regard, I'm not one to let the past influence the future if it can be helped. I'd like to meet my half-sister under better and happier circumstances.'

'If I find the right moment I'll pass those sentiments on.'

'You do that.'

Documents were read through and signed on a makeshift table and returned to their case, and Meadow wrote down details of the family bank account.

'There, that's done, now all you have to do is wait for the money.'

'Well, thank you again, Sebastian.'

'My pleasure....So can I call you sometime to set up a somewhat longer and less official meeting?'

'Yes, I'd like that.'

'Good, so would I, and thanks for the tea.'

Sebastian made ready to leave, but Meadow had another question.

'So, I mean, how are you coping with father's death, we haven't spoken about you at all, have we?'

'Well, we've been without him in our lives for so long that I suppose it's made little material difference, and one is sad, of course, at his death, but the sadness started long before that. I knew him when he was a better and more capable man. Still, as I say, without his demise he might never have found you, and you and I may never have met, so one must try to look for the good in things, must one not?'

'Yes, indeed one must.'

'Also….Well, it's just the germ of an idea, although it's been growing for some time now, but I'm thinking about doing a correspondence degree in psychology, with a view to one day perhaps becoming a practising psychiatrist. I've always held an academic interest in the workings of the human mind, and it might help me to better understand, at least. Anyway, that's all for the future, and for now I should be going. Good to see you again, Keith.'

'Yeah, you take care now, and don't be a stranger.'

Meadow approached her half-brother, who read the signs and kissed her cheek. Smiles were shared, and the visitor turned, and with no backward glance trod the lane upon which he had come. Meadow and Keith sat down, and Keith picked up his guitar. He was playing nothing in particular, but now and again he would play the chord and note sequences which were a part of his contribution to the next Tara album.

'Seems like a nice boy.'

'Yes, he does, I hope we can meet again soon.'

'I wouldn't doubt that, he'll be back. What the hell does he do, anyway?'

'He's medically trained, like father, and I think he practised as a hospital doctor for a while, but he gave that up to become an art or antiques dealer, or some such. We've never really talked much about it, because we've never really talked.'

'Well, I'm sure you will, and in the meantime, you've got some money coming.'

'*We* have, Keith, the money's for all of us.'

'Well put me down for some new cricket whites, otherwise I'm sorted, and I'll be contributing to the family coffers anyway when the album comes out. We won't know ourselves soon, will we, what with our eldest daughter singing so well for her supper.'

'No, things aren't the same anymore are they? That was what father was worried about.'

'What, that the money was somehow going to corrupt his own eldest daughter?'

'Something like that.'

'I think he knew you better than that.'

'Yes, I think he did. Anyway it's getting chilly, shall we go inside?'

'Sure, I'm quite tired anyway, think I'll retire early, I've got an old house to rebuild in the morning, and I'm due to meet Mike first thing to talk about the church.'

'So when are you going to Ash's place again?'

'I don't know, he's going to call me when I'm needed. So will you be retiring early as well?'

'Why do you ask?'

'Oh, you know, just asking....'

'I thought you were tired.'

'I might wake up a bit.'

Meadow smiled; it had been a particular and unexpected evening, the so varied men in her life were having their so varied influence upon her, something which looked set to continue, and that at least was something which she hoped would not change.

Sebastian had parked his motor vehicle on the road at the end of the lane, and as he began his journey home he contemplated the evening as it had been so far. Gypsies, Veronica had called them, and not in a complementary way, in fact *'Bloody gypsies'* had been her actual words, but gypsies they clearly were not, however one perceived the term. And yet, the way they lived, in harmony with the natural world around them, and with apparently so little regard for the material things in life, there were similarities with the traditional life of Romany travellers as he understood it. Keith seemed amicable enough, with an underlying threat of becoming something else should the need or wish arise, and then there was Meadow herself, his half-sister, who carried about her an aura which was hard to define, but which drew him to her in a way that he had not experienced before. It was something about the way that she bore herself, which had a lightness about it, but she also had her hidden depths, he was sure. It was nothing sexual, despite her obvious femininity, and they were in any case related by blood, but the aura was there, nonetheless, and she was a person who he wished to see again, and to better get to know. Veronica, he was sure, would take some convincing, and may never be convinced, but he would 'phone Meadow after a decent length of time had elapsed, and he would return here, because he wished to return here, and regardless of whatever his beloved other sister may say or think of his so doing.

'Will, how much water have we got?'

Will and Emily were now headed in an approximately and generally northerly direction. They had reached the south coast of Turkey from Izmir in a single day's drive, and had arrived at the town of Marmaris, where they had rested overnight and formed a plan for the next stage of their road trip. They would set off after breakfast from wherever they were, drive for the morning, and wherever they ended up, to the nearest place where there was accommodation to be had, there would they spend the afternoon and night. This would give Will a break from the intense, hard miles of driving which had been his lot since they had left Istanbul, and avoid their having to drive during the hottest hours of the hot Turkish day. Thus had their afternoons seen them swimming in the clear, blue ocean, or exploring the remains of the many Greco-Roman settlements and fortifications which had been so much a part of the history of this part of ancient Turkey. Their accommodation had ranged from the most basic to the somewhat more luxurious, depending in part on their mood, and in part whatever was easily and quickly available, and they had dined each evening on always fine Turkish fare, and enjoyed the always friendly and welcoming Turkish hospitality which they had by now come to expect. Total strangers in cafes and restaurants had given them small gifts of perhaps a bunch of grapes or a small, wooden carving, and always people wished to know where they were from. *'Ah, England....'* As though it was a place which people knew well, whereas Will and Emily suspected that these so local people had not ventured very far from their particular part of their own country. In any case in this manner had they at least in part explored the magnificent southern coastline, until they had reached the town of Mersin, and thus almost the Syrian border. Here they had decided that it was time to head northwards. It was a long way back to Istanbul, where they hoped to rest for a day or so before their flight home, they had yet to visit Cappadocia, or Ankara, the capital city, and so upon a certain morning and with some reluctance they had fuelled up the car, which by now was beginning to show signs of having been worked hard on the long miles, and begun the homeward journey; hard miles now once more lay ahead, as did the hot, arid Turkish interior, and at about midday of their first day, Emily had asked the question.

'Water...?'

'Yes, you know, water, that stuff you have to drink to stay alive.'

'About half a bottle I think, why?'

'Well, I mean look where we are, this sort of redefines *"the middle of nowhere"* don't you think, and I haven't exactly seen many cars for the last hour or so, or anywhere where anyone lives for that matter.'

'Yeah, it's sort of arid, isn't it, you can see why not much goes on here.'

'It's a bloody desert, Will, and I mean supposing the car breaks down, we'd be stuck out here forever.'

'With no water…Yeah, I take your point.'

'We'd better make sure we have some food and a lot of drink with us in future.'

'Sure…'

'Do you think the car is in fact going to break down?'

'Well, so far so good, but it's making some weird clunking noises, and I'm having to steer right a bit in order to keep going in a straight line.'

'What does that mean?'

'You mean in mechanical terms?'

'Yes, in mechanical terms.'

'It means there's something wrong with the car.'

'Very helpful…'

'I mean, I don't know, Em, it's got something to do with the transmission, but it's nothing I can fix, so there's not much point in theorising about it.'

'Do you think we need to take it to a garage, assuming we ever find a human settlement with anything which looks like a garage in it?'

'I think that would have to be a last resort, whatever it is could take days to fix, and it would cost, you know? Let's just keep going and hope for the best, shall we?'

'Okay, but I think from now on we'd better prepare for the worst.'

'Agreed….I mean civilisation must be out there somewhere, we should get somewhere by evening.'

'Let's hope so…I'm getting hungry, and hot, and thirsty now we're talking about water.'

'It's all part of the adventure, Em, and it's been great so far, don't you think?'

'It's been wonderful, I could have spent days just at Ephesus.'

'Yeah, it's been mad, I can't even remember the names of all the places we've stayed, we should have been making notes, or keeping a diary or whatever.'

'Marmaris, Fethiye, Kas, Side, Alanya and Mersin, in that order….'

'Right….'

'I won't forget any of it, just get us safely somewhere by this evening, okay?'

'Doing my best….'

Louise's return to the village was from anything other than a private perspective a quiet and understated affair, which happened quite late in the evening. Percival had returned to the cottage from Brighton in the afternoon, stopping en route in town to buy provisions and candles, and had cooked lasagne before securing the loan of Will's Land Rover by way of Keith, who was pleased to oblige on Will's behalf. On her arrival home, Louise and Percival took the by now considerable luggage containing her personal belongings upstairs, and she took a shower whilst Percival returned the borrowed vehicle, reheated the pasta and set the dining table for supper, upon which he had placed and lit the purchased candles. Louise, who was now in possession of her full wardrobe, wore a dress that she had not worn for a long time for the occasion, and they sat by candlelight as Percival poured wine, and they broke bread.

'This is almost biblical, the man has made an effort.'

'Well, you know me, all consideration and thoughtfulness.'

'Indeed…One thing, though, have you started using skin products?'

'Sorry….?'

'There's moisturising cream in the bathroom, and it's not mine.'

'I don't know, I don't know what stuff's up there, I suppose Sally must have left it, I told you she stayed over.'

'Yes, you did, and she left these in the spare room.'

Louise held up a pair of white, lacy knickers, which were in truth little more than a delicately decorated thong.

'They're not mine either, never seen them before…'

'One would hope not, dear heart, especially if she was wearing them at the time.'

'I haven't been in the spare room lately.'

'Careless of her, wasn't it?'

'Yeah, I guess…'

'Unless of course she left them deliberately, women don't usually leave their underwear behind.'

'We didn't sleep together, Louise.'

'I know you didn't, you'd have been more careful about covering your tracks, and they were in the spare room, there for all to see, so one must conclude that that's where she slept.'

'It was….'

'So do you think this was a sort of *"Look what you missed"* token, or maybe they were left for my benefit, a sort of *"I was here"* message.'

'I've got no idea, Louise, better men than I have tried to fathom the workings of the female mind. Maybe she just left them by mistake, you know?'

'Maybe she did. So what should we do with them, do you think?'

'Whatever you want, you can throw them in the bin as far as I'm concerned.'

'No, I won't do that, they look expensive, and they are rather nice. I'll wash them and keep them for her if she comes back. I assume she'll be back to sort out the mystery of the missing tenants?'

'I assumed so, although if they don't show up or stop paying rent the agents will have to clean the place up and find new people, it could all be done remotely, but yeah, I expect she'll be back in due course.'

'Well, we'll keep them, then, and you can give them back to her, it would sort of complete the symbolism.'

'Like I say, whatever. Anything else you've found lying around the place?'

'Nope, don't think so, everything else just looks like you've been living here on your own for the duration.'

'Meaning what?'

'Nothing, dear heart, just let's change the sheets tomorrow, shall we?'

'Sure…I did have a bit of a tidy up, but this was all a bit unexpected, I mean I didn't take your return for granted, or wish to tempt fate, you know?'

'Of course, and this is lovely, a candlelit dinner to welcome me home. Thank you, my love.'

'This is a big day for me, Louise, the last weeks haven't been easy for either of us.'

'I know, and I do know that everything you've done has been to try to keep me safe, and if you say that it's all over then I have to believe you, don't I?'

'We'll just…We'll just be careful for a bit, that's all, and I'll be picking Lulu up in the morning, so we'll have a dog.'

'Of course….But I mean are you okay?'

'What do you mean?'

'Well as you say, we've both been through it. I've suffered the inconvenience of living somewhere that I wouldn't have chosen to live, but you've been through far worse things since all of this started.'

'You mean like being drugged, tied to a stake and almost killed, and then abducted and drugged again, unconscious this time, and left in the middle of nowhere, that kind of thing.'

'Yes, that kind of thing, and then there was the one about the cottage being trashed and left with death threats. Any and all of that could be said to be traumatic, and professional help is available, if you felt you needed it.'

'You mean like counselling, or therapy, or whatever.'

'Yes.'

'You think I'm showing signs of needing it?'

'No, I don't, but these things can be delayed, reactions, I mean, and all I'm saying is that you don't always have to brazen things out, you know?'

'I'm still alive, Louise, and now you're back I'll be fine. I was raised on the mean streets of London, don't forget, I've seen bad stuff happen to people since I could walk. All I need is a life more ordinary for a while, a few long walks with a dog and whatever.'

'Yes, you're probably right, and you're Percival, after all. Maybe I've just been living amongst the snowflakes for too long, if anyone sneezes in certain sectors of Brighton society everyone runs to the therapist, and everyone's struggling to define and come to terms with their sexuality down there.'

'Yeah, well it's the way things are these days.'

'Not for you though.'

'Life's too short, especially when you almost didn't have one.'

'Yes, well there's that….I was talking to a doctor down there, just an ordinary GP, you know, and the practise is overwhelmed by people self-harming or attempting suicide. He's convinced that social media is causing most of the problems, young people being bullied twenty four-seven, or made to feel inadequate, or whatever. It's a terrible thing.'

'Whereas all I have to deal with are a few nut-jobs in hoods and a couple of good old-fashioned witches, it's a piece of cake.'

She smiled, they raised their glasses and touched them across the table for no particular reason, so Louise invented one.

'Well, here's to a life more ordinary, then.'

'And to our reunion...'

'Yes, that too....So talking of witches, what now..?'

'I'll go see Rebecca, find out how the land lies, and I'll have to speak to the big white witch, even if that means going to the white house, but I'll do that when I'm ready.'

'Of course....'

'In the meantime there's lasagne to eat, if you're hungry.'

'I was, but now I'm not anymore, can we just sit and talk for a bit, we can eat lasagne tomorrow.'

'Sure, I'll turn the oven off. I made salad and garlic bread, we can graze on that and talk at the same time.'

'Sounds good to me...'

He lit a cigarette, and offered the packet over the table.

'Are you...?'

'Not really, not cigarettes, anyway, but I bought some weed up from Brighton if you want.'

'Seldom been known to refuse....You skin-up, I'll take care of matters culinary, I'll be five minutes.'

'I'm not going anywhere. I'm back, Percival, and I won't leave again.'

'And I won't ask you to.'

'Whatever happens from now on, we do it together, okay?'

'Sure, of course, and I'm sorry for everything, Louise.'

'I know, and you don't need to be. I understand your motivations, at least in my regard, and I think I'm even beginning to understand you, and you're the person that I love, so from now on I'll take whatever's coming.'

'Selfish bastard though I am?'

'Well, we're none of us perfect, are we, and you're not that all the time.'

The remainder of the evening was spent in conversation, which was in large part a reliving of all that had happened to them during the last weeks, and it was well into the small hours of the morning before they retired, and the dawn of the new day was not long away before they slept.

Chapter 6. Concerning a Party, and the Buying of Olives

On the evening of Ross's birthday party, Abigail had a particular problem to overcome. She was dressed for a party, had applied more makeup than anyone at the Manor would have seen her wear before, and had decided upon a black, partly sequinned dress, which was rather revealing above and fell only just far enough to be decent, depending upon how one might define such things. It was in fact a dress which she had bought several years previously, but had not in fact had occasion to wear, and after some deliberation had decided that on this occasion she would put this to rights. She was also wearing strappy, high-heeled shoes, the straps being buckled just above the ankles, and the whole ensemble she considered rather risqué in anything other than a party environment. Under normal circumstances she would have caught a bus to town and walked the quite short distance to Ross's house, but on this occasion she decided better to treat herself to a taxi, thus avoiding unwelcome eyes which might fall upon her if she used public transport, and avoiding having to walk very far in her chosen shoes, which were not really designed for walking in for any distance. Ross would have come to collect her, she was sure, but he could not have driven to the Manor House doors, since in doing so their being together outside of the working environment would be revealed, and Abigail was still keen that this should not be so, not yet. In any case having spoken to him in the late afternoon, he and others were still busy with party preparations, so she had insisted that she was okay to make her own way there, a decision which she had now begun to regret. So, a taxi, then, which took care of the better part of the journey, but there was still the matter of how to leave the Manor House without drawing attention to herself, or more specifically to her attire. That which she wore was her business, of course, but still there was a certain discomfort in being seen so dressed by her employers, and Victoria in particular. She had left the children in Victoria's care, so she would be otherwise occupied, but still, there were her Ladyship and his Lordship to avoid if possible. She would carry with her a small overnight bag containing jeans, flat shoes, underwear and a T-shirt for the wearing of in the morning, and she had even considered wearing these now and changing at the venue, but decided that this would be silly, and wished to arrive at the event in her party attire. In any case it was likely that Ross and the others would begin the evening in a public house, which rendered the idea less viable.

So, she would have to brazen it out, and hope that her departure went unnoticed. At the decided hour, which was a little after eight o'clock, she messaged the taxi company, and the taxi would be here within fifteen minutes, and would drive to the steps of the Manor. She checked herself once more in the mirror, adjusted her shoulder straps, and sat down on her bed to wait; she would emerge from her room only when she heard the taxi arrive.

Percival and Louise awoke late and somewhat hung over on the morning after their domestic reunion. Soon enough they would need to get on with the more mundane aspects of living together again, and Louise would return to work the next day, but today could in large part be put aside for the enjoyment of one another's company, and an acceptance that past events could now be consigned to the past. They cooked breakfast together, which in truth was nearer to lunchtime than breakfast time, and they agreed that the evening would be spent watching a movie in a state of sobriety. Nobody in the village yet knew of Louise's return, and they could have maintained this state of affairs, but by the afternoon both began to think that something else should be done, and the catalyst for this was a jar of preserved fruit, or lack thereof, and it was Percival who began the process.

'We've run out of olives.'

'That isn't a problem for me.'

'It is for me.'

'Better go and buy some, then.'

'It'll mean going to the deli.'

'I know, but I suppose you'll have to see her sometime, so it might as well be today, just don't be gone too long.'

'I won't.'

Percival would meet and speak with Meadow, but it was not her to whom they were referring, for both knew that Percival could scarce ignore the fact that a certain witch now resided above and behind the delicatessen, and that he could scarce avoid seeing her if he visited the establishment.

'So go, then, I've got some things to do anyway, like wash the sheets, and I'll probably take a long bath.'

'Okay, I'll see you later. I mean she may not be there.'

'I thought she was hiding, and she probably won't hide from you.'

'Yeah, she'll probably be there.'

Percival took a quick shower, changed his clothes and walked to the village Green in search of olives, and whatever else he might find as a consequence.

In the event, Abi did not see Victoria on her way to the taxi, but by that which she considered to be somewhat milder misfortune she encountered his Lordship, who emerged from his study under the stairs as she was approaching the front doors. She smiled, sweetly, and the smile was returned.

'Hello....'

'Good evening Abi, I assume the newly arrived vehicle is for you, then.'

'Yes, it's a taxi.'

'One may not quite have all of one's faculties as one used, but one's hearing is still sharper than the average, and one did wonder...Anyway, mystery solved.'

'Indeed....Well, best be going, then.'

'Yes, best had...I have received no intelligence as to your leaving us this evening, and won't ask to where you are bound, but I assume this is not an attempt to escape our clutches forever?'

'No, just for one night, I'll be back in the morning, or maybe the afternoon.'

'Glad to hear it, we'd be quite lost without you.'

'I don't think I'd get very far dressed like this, do you?'

'I suppose that would depend upon where one was trying to go, but if in these delicate times an old man may be permitted to voice opinion, you look quite stunning, my dear.'

'Thank you.'

More smiles, and Abigail made the front door, descended the ancient steps and entered the taxi.

'Hello...'

'Where to, love?'

'Town, please...'

'Anywhere in particular..?'

'Hang on, well don't hang on, but just wait a minute...'

The taxi driver turned the vehicle and began the return journey to the gates of the Manor as Abigail made a 'phone call, and spoke into a clearly crowded room.

'Where are you?'

'We're in the Kings Arms, Merchant Street.'

'Okay, I'm in a cab, see you in a bit.'

'Sure....'

The call was ended.

'Kings Arms, please, Merchant Street.'

'On our way....'

It was not a pub to which Abigail had ever been, but she knew its location well enough. Victoria had looked out of a window when the cab had arrived, and watched now as Abi walked to it, dressed and looking as she had not seen her before. Something was happening in Abigail's life which she was keeping to herself, which was her prerogative, of course, but for a moment Victoria wondered what the something might be. She had spent more time in the garden with the children than was usual since Ross had taken up his position, and she had noticed their speaking and laughing together on occasion. Perhaps this was just coincidence, but the seed of a thought had been planted in her mind, and she wondered whether the general lightness of demeanour which she had noted in Abi of late had something to do with the newly appointed gardener. She could be quite wrong, of course, but the seed had germinated, and had been further encouraged in its growth by a general reticence as to where Abi was going this evening, and she would see how it grew from here. She turned her attention to her two charges, and let the matter be for now.

The wind chimes sounded an uncertain but somewhat relieved tone as Percival entered the delicatessen, and Meadow found herself surprised at how pleased she was to see him, and looking so well, if a little tired, perhaps, although she was at pains to think how else he might be looking.

'Percival, how good to see you.'

'You too…'

'So, I suppose the obvious question is, how are you? Keith has told me all about your ordeal, of course, or as much as he knows of it, anyway.'

'I'm fine, Meadow, a lack of olives notwithstanding.'

'Well, I can help with that, at least.'

'I don't know what I'd do without you.'

He took his intended purchase from the shelf, and came to the counter.

'Quite a lot's happened since we last spoke, has it not?'

'It has indeed…'

'Not all of it good, but one positive is that Louise is home, I picked her up from Brighton yesterday.'

'Oh, that is good news, so is this to be a permanent arrangement this time?'

'For as long as she'll put up with me, that's the plan, anyway.'

'Well, I'm very pleased for you both, and I've missed our occasional conversations. I mean I don't wish to dwell on unpleasant things, but what happened to you was horrible.'

'Yeah, I've had better things happen, and I owe Keith for the rescue, and for breakfast.'

'I'm sure you owe him nothing, and you seem to have quite recovered yourself.'

'No point crying over spilt milk, as they say, and it could have been worse, they could have killed me, like they were going to when you and Keith came to my rescue the first time.'

'Well, that wasn't just us, was it, and we still can't know what would have happened had Rebecca and the witches not intervened.'

'That we'll never know, and I understand that the witch in question is living here now, secretly, of course.'

'Yes, she is. There's another witch looking for her, as I understand it.'

'There always seems to be someone looking for her, she's ever popular, it seems. I mean I needed the olives, but I suppose I should call in upstairs. How much does she know?'

'Nothing, not from us, anyway...'

Percival smiled.

'What's funny?'

'I was just wondering how many people have this kind of conversation when they buy olives.'

'Not many, I would think. It really is good to see you, Percival.'

'You too… So how much do I owe you?'

'It's okay, look upon them as a coming home gift.'

'Are you sure…?'

'Quite sure….'

'In that case I'll put it on the owe-you list, and look upon it as karma, good things balancing out the bad, that kind of thing.'

'Well, if it helps….'

'It does, and not just the olives.'

'What do you mean?'

'Never mind…So, how's the best way, down the side passage to the back door?'

'Yes, that's the way, and I hope your meeting goes well.'

'Me too… Meetings between Rebecca and I are seldom mundane, anyway.'

Now they both smiled, and Percival put his gift in his jacket pocket as he turned to leave.

'Thanks, Meadow, I'll see you soon then.'

'As long as there're olives…'

'Yeah, that too, and next time I'll pay.'

'Well, whatever…Good luck, Percival, and I'm so pleased that you and Louise are back in the cottage.'

'Yeah, so am I. Can you keep Lulu for one more night, I'll pick her up tomorrow if that's okay?'

'Of course….Tara's away at the moment, but she's been primary dog-carer, and she enjoyed it, actually.'

'Well, thanks, you know?'

'So will you tell her, about what happened, I mean?'

'I don't think I have much choice, do I?'

'No, I suppose not.'

He left, and as the wind chimes became quiet, waiting for the next person to walk through the door, Meadow was struck by the symbolism; Percival's love of olives, his constantly craving the bitterness of the fruit, as he tasted and swallowed the life which he led, but it was never enough, and he would always return for more. She leaned on her counter, and let her thoughts go where they may.

Percival walked the passageway and knocked hard on the wooden door, and spoke in a quite loud voice.

'Rebecca, it's Percival.'

The Kings Arms was well patronised on this evening, and was busy and noisy as Abi entered through its front door. She attracted little attention, aside from the attention which may be generated by an attractive young woman entering a premises, and she found Ross sitting at a table with half a dozen or so others, who had clearly already begun the night's celebrations.

'Ohhh….Here she is. Everyone, this is Abi…'

All eyes around the table were now on her, and Abigail counted four boys and three girls.

'Hello everyone...'

Smiles and looks were exchanged, both around the table and between Abi and its occupants, and an integration was needed.

'Don, you're nearest, get the lady a drink, will you, and get another round in while you're at it.'

Don stood up.

'What's your poison?'

'Gin and tonic, please...'

'Make it a double,' said Ross 'the girl's got some catching up to do.'

Ross was sitting on a bench-seat against the wall, and positions were shifted to allow Abi to sit down next to him, which placed her between and very close to two of the boys.

'So let's do some introductions. This is Gina, and that's Steph and Ruby, who share the house with me and Don, and the other two degenerates are Mick and Bren.'

More smiles were exchanged, and further assessments were made. The boys were about as Abi would have assumed, and all of an age and appearance which she would have expected of Ross's friends. Gina was blonde-haired and pretty, Steph was tall and dark-skinned, probably of African or half-African descent, and Ruby was by contrast of pale, Anglo-Saxon complexion, with cropped, mid-brown hair, and in Abi's opinion quite beautiful, in fact all of the girls were lovely, and dressed in a way that for the first time this evening made Abi feel quite at home in her own chosen attire.

'It's very nice to meet everyone.'

'You too,' said Ruby 'Ross's spoken about you a lot since...Well, since you met.'

'All good, of course...' Said Ross, as Don returned with drinks, and placed a Gin and Tonic before Abi. He took his seat, and all raised their glasses as he spoke.

'Well, here's to old friends and new meetings, and to our birthday boy, of course.'

Abi drank, and for her the evening had begun.

Rebecca opened the door.

'Hello Percival, there's no need to be so loud, I knew you were there.'

He walked through the door, and here was a meeting of two people who had been many things to and for one another, waiting now to see how they would be today.

'Coffee...?'

'Of course, and make it strong, I'm fighting a hangover, which seems to become a less even fight as one gets older.'

'Celebrating, or is this a return to your old ways?'

'Louise has come home...'

'Oh, I'm very pleased to hear that.'

'Are you?'

'Of course....I may not be able to entirely fulfil my own emotional or physical needs, but that doesn't prevent me from feeling happy for others who can.'

'She's not that far away, you know, the Manor House is but a short walk from here.'

'Sometimes it feels as though it might as well be a million miles. Anyway, if it's not a stupid question, what brings you to my door?'

'Yeah, it is a stupid question, so let's just say I heard you'd moved back into the neighbourhood, and thought I'd find out what the fuck you were doing back here.'

'That doesn't sound very neighbourly.'

'Well, I have to be honest, I'm struggling to work out how this is a good idea.'

She poured coffee, and then tea for herself, whilst Florence observed the goings-on from the doorway. Percival was struck once again by the similarity in looks between mother and daughter; whoever was the father to this child he apparently had had little influence on the matter of her facial appearance.

'Good, well I'm glad we're being honest, at least. Shall we take our drinks upstairs?'

'Whatever you like...'

They ascended the stairs, and entered the room which was both sleeping and living area, and Percival walked to the window, having to bend down slightly in places to avoid the lowest timber beams.

'I've not been up here before.'

'You get a nice view of the Green, and the Manor House, of course.'

'Indeed….So, do you want to give me some kind of an explanation?'

'I had to move out of my last place, the bad witches found out where I lived.'

'I think the badness of witches might depend on your perspective.'

'As might the goodness or otherwise of people, be they witches or otherwise…'

'I never claimed to be a good person.'

'And I never claimed to be a good witch, let's call it a figure of speech, shall we?'

'Fair enough, so….?'

'Actually it wasn't me who thought of my living here, Victoria approached Meadow on my behalf, and I needed somewhere, you know? And well, once I was here I decided that I wanted to stay.'

'That still doesn't make it a good idea, don't you think this might be the first place that the bad witches will look?'

'There's only one of them now, and I can deal with her if the time comes, I can go bad again if I want to, if there's a good reason.'

'Yes, I'm sure, but I'm here to tell you that witches might be the least of your problems, our hooded friends are still baying for your blood.'

'You know this? How…?'

'Well, aside from it not being that hard to work out, I've just spent a day and a night at their pleasure, and you are not forgiven.'

'What….?'

'Yeah, they came for me, and I didn't make it back here until the next day. I had a few of them killed, and they think that was you, and I confess I didn't enlighten them, under the circumstances.'

'You did....What?'

'I know some people, from London, you know, and beyond that I'd rather not embellish...'

'But....'

'Look, forget it, Rebecca, that isn't what I've come here to talk about.'

'Okay...Okay, but....So they are after me for things that I didn't do, is that what you're saying?'

'They were after you anyway, Rebecca, so I figured that you might as well be hung for a sheep as a lamb, even if you didn't kill the sheep.'

'Well, thanks for that.'

'Getting out of there alive was also something of a priority for me, and on that subject, I believe the only reason you and I are talking now is that a certain other witch was involved, who I think we can't describe as being anything but good.'

'What do you mean?'

'I mean that...You know even now I can't be certain, everyone apart from me was all dressed up, but I'm as good as sure that Charlotte was there, as one of them. She left me a cryptic note just before I was invited to the party, which said that I should trust her, whatever happened, and the only thing that makes any sense is that it was her, and I'm sure she would have had some influence over events.'

'In other words she saved your life, is that what you're saying?'

'What I'm saying is that I believe she set the whole thing up, I could have stayed away from the village, but she told me to go home, so I did. I put myself entirely in her hands.'

Rebecca took a moment to consider all that he was saying. It was though her disobedience and her breaking the code of secrecy of the coven that Percival had once found his way to the white house, and spoken with Charlotte, and now perhaps Charlotte had infiltrated the ranks of the sect. Yes, she supposed that she could have done that, but what had been her motivation? She had put herself in great danger, but why? Had it been for Percival, or for her, and if for her then why were they still looking for her?

'This raises a lot of questions, Percival.'

'Yeah, I know, and she's a person that I need to speak to.'

'Yes, I think we both do, so why don't we go together?'

'That would be cosy.'

'I'm serious....I've had no word from Charlotte for some time, and this would explain why, but there's a lot which still needs to be explained, so we should go to the white house, don't you agree?'

'I suppose that makes sense, but let's give it a few days, I've had enough excitement to be going on with.'

'Of course...Whenever you're ready, but I think we have to go, she would know things about the sect that I need to know, if I'm to survive this. I don't feel safe living here, Percival, but this is where I want to be.'

'To make your final stand, as it were...'

'If it comes to it, yes...I can't run and hide for ever.'

'Well that isn't true, is it, I doubt if they'd find you on some remote Indonesian island, or whatever.'

'No, but...'

'Home is where the heart is, right?'

'I still live in hope, Percival.'

'Sure, and without hope what else is there, I get that.'

There was only a sofa in the room upon which to sit, so Percival sat upon it and Rebecca sat cross-legged on the floor before him, with Florence beside her.

'But hang on, you say that you were with the sect for a night, so what happened?'

'Actually our meeting was surprisingly brief, then they put me to sleep and I woke up in Hampshire, of all places. Keith came to get me.'

'I see....I think...'

'Mostly they were looking for me to tell them where you were, but they didn't press all that hard, and perhaps again that had been Charlotte's influence, but anyway, finding you is still on their to-do list.'

'So what about you, will you be living at the cottage from now on?'

'Yeah, I won't leave again, and nor will Louise. I have a sense that they're done with me, and perhaps think that I'll lead them to you, so they'll be watching the village, I'm sure.'

A further moment was taken for thought, and Rebecca attended to her child before she spoke again.

'It doesn't matter, I'm still going to stay here.'

'Well, that's your call, of course, but just be aware, that's all.'

'I will, and always am, and thanks, you know, for not giving me away.'

'I wouldn't do that.'

'No, I know…'

'So what will you do, I mean you could be here for a while, all being well.'

'I'm going to buy a potting wheel and work from here, I still have a lot of commissions to fulfil, so we'll be fine, and I really need to start working soon. So what about you…?'

'I'll keep writing the articles and such, it doesn't pay well but it buys the groceries. First priority is to bring Lulu back home, and talking of which, what the hell happened to your dog? It's something I've meant to ask before.'

'Lady….She died.'

The statement was accompanied by an expression which told Percival to make no further enquiry, so he let the subject be; perhaps it was too painful a subject, or perhaps there was something else, but there it would rest. They talked further about witches, and cults, until eventually Percival decided that it was time to leave, and they parted with an agreement to go together to the white house, unless Charlotte was first to make contact with either of them, but that was something for another day. For now their ever-complex relationship had done all that it had needed to do, and both had much to think about before they would meet again.

Last orders had been called in the Kings Arms public house by the time the assembled party made their move to the party venue. Alcohol had flowed freely, the conversation had been light and convivial, and Abigail had thus far very much enjoyed the evening, and the meeting of the people who were clearly significant in Ross's life. A natural assessment of those present told her that none of them were romantically engaged, that of the girls, Gina was the most flamboyant and extroverted, and that Ross was pivotal to the social gathering; his natural wit and outgoing nature, particularly when under the influence of alcohol, saw to it that it was to him that the others most often deferred. Inevitably, given the close proximity of the seating arrangements, there was a deal of close physical contact between Abigail and Bren, who was sitting to Abi's left, and he made no attempt to lessen the contact, and no secret of the fact that he was enjoying it, but Abigail made little of this aside from noting it. In any event the party now made their move, and walked to the house, where loud music was already being played, and the early stages of the party were already underway. Ross escorted Abi to the kitchen, where wine and other bottles had been placed on the work surface, and where a flagon of beer had been placed.

'So, what can I get you? I can't see the wine lasting very long, so if you're a wine drinker I would make the most of it.'

'I'll have wine, then, red please...'

He poured wine into a paper cup, and a beer for himself.

'Well, make yourself at home, then. Oh Christ, we should put your bag somewhere, follow me...'

They walked the narrow hallway to the stairs, carrying their drinks as they did so, and passing others on the way. On the way up they navigated past those seated on the stairs in deep discussion, and thereby found their way to the landing, upon which other people had formed an informal line.

'Okay, so the bathroom's there, obviously, and this is us.'

He opened a door, and they were at once greeted by the pungent smell and smoke of marijuana. People were seated on and around a double bed, and otherwise the room was a mess of clutter and pot plants, which had probably been moved here from elsewhere for the occasion.

'This is where you'll be sleeping, it's okay, we can eject this bunch of degenerates when the time comes.'

'It's fine, really…'

'Just leave your bag somewhere….'

She put her overnight bag down in a corner. One of the boys passed Ross a marijuana cigarette, which he drew on and passed to Abigail, who shook her head.

'Right, shall we join the party, then?'

'Okay….'

'I'm sorry, I didn't know they were going to turn your bedroom into a dope den, although I suppose I might have guessed.'

'It's okay, really…'

They re-navigated the stairs in a downward direction, and entered the party room, which was the entire rest of the ground floor. Ross was distracted by a conversation with someone, which could only be had in very close proximity because of the loud music, and the general noise of people dancing and talking loudly with one another. Abigail took a moment to observe and absorb the crowded atmosphere, and drank the rest of her wine. She was already feeling quite drunk, and decided that this was no bad thing; she had been to occasional parties during her mostly quite sheltered life, but this had the appearance of becoming of a level that she had not experienced before, and she determined to enjoy herself. Her momentary reverie was interrupted by a male presence before her and a voice in her ear.

'I see you've been deserted, that's no way to treat a lady.'

This was Bren, who now took her by the hand and led her into the main throng of dancing bodies.

'Come on, let's dance.'

And so they danced; it was the time of a party where dancing was the primary activity, and physical contact was at a minimum and not the point of it, but Bren seemed determined to ignore this general principle, and held her and touched her sporadically in ways that Abigail felt inappropriate, even under such circumstances of reduced inhibition. She knew nothing of Bren, other than that he was a friend of Ross, and had made the inner circle during the early part of the evening, and was therefore likely a close friend, so for now she ignored his presumptuous advances, and after a few minutes made her excuses.

'I think I need a drink.'

'Sure, me too....'

They left the party room and made the kitchen, where she poured the last of the last bottle of wine into another paper cup, and Bren helped himself to beer. Abi looked for Ross, who was presently nowhere to be seen, but now Ruby appeared beside her. Ruby was clearly a little drunk, but she glanced at Bren, and looks were exchanged between the two young women.

'Okay, it's girly time, I'm taking her off your hands.'

'But we were getting on so well...'

'Fuck off, Bren, she's mine...'

Abi and Ruby returned to the party room, and the two young women caught the rhythm and danced closely, a situation which Abi found altogether more acceptable and enjoyable.

'Bren's okay, but you have to watch him, he's a lecherous bastard, especially when there's new blood around.'

'I gathered that. So, no girlfriend, then…?'

'He doesn't seem very good at that, you know, the whole relationship thing. So it's you and Ross, then.…'

'Well, we've sort of been seeing each other, but we've actually only been out once.'

'You'd never think so.…'

'What do you mean?'

'He's…Never mind…'

'Come on, you can't leave that hanging.'

'Okay, well, seems like he's crazy about you…'

'Is he…? I mean how do you know?'

'I mean he doesn't actually talk about it much, but I can tell, you know?'

'Well, I'm sure you know him better than I do.'

'Where the fuck is he, anyway?'

'I haven't seen him for a bit.'

'Fucker's disappeared on you, that's not nice…'

'Well, it's his birthday, so, you know, he's probably got people to talk to.'

'Yeah, I guess, anyway, rescue over, and I need a pee, which could take ages. You be okay…?'

'Of course, don't worry about me.'

Of the two young women, it was in fact Ruby who would next encounter Ross as she was ascending the stairs, and they met halfway.

'I think your woman needs some looking after.'

'Yeah, I got caught up in something.'

'She doesn't know anyone, Ross, and Bren's circling…'

'Right, I'll get on it. So what do you think?'

'I think she's gorgeous, but she needs attending to, so go to it.'

Ross found her in the party room, where she had for now been invited by means of body-language to join a small group of people who were dancing with nobody in particular.

'Hi, sorry, got called away….Are you okay?'

'I'm fine, just…'

'I know, sorry…'

They had not danced together before, and whilst neither of them were particularly adept at the art, and neither had danced for a long time, it was no matter. It was also the case that Ross had not previously seen the lady so apparelled, and the business aroused in the young man feelings which he had hitherto for the most part tried to ignore, although there had been occasions of an evening when the thought of her had led him to seek solitary fulfilment. For the young woman, this was an altogether different experience from dancing with Bren; this was enjoyable, and now she did nothing to discourage occasional physical contact, something which the young man took as a positive sign. She smiled, he smiled, and they spoke sometimes as best they could over or between the music, but mostly they danced, and were now there for one another to the exclusion of all others in the crowded room, and a ritual had begun.

During the mid-evening, as she was seated in her bedroom with her laptop, Victoria received a telephone call from Anna Merchant.

'Hi…'

'Hello Victoria…Right, so Monday it begins.'

'I see….'

'A man called Roger Altman will be acting artistic director, so he'll be with you in the morning sometime with about six technicians and a removals van.'

'Oh, okay, fine.'

'Sorry it's short notice, but I only heard myself an hour ago, that's how things are in the film industry, I'm afraid.'

'It's fine, it had to start sometime, and thanks for letting me know. So otherwise how's everything going?'

'Well, we're behind with rehearsals and final auditions, and the costumes are causing us some problems, so it's all the usual crap when you're working to a tight budget and schedule, but it's going to get worse before it gets better, so, you know….'

'Well, good luck, then, and I suppose we'll be seeing you soon.'

'It won't be soon enough, but yes, you will. In a perfect world the set and actors will come together and prepare in unison, but it's not a perfect world, is it, so all I can say is that I'll see you sometime.'

'Of course…Well, thanks again.'

'You're welcome.'

The call was ended and Victoria turned off her computer screen. She checked in on the children, who were fast asleep, so she walked out onto the back terrace and lit a cigarette. The by now familiar emotions fought for precedence in her mind; this was exciting, and something to which she had at once been looking forward to and dreading in about equal amounts. Contracts had been signed by her father, and he would be paid for the inconvenience, but still, none of them could yet appreciate the extent to which their domestic circumstance was about to be disrupted. The agreement was that any and all furniture in the rooms to be used which was not of the period would be taken into storage for the duration, since otherwise there was nowhere else really to put it, and it had seemed to all to be the best way. Then as she understood it, light switches and such things would be disguised or covered, and inappropriate paintings removed from walls, which would give a blank canvas for the importation and placing of period furnishings, against which the actors could play their parts. So that was the theory of it, and now came the practice. She checked her watch; her mother would likely have retired by now, and her father likely not, so here was a time when she could speak to him without her mother being present, and she had better take advantage of this as she had done on many occasions before; this would be an easier way for her to break the news to them.

Firstly, though, she had a telephone call to make. She was not aware of any special duties for her to perform at the gallery on Monday, so she would call her superior to try to get the day off. Again it would be short notice but she was owed annual leave, so under the circumstances she didn't anticipate any resistance to the idea. In any case she had better try to be around on the first day at least, to calm any troubled waters; Roger Altman was not a name that she had heard before, so it would be his first visit to the Manor, and he would be a significant person for her to meet. She put out her cigarette, took a deep and conclusive breath, and went in search of her father.

It was not until the small hours of the morning that the party began to lessen in its intensity. Mick, who had taken it upon himself to be DJ for the event, lowered the tempo and volume of the music to better fit the mood of the party-goers. Some had already left, others had found convenient places to fall into an intoxicated stupor, or had in such a state and atmosphere of disinhibition begun sexual relationships with others who were similarly disinhibited, which may or may not survive the cold light of day. Someone had vomited on the pavement outside, all available alcohol had been consumed, and one young lady whom Ross did not know had quite lost control of her emotions, and was being consoled by others of her gender. Ross and Abigail had for the most part stayed together, given that Ross had been called upon on occasion to deal with situations, and their dancing together had become ever closer and more intense. They had made occasional visits to the kitchen for further refreshment, or to the bathroom, but otherwise had remained together, and now Ross decided that it was time to ask a certain question.

'Are you okay, I mean do you need to sleep, or whatever?'

'I'm fine, I mean sometime, you know?'

'Sure, well, let's go find you a bed, then.'

They negotiated the stairs, and somewhat to Ross's relief they found that aside from a residual smoke-infused atmosphere his bedroom was now unoccupied.

'Well, this is you.'

'So where will you sleep?'

'I'll be fine…I'll find a sofa or something.'

It was a moment which both had been awaiting with some anticipation; they were both a little drunk, although neither were by now very so, Ross having curtailed his drinking in order to better deal with this moment with his lady friend. They smiled, and they kissed, and he waited.

'I mean, okay, you know?'

'What…?'

'I mean I wouldn't want to evict you from your own bed, not on your birthday and everything.'

Their eyes met in understanding, she quietly but significantly removed one shoulder strap and he removed the other, and with one deft movement she lowered and removed her dress, and unbuckled and kicked off her shoes. They fell together as he undressed and removed the last of her underwear, and for the first time she had knowledge of a man, and the night was old and the day new before they fell into sleep together, as the first rays of morning light shone through the thin and shabby curtains.

In the evening, and in compliance with an agreement between them to from now on speak openly regarding all matters, Percival recounted to Louise his meeting with Rebecca, after which they ate the lasagne which had been intended for the previous evening. During the latter part of this evening they sat closely together on the settee, and watched a movie; after the excesses of their initial reunion, here at last was comfort in one another's company, which both had in their own ways craved for so long. In the morning, Percival would fetch his dog home, and his domestic life would be complete, but for now he ate his olives, and let the film and the evening distract his thoughts from places that he had no need or wish for them to go. He was at this moment with Louise, and for this moment this was enough, and all that he wanted.

In the morning, Abigail awoke with initially confused thoughts and questions, primary amongst them being where was she? She sat up in bed, and then she remembered, her memory being aided by the site of Ross still sleeping beside her. It was a somewhat informal arrangement, but she would return to the Manor and the care of her charges sometime in the afternoon, so life would return to its usual patterns, and nothing would change, but a feeling now awoke in her and with her that nothing would actually from now on be the same again. Her monthly cycle was predictable almost to the day, and she was sure she was safe, and they had used contraception in any case, but the point was that she had given her maidenhead to the young man beside her, who now turned in his sleep, and would likely awaken soon.

She had drunk more alcohol last night than had been the case for a long count of days, and she had not yet reached for her telephone to check the hour, and there was no bedside clock, but she assumed that she had had only a few hours of sleep, or perhaps only two or three, but she felt okay, all things considered. In fact she felt vitalised and alive in a way that she had also not felt for a long time. She was in a relationship, a matter which had been confirmed not only by she and her beaux having had their first full sexual encounter, but also in his eventual care for and attitude toward her during the party, which had after all been his party, but he had in the end only had eyes and time for her. The next thing that came to the forefront of her thoughts was that she needed to pee, so having confirmed that the time was a little after nine o'clock, she found her overnight bag and dressed quickly in fresh underwear and a long T-shirt, and crossed the small landing to the bathroom, in which she locked herself. She had brought with her a small bag containing some essential toiletries, and she cleaned her teeth and washed as best she could. The bathroom was a mess of empty or half-empty paper cups and other detritus, which she assumed would be the case or worse in the rest of the house, and she would in due course help to clear up. She returned to the bedroom, where Ross had now awoken, at least to some degree, and he yawned as he spoke his first words of the day.

'Good morning...Fuck, what time is it?'

'Just after nine, and good morning to you, too...'

She sat down beside him on the bed, and he pulled her to him and lifted her T-shirt, which she allowed him to do.

'Ummm, what are you doing, I'm dressed.'

'No you're not.'

'Well, I'm sort of dressed, I needed the bathroom.'

'Well don't get too carried away with the dressing thing, I prefer it when you've got less clothes on.'

She smiled, and pulled down her T-shirt, and he was the next to speak.

'So....Are you okay, about last night, I mean?'

'Yes, I'm fine about last night...'

'Good, thought I'd better ask...'

'Well thank you for asking.'
'So, we're cool, then?'
'Yes, we're cool.'
'So shall we do it again, then?'
'What, now?'
'No time like the present....'
'Are you sure you're awake enough, and don't you have a hangover?'
'Yes to the latter, and I find myself awakening in your presence, if you know what I mean. Is there anything to drink?'
'No....'
'Man I need water, or coffee, preferably, and tablets. So what's it looking like out there?'
'Well, I haven't been very far, but it's not looking good.'
'Hmmm, better get up then, I suppose, see what the damage is. You're not rushing off today are you?'
'No, I can stay 'til the afternoon.'
'Good, I may request your presence in my bed again before the day is out.'
'Well, I suppose there's no harm in asking.'

They both smiled, and both now stood up; she dressed properly as he was dressing, and they descended the stairs, where the party room and kitchen did indeed bear the marks of celebration, but there was no apparent damage, aside from a few cigarette burns on floors and the upholstery of the anyway less than new furnishings; clearing up would be a laborious but mostly superficial affair. Someone was asleep on the sofa, which both quickly identified as being Bren, and an as yet unidentified form was wrapped in a sleeping bag in the corner of the lounge floor. Ross boiled the kettle, found painkillers in the kitchen cabinet and made coffee, whilst Abi began filling a plastic bin-bag with used paper cups and the contents of ashtrays. They were joined in time for coffee by Ruby, who looked even paler in the cold light of morning than she had the previous evening, and in Abigail's eyes just as lovely with smudged makeup and tousled hair, such as it was, and wearing jeans and sweatshirt as she had in her party finery.

'Morning everyone, how bad is it?'

'About as bad as could be expected, which isn't too bad.'

'Who's the body in the corner?'

'No idea, I think it's alive though, and probably male.'

'Is that coffee…?'

'Yeah, that's yours.'

'Thanks…'

Abi and Ruby shared smiles, and the knowledge that Abi and Ross had spent their first night together, but no words were spoken, as none were needed, and Ross was the next to speak.

'Who's hungry?'

'I'm starving,' said Ruby 'why?'

'I was going to suggest we leave this for later and hit the café for breakfast, soak up the alcohol. I'm paying…'

'Sounds like a plan, only let's get going before Bren wakes up, I don't think I could take Brennan this early in the morning.'

'What about Steph?'

'She'll be asleep for hours, yet, she could sleep for England, you know what she like.'

'Yeah, she wasn't holding back last night, was she? Go and wake her up, she won't want to miss breakfast, especially if it's free.'

'No, best leave her. Anyway I need to freshen up, let's say ten minutes?'

'I need the bathroom too.' Said Abi

'Okay, you first then…'

She left, which left Ross and Ruby drinking their coffee, and exchanging looks through still hung over and still not fully awakened eyes, and she spoke.

'You've got a smile on your face this morning.'

'I don't think I've smiled once.'

'You don't have to have a smile on your face to have a smile on your face.'

'So what do you think?'

'She's sweet, not the most street-wise of people, but yeah, the boy done good, and just so that you know, Steph entertained a young gentleman last night, so she wouldn't appreciate being disturbed...'

'Right....Who?'

'Tallish guy, longish hair, goes by the name of Saul, or Paul, or something.'

'Don't remember him.'

'You two only had eyes for each other.'

'Must be love, then...'

'Looks like it...'

'Anyway, I'll go see if Don's conscious yet.'

'He's not, trust me.'

'You've seen him?'

'He didn't sleep alone last night, either, and nor did I.'

'Fuck, really...? Was that a good political move?'

'I wasn't thinking about household politics at the time, but it'll be okay, I'd just rather not face him over breakfast, we might need some private coming to terms time.'

'Sure...So let's get going then, shall we?'

The café was a short walk away, and rested somewhere between a transport café and a low-end coffee house, but their full-English breakfast or fine omelettes on offer had been appreciated by the residents of the house on numerous occasions and in various combinations. Abigail had thought it important to ingratiate herself into Ross's household, and although she had scarce spoken to Don or Stephanie, she regarded Ruby as being a good start, and the shared meal was enjoyed by all in attendance.

By the time they had returned to the house, the body in the sleeping bag had departed, and nobody would ever know who they had been, and Brennan had also awoken and left, as had Saul, or Paul. By now the others were awake, and Don played gentle, low-volume music whilst the remainder of the morning and some of the afternoon was spent in a clean-up operation by the four residents, ably assisted by Abigail, which at least returned the domicile to some semblance of order and cleanliness, the rest by general consensus being left until another day.

Abi and Ross made love again, and the afternoon was drawing on by the time she reluctantly decided that it was time to go.

'I can drop you off if you want, at the gates anyway.'

'It's okay, you've probably still got too much alcohol in the bloodstream, I'll catch the bus.'

'If you're sure...'

'I'm sure....'

'Well, I'll see you in the garden, then.'

'Yes, I suppose....'

'So what are we going to do about our employers?'

'We'll have to tell them, I suppose, I mean why not, we're consenting adults, after all.'

'Sure....'

'Only maybe not just yet...'

'A secret love affair at the big house...Yeah, I'm cool with that, if you are.'

'Let's talk about it later.'

'Okay.'

They kissed and she departed, differently apparelled now and carrying her party finery in her overnight bag. The bus journey would take her to the village Green, from whence she would walk to the Manor, and as she watched the world go by from an upstairs window, the world seemed and looked to her to be a fine place, and her life to be a fine thing. It was a life which had become becalmed, and stagnant, and she had needed change, and now there was the likelihood that she would be living in Glebe House for at least some of the time, and the Manor House was soon to be thrown into chaos when preparations began for filming, so there was something interesting, and her two charges were growing into fine young children, and she loved them both. Nathaniel, who had been born so tragically, and who was next but one in line to the Lordship, was not Michael's child, but was son to the man called Percival, who was friend to Victoria, she was certain of that now, and little Henry had no father who lived beyond Victoria's secret knowledge, so there was all of that. And now and by far most importantly, there was Ross, and their thus far clandestine love affair, for now surely this was how it could and should be regarded, and she now had the answer to a question. She had oft times wondered how and to whom she would lose her maidenhead, and now she knew, and as her journey continued she came to a decision, and a practical matter must now be seen to, and as soon as may be. In the meantime, perhaps it was the alcohol, or the lack of sleep, but now and not for the first time it seemed to Abigail as though her life was not a real thing, but that she was living as a part of a novel, which was writ anew each day, and the next pages were quite unknown to her or any of the characters who dwelt and lived out their lives therein, but they and she would know soon enough. Perhaps and indeed it was the case that the writer themselves did not yet know how their story would unfold, or had only a vague sense of it. In any case, on this page and in this chapter, the character which was she, and which she lived out every moment of each day, was no longer a virgin, the writer had seen to that; a young woman, looking out of the window of a bus bearing no expression, and none but those who knew her well would see the smile on her young face.

Chapter 7. Concerning the Manor House, and a Continuing Journey

May Thomas was the first representative of the film company to arrive at the Manor House, on the day when everything began there in earnest. She had spent the previous evening and night at her brother's house in the village, where she had assessed his emotional state and used his bath, both of which she regarded as being important aspects of her stay, and both she concluded were in good working order. Barrington she knew was a sensitive soul who had been hurt before, and Sandra Fox, the clever, beautiful and depressive object of his love and desires, had in the recent past proved to be less than reliable when it came to matters emotional, but all was apparently well between them at present. We will hear more of Barrington and Sandra later in our story, but for now we will rely upon the impressions and word of his sister, who had also slept well that night, as she always did in the house on the Green. In any case she arrived at the Manor a little after nine o'clock in the morning, feeling refreshed and ready to face the challenges of the new day. She had pulled her car up outside the house, and Victoria, who had secured the day's leave from work, answered the door to her.

'Good morning May.'

'Good morning.'

'Coffee…?'

'Thanks, that would be great.'

They walked to the kitchen, where Victoria set the kettle to boil, and May placed her briefcase on the work surface.

'That looks official…'

'You'd be amazed at how much paperwork is involved in something like this, even in our technological age. So, is everyone prepared for the invasion, then?'

'I think so, as far as we can be. Mother may be in evidence a bit, but I expect my father will retire to his study for a majority of the time.'

'I'm glad that you're here, anyway.'

'As am I that you're here, I didn't really know who to expect...'

'Well, I've been promoted to co-producer, so I'll be coordinating things, for now anyway. We have a new artistic director who hasn't been here yet, so I'll be showing him the rooms we'll be using, and after that I'll sort of let him get on with it.'

'I see, so what's he like?'

'I've not met him personally, but by reputation he's very good, and Anna and David have both worked with him before on different projects. Otherwise all I know is that he's a rather flamboyant gay and a stickler for detail, which was what we need, of course, I mean the stickler bit, not the camp-gay bit.'

They smiled, as Victoria poured hot water.

'Of course….So how are things in general with the production so far, Anna didn't paint a very happy picture when I spoke to her.'

'Oh, you know, there are always problems early on in any production, and period dramas present their own issues, it seems, but we'll get there. One must remain positive or go mad, and we've at least found somewhere for the kitchen scenes now.'

'Oh, that's good, I understand we weren't suitable for those.'

'Well, this kitchen's far too modern to be easily tailored to our needs, and too small to be honest, they needed bigger kitchens in those days for all the staff and such.'

'Indeed….Anyway whatever happens elsewhere in the house, at least we get to keep our kitchen. So what time are we expecting people?'

'Any time now I would think, starting time from now on will be eight a.m., but there're things to organize on the first day, and by the way, the coffee's great, but please don't feel obliged to make coffee for everyone, that would be asking too much, there'll be loads of us when we really get going, and people bring thermoses and such.'

'Okay, I'll bear that in mind, and keep coffee strictly between the two of us. So what happens with catering in general?'

'Well, there'll be a catering truck here when the actors arrive, but for now it's sandwiches, although I daresay I'll be sent out for burgers at some stage.'

'Isn't that a bit below your pay grade?'

'You'd be surprised what I have to do. I mean I could delegate, but my primary task is to keep everyone working productively, otherwise I'm a bit surplus to requirements when people are moving furniture around, and Roger will be giving the instructions.'

'Yes, I see.'

The sound of a large vehicle approaching the house intervened in their conversation.

'That sounds like us, I'd better go to it.'

'Okay, so do you need me?'

'Only for a quick introduction, if you want, then you can leave us to it.'

'Right you are....Well, here we go, then.'

They left their newly poured beverages on the kitchen table for now, and both had mixed feelings as they approached the front door. May had found the house, and had had to work somewhat to convince David Bates as to its suitability, and Victoria had rather persuaded her parents to allow its use, so both had considerable investment in seeing that all went well, or at least as well as could be expected.

It was with some relief that Will Tucker and Emily Cleves arrived in the province and then the city of Cappadocia, where they found themselves some fairly mid-level accommodation and allowed themselves a two-night stay, in order to spend an entire day visiting the vast and complex warren of man-made tunnels, churches, chapels and living places which had been carved into the bare, volcanic rock over many generations. One day, however, was scarce sufficient time to see and appreciate this strange and unique place, but time was pressing, and during a mid-day break for Turkish coffee, Emily saw fit to comment upon their limited time.

'It's such a shame, I could spend a week here.'

'Yeah, I know what you mean, but that applies to a few places we've been. I think we'll be okay, though, we should make it from here to Ankara in a day, then if we can do the Ankara to Istanbul run in another day, we should make it back in time for some R and R before the flight, so we've got some slack, just about, and the roads should get better from now on.'

'Yes, we do seem to have made it back to civilisation again.'

'This place is amazing, though. I mean imagine living here when it was a thriving community. So you get married and leave home, and dig your own hole to live in, and then dig more holes when the kids start arriving.'

'Yes, it is extraordinary. And talking of kids, I don't want any.'

'What, can't handle all the digging, is that it?'

'I'm being serious, Will. I mean I know we've talked about it before, and what not, but I've been thinking about it a lot whilst we've been driving.'

'Mostly I've been hoping that the car isn't going to break down, but sure, I mean whatever, Em, although it's a funny time to bring it up.'

'I know, but…It's important, you know? Probably about the most important decision that anyone has to make, actually, and I don't want that in ten or twenty years' time you start resenting me, for not having sprogs, you know?'

'Look, I can't even tell you what I'm going to resent tomorrow, never mind in two decades' time, but if that's you then I'll live with whatever happens. I mean I'm not going out on the pick-up to find someone who wants kids, sort of.... *'Hello, you look nice and my name's Will, and I was just wondering whether you would mind having some children with me...'*

'That might not work.'

'It'd be a long-shot, but my point is that you're a bit more to me than a breeding machine, you know? Anyway I'm not exactly bursting at the seams with paternal instincts myself, so, you know, it's not an issue, Em.'

'So if I said that I did want kids, would you be okay with that, too?'

'Yeah, I suppose...I mean you've never expressed any serious desire to procreate, so I've not really thought that much about it, and at the end of the day it's your body, so you do what you want, and if I had any issues I'd tell you. Anyway, here we are drinking coffee in Turkey, and you bring it up, so why now?'

'Well, in the first place you mentioned kids, and this has been such a great holiday, and Turkey's a wonderful country, but it's not the only country, is it?'

'No, I think are some other countries...'

'Exactly, and I want to see them.'

'What, all of them?'

'Well no, but I want to go to Japan...'

'Yeah, that would be cool...'

'And China...'

'Sure...'

'And India, and Malaysia, and Indonesia...'

'South America...'

'Africa...'

'Yeah, there're quite a few other countries when you come to think of it.'

'Yes, there are, and the furthest I ever went with Mum and Dad was France, and if we had kids we'd never see half of it, or hardly any of it, probably.'

'People travel later in life, Em, it's not a preserve of young people.'

'I know, but I just can't see myself putting everything on hold while I change nappies, or whatever, and see it through school, and pay for university...We'd probably never have enough money to do it properly.'

'Yeah, kids are expensive.'

'Do you think I'm being selfish?'

'What...? No, no more selfish than people who do have kids, I don't think people have children for the sake of the children, otherwise everyone would have loads of children. People have kids because they want to, and the world can't sustain our ever-growing population as it is, but nobody thinks of that when they have kids, do they?'

'No, I suppose not, so I suppose you could say that people who do have kids are more selfish than people who don't.'

'All I'm saying is that it's not something you have to feel guilty about, that's all. It's up to us, Em, we can make the decision, and if we think our lives are going to be better without kids than with them, then it's nobody's business but ours.'

'And you really don't mind?'

'Of course not, I mean I have thought about it sometimes, and if there was a problem I'd have told you.'

'Yes, I know you would.'

'Well then...Anyway I suppose we'd better go and look in a few more holes in the ground, we've only got today here.'

'Yes, I suppose...On the other hand we could just go back to the hotel.'

'Oh, okay.'

'I mean we can stay here a bit longer if you want, but I'm boiling hot, and we've seen quite a few holes already. We've been here, and it's something I really wanted to do, but you know…'

'See one hole and you've seen them all, right?'

'Something like that….'

'I thought you could spend a week here.'

'Well, I could, but just not today, and it's today that matters, isn't it?'

'Sure…Let's go take a cold shower, and prepare ourselves for the onward journey.'

'Yes, well that's one reason for going back I suppose.'

'What do you mean?'

'What I mean is that to me at this moment there are more important things than amazing landscapes, seeing the world is only one aspect of life, after all, and whilst conception might not be what's looked for…'

'There's no reason why we shouldn't keep practising.'

She smiled, and they both went in search of the car.

That which became immediately clear was that Roger Altman was not a person who could be easily ignored. A small removal lorry had arrived, and six young, male employees of Magic Hour Media Productions emerged from its various doors just as their somewhat older artistic director had rather breezed from his sports car, clipboard in hand, as May and Victoria had descended the steps of the Manor to meet him. He quickly made assessment of them as he was also clearly assessing the house, and they met.

'Hello Roger, I'm May Thomas, and this is Victoria Tillington, who'll be your main point of contact with the family during production.'

'Delighted, I'm sure...So this is our pile, is it....Nice steps...Okay boys, get ready...So, shall we into battle, then?'

May and Victoria exchanged looks, as did the removals crew, whose getting ready seemed mainly to involve lighting cigarettes, but Victoria supposed there was not much for them to do prior to receiving instruction. She also now followed May and Roger up the Manor steps and into the reception room, of which Roger was clearly and with quick eyes taking in every detail as they walked. She was surplus to requirements now, it seemed, and she let them walk ahead: May would likely take him first to the library, dining room and main study and music room downstairs, before ascending the main staircase and showing him the bedrooms which had been agreed would be used. She next went to the kitchen, where she now found her mother and father preparing a light breakfast for themselves and the two children, and whilst quickly drinking her coffee she informed her parents of the goings-on. She next went upstairs herself, where she next happened upon the pair as she was making for her bedroom, and just as they were walking past a certain portrait which hung in the upstairs hallway. They had not, however, walked past, but Roger and therefore May had stopped beside it.

'My God, who's she?'

'She's a family member,' said Victoria 'now deceased, unfortunately.'

'Christ, such wasted beauty...'

Victoria was unsure whether by this he referred to the painting or its subject, and awaited clarification.

'We'll have to use the portrait, it's lost here, she needs more space and perspective...So who was she, exactly?'

'She was wife to my brother, Michael, and mother to Nathanial, who's next in line to the title after my brother.'

'So how old was she when she died?'

'About the age that you see her, in fact she died a little less than nine months after this was painted...She died during childbirth.'

'So she was carrying the child when this was painted?'

'Yes, she was.'

'Such tragedy....We write scripts and produce films, but real life can get the better of us all, can it not?'

'Yes, I suppose it can.'

'And your portrait in the banqueting room, that was by the same artist?'

'Yes, it was.'

'Yes, one can tell....He or she has captured you perfectly, and the blue dress was a stroke of genius.'

'Thank you...'

'Anyway, we'll start downstairs.'

'So, what are your first impressions, of the house I mean?'

'It's doable, some of the rooms are smaller than one would have wished, but we were aiming for mid-level aristocracy, so I'm sure we'll make do.'

'Oh, well, good...'

'So, best get on, then, we're already running late due to a cock-up with the bloody removals lorry, and there is much to do. Thank you, May, I can take it from here, if I need anything I'll find you.'

And with that, Roger and his clipboard strode purposefully along the corridor; he was casually but expensively dressed, with a cravat which completed the ensemble perfectly and archetypically, and now Victoria and May exchanged looks, and smiles.

'So, that's Roger, then.'

'Indeed....'

'He seems to know his stuff, anyway.'

'That he does.'

Victoria was impressed. To have made such quick connection between her and her portrait, and to have even noted and remembered the colour of her dress indicated something in itself, but he had apparently in such a short meeting made assessment of her character as well; here was a man who despite his rather brusque and dismissive manner missed very little about the world and people around him, it seemed. She also wondered where May and he stood in the hierarchy of the company; May was now officially a producer of the film, which she supposed ranked higher than artistic director, but in regard to this day and the days to follow, the man would it seemed reign supreme, and all would be done in accordance with his wishes, and his apparently considerable talents.

On this day, Ross had arrived for his day's work at the usual time, and had known nothing of the events which he would bear witness to in the latter part of the day, as he was attending to matters horticultural in the front garden of the Manor, and items of furniture were removed from the house. So, it had begun then, and soon, he assumed, his duties as head and only gardener would include the removal of inappropriately modern cultivars from the borders surrounding the house, and perhaps some replanting would be required. For now, though, his duties were nothing extraordinary, just his usual attempts at taming a wilderness which had been let go for too long under the care of the last groundsman. His thoughts during this day were otherwise distracted by a certain young lady, who would also be about her duties today, and his feelings were mixed in this regard. They had slept together, and his buying of contraception prior to the event had proved to be a foresighted thing, if only retrospectively, so there would be no physical consequences, but there was an emotional aspect to the business about which he was less sure. The sex had been quite consensual, he was certain of that, although they had been a little drunk the first time, and they had made love again the next day, which had been a sort of reaffirmation that all was well, but it had all rather been in the heat of the moment even so, and now would come their meeting again in a working environment, and now would come any adverse reaction on her part, if there was to be any. So anyway he worked, and at the end of the working day there had been no contact between them, which sowed a further seed of doubt in his mind. The day had been overcast, so there was no reason for her to bring her two charges out for a walk around the grounds, as was her habit on sunnier days, so he should not read too much into that, and today had turned out not to be a usual day at the Manor in any case. But still, he wished to see her again, not only for the seeing of her, but also now to make certain that she had no regrets about the weekend, that her avoidance of him was not deliberate, and that all was well between them. As he drove home at the end of the day, however, he concluded that such reassurance would have to wait for another day. He could 'phone her, of course, or message her, but he was unsure what to say, or to write, so he thought best to leave it, and hope to see her soon.

Furniture was removed from rooms, until in some instances little was left, and Victoria noted that the technicians or removals men or however she might choose to define them went about their business in conscientious and jocular manner, who took to saying *'Roger that...'* behind their director's back whenever given instruction, something which they apparently found endlessly amusing. May Thomas found herself a quiet place in which to work on her laptop, no doubt on other aspects of the production, and only occasionally did she emerge to update herself on proceedings.

Victoria ate lunch with her parents, who had little to say about events going on elsewhere in the house, for there was nothing really to be said, this particular die having been cast, and only brief and cursory introductions had been made. Abigail had charge of the children, having arrived yesterday in the afternoon looking somewhat tired but quite contented, and Victoria had not asked for comment or intelligence as to her night away, and none was offered. The only noteworthy thing which occurred between them was a brief conversation just after luncheon, when Victoria had checked on the children.

'I wasn't expecting you to be home today.'

'I wasn't expecting to be here myself, this was all rather eleventh hour.'

'Yes, I see….Still, since you're here, I wondered whether I might take a couple of hours off this afternoon, there's somewhere I need to go, but if it's a problem then it's not a problem, if you see what I mean, I can go another time.'

'I see, well, I'm sure we'll cope, if it's only for a short while.'

'Well, I can't exactly say how long, yet, but it shouldn't be for long.'

'Okay, well, do as you wish then.'

'Thank you.'

Thus otherwise did the day pass, until at a little after six o'clock, Roger Altman and Victoria met in the reception room.

'Right, well I think we're about done for the day, so tomorrow we start the clean-up and rebuild.'

'So, is everything going okay?'

'Nothing insurmountable that I've seen….We're fortunate that the walls are tastefully painted, radiators are a bane, of course, so we'll have to be creative there, but the fireplaces seem to be in good working order should we need them, and most of the paintings we can use. Some of the portraits in the banqueting hall will have to go, including that of your father and you and your blue dress, I'm afraid.'

'Far too modern, I suppose.'

'Indeed….Still, all things considered we should be okay. Some of the crew will be in first thing and they know what to do, the rest will be with me picking up period furniture, so I'll be in later.'

'Okay, well, I'll be in London tomorrow, but I don't think you'll need me, and my father will be around if anything's required, and you have my number.'

'I'm sure we'll manage.'

'Well, thanks, then, see you soon.'

'Indeed…'

Man and clipboard left, and the removal lorry departed. Victoria walked briefly around nearly bare rooms before retiring for her shower, and thence in search of her parents, with whom she shared the evening meal. When eventually she lay down to sleep, she did so with a sense that that could have been worse. Molly had refrained from comment; this was of course the very stuff of nightmares for a housekeeper, but she had seen her working world being torn apart with stoicism. Her father's tone had been characteristically conciliatory, and had quieted her mother's equally expected complaining spirit, for which Victoria had been grateful to him. She also lived with the hope that this would be the worst part, and that once the actors were on site and filming began, the ambience would be one of creativity rather than demolition, but they were she assumed some way from that yet. In any case it had begun, and she fell into sleep with a sense of relief that the waiting was over, and one of anticipation of that which would follow. It was also the case that she currently remained grateful for any form of distraction from darker thoughts which had grown and festered in her mind of late. Her brother had been murdered by a witch, or as good as, and this was something which try as she may she could not come to any kind of terms with. Perhaps if the witches were now history, or now only a power for the good it would have been possible, but they were neither of these things, and the fact that she was in love with a witch who had carried out horrible acts herself did nothing to allay her confusion. And now another witch was looking for Rebecca, and as she understood the matter this witch was a part of the same coven as she who had bewitched Alexander as a part of some ancient curse upon her family, and the same coven as she who had threatened her child on the steps of the Manor House, so what was to be made of that? She wished so much to see Rebecca, and to seek further clarification and understanding, so that perhaps some resolution could be found, but at one and the same time the thought of speaking with her on such matters was something which Victoria found repulsive, and how could she otherwise speak to her? The curse had not been Rebecca's fault, but she was a part of it all, and perhaps she and her family were safe, now, but perhaps they were not, and not for the first time feelings of love and hatred fought for ascendancy in her mind, for who was to hate, and who to love? So for now she slept, and turned her mind to the business of a film being made in her house, in the hope that perhaps soon she would find answers to the questions which so plagued her waking thoughts.

The last days of Will and Emily's journey through Turkey were for the most part concerned with the journey itself. Having left Cappadocia the next morning they arrived in Ankara, the modern and quite cosmopolitan city, which neither had had much desire to visit, but here they found and booked into a better quality hotel, where they rested and ordered room service, despite having seen several restaurants within easy walking distance; it had been a hard day's driving, with another to follow the next day, and their sights were now firmly set on Istanbul. The hired car was by now in a condition where under normal circumstances Will would not have attempted any sort of a journey, but they did not have time now to effect any kind of repairs, and all being well they would only ask one more day of it.

In fact the car did make it to Istanbul, where their arrival at the same hotel which they had left some two weeks ago was hailed as something of a triumph by themselves and the hotel receptionists, when they briefly recounted their journey. Will returned the car to the depot, and felt obliged to point out the fact that top speed was now considerably less than it had been, and steering the car at all had become something of a challenge, but nothing was made of it by the hire company, who had no doubt seen it all before. So it was done, then, and they had one more day in Istanbul and one more night before an early morning taxi to the airport and a flight home.

Having returned the car, Will took a shower and fell on his back onto the hotel bed, and closed his eyes.

'Christ, what a relief...'

'Well done, hero boy.'

'Next place we go, let's travel by rail, or boat, or donkey. I'll be having nightmares about Turkish roads and Turkish drivers for weeks.'

'I know, but we're here now, and it was a great trip, wasn't it?'

'Yeah, but I daresay it'll seem more like a great trip when I've recovered from it, maybe I'll only remember the good bits...'

'Yes, I'm sure you will. So, what do you want to do tomorrow?'

'Sleep....'

'There're a couple more mosques I'd like to visit.'

'Sure, whatever, just as long as I don't have to drive to them...'

'No, from now on it's taxis or walking. So shall we eat in the hotel tonight?'

'Sounds like a plan.'

'I've just about got something to travel home in, but we may have to buy you a shirt for the flight, there's not enough time to get laundry service.'

'And some pants, I haven't seen a clean pair of pants in days.'

'I don't think I wish to know that. Okay, well find you some clothes somewhere, then. I mean I know we've got another day in this wonderful city, but I'm looking forward to getting home now, seeing Monty and everything. Are you looking forward to getting home...? Will....?'

Will, however, had fallen asleep.

This day also saw the reunion of Percival and his dog, which he had collected from the bus in the early morning, and this had been an emotional event for both parties to the meeting. He had the usual options for their first walk together since he and Sally had taken her over the heath, but he did not go to the heath; that was a place which now in his thoughts belonged to him and Sally, and for now he did not wish to go there alone, something which in fact surprised him rather. Hitherto he had not consciously realised how their quite brief time together had found its way into his emotional being, but there it was, and there she was, and so he did not go to the heath.

Thus it is that we now find him sitting by the lake, on one of the rustic benches which has been placed at intervals on the pedestrian pathway. The pathway had no formal structure or hard surface, but rather had been worn by the passing of thousands of feet, where people had come here to seek solace or a more natural place to be, and on rainy days the path was hard to traverse without coming away with wet or muddy shoes for one's trouble. Today was dry, however, and Lulu played contentedly in the shallows, as a kingfisher went about its business, and the now thriving population of ducks went about theirs at a safe distance across the water. The ducks had been first introduced to the lake by a certain Reginald Pratt, ably assisted in the end by others, and Percival could not but smile inwardly at the thought of it.

Louise had done her commute to Brighton on this morning, and would return in the early evening, and life now for them would resume its once normal patterns, and Percival was more glad of this than he could easily express to himself. There, however, any semblance of normality about his present circumstances ended, and Percival sat for a considerable time in contemplation of all that had recently happened, not only in his life but also in the lives of others whom he cared for. Sally had her missing tenants, who had apparently still not returned to number three, and there was something which no doubt she would be in touch with him about in due course, and she would likely wish to see him, and this time Louise would be here, for which Percival was grateful. He had resisted her charms the last time, or had resisted making a fool of himself, he was not sure which, but when it came to such matters of the flesh a man may act in a way which is in nobody's best interests, least of all perhaps their own, and Percival was no exception to this general rule, as he knew well enough himself. His dealings with the cult had perhaps come to a dramatic conclusion, at least for now, but now there were the witches and Rebecca to think about, and the two things were it seemed more closely intertwined than ever. A witch was hunting Rebecca, and she had apparently put herself in a place where a witch might easily find her, so perhaps that might be an even contest, but the cult were also seeking her, and what power she had against the chicken stranglers Percival could only guess. Rebecca was clever, and kept her own council when it was needed, this he also knew, and she would surely not put her daughter in such apparent danger, but when it came to the witch Rebecca, not everything was apparent. And now there was Charlotte, the quiet, polite and unassuming woman who had somehow infiltrated the cult in so short a time and had influence upon their actions, which had been an act of considerable bravery, and had amply demonstrated her own particular and exceptional powers; when it came to witches, she was it seemed the greatest of them all, and all others, including Rebecca, would it seemed defer to her. The day would soon come when Percival would have to see her, one way or another, but that day would not be yet, it was too soon, and if she wished to make the first contact he was also someone who was now easy to find.

Victoria remained ensconced in her ivory tower at the Manor House, and word had reached the village of a film which was to be made there, which was at least something somewhat more of this earth than much else that was happening. She it was who had instigated Rebecca's moving back to the village, but as far as Percival knew she had not much been in evidence herself, so the complexities of their particular relationship remained beyond his male understanding.

Meadow remained her usual somewhat aloof and always charming self; there was someone else who it was at times hard to read, and Keith he would also have to see soon, if only to buy him a beer and thank him again for coming to his aid in the morning after his abduction. That which Percival knew of himself was that he was not an easy friend to have, but Keith had always been there when he or others had needed him, and something like a deep bond of friendship had developed between them, regardless of their so obvious differences, and the little time that they usually spent together away from the cricket field.

In any case, there was a match at the weekend, so he would see him there, and Percival could now at least bask in the warmth of his return to the mainstream of village life and its usual and comforting rhythms, and most importantly of all, Louise was home, so there was something else for which he could be grateful.

Lulu now emerged from the shallows and shook herself dry before coming to him and putting her head on his knee, her tail working furiously.

'Yeah, okay, I know, time to move on. What do you reckon, once around the lake and then home for coffee?'

This apparently was a very good plan, and his best and most loyal friend of all strode off purposefully, turning only occasionally to make sure that her master was following. His time in hiding had been a hard thing for Percival, and not the least hard thing had been his estrangement from his canine companion, whose association with Sally he could not entirely erase. One day soon they would walk the heath, so that the ghost of her and that which they had been, which still at times haunted his thoughts could once more be laid to rest, this time perhaps for ever, but not today. Today and this moment were for the lake, and his dog, and this fine, English summer's day, and everything else could wait, for now at least.

Abigail had not made an appointment at the clinic, but did not have to wait very long before her turn was called. She had kept the children indoors on this cloudy day, both had slight colds, and she had not seen Ross, except once at a distance through the window of the nursery as he had been going about his work. She had in any case not spoken to him, and he knew nothing of her present activity, which she had decided upon the day before on the bus journey home. They were still in certain ways, she supposed, at the early stages of their relationship, but sexually they had reached fulfilment, and were now at a point of no return, or at least at a point from which she did not wish to return, and neither, she supposed, would he. A swift medical examination and interview with the doctor was all that it took for her to leave the establishment with the requisite and appropriate pills, and she would have to wait for seven days before she would be certain of safety, but from then on the visit would give her the freedom and liberty from any concern which her young mind and body now desired. It had not taken very long, but it seemed to Abigail that she had just taken an important step in the journey which was her life.

Chapter 8. A Breakfast of Fried Rice

'Hi mum...'

'Hi darling, is everything okay?'

This was early in the evening, and Meadow was on the bus, preparing a rice dish for supper, although as yet and as often was the case she was unsure how many of her family would be in attendance to eat it. Rosie she knew was in Brighton, continuing her preparation for moving into her student accommodation, but of Basil and Emma's whereabouts on this evening she had received no intelligence. In any case it was her eldest daughter who had 'phoned, to whom she had not spoken for a few days.

'I'm not sure...I mean I'm okay, but our great one and leader has gone walkabout.'

'What do you mean?'

'I mean he told Sam that he was taking time out from rehearsals, and it fell upon her to tell the rest of us.'

'I see, I think...So, any explanation?'

'Not really...I mean everything's going okay here, I think, we're making good progress with the music, but Ash is unhappy about something, and left early this morning, with no indication as to when he might be back. Apparently he's done this before, when the band were together, but mostly that was about his having fallen out with Al about something or another, but this is a bit of a mystery.'

'So is it something personal with any of you?'

'No, I don't think so, and Rick says not to worry about it, just wait until he works through whatever it is, but it sort of leaves us in limbo, so I thought I might come home for a bit.'

'Oh, well that would be lovely, of course, so when, and how? Do you need your dad to come and get you? He's not back from work yet but he'll come as soon as he gets home.'

'No, it's okay, I'll manage, Mick says he can pull in a favour from a friend with a car if I want, and I think I want, so I should be home in a couple of hours.'

'Okay, well I'm making Nasi Goreng for supper.'

'Then I need no further incentive, keep some for me, I'll be there as soon as I can.'

'We'll wait for you.'

'Okay, well if I'm delayed for any reason I'll let you know, otherwise I'll see you soon.'

Whilst Rosemary was away preparing the way for the beginning of her studies at Sussex University, another young lady who was similarly occupied was a certain Isabella Baxter. Isabella, by virtue of her natural and exceptional mathematical abilities, had gained entry to Trinity College, Cambridge, and was thus about to begin a new phase of her life, which promised to be very different to the last. In the first place she would be leaving the parental home, the place where she had been born, for the first time, and had secured a place in college dormitories for her first year at one of the most prestigious and iconic universities in the academic world. There were, therefore, certain matters which must be dealt with prior to her departure, some of them practical, and others of a more esoteric nature, the uppermost of the former being how she would live for the next years of her life. Her father, Norman Baxter, had agreed with scarce any thought upon the matter to pay all of her tuition and accommodation fees, as well as providing a certain allowance to his only daughter for her living costs. Norman Baxter, however, was not a rich man, having only a quite modest monthly income to cover his own outgoings, and this commitment would likely use up in their entirety such savings as he had, and may in due course require him to secure a bank loan, but all of this he would do willingly to see Isabella through to her graduation. Benjamin, his only son, had inherited none of his sister's exceptional academic abilities, and would likely not attend any significant further education after his school years, and Norman Baxter could think of no better use for such wealth as he possessed than paying for his daughter's immediate academic future. The only proviso to this arrangement was that Isabella would find such temporary employment as she could during the Easter, summer and Christmas breaks in the academic year, and with this agreement in place, Isabella had at least secured this most significant aspect of her forthcoming university years. There were other matters, however, which required her deeper thought. Isabella had in an emotional and indeed sexual sense lived a life which belied her still young years; there had been Jed, her first lover, whose swift and to her still inexplicable departure from her life had led her to seek her revenge upon men, and this had in turn led her down a dark and dangerous path, which had culminated in her having been drugged and gang raped, and suffering the trauma of such a traumatic experience, from which she had still but recently recovered.

And then into her life had come Richard Templeton, who had, she was quite convinced, murdered Barnabus Overton, whom she regarded as her chief assailant, and had given her some manner of emotional safe haven, and had to a large degree quieted her unquiet spirit, and restored in her some faith in the male gender. And then had come Richard's son, Stuart, with whom she had made love, and thus in a way had she come full-circle, back to an innocence which she had quite consciously cast to the four winds during her turbulent recent and still young past. Isabella had few if any close friends, her character and bearing had seen to that, so she would leave for her new life with a deep history but carrying no emotional baggage, save for the love that she held for her father, and for these two men, and it was to these two men that she now turned her thoughts, as she awaited her time to leave.

Meadow was little further forward with the preparation of food and the addition of more vegetables when the dial tone on her telephone sounded again, and this time it was Keith.

'Hi love, you still at work..?'

'Just leaving now, I've had a 'phone call from Ash.'

'Oh yes....?'

'Yeah, he's on his way to the village, wants to sink a couple of pints of ale with me in the Dog and Bottle this evening.'

'Really...? That's interesting.'

'Maybe he wants to take a look at the church tomorrow, see how the work's going.'

'That's not really the interesting part. I've just had Tara on the 'phone, apparently Ash left his house this morning with no explanation, I think she thinks he's having some kind of meltdown or something, so she's coming home, she'll be here in a couple of hours.'

'Is that so....That's curious...'

'Yes it is. It's a bit awkward, too...Is it awkward?'

'I don't know, I mean if he's having some kind of freak-out...'

'How did he sound?'

'Oh, you know, Ash-like, but nothing to indicate anything was wrong in particular. Maybe he needs a shoulder or whatever....Anyway he can hardly stop our daughter from coming to see us, can he?'

'No....I mean maybe it's nothing to do with Tara or the music, but if it is then it does get awkward, maybe.'

'Yeah, could be, but what can we do?'

'Did he tell you what he's been doing since this morning?'

'No, just that he's on the train. He and I should arrive at about the same time, I said I'd meet him in the pub.'

'Right...Well, I suppose all we can do is stay with that plan, and I'll talk to Tara when she gets here.'

'Sure...Could be an interesting evening. What's for dinner?'

'I'm making fried rice.'

'Better make enough for all of us, then, and prepare some floor space, we may have a house guest.'
'Yes, we may....This is all a bit odd, isn't it?'
'Did Tara say there're any problems between her and Ash?'
'No, I mean she doesn't think so.'
'Well, it's probably nothing to worry about then, it's just rock and roll, you know? A bit of artistic temperament which we artists suffer from sometimes...'
'Must be dreadful for you...'
'You've no idea....So I'll tell Ash that Tara's home and you tell Tara that I've got Ash, and we'll see how it goes from there.'
'Okay, speak to you later, then.'
'Sure, and don't worry, we'll sort whatever it is, it's all part of having a talented and famous daughter.'
'I blame you for that, you're the musical one.'
'That isn't fair, she's half your genes as well.'
'Go, I'll see you later.'

Meadow put more rice on to boil; she was now still less clear as to who would be eating, but she decided to err on the side of caution. Despite the new and somewhat strange circumstances she smiled to herself as she went about her culinary preparation; she had no idea what to expect from the evening, but she had Keith, who could make light of any situation, and could bring her doubts and uncertainties firmly down to earth, and usually did. She received one more 'phone call before the meal was ready, which was from Basil, to say that he and Emma would be eating in town, so there would be too much food, but Basil's absence might make a potentially complicated situation a little easier. Now whatever was the problem with Ash could receive everyone's full attention, and all that she could now do was to wait for Tara, and see how the evening would unfold from then onwards.

Isabella and Stuart met at Dawson's coffee shop, which had been on her instigation. Since the night that they had spent together at his father's house they had met only once for drinks, and the conversation had been light, they had kissed goodnight at the bus stop and made no firm plans to meet again, other than agreeing that they would see each other soon. In truth Stuart was waiting for his father and step-mother to be absent from the house again, so that they might repeat their secret dalliance, which was in fact no secret, the only secret being that she and Richard had agreed to keep his knowledge of it from Stuart. The occasions when his father and step-mother were both away, however, were occasional indeed, and this fact was causing the young man much frustration. In any case she had 'phoned him, and here they were.

'So, how's life?'

'Okay, I'm just getting ready for Cambridge, really, not that there's much left to get ready. Freshers Week is in three weeks' time, so I'll be leaving just before that, I would think.'

'Right....So you'll be living on campus, then.'

'Yes, everyone lives on campus, for the first year anyway, and I'll probably be there the whole time.'

'With little chance of escape, I daresay, or inviting guests to stay.'

'Well, it's an all-girls dorm, and it's Cambridge, you know, so I expect I'll be working hard.'

'So what about weekends and such..?'

'It's not a prison, but who knows, I won't know until I get there, really.'

'Sure....'

'So, what's your news?'

'I've got a job, behind the counter in a filling station, I start next week.'

'Oh, well done.'

'Is it? Hardly the heady stuff that you've got to look forward to...'

'Well, it's something, at least.'

'At least I won't be so dependent on the old man, I suppose.'

'Which is a good thing, isn't it?'

'I might even be able to afford for us to go out occasionally, I mean properly, maybe have weekends away or whatever.'

'Yes, I suppose you might.'

Taking Isabella out in this fashion had in fact been the primary motivation in Stuart's finding employment; his paternally-provided allowance would be insufficient to pay for hotel rooms or other accommodation, but her somewhat reticent reaction to the idea and her general demeanour gave the young man pause. They had only touched upon their immediate future at their last meeting, and had not at any time discussed any longer-term plans, and he sensed now that it was not something which she was keen to speak about, and she was about to embark on a new life, in a new town, so he was on his guard. What, after all, did he have to offer her, other than their occasional meetings, which would likely soon become very occasional? In any case the subject was let go, and conversation now revolved around life at university, which was something which his sister and brother would understand, but that he would not, having opted during his own post-school years to travel the world. By the time they had finished their coffee, he had become quite convinced that she had instigated this meeting in order to make it their last, but he allowed himself one more chance to at least assuage his most immediate sense of frustration.

'So, what now..?'

The question could be taken either way, and he left it to her to decide which way to take it.

'What do you mean?'

('What do you think I mean?')

'Fancy going for a walk along the river..?'

A place where they had made love again on the morning after they had first slept together, and her answer would answer everything.

'No, I don't think so.'

So, that was an end to it, then, which he could and perhaps should have seen coming. Isabella Baxter, this strange, highly gifted and sexually experienced young woman, who was in any case first and foremost friend to his father, was not to be his future, and if this was not to be his future, then his future must lie elsewhere than where his life currently lay in its stagnation. Before they had even said goodbye, and before she had walked out of the coffee shop and out of his life, Stuart Templeton had made a decision. The world was calling, and he would leave, as soon as he had accumulated enough money for his fare, to whichever part of the world the wind might take him. He had in any case met Isabella largely on his father's instigation, and he had liked her well enough, although she was of nervous disposition and unpredictable temperament, and so perhaps this was after all for the best. There were, as his step-mother might have put it, other fish in the sea, and it was his hope that the next fish would swim in warmer waters.

The Dog and Bottle public house was moderately attended at this early hour on a mid-week evening; there were a few office workers from the town, putting some time and alcohol between their work and home lives, and others enjoying the wholesome fare offered by Susan, worthy wife to Nigel Hollyman, the worthy landlord, rather than cook their own evening repast. The notoriety of the village Green, in the quiet and picturesque village of Middlewapping, which was due in very large part to the infamous meteorite which had landed close to its centre some years past, had seen to it that the establishment had since thrived, and although interest had waned over the years, and the small piece of extra-terrestrial rock had to some extent entered into common folklore, the pub continued to benefit from its presence. In any event on this evening, Ashley Spears, once and now once again famous rock musician, whose occasional presence in the village had done nothing to lessen its notoriety, had ordered his beer and found a corner table with no difficulty. Such a man as he also still attracted some interest and attention; his physical appearance and quiet and effortless charisma alone set him apart from the crowd, and it was well known thereabouts that he had bought the village church, and that *'Tara'*, a new young talent to arrive on the music scene, lived hereabouts, although nobody was quite sure where, or why he had bought the church, and Nigel and Susan Hollyman if asked gave nothing away.

In any case Keith, father to Tara and friend and occasional fellow musician to Ashley, now joined him at table, and his long, tied-back quite blonde hair led those others present to assume that he too must be a famous musician, although nobody could quite place him, and he had all the appearances of being a builder, which further added to the enigmatic nature of the two men who now sat opposite one another.

Keith supped his ale, and such was the understanding between these two that for a moment neither spoke, until Keith broke the friendly and amicable silence.

'So, what's up, Ash?'

'Yeah, you know, just wanted to get away.'

'What, all getting too much or something?'

'Not so much that…'

'Thing is, Tara spoke to Meadow and she's coming home, she said that you walked out on rehearsals or whatever.'

'Well, we weren't actually rehearsing at the time, but I guess you could say that, and I'm glad she's around, we should talk anyway.'

'So what, things not going so well with the album..?'

'The album's going fine, as far as it goes. Like we've got sixteen songs at various stages, and I guess thirteen or maybe fourteen of them will make the cut, and we're close to studio-ready with most of it. I've got some orchestral backing to work on with some of the tracks, but Sam's helping with that, and Aiko's got the base lines working well.'

'So…Why the need to get away..?'

'Just needed some space, I guess, it gets fairly intense, you know?'

'Sure, but I still sense a *'but'* coming.'

Ashley drank his beer, and was clearly thoughtful before he replied.

'It's the third album, you know?'

'Meaning what?'

'I mean with the first album you ride on the novelty value, new voice, new direction, and Tara's got a great voice, so that worked, and the second album reinforced that well enough, I guess.'

'Sure…'

'So then what..? I mean sure, we could carry on and make maybe four more albums, but then it gets to feel like a product, you know? Just another female voice making moderately good music which sells moderately well, the record company keeps signing the contracts, and we all make money and go home, but that was never it for me, and I don't think it should be for Tara, either. I mean she and I have talked a lot about the philosophy of the whole thing, and I think Tara agrees that none of us are in this for the money, any more than are you, but it feels like we're walking into something which was never the point of it, and maybe we need to reassess, you know? I mean the music's good, man, don't get me wrong.'

'But in your opinion it's not *that* good, right?'

'It's good enough to ensure some kind of a future, but we need to take control of that future, and not let past success dictate what happens next, is how I feel right now, and I suppose that's how I've always felt.'

'Right…So have you let Tara know how you feel?'

'Not in so many words, and of course she's the most important person in all of this now, and the album's going to get made, whatever, and for her to sing is the main thing, and I want to make that happen, but musically she and I have what one might call a complicated and interesting relationship.'

'Sure, I mean I get that. She's the voice but you're the writer and creative input, and you both have to be cool with what's being produced, right? I mean as far as I've heard, she thinks the songs are good songs.'

Ashley smiled, and drank more beer.

'I know, and I bless her for that, and maybe it's just me, you know, but I don't want us to make good music, I want us to make great music, which a year down the road isn't going to be covered by some kind of idiots and played in supermarkets. Tara's got soul, you know, but she can only sing what she's given, and I don't want to be letting the lady down.'

'Without you she'd never have sung anything, Ash.'

'Yeah, but we're past that now, man. However this all started, Tara's her own woman now, in her own right, with her own talent, and that deserves more than just a good album, and a better thing than just being, I don't know….'

'Another female voice…'

'I guess…And I suppose I just wanted to talk it through with someone who isn't so close to it.'

'I'm kind of close to it, Ash, I mean I'm playing on the album and I'm father to the lady in question.'

'Yeah, and your songs stay, they're good album tracks, and we'll need you to give some time to it soon, so maybe that isn't it. Maybe I wanted to talk to a friend, and someone who knows Tara better than I, and someone who'll understand when I say I love the girl, and want the best for her.'

'Well then you've come to the right place, but what does Sam have to say about all of this?'

'Well there's another complex relationship. I mean there's Sam and I as lovers, man and wife or whatever, and Sam who plays keyboards, but Sam's been there since the beginning, you know? She knows how it used to be with the band, and how much shit we went through making any kind of music, but with Tara she's kind of taken a back seat, and she's been through enough of my doubt and insecurity, and I don't want her to go through that bullshit anymore, or for it to be anything between us, if you know what I mean.'

'Yeah, I think I get that...So is the doubt and insecurity something which has always been there, I mean when the band were together?'

'Always, but back in the day we used to just take more drugs and get on with it, and live on the adulation, and I had Mickey to go to when things got heavy, before the fucker killed himself, but I don't have that crutch anymore, and as a man grows older, you know?'

'Sure...'

'Now it feels like it's just me against the fear.'

'So what's it fear of, Ash? Failure...?'

'I don't know, mediocrity, maybe, or a fear that one day I'll wake up and can't do it anymore, or that it's all been for nothing, so yeah, I suppose you could call it failure, which was different when I was front-man, back then I stood or fell on my own abilities, and if people stopped listening I'd have stopped playing and been cool with that, but now there's Tara, and her success or otherwise to think about, and that's a responsibility which weighs heavy sometimes.'

'It would never have been for nothing, Ash, even if you stopped now you've made some great music, and the fact remains that her success so far is all down to you, and she's made two critically acclaimed albums which have brought pleasure to a lot of people, and Tara's big enough to stand up for herself, you know?'

'I know….'

'If she thought the songs were crap she'd tell you, so have some faith, man, in yourself, but also in her. I mean she's always had this self-effacing way about her, but deep down she's all there, otherwise she'd never be able to stand up and sing in front of thousands of people, and she sings because she believes, not just in herself but in you, and in the music, so, you know, stay with it, and trust the people around you, you're not in this alone, man, however it may feel right now.'

Customers now began to leave the premises, in greater numbers than they entered; the early evening was over, and the establishment now waited for the later evening clientele. The two friends were quiet for a moment, until Ashley spoke.

'You know, I love this place. I've travelled the world with the music, and been to some places, you know, and Sam and I have found some kind of domestic and emotional harmony which I never thought I'd find, but coming here always feels like coming home.'

'Yeah, well, we like it here, and it's been a great place to bring up the kids. We should take a look at the church tomorrow.'

'Sure, I mean is it okay if I crash at your place tonight?'

'Of course, take it as read, and stay as long as you need.'

'Thanks, man…'

'Think nothing of it, Tara's not the only person who owes you, you know? You've given our eldest daughter a kind of life that none of us expected her to have, least of all her.'

'Tara owes me nothing, and nor do you, despite my current state of mind Tara's given me a whole new musical direction which I didn't expect, either, and I've got a new guitarist. Talking of which, you do need to put some time aside soon, we need you at the house and then we start studio work, so be ready for that,'

'Just say the word, Will's back on site from Monday, so he and Damien can handle things whilst I'm away, I can give you as long as you need.'

'Okay, well let's say from Monday, then. I'll take a day out tomorrow and get back in the saddle next day, and thanks for this, Keith, I appreciate it.'

'Think nothing of it, but Tara might be wondering what's going on, I should call her.'

'Yeah, and I should call Sam, she can steady the ship 'til I get back. So shall we invite the ladies to dine with us, the least I can do is to buy everyone some pub food.'

'Sure....I need the gents anyway, so I'll leave you to deal with Sam and I'll 'phone home. So is everything cool?'

'Yeah, everything's cool, just, you know....'

'Sure, not a word...'

It would be better than a week after her meeting with Stuart that Isabella would meet his father. She had 'phoned the house, but Richard had been away on business for a few days, and they met by appointment one early evening at the chess club. By happenstance, her annual subscription to the club was due to expire shortly, and she would not be renewing it, and this would be their last meeting here. They smiled a greeting for each other, and by force of habit found a table and board.

'One for the road, then..?'

He held his fists out to her, containing respectively a white and black pawn, and she drew the white pieces, and moved her e-pawn two squares. Talking was discouraged at the club whilst play was in progress, and loud talking was forbidden, but they were far enough away from other occupied tables to allow low-volume conversation.

'So, you're about to leave us, then.'

'Yes...'

'We're going to miss our highest-ranking player.'

'And how about you, will you miss me?'

'Of course, and not just for the chess, I'll miss our post-match coffees as well.'

'Yes, so will I.'

They played a variation of an opening which both knew well, and made their moves quickly and with little thought.

'Still, onto bigger and better things.'

'I suppose so. I've, ummm, I met Stuart.'

'Yes, so I understand.'

'Did he say anything?'

'Not in so many words, but apparently he's been moping about the place when he's been home, and staying in his room even more than usual.'

'Oh, I'm sorry.'

'He's not your responsibility, Isabella, and this was bound to happen under the circumstances.'

'Yes, I suppose it was.'

They had moved quickly into the middle-game after swift exchange of pieces, and now more thought was required between moves, but the silence hung heavy between them, and Isabella saw fit to break it.

'So, where are you ranked at the club now?'

'About fifth or sixth, I think, I've hardly been here recently, and been a bit off my game when I have been.'

'Not like the heady days of Copenhagen, then?'

A quick exchange of looks for that one; she knew what had happened in Copenhagen, and he knew that she knew, or at least was as good as certain of it.

'No, nothing like that...'

'Still, I regard that as being a high point in my life.'

What, he wondered, had been the high point, the city and her time with him, the chess, or the matter which would not be spoken of?

'Yes, you played well.'

The game now required full concentration, and both were grateful for the distraction, and for a while neither spoke. By move twenty-six the position was equal, neither player could see any way of gaining advantage without a long and protracted contest, and neither now wished to prolong this meeting; there would be no end game, and Richard was the first to express their mutual feeling.

'So, what do you think, shall we call this one a draw?'

'Yes, let's do that.'

She sat back in her chair, as did he, and both smiled again. Under more usual circumstances one or other would have suggested another game, or coffee, but these were not usual circumstances.

'Well then, I suppose I should go.'

'Yes, I suppose you should. Don't be a stranger, Isabella, come back and see us sometimes.'

'Yes, I'll do that.'

Words to fit the occasion, but both knew that in all likelihood this would be their last meeting, whatever may be the intent.

'So, goodbye then, Richard, and thanks, you know, for everything.'

'The pleasure's been all mine...'

A final smile and she stood up, and now it was Richard Templeton who watched this strange and enigmatic young woman walk quickly across the hall and through the door. Isabella had not wept after her parting from Stuart, but as she stood now at the bus stop in the fading light of the evening, tears welled up in her eyes; this had been the hardest goodbye, and now perhaps for the first time she understood that her love for Richard had been the deeper love, and he it was that she would miss the most.

'Hi...'
'Yeah, it's me.'
'I know it's you, Keith, so what's happening?'
'The man and I are just having some beers and a quiet chat, but that's done now, the chatting part anyway, so is Tara there?'
'Yes, she's here, and she'd quite like to know what's going on.'
'Nothing to worry about, it's just man stuff, you know?'
'What kind of 'man stuff'?'
'I'll tell you later, just keep Tara away from it. So is she okay?'
'Not particularly, I mean none of this is making her feel good, you know?'
'Sure, but tell her not to worry, it's cool, and bring her to the pub, Ash's buying supper for everyone, and there's vegetable lasagne.'
'Oh, okay....Where are you, anyway?'
'I'm in the gents, you know me, ever the incurable romantic. I'm about to get the beers in, shall I get you an orange juice?'
'Yes, and put some Vodka in it, will you, I think I need it.'
'Sure, see you in a few minutes, and don't worry, we're all sorted here.'
'If you say so...'

Keith returned to the bar, and purchased two beers, a Vodka and Orange for his beloved woman and Vodka and Tonic for his equally beloved daughter, and re-joined Ashley, who was just ending his call with Samantha.

'So, all good at HQ...?'
'Yeah, Aiko sort of freaked out, then meditated her way through it, and Rick went to the pub, but Sam's got the situation under control, I think.'
'Good...'
'Man, I didn't expect this....'

'What didn't you expect, that you'd have a crisis of confidence or that people would react to your sudden and inexplicable disappearance?'

'I don't know, both, I guess...'

'Well, the former's understandable, but the latter you might have seen coming, man, people are putting heart and soul into this, each in their own way, and the reason they're there just walked out of the door, so, you know, it was going to happen. If I might suggest that in future you talk it through with the people who matter, who are all great people, you know, and they all love you, so don't take the whole thing on yourself.'

'Yeah, I love them, too, which I guess is a part of the problem...Anyway, I'm sorry I brought this to your door, Keith....'

'Don't be that, either, it's what friends are for, just go and make the album, Ash. Do it for Tara, man, she won't understand.'

'I know, or I should have known. I'd move the earth for her, man, and I've just fucked this, haven't I?'

'It's not fucked, it's just temporarily derailed, and like I say, it's understandable, and not just by me, so put it down to a bad day. We all have bad days.'

'Sure...'

The masculine philosophy was now interrupted by feminine presence, as Meadow and Tarragon entered the establishment and took the two remaining, opposing and vacant chairs, and whatever feelings and senses exist between people who know each other as well as did these four people, each in regard to each of the others, took precedence, before any words were spoken. Words, however, needed to be spoken, and Tara was the first to speak.

'So, what's going on?'

The question hung in the air for a moment longer than its sound, and Ashley could not explain, but some explanation was needed.

'I just needed time out, it's nothing.'

'It isn't *'nothing'* Ash, is everything okay with the music?'

'Yeah, everything's cool with the music.'

'So....'

Keith and Meadow exchanged looks, and both agreed that intervention was needed between the musician and his protégé, so Keith intervened.

'It's just us men have to sort our shit out sometimes, but that's done now, right Ash?'

'Yeah, it's done.'

'But....'

Keith now looked at his daughter, who was clearly not content with the explanation thus far given.

'It's all good, Tara, Ash and I just needed to talk some things through, and I've agreed to join the band from now on, so we can move on to the studio.'

Meadow had thus far watched and listened in silence, but Keith needed help, and the conversation needed to be brought down to earth, and practicality.

'So when are you going up?'

'Monday, Ash needs to see the church, then I'll be going into rock musician mode for as long as it takes.'

Tarragon studied all three people, and her relief that all did indeed seem to be well was tempered by a sense that she was not being told everything, but she quickly concluded that this was all that she would be told.

'Well, good then...'

'Yeah, I should have come sooner, so you can blame today on me.'

Tarragon would do no such thing, but she smiled her thanks to her father for the distraction.

'Anyway, we builders get hungry, so I suggest food. I'm for the lasagne.'

In the late evening of her meeting with Richard Templeton, Isabella sat up on her bed as was her wont, arms wrapped around her knees and chin resting on her arms, rocking gently backwards and forwards. She was in her nightdress, but was otherwise not quite ready for the night. So, it was done, then, although it had not been an easy thing to do, and her reaction to saying goodbye to Richard had surprised her somewhat, but it was done, at least, and now she must look to the future. Soon she would leave a world where her exceptional abilities set her apart from those around her, and would she supposed be living and studying with her intellectual and academic equals, and this was something to which she looked forward. A new future awaited her, away from home and amongst new people, and here was a chance to at last put the past, with all of its hatred and confusion, and now a little sadness at love lost, behind her, and to remake her life into something better, and into something with which she could live. For a while she lost track of the passing of time, as her thoughts wandered where they would through her life, and chess games, and Copenhagen, and it was at some uncertain time that she lay down under the covers and turned off her bedside light. She closed her eyes on her old life, and would open them in the morning to a bright new world; the next part of her history was about to be writ, and at long last she felt ready for the writing of it.

The remainder of the evening in the Dog and Bottle passed in quite light and amicable fashion, although the undercurrents of the reason for the gathering remained, and threatened at any time to pull the conversation into deeper and darker waters. In due time the party retired to the bus and trailer, Keith showered whilst Meadow made up a sleeping place for Ash, and finally she and Keith retired to their futon, and she had a question.

'You haven't told me what this has all been about, Keith.'

'Yeah, it's just stuff, you know?'

'No, I don't know, that's why I'm asking.'

'Ash is thinking about the future, where everything goes from here.'

'You mean with the music?'

'Yeah, that kind of thing…With Tara, you know.'

'And what did you and he conclude?'

'Nothing, really, but it's okay, he just had some kind of an existential mid-album crisis. He's worried about doing his best for her, that kind of deal.'

'I see…But the album's going to go ahead, I take it.'

'Oh sure, he came around pretty quickly, I think he just needed to talk it through.'

'Tara was quite upset when she first got home.'

'Sure, but she's got nothing to worry about, the show will go on…'

'And how much influence did you have on that?'

'Hard to say, I mean in practical terms nothing, I suppose, I mean I don't write the songs, but sometimes people just need some reassurance, you know?'

'Yes, of course, and you can reassure with the best of them, can't you.'

'One does one's best. I might be away for a while.'

'Well, whatever, I'm sure I'll cope. Anyway, well done, Keith, you seem to have averted the crisis.'

'Yeah, the things one does for one's family, all that beer I had to drink.'

They held one another and sleep took them, and the next morning dawned fresh and new, and everyone ate fried rice for breakfast.

Chapter 9. A Witches Coven, and The Trials and Triumphs of Ross Farrier

Fifi Fielding arrived at the Manor House in the morning at the appointed time, where she was to meet May Thomas, and thence she assumed the resident gardener. It was in fact quite by happenstance that she had read in a horticultural publication an advertisement placed by a film company, which required a consultant to work on an upcoming production. Fifi had more than sufficient work at present, and would likely have ignored the advertisement, had she not noticed the location of the film set; Middlewapping Manor, family home to Michael Tillington, her client at Glebe House. This piqued her greater interest, which had motivated her to respond to the advertisement, mentioning her connection with the son of the household, and whether this was influential in her gaining the consultancy she did not know, but in any case she got the job, and here she was. It was true to say that Anna Merchant knew little or nothing about plants, and cared about as much, but in the interests of making her production as authentic as possible, she had rather persuaded David Bates, producer and budget-holder for the film, to pay for a one-off consultancy. Most of the people who would she hoped in time watch the film would not, she was sure, know the difference between a Viburnum and a Veronica, but in such productions as this detail was everything, and there would always be somebody who would point out a plant which would not have been there in Elizabethan times, and although she knew well enough that the budget would be tight, she considered the cost to be worth the bearing.

And so, Fifi Fielding arrived, at a time when there was still much activity about the place, with technicians wielding drills, paint brushes and such equipment and materials as were required to bring the Manor back a few hundred years in time;

a meeting was held, and she was introduced to the gardener, with whom she would walk the grounds.

Victoria Tillington was in residence on this day, and out of a general interest in that which was happening, she was also briefly introduced to the consultant, who thought that she would make her connection to the family known.

'Actually, I know your brother, Michael.'

'Oh, really..?'

'Yes, on a professional level. I've designed and will I hope eventually be involved in landscaping the gardens at Glebe House.'

'Of course, now I recognise your name, he's spoken of you. Well, good luck with trying to sort out our mess of a garden, Ross is doing his best, but he's still quite newly arrived here, and he's on his own, and there's a lot to do in any case.'

'Well, first impressions are that most of the planting will be fine, you've got some lovely mature trees here which are mostly native, so there shouldn't be anything too drastic, just some shrubs around the house I would think, but we'll see.'

'Indeed, well, I'll leave you to it, then.'

Since her return to the white house, Charlotte, head of the coven of witches, had spent her time in quiet meditation as she had been going about her daily and solitary life. She had yet to speak with Rebecca, or Percival, and had no current contact details for either, so would for now have to wait for them to contact her, however that might be done. Much uncertainty still surrounded both of these people, and this was something she must address soon, but that which by degrees became foremost in her thoughts was that the inner circle must be gathered together as soon now as may be. She had acted quite alone in her attempt to resolve the matter of the sect, and knew that in doing so she had put her own place as head of the coven at risk, so her own future was also uncertain, and this state of being could not be allowed to continue. Thus it was that she first 'phoned Sophia, and then Maria, Sylvia and Amanda, and last of all Rosalind. Each of them had a contact number which was known and used only amongst the inner circle, and each of them had quite naturally wished to know everything which had occurred since they had last seen her, but to each of them she said the same thing; that she would address them all at their next meeting. To Sophia in particular she would gladly have unburdened herself, but she did not wish to be seen to be showing favour to any of them; let them all meet, and be told, and let them individually and collectively judge her as they would.

Thus was a meeting convened, two days hence, and thus could Charlotte do little more in the practical sense than make ready the cellar which now served as a meeting room, and wait for the appointed day.

Ross accepted the intervention of the consultant into his working life with silent contempt; he could have told anyone which plants should be there and which should not with sufficient accuracy, but here was a consultant, and it was their money, so it was up to them. In any case, to turn the Manor House grounds as were into anything like an Elizabethan garden was in his considered opinion akin to making a silk purse from a pig's ear, but there it was. He wondered briefly who he was now working for. His wages were of course to be paid by the Manor as usual, but he was now he supposed de facto working for the film company, so some accommodation had likely been agreed upon, or more likely he had been loaned to the film company for the duration. So in any case he and said consultant walked the grounds, and he received instruction as to which plants would be removed, and which severely cut back to allow later regrowth once filming was over, which looked like about three or four day's work. The director had wanted more colour, it was the wrong time of year to be planting summer bedding, or anything else for that matter, and the gardens in general were no longer a matter of pretty herbaceous borders as would once have been the case, with a gang of gardeners to tend them, but rather the order of the day was low-maintenance, so quite where the colour was to come from Ross was unclear, but he would leave all such matters in the no doubt capable hands of the consultant.

Ross had seen Abigail only occasionally since the weekend of the party, and mostly this had been from a distance as she had been walking abroad with her charges, and they had spoken in person only once. Her manner at this meeting had been friendly enough to reassure him that she held no regrets at their having slept together, and their telephonic communication since that weekend had also been friendly enough, but Ross was aware from his own experience and the experience of others that with women one could never be certain, and time alone together was still something which evaded them. That was until late in the afternoon of this day, by which time the consultant had gone, and would leave him to carry out her instructions whilst she sourced some plants to provide at least some degree of supplementary colour. She came to the tool shed as he was preparing to go home, and she looked different today, in an immediately obvious way.

'Welcome to you all, and I apologise that it has been a longer time than usual since our last gathering.'

The witches had all arrived within close proximity of the appointed time, Charlotte had made tea, and after the traditional and time-honoured ritual, discussion could begin amongst the inner circle, and it was Maria who first responded.

Maria, Charlotte knew, would likely waver in her support for her, Sophia she could rely upon to take her side, Sylvia's quiet sensibilities she could not predict, Amanda would likely take a neutral stance, and would await discussion, and Rosalind made no secret of her disapproval of Charlotte's actions or her disdain for Rebecca, or indeed her wish to take Charlotte's place as head of the coven.

'Then you apologise for something which was inevitable, and of your own making.'

This was somewhat more aggressive a stance than Charlotte would have hoped for from Maria, and she wondered whether this would set the tone of the meeting.

'Yes, thank you, Maria, and you are right, of course. Nevertheless I could not have predicted the duration of my absence with any certainty, but I do apologize, and hope that you will at least all see and accept the sincerity of my apology.'

'I think that will depend,' said Rosalind 'upon whether the effective disbandment of our coven was a price worth paying for that which has been achieved, and of that we await your words.'

'Indeed,' said Charlotte 'and you will all judge that as you may, but in my defence I would point out that our *disbandment* as you have seen fit to call it was only ever to be temporary.'

'Nevertheless it is unprecedented in our history, and was not done with our approval.'

'We cannot know the history of our coven in its entirety, Rosalind, but your point is made, and noted.'

'So,' said Amanda 'before we proceed I think we'd better hear what's been going on, and what you've been doing these past weeks, since we last heard any news of you.'

'Yes, of course, and for my lack of communication with any of you I can also only apologize, but for reasons you are about to hear I have had no access to a telephone.'

'So, what have you been doing?'

'I will tell you my story as briefly as I can, then you are of course free to ask any questions that you have. I have been mostly in the town of Headwater, where I infiltrated the sect, and became its member, and where I did my best to influence its decision making.'

'You did what?' said Amanda 'How on earth did you do that, get in with the sect, I mean?'

'It was not easy, Amanda, but I have used such powers as I have, and otherwise would rather not expand upon that.'

'But wasn't it dangerous?'

'Yes, there was a certain danger to the matter, of course, and as I indicated at our last meeting, it was not a decision which I took lightly, but I deemed the risk worth the attempt, and I was in that regard at least successful.'

'So are you still a member of the sect?'

'Yes, I could return there if I so wished, but I have no wish to do so, and I can at present see no gain to it, in that regard I believe I have achieved as much as I am able to achieve.'

'And what, pray, have you achieved?' Said Rosalind

'Wait a minute,' said Amanda 'I think first we should know more about this sect, like what is it, and what are its aims?'

'That I will not tell you…I have taken a vow of secrecy which I will not break, any more than I would break the vows of secrecy which exist between us. I will only say that the sect is a very ancient one, and exists for reasons that none of us would have predicted or assumed, and however we may judge their actions, at their core I no longer regard them as a force for evil.'

'They were going to kill Percival, and we all remember the night at Howard's Bench.'

'Yes, of course we do, and I still believe that our actions in helping Rebecca to confront her alleged tormentors were justified, but they would also tell you that their intent on that night was justified, and I see no need to make judgement upon that, nor for us to further discuss the sect or the reasons for its existence. Suffice to say that we as a coven have nothing to fear from them, it is only now against Rebecca that they seek vengeance.'

'So what about Percival, is he in the clear now?'

'Yes, I believe he is, so long as he takes no further action against them himself. Largely on my instigation, Percival was recently once more brought before the sect, and I was able to use my influence in so far as to convince them that Percival no longer represents any kind of existential threat to them, indeed that he never did, and that he should be let alone. Indeed the view was taken that Percival may be the way to Rebecca, so he was in the end allowed to live, and was let go, and has now returned home. Percival in my view was and is an adventurer, who took it upon himself to avenge Rebecca, in part at least because of his love or regard for her, but also I believe this was a manifestation of a restless spirit, which thrives on danger, or the possibility of danger, and all that has happened may I think at least in part be seen as a manifestation of that spirit, and nothing more or less than that. Percival has no knowledge of the sect, its philosophy or ideology, and nor I believe does he care about it, so there is no longer any need for his death. He it was, with others, who saw to it that Rebecca was rescued, but that act alone has now I believe been forgiven, or at least consigned to history, and the sect knows well enough that Percival has protection, and they will not in any case risk open warfare with the witches. As I have said, the sect is not in my view essentially evil, and they do not kill for the sake of killing, but rather and only as a way to assure their own continuation. Percival was to be killed, and had he been killed this would be the first time in living memory that such a thing would have happened, but if I am any judge of the matter he is no longer or at least as things stand in any danger.'

For a moment there was silence around the table, whilst all considered the magnitude of that which she who was still for now their leader had achieved, and in so short a time. To have infiltrated the sect, alone, and to have gained such intelligence and had such influence was indeed an extraordinary feat, and one which must be considered, and in various degrees by those gathered respected, however grudgingly that respect might be given.

'So, that briefly is my story, and I should add that I have not spoken to Percival or Rebecca since I returned here. I have needed the time since then to come to terms with and frankly recover from my own particular adventure, and my first priority was to call this meeting and speak with you all, so that you may pass whatever judgement you will upon me. So, I pass the matter over to you.'

'Well,' said Amanda 'I think we're all frankly amazed, at least I am, anyway, but I suppose the next question must be, what about Rebecca, is she still in danger?'

'There I was able to have less influence, and Rebecca is still the sworn enemy of the sect, and yes, she is still in danger.'

'So,' said Rosalind 'all of your efforts, however impressive, have only served to save the life of one man, so far anyway, and Percival is a name that we have heard so often, is it not?'

'If you are implying, Rosalind, as you have done before, that saving Percival was my prime motivation and intent, then all I can do is to once again deny that absolutely.'

'Anyway,' said Sophia 'that is not *only* what Charlotte has achieved, is it, which could be said to be enough anyway. We now have deep knowledge of the sect which we did not have before, and what their aims are.'

'Do we...?' Said Rosalind 'Apparently we are not to be privy to any information which might enable us to judge the sect for ourselves in any meaningful way, since our leader has seen fit to keep any such intelligence from us...'

'And amongst other things I have thought long and hard about this, Rosalind, since my return, but on this I will not be swayed, however much I may wish to tell you. I will not break my vows.'

'Anyway,' said Sophia 'we also know that we don't need to worry about the sect any more, and that was never a given, was it? We beat them absolutely at Howard's Bench, and they might well have wanted a re-match, but that isn't the case, apparently.'

'No, my dear Sophia, there need be no *'rematch'*. Let me say that since Howard's Bench there has been much soul-searching within the sect, and they have changed their leader twice since then, and not everyone is in agreement about how their future should be.'

'So even now we cannot be certain of anything,' said Rosalind 'if they change their leader again then everything else could change, could it not?'

'If you seek for absolute certainties in any of this, Rosalind, then you seek in vain. Everything can change, that is the way of things, but you should bear in mind that the sect has its own survival and future stability to consider. Howard's Bench was a long time ago, now, and the intervention of the witches was something that nobody in the sect could have predicted, and the events of that night have echoed ever since in the collective consciousness of the sect. It was for them something traumatic, and trauma can take and has taken a long time from which to recover, and they have higher things to consider, which in the end it is my belief will always take precedence over their wishing to avenge themselves upon us. They have seen our power, and it is my firm belief that they will not seek confrontation with us again, even if they were able to find a means of so doing. We have nothing to fear from them.'

'So,' said Maria 'all of this in the end comes down to Rebecca, does it not?'

'Yes, Maria, I believe it does, and there lies the far more traumatic event in their recent history. Their temple was burned, and many of them died cruelly at Rebecca's hands, and still more recently an assassin was sent amongst them, and more of them were killed, and for that they also blame Rebecca.'

'What…? So, I mean was that really her?'

'I don't know, Maria, but I suspect not. I believe that in her current state of mind and being Rebecca would not have done such a thing, and they may have other enemies besides anyone whom we are aware of.'

'Well,' said Rosalind 'it seems to me that so much of this is based on your beliefs and suppositions, one is left to wonder how much of it we should take at its face value.'

'You may and will take it as you wish, Rosalind, and this is what today's meeting is for. I am aware that there are matters pertaining to other members of the coven to be dealt with and judged upon, some of them as quickly as may be, and I take full responsibility for all such delays, but before and above all else it is for you to decide whether you wish me to continue as your leader. That is the only decision which we will come to today, and we will come to it in due course, but please, for now, let us continue our deliberations regarding Rebecca, for as Maria has rightly said, her future and ours are bound together, and all in the end comes down to how we regard her, and what we do about her.'

'Well,' said Rosalind 'not for the first time let me say that I regard her as a murderess, since by your own admission, that is what she is.'

'I don't regard speaking the truth as an admission, Rosalind, and I have never denied any of Rebecca's acts, horrific though they were, but they were done at a time when all of her thoughts and energies were focussed absolutely on taking her own vengeance against the sect, and the way that she claims to have been treated by them as a young girl. For ten years and more she was kept by them, and if we are to believe her, abused by them, and her actions must be seen in that context. She was once a powerful witch, perhaps the most powerful of us all, but she has changed now, and is not as she was, and she has a child, and so it is my firm belief that even if we now abandon Rebecca to her fate, we cannot so abandon her child. Rebecca is one of us, she is a member of our coven, and I for one will not desert her, any more than would our dear Helen, our former leader.'

'Who was killed, and we have never understood why, or by whom, and Helen's daughter, Helena, has also we must assume met her untimely end. So much death and mystery surrounds Rebecca, and it is and has always been my view that we must be rid of her, once and for all, and in this I will not be moved. As you say, we have only her word for what happened during those ten years, and if as you say the sect is not intrinsically evil, it throws more rather than less doubt on her story, does it not? I have listened to your words, Charlotte, and understand the risks that you have taken, but unless you can find greater justification for your unilateral actions, I hereby challenge you for the leadership of our coven, and if the vote should go against me then I will leave the coven, and the sisterhood, and I will not return.'

Silence again now found its rightful place amongst them, as each of them came to terms with this sudden development, which was in truth not entirely unexpected, but it had come swiftly, and needed a moment.

'Well, thank you for your candour, Rosalind, which I'm sure we all appreciate. Very well, then, we must each of us decide as we may, and I suggest an adjournment for one hour whilst we all decide upon this stark choice. I have not been your leader for very long, and we have since lived through turbulent times, unprecedented in our collective memory, and I have done as I have seen fit, and always in the best interests of us all as I have perceived these to be. I have asked myself why we are here, and what is the point of all of this if not to protect the interests of our sisters, and to keep them safe. Our order has a deep history, and has lived through persecution for many centuries, and I could not and cannot stand by and see one of our number killed, without doing all I could to protect them, and this is why I have taken the decision to act, and for that I offer no apology. There are no moral absolutes here, Rebecca has killed, we are all aware of that, but she has lived in fear of her own life for a long time, now, and who amongst us can say how we would have acted in her place, and given her experience? There need be no more death, all that I know of Rebecca convinces me that she now wishes for nothing more than peace, with herself and with the world, and for herself and her child, and to this end have I and will I continue to work, whether in the end I succeed or not. I have great respect for you, Rosalind, and believe that you would make a fine and worthy leader of our coven, but in the matter of Rebecca I believe that you are wrong, and not merely because of who she is, but that which she represents. So, let us take some time for quiet and solitary contemplation. We will reconvene in one hour, and then each of us will say our piece, and make our choice.'

'Hi….'

'Hello…So you lost the kids, then.'

'Yes, Victoria's got them for an hour or so, so I thought I'd come and see you before you left.'

'Oh, well, thanks for that, or this, rather.'

'Thing is, I've got some news. I'll be taking the children away for a while, we're going to Glebe House whilst the conversion goes on.'

'Oh, I see…'

'I've tried to resist, but there's so much noise and disruption that this really isn't a good place for them to be at the moment, and I can't really argue with that.'

'So can they do that, just tell you where to live?'

'It's what we agreed, before you and I were, you know…'

'Right…So is Glebe House ready for you now then?'

'Well, ready enough, I suppose. I mean both places are building sites, but I think Glebe house is currently the lesser of two evils, so to speak.'

'So when do you go?'

'Tomorrow, actually…I hope to bring them back once the place is ready and filming starts, but it's not really my decision.'

'So you could be gone for some time, then.'

'Possibly…'

'So how will I see you? Are you going to get any time off at weekends?'

'Well, I hope so, I mean one good thing is that Elin, that's Michael's wife, works Monday to Friday, so the best time for them to have the children will be weekends, so I hope I'll get some time off then, so we'll be able to meet somewhere. I'm just not quite sure when yet, until we get settled.'

'Does Elin actually want to spend time with the kids then?'

'Well, yes, I think so, with Michael's child, anyway, as long as it's not all the time, and they sort of come as a package, which is what everyone seems to want.'

'Seems like a weird arrangement to me.'

'It's not conventional, but it sort of makes sense, I think.'

'Sure…Well I'll come to wherever, you know that. This is a bummer, isn't it?'

'It's only temporary, I mean I expect I'll be spending some of the time at Glebe House from now on anyway, that was always the plan, but I'll be here, too, so it'll all work out in the long run, I'm sure.'

'Ay, I daresay. I mean it's bloody frustrating seeing you around the place and not being able to talk, and whatever.'

'Yes, it is, isn't it...Very frustrating, still, I'm here now.'

She moved in close to him, he put down whatever he was holding and they kissed. Seeing Abi today was not something that Ross had been expecting, but that which she now encouraged had been still further from his expectations.

'Look, I don't, you know....'

'We won't need that anymore, I've been to the clinic.'

'You've....Oh, right, so....'

'Indeed....'

This was not the most convenient or comfortable of locations for such intimacy, and the setting could scarce be called romantic, but by now the setting was about the last thing on Ross's mind, and here was an end to his somewhat annoying working day which banished such annoyances far from his thoughts. The future may be uncertain, but the future could wait, and any doubts about her feelings toward him in certain regards, or in any regard, really, had just been cast to the four winds.

Victoria had readily agreed to give the children their tea, Abi had a slight headache, apparently, and was feeling a little under the weather. She had, however, happened to see her as she had walked from the Manor, and she was wearing a summer dress, which Victoria could scarce ever remember her doing before during a working day, and she looked anything but under the weather, and where was she going? Something was definitely going on, and Victoria now believed that she understood what that particular something was.

The hour had passed, during which each of them had found their own place to be alone, within or about the house, and all now sat once again at table, and Charlotte spoke.

'So, who will begin? Rosalind and I will take no further part, but the others may now speak. Maria, will you speak first?'

'I, ummm...I have thought long and hard, and listened to all that has been said, and I'm afraid I cannot find sufficient justification for your actions, Charlotte. I don't think that any of us, least of all you as our leader, can leave the coven at will on some personal crusade, without there being consequential doubts regarding your commitment to our order. I regret therefore that I must vote against you, and in favour of Rosalind.'

'Very well, thank you, Maria...Sophia, what do you say?'

'I'll tell you what I think, but first can I ask you whether if you are replaced as our leader, you will stay in the inner circle?'

'I think not, Sophia. I believe that the differences which now exist between Rosalind and I make that next to impossible, from both of our perspectives.'

'Right, well then here's what I think. I believe that I know Rebecca as well as any of you, she was the reason that I was sent to the village in the first place, and since living there I have made a better life for myself, and have found love and contentment. I know that this is of no relevance to the discussion, but it has allowed me to better understand who Rebecca is, and why she has acted as she has in the past. I would have helped you, Charlotte, in all that you have achieved, and I too will do whatever I can to protect Rebecca from now on. I'm with you, however the vote goes, and if it goes in favour of Rosalind then there is no longer a place for me here, and I will leave the coven with you.'

'Thank you, Sophia. Amanda, what do you say?'

Amanda held her own silence for a moment longer, merely closing her eyes and inhaling and exhaling deeply.

'I confess that this is a hard decision. I agree with a great deal that Rosalind has said, and have great respect for her. I think that your acting alone was against our code, Charlotte, and have no great love for Rebecca. However, I do agree that there are greater principles at stake, here, and that above all else we should look to protecting our own, whoever they are, and whatever they may have done. There is much doubt still surrounding all of this, and even I doubt my own judgement, but I think that this must now be seen to its end, whatever that end. I would that Rosalind stay with us, but if that is not to be then I'm sorry, Rosalind, but I will put my faith in Charlotte, for whom I have also hitherto always had the greatest respect.'

'Thank you, Amanda. So, since I don't have a vote, and since we can take Rosalind's vote as a given, we have two for a change of leadership and two against. So, Sylvia, it is it seems down to you to decide. You are ever the most thoughtful and quiet of us, and you have been silent throughout our meeting, but now it's time for you to speak, and to decide our future, and I can think of nobody in whose hands I would sooner leave such a decision.'

Charlotte smiled, and waited.

'Then I am afraid that you will be disappointed, my dear Charlotte. I too have thought long and hard, and my decision would have been the same without foreknowledge of how all of you have expressed your thoughts.'

'Of course,' said Charlotte, 'and perhaps we should have held a secret ballot, but that has never been our way, we have always spoken openly amongst ourselves.'

'Indeed we have, and until now we have always reached consensus, that has also been our way, and in all conscience I cannot condone your recent actions, Charlotte, however much I may admire them, and I cannot vote in your favour.'

This nobody had expected, and all present looked from one to the other. So, Sylvia, the quiet and unassuming Sylvia, had seen to it that there would be a new head of coven, and of the sisterhood which spread its web far and wide in their own country and abroad. All now looked to Charlotte, who now spoke.

'Very well, then it is decided, and I will make arrangements to leave the white house as soon as may be, and I....'

'Wait, I'm not finished....'

'I apologize, Sylvia, please continue.'

'I also wish to say that even after so much consideration, and with so much which is still unclear, I don't feel that I am presently able to make a decision either way. I love and respect both of you, and if I cannot condone your actions, Charlotte, neither can I yet condemn them. I abstain, which I believe it is my right to do.'

'Indeed, that is your right...'

'And in that case....' said Sophia 'In that case, since no definitive decision is made, the status quo will prevail, that's right, isn't it?'

'Yes, Sophia, that is correct,' said Charlotte

'So, you will remain as our High Priestess, then.'

'I have never called myself that, but I believe you are right again, Sophia. All votes have been cast, and since the vote is inconclusive, our traditions dictate that I will remain as head of our order, and those of you who wish to stay with me may do so. I invite you, Rosalind, in the light of all of this, to change your mind and remain with us, which I'm sure we would all wish for, but I will of course respect any final decision that you make.'

'You know my decision, and it is indeed final. I'm sorry it has come to this, but aside from Maria I believe you are all mistaken in your continued acceptance and support for the witch Rebecca, and that this decision is wrong, and ill-fated. I have no choice, therefore, but to bid you all farewell.'

Having first offered a look to Sylvia which indicated that she could at that moment have committed murder herself, and with one final glance to Charlotte, Rosalind stood, placed her telephone on the table, and with no further ado or formality left the room. By the time the others had ascended into the still bright light of the early evening, there was one less vehicle parked outside the white house.

Abigail emerged from her room after that which she considered to be a respectable length of time, and took over care of her charges for the evening, and Victoria had a question.

'Are you feeling better?'

'Much better, thanks.'

'Good, headaches can be horrible, can't they?'

'Yes, but I took some tablets and I'm fine, now...'

'Good....So, are you all set for tomorrow?'

'I think so, I mean I think I've got enough clothes now to take with me this time and leave there for future visits, and I'll take whatever I need for the children, and Mike has said that I can buy whatever else I need once I'm there.'

'Of course....I hope all of this won't be too inconvenient for you.'

'It's fine, and Glebe House is nice, anyway.'

'Yes, it's a beautiful house, or will be when it's done.'

'I hope....'

'Yes...?'

'Well, it's up to you of course, but I'd like to come back sometime during the filming, I don't want to miss all of the excitement.'

'Yes, I'm sure that will be possible, let's just see how things go, shall we?'

'Sure....Well anyway, thanks for taking the little ones off my hands.'

'I'm sure you had good reason to take the time off, what with the headache and all.'

'Yes, well, thanks, and like I say, I'm okay now.'

'Have you spoken to Ross lately?'

'What...? Well, no, I mean not lately, why?'

'I don't think he's very happy about having a consultant to work with, at least I get that impression, but he appeared contented enough when he went home, so I assume all is now well.'

'Well, I wouldn't know about that.'

'No, no of course you wouldn't. Anyway I'll leave you to it, then.'

So what was this? Did Victoria suspect that she was in a relationship with the gardener, or were her slight feelings of guilt making her paranoid? Abigail saw the children to their ablutions and to bed, and for now she was leaving the Manor, so nothing else for now need be done, but the situation could not continue indefinitely, and probably not for much longer. Either she or they would have to tell her, and why not, or she would have to be more careful in her subterfuge. Abigail also had to admit something to herself though. She had felt so much better about herself and the world since she and Ross had begun, so that was all to the good, but then there was the secrecy of it, and that which she had to admit was that the secrecy had become a part of it, and a part of it which she was for some reason reluctant to let go. A tryst was one thing, but a secret tryst was one thing better, so she would not decide what to do, not yet, anyway.

Ross Farrier drove home from work on this day with a particular feeling, other than a slight aching in his loins, which a young man is in general content to endure for its short duration. After their lovemaking, she had left him with little ado or fuss, merely saying that she should get back to the Manor before any suspicions were raised; she was supposed to be feeling unwell, and had better retire to her room for a while before announcing her recovery. They had kissed and she had left, and they would speak soon about future arrangements to meet. So, there had been that, which had seen to their saying goodbye for the present in that which Ross regarded as being in quite spectacular and quite unexpected fashion, but this was not the thought which was now uppermost in his mind. The young lady had, with no encouragement from or even suggestion by him, taken it upon herself to make safe any and all future intimacy between them, which spoke loudly to him of her intent that their relationship should continue, despite any logistical difficulties for its continuation, given the circumstances of their working for the same employer. And there was something else which now occurred to him, and that was the general nature of the lady herself. How had Ruby described her on the morning after the party;

'Sweet, and not the most streetwise of people' and yet that which had just happened made him think that he may have to reassess this quite reasonable and understandable assessment; perchance his newly beloved possessed hidden depths which she had yet to reveal to him, and certainly this was the case given their most recent history. In any event, Ross Farrier turned up the volume of his in-car stereo to a higher than usual level, and considered that all things considered, and however the future may go between them, in the end this day had been a very good day indeed.

During the next hour and more of the day, the five remaining women who now constituted the inner circle of the oven spoke informally amongst themselves, and Charlotte provided light refreshment. Most of the conversation was of a general nature regarding Rosalind's departure, and its implication, and who might replace her, and need not be relayed here, but there was one private meeting between Charlotte and Maria which the author thinks worth the telling, which was instigated by Maria, and went as follows.

'I'm sorry to have voted against you, Charlotte, but it was in all conscience.'

'Of course, my dear Maria, we all of us can but judge according to our own judgement, and our own conscience.'

'I mean aside from this one thing, which was an amazing thing, actually, I think you've done a great job under difficult circumstances, and hope....Well, I hope I may be allowed to continue to come here, and be a part of the inner coven.'

'That was never in question, you are most welcome to stay with us, of course. I also acted upon my own conscience, and knew that there would be consequences, and would have accepted the decision of the coven, whatever that had been.'

'So, no hard feelings, then..?'

'None whatsoever...However I may do my job from now on, this will never be a dictatorship.'

The two women smiled, and that was an end to the matter, which was to say the least of it somewhat to Maria's relief.

The last of them to leave was Sophia, and the two women stood at the head of the steps in conclusive conversation.

'So, what now, Charlotte..?'

'What indeed...I can only assume that Percival is okay, and will come here, in due time. The last time I saw him he was being lifted unconscious into a car, and I've no idea where they would have taken him. All I know is that he was not to be killed, but beyond that I had no say in the matter. Your news that he has returned to the village was a great relief to me, to be honest. So you've not spoken to him, then?'

'No, but I'm out during the day and at home mostly in the evenings. Should I, you know, approach him?'

'No, let things take their course, for now, anyway.'

'Okay...'

'I'll be glad to see him again, to be honest, although I daresay he'll be angry.'

'You saved his life, didn't you?'

'Yes, I believe so, but still, he was maltreated, however that ended up, so I'll have some explaining to do.'

'So, what about Rebecca..?'

'Again, let things be, and let her come here, which she surely will. I have a feeling that I will not be rid of Rebecca so easily.'

They smiled at that thought, and Sophia had another.

'Well, at least now you'll be here when she does arrive. She might not have received such a warm reception had things gone differently today.'

'Yes, it was close, wasn't it?'

'Too bloody close....I'm surprised at Maria, though.'

'Are you? I have long known that she had certain sympathies with Rosalind's position, but I don't expect any problems from her from now on.'

'Well, at least we now know where everyone stands.'

'Indeed, and thanks as ever for your support, Sophia.'

'Take it as a given. As you know I'm not so much involved in the sisterhood as I once was, but you have my support, you know that. Anyway, better be going I suppose.'

'Off you go, then, and we'll speak soon. There are other matters to resolve, and I'll convene another meeting shortly, and let's hope the next one will be less controversial.'

One final smile between them, and Sophia descended the stone steps and took her leave. Charlotte turned and entered the white house, a place which she could still call home, and with an almost overwhelming sense of relief, she closed the door behind her.

Chapter 10. More than a Kiss

Elin Tillington had, by her own volition and decision, forgone the nowadays more common custom for younger Norwegian women to retain their given surname upon marriage. Hers, after all, was not a common marriage, and in English parlance she had not married a commoner, but rather a member of the English aristocracy, whose forbears had retained an entitlement since the sixteenth century, and the reign of the eighth King Henry. Due to the ofttimes complex vagaries of said aristocracy, therefore, and since in common with many women of her age and original nationality she had no middle name, she would in time become simply Lady Elin Tillington, since even before Michael had formerly proposed to her, she had decided that in such an event it would be appropriate for her to adopt her husband's name. It is also true to say that this was not the only concession which she had made upon marriage, having given up a better-salaried job and more prestigious and stimulating employment in favour of a lesser paid position in a much smaller law firm, from which she was unlikely to progress beyond a partnership, which she fully expected to attain in due course. Her former life of domestic solitude and long working days had thus become one of regular, predictable hours, a shared domicile, and a shared bed, wherein metaphorically speaking at least nowadays lay her entire carnal life. Since reaching sexual maturity, and even before reaching the age of consent, she had regarded sex as something to be had as and when desired, and over which she had complete control. She was herself, after all, descended from Viking stock, wherein ofttimes women as well as men had been warriors, and had hardened themselves to a life of hardship, conflict, and fierce independence of spirit, an emancipation of her gender long before the word had in this respect entered common parlance in her adopted country. Men had hitherto for her been something to be used to her own advantage and for her own fulfilment, and once so used gently discarded, or sometimes not so gently discarded, before the inconvenience of emotional engagement had entered the arena, and she had, she supposed, broken a few hearts along the way. Now, however, there was Michael, her chosen husband, who had accepted the vagaries of her sexual preferences, which had seen them consummate their relationship in unlikely places, such as in the public convenience of an airplane, with English stoicism.

Aside from her work, which nowadays was confined to a more conventional working day, that which took precedence in her thoughts was the renovation of her home, over which, once all more fundamental and practical decisions had been made, Michael had left almost entirely to her. She it was who chose bathroom tiles, and decided which elevations would be plastered and painted, and which left to bare brickwork; where light switches and electrical sockets should best be placed, and so on. In all of this she worked closely with Keith, who would exchange notes with her, or occasionally 'phone her at work, or more often would arrive on site early, or stay late, in order that they could meet together for discussion on working days. Elin liked Keith, who despite his unkempt appearance went about his work with skill and diligence, and controlled his workforce with friendly efficiency. He was tall, and strong, and Elin had early on decided that in a different age and place, Keith would have made a good Viking, and would now make a good lover, were she of a mind to take one.

And so, for the most part, the future Lady Elin went about her daily life in contented fashion; after its somewhat faltering start, her marriage to her future Lord ran well, and her occasional visits to the Manor House in her new role within the family were a quite easy and enjoyable thing. She had accepted without question or doubt the existence and influence of Michael's son, and could quite see the sense in his sister's illegitimate child, Henry, taking up residence at Glebe House for short periods of time; the children would, after all, come with a nanny, and her time spent with them could and would be something else quite within her control. So, all was well, then, aside from one remaining uncertainty, which was Michael's other and secret child, a girl whose name was Florence, who she now quite accepted had been conceived out of a bewitchment, by the witch Rebecca. She had grown up with tales of Norse mythology; of witches and sorcerers, but now such things had entered the realm of her real and adult life, and even now at times this was something which she fought with in order to come to terms. Experience had taught her that she could seduce, and that for the most part she could take most any man to herself, almost whenever she wished, but to take a man against any conscious will on his part was a different skill altogether, and one which under different circumstances she might almost have admired, but the circumstances were as they were, and it was her beloved Michael who had been so misused, and another child had entered their lives, as had the mother to that child, and who knew what influence that might have on their future? Michael had accepted the witch's daughter, and even would play his part in her upbringing, which spoke to Elin of her husband's magnanimous nature, and although it was true that she had no wish to meet the witch Rebecca again, the woman held a fascination for her, and the child was without doubt a beautiful child, and she was Michael's child, however that had come to be. Michael had spoken to her of the likelihood that Florence would come to Glebe House in the near future, so there was something to consider, when the time came, whenever that might be.

In any case, for the present, Abigail was soon to bring Nathaniel and Henry to reside at the house for the first time, and preparations must be made for that, and she had had a final conversation with Keith prior to his temporary departure to make his music with Ashley Spears, so for now she would liaise with Damien, or Will, who would be returning to site after his own absence. In essence she had no problem with this, since most significant decisions had by now been made, and the renovation of the house was nearing its completion, after which and in due time and as money allowed, a garage would be built, and the gardens would be landscaped, which would fall under Damien's speciality and remit, and Damien was someone else with whom Elin saw no problem working, doubtless under the watchful eye of Fifi Fielding.

Such were the thoughts of Elin Tillington on this evening; another working day awaited her tomorrow, and for the most part her life seemed to her to be a good thing. Later she would see to the matter of sex with Michael, fully awake and conscious, before they slept away another night in her beautiful house, which now felt to her like home.

Meadow was behind her counter, distractedly watching people alight from the bus on the other side of the village Green, when the wind chimes awoke her from her revelry, and the person who entered was someone who had at all times evoked emotions within her, whatever those emotions might have been; here was a person who, however one might feel about him, could not easily be ignored. She smiled, and the smile was returned.

'Good morning Percival....Olives?'

'How did you guess? I also need bread, and some other stuff.'

'Well, I'll do my best to provide, we have plenty of stuff here.'

They smiled again.

'And some of Em's cheese if there's any going.'

'There is, as it happens, the lady herself made delivery this morning, you haven't long missed her.'

'I heard rumour they'd been away, to Turkey or somewhere.'

'Turkey it was, and they had a fine time, apparently.'

'I should visit Jacob's Field sometime, I haven't seen either of them for a while.'

'Yes, you should, they'd like that I'm sure.'

'Anyway, apart from food I came here for another reason. I suppose it's a stupid question to ask whether she's in residence at the moment?'

'Whether who is in Residence…?'

'Ahhh, you know, the name escapes me at the moment, Rebecca, or some such.'

'Rebecca…? Haven't seen her for some time…'

For a third time they smiled, a different kind of smile this time, born of a long history and shared experience.

'You can come through the shop if you like.'

'Sure, okay.'

'What kind of cheese do you want, and how much?'

'Whatever you've got in quantity, within reason, of course…'

'Of course…I'll get it ready for you.'

'Thanks.'

Percival walked behind the counter to the back of the store.

'Just go in, if she's upstairs she might not hear you if you knock.'

'She might not be decent.'

'Could be your lucky day, then…'

Meadow returned to her counter and began preparing cheese, and Percival entered that which served Rebecca as her kitchen, just as she descended the stairs.

'Hi…'

'Hello, shall we talk?'

'Yes, let's do that.'

Rosie had arrived from the railway station at the Kemptown house, laden with items which she had bought on the way there from central Brighton. These included towels and bed linen, some toiletries, and two bedside lamps, one for her bedside and one to place on her desk, which aside from its chair and a small bedside table was the only other item of furniture in her small room. Hers was the smallest bedroom of the three, but she had a window overlooking the street, whereas Grace's bedroom overlooked the backs of other terraced houses, so she was happy to forgo the extra couple of square metres of space for a better outlook. She had let herself in, and finding nobody in residence, had gone about the business of arranging her few furnishings where she thought best. The window was central within the room, and she wanted her desk slightly out of adjacency with it, so that she could sit at her studies and see out, and she wanted to face the door as she worked. The length of the bed, which was a single bed, and the desk constituted the entire length of the room, there being insufficient width for the bed to fit sideways, so she would have to climb over the bed to attain her seating position, but she considered this to be a small inconvenience, and in any case aside from an electrical socket beside her bed, the only other source of electricity was in the far corner, so this worked better for her desk lamp. She had bought a multi-socket extension lead, which aside from the lamp gave her somewhere to plug in her personal computer and telephone charger, with one additional socket for anything else that she may need. She removed the items from their boxes and wrappers, which included a small cushion for her chair so that she could sit more comfortably, and within the half-hour, and having plugged in her lamps, she decided that she had made the best job of it that she could, and that the room would be quite cosy after dark. Her few toiletries could be left in the shared bathroom, which left the only remaining problem, which was that there was nowhere to store her clothes. Mal and Toni had the only wardrobe in the house, in which Toni had said that she could hang a few things, her spare sheet and pillow cases could be kept in the airing cupboard, but for now her day-to-day clothes would have to live on the floor, pending a first visit by her parents. At this juncture her father would borrow Damien's vehicle and bring a small wooden box which he would fashion, in which she could keep her underwear, and some shelving for her other clothes, which would fit well enough beside the bed. Having completed her tasks, she sat at her desk, and decided that all things considered, she would be quite comfortable enough in her small, personal space, which was in any case comparable in size with the trailer in which she had spent the last years of her life; Rosie was used to making do as best she could, in all domestic regards, and at near nineteen years of age, this was the first time in her life that she would live in a house.

Mal and Toni, who shared the master bedroom and only double bed, she had met so far on only two occasions, once when Grace, her former school contemporary, had introduced her to them and them to her, and on the only other occasion that she had been to the house, and both meetings had been fairly brief. Mal was tall, slim and passably good looking, and seemed pleasant enough, and Toni was petite and not unattractive, with mid-length, mid-brown hair, and of the two Rosie had taken to Toni the better. They were second-year students who had met in their first year, Grace had answered an advertisement for the shared house, and had contacted Rosie with the intelligence that there was another room to be had, and so here she was, about to embark upon her first independence from her parents, and the furtherance of her academic life. She and Grace had not been particular friends at school, but it was true to say that Rosie had not had any particular friends, but had rather relied upon her enigmatic and aloof former self, by which she had attracted certain of the other girls to seek out her company, and Grace had been amongst them.

The road upon which the terraced house was situated was relatively quiet, adjoining as it did the seafront and the main arterial road through Kemptown, which Rosie assumed had once been a village in its own right, before it had been joined and integrated with the town which had once been Brighthelmstown, and was now merely Brighton. Kemptown was a popular area of residence for students, having its own cafes and public houses, and having an independent sense of itself, whilst being a convenient walking distance from the city centre, and there was a thriving gay community here. In any case Rosemary considered that here would be a good place to live, having a quite easy daily commute to the university, and she looked forward to the beginning of term time, when the point of being here would begin. She would 'phone Quentin later, she wanted him to come and see her, as soon as his shifts allowed; whatever memories she would one day take away from this place, she wanted them to begin, and she would stay here for a few days to better get to know her housemates, and better familiarise herself with her immediate surroundings. Grace had proposed that the four of them go out together one evening, and Rosie considered that this would be a good idea. In any case her contemplations were interrupted by the sound of the front door opening, so she left her bag of clothes to be unpacked later, since in any case she had nowhere as yet to which to unpack them, climbed over her bed, and went to see which of them it might be.

'Would you like coffee?'
'I'm okay, thanks.'
'Let's go upstairs, then.'

Rebecca led Percival up the staircase to her living and sleeping quarters, where Florence was soundly asleep on the only bed.

'She's becoming a night owl, and needs her daytime nap. I'm glad to see you, Percival.'

'Well, I don't suppose you get many casual visitors.'

'No, I don't, and the day you become a casual visitor will be the day that reality takes a sea-change. So, how have you been since we last met?'

'Oh, you know, nothing special, just getting back into some routines with Louise, there's comfort in that.'

'Yes, I'm sure….Things haven't been very comfortable for you lately, have they?'

'You might say that, and that's why I'm here.'

'And there was I thinking that you just wanted to see me.'

Percival walked to the open window and took out a pack of cigarettes.

'Do you mind….?'

'Just stay by the window, it's not me, it's the little one.'

'Of course…'

'Listen, Percival, I didn't really say how sorry I was about what happened to you, the abduction, I mean. We didn't really talk much about it, and well, it must have been horrible.'

'I've had better days, and I think we're a bit past being sorry, aren't we? Shit happens to you and me, and how much of that is of our own making and how much isn't has become a somewhat moot point, so let's not go there. How it goes from here is what we need to talk about.'

'Indeed….'

'So, how's life going in your secret hideout?'

'Oh, you know, okay. I'm taking delivery of the potting wheel any day now, so I'll be able to get down to some serious work at last, which will take my mind off things.'

'Well don't let your mind drift too far away from things, you're still in danger, you know?'

'I'm well aware of the situation, Percival, or at least as aware as I can be.'

'Yeah, well that's the thing, I think we both need to become more aware, and last time we talked about going to the white house together.'

'Yes, we did.'

'So, shall we then? I mean I considered going alone, to be honest, but I think having two of us there would be better.'

'I agree…She's probably still angry with me for revealing the location of the place anyway, so having you there will help, and we both need to know what's going on. Anyway, we'll be company for each other on the journey.'

'We can talk about the state of the economy and such.'

'So, how do we get there?'

'I'll hire a car.'

'We'll need a child seat to be legal.'

'Sure, I'll organize that, we mustn't be illegal, must we?'

That raised a smile between them, given all that between them they had done, and seen.

'Should we give her fair warning of our arrival, do you think?'

'I don't have a current telephone number, or maybe I did once but I've lost it, do you?'

'No, our last communication was by cryptic note, and that was all one way. So I suppose we just turn up, then, and hope she's there.'

'Yes, I suppose so, so when shall we go?'

'That's your call.'

'How about tomorrow…?'

'What about your potting wheel?'

'I'll ask Meadow to take delivery if it comes, they didn't give me a definite delivery date, and it's paid for. Anyway, once it's here I'll need to start work, so let's do it now.'

'Sure, I'll get the car today and pick you up in the morning.'

'We should leave early, don't you think?'

'How early's early?'

'I can be ready by six.'

'Six it is, then. I'll tell Meadow on the way out, shall I?'

'Sure....I'll talk to her later, anyway.'

Percival stubbed out his cigarette on the outside wall, and put the butt-end in his jacket pocket. It always seemed to both of these people that there was more to talk about between them than was talked about, but as a rule neither knew how to begin, so nothing was begun.

'Percival....'

'What?'

'Oh I don't know, just, you know....'

'Sure, but not now, I've got some groceries to collect. Perhaps by this time tomorrow things will be clearer.'

'Yes, perhaps they will.'

'Like how the hell did she infiltrate the sect, for one thing.'

'She may not tell you, we witches like to keep our secrets, you know? Don't press her on that.'

'If you say so...'

'It can't have been an easy thing that she did, she risked her life, Percival.'

'Yeah, I figured that.'

'And I find myself wondering who she risked her life for.'

'What do you mean?'

'Well, you're in the clear now, apparently.'

'I think that's just the way things turned out, assuming it's true.'

'If you say so... Are you sure I can't offer you coffee, I could do with the company, to be honest.'

'Thanks, but I'd better go.'

'Of course....'

'I suppose it must get lonely, your self-imposed isolation.'

'I've got Florence, and it'll get better once I start working, and I can put my mind and energy to something.'

'So how will you go about selling stuff from here?'

'I've got orders to fulfil, for now, and I'll find a way to get those delivered. After that I'm not sure, but since I'm not sure of anything at the moment that sort of fits, you know?'

'I expect Victoria will visit sometimes.'

'Yes, I expect so, but I can't rely on that, she and I still have a long way to go before we can be anywhere near together.'

'I'm sure she loves you, underneath all the present goings-on.'

'I know she does, and I love her, but ours has never been an easy relationship, and it's not getting any easier. The goings-on just keep on coming, or going, or whatever, you know?'

One final smile, this time with irony, and Percival departed, and went about the business of buying his provisions.

'So, did you find her then?'

'Did I find who?'

'Of course, I'm sorry, silly me, there's no one there, is there...'

'Didn't see anyone, and there'll be no one there tomorrow, either, we're going to see the big witch.'

'Oh, well good luck with that.'

'Thanks, I'll let you know how it goes.'

'Yes, please do. Don't be a stranger, Percival, now you're back, come and see us at the bus sometimes, and bring Louise.'

'I'll be sure to do that. I'll see you both at the match at the weekend anyway, we're playing Weybridge, apparently, which is usually a good game.'

The wind chimes sounded a note of uncertainty as he left, and Meadow leaned on her counter, and watched the traffic pass. Since she and Keith had helped in the rescue of Percival from Howard's Bench, she had been keen to limit Keith's involvement in his affairs, but Keith seemed to have the matter under control, and the two men were close friends, in their way, and one thing which they shared was the love of the game of cricket. Even during his dark and dangerous recent days, when he had not felt able to live at home, Percival had most often turned up on match days; it was such a mundane, ordinary thing, and perhaps that was the point, but in any case he was back, now, and Meadow found herself being pleased at his return. In truth she had not particularly missed him during his absence, but his presence about the village and their occasional conversations were something which she enjoyed, nonetheless, and she wished nothing bad to happen to him, however he brought so much of the badness upon himself.

The person whom Rosie encountered in the small hallway as she descended the stairs was Grace, and they both made for the kitchen, Grace laden with two rather full supermarket bags.

'Hi, I didn't know you were coming down today, are you staying?'

'Just getting myself sorted, you know, and yes, I think I'll stay and get settled in for a few days.'

'Good idea, we could do with having you around at the moment, I could, anyway.'

Rosemary let that rather enigmatic statement be, and began to help to unpack the groceries, whilst Grace set the kettle to boil.

'I need coffee, I bought you some of that herbal stuff.'

'Oh, thanks....So how do we work this, I mean who pays for food?'

'I think Mal and Toni like to be quite independent, you know, cook their own meals and whatever, so that leaves you and me, possibly, anyway.'

'Right...Well, we may as well work together then.'

'Two can live as cheaply as one, right?'

'Well yes, but I was more thinking about the cooking, you know, we could take turns or something, as long as you don't mind going veggie sometimes. I mean I don't mind cooking meat for you.'

'Sure, and veggie would be fine, if I ever got meat cravings I could save that for my days, and cook you something else. There's a health-food shop not far away which does all the meat substitutes.'

Something was off. Grace was not her usual enthusiastic self, and seemed depressed or worried about something, and the idea of cooking together seemed more theoretical than actual. The words were all there, but they weren't coming out right.

'So, where are the others, anyway?'

'I think they've gone to see his parents in Wiltshire, ostensibly, anyway, but I think they're also trying to make a decision.'

The groceries were by now for the most part unpacked, and Grace opened the pack of herbal tea, and made their hot beverages.

'What kind of decision?'

'They're, ummm...They're not getting on too well, got to sort some stuff out with their relationship, partly, anyway.'

'Right....So has something happened, then?'

'She caught him snogging someone at the weekend, in a club in town.'

'Oh, I see...Well, these things happen, I suppose.'

'Yes they do, unfortunately....Trouble is, it's not quite as simple as that.'

'What do you mean?'

'I was at the club, too.'

It took Rosemary a second or two, but then came the realisation, and the explanation.

'What...? Christ, Grace, that was bloody stupid, wasn't it? I mean what were you thinking?'

'I wasn't, obviously, I mean everyone was pissed, it was just one of those moments, you know?'

'So where did it happen?'

'Outside the toilets... I went for a pee, came out and we sort of bumped into each other in the melee, and then Toni bumped into both of us, the timing was all off, I mean it was just a couple of seconds, you know? Well maybe five seconds, but it was a fateful five seconds, you might say.'

'Yes, it certainly was....'

'It was just a kiss, for Christ's sake, and he came on to me. Took me by surprise, to be honest, but I was too drunk to resist his charms, you might say, and in a moment of temporary madness and with all the loud music and flashing lights I sort of got into the spirit of things.'

'Bloody hell....It wasn't just a kiss, though, was it? I mean sure it was just a kiss, but it was a kiss with someone you share a house with, which makes it more than a kiss, doesn't it? So I mean what happened then? Was anything said?'

'Not at the time, and it's all a bit vague, now, but she sort of shot me a look which could have killed me on the spot and dragged him off. They went home and I followed in a separate taxi, and went straight to bed. Woke up next morning with a terrible hangover, and a feeling that I'd committed the ultimate sin, or whatever, and we've been avoiding each other ever since, which was only about a day, actually, and she left a note saying that they'd gone away. I wanted to get either of them on their own, her to apologise to and him to ask what the fuck happens now, but she was sticking to him like glue and I never got the chance, with either of them.'

Rosie drank her tea, and took a moment to contemplate the implications of all of this, and the perhaps wider implications.

'So...'

'Yeah, so...It's all sort of left hanging, you might say. I mean in the good moments I think that she'll just overlook the whole thing and see it for what it was, which was nothing, really, and come back and everything will be normal, not that there's much to be normal about, I mean I've hardly spent any time with them, and that was the first time we've been out together.'

'So what about the bad moments..?'

'In the bad moments they ask me to leave the house, which in the worst moments I wouldn't blame her for, and she sees me as some kind of a hussy, out to get her man, which is absolutely not the case, but who knows what she's thinking? I don't know either of them that well, that's part of the problem, but you know, it takes two people to kiss, right?'

'Yes, but that's not the point, is it? Whoever instigated it, which you say was him...'

'It was him, like I said, I was sort of in a state of shock, and sure, I could have said no, just told him to fuck off, or whatever, but I sort of got caught up in the moment. None of it was premeditated or intentional on my part, and for all I know it wasn't on his, either, and as you say, these things happen.'

'Even so, she's maybe more likely to forgive him than she is to forgive you, girls can be like that, and she's got a lot more invested in her relationship with him than she has in you.'

'So I'll be the fall – guy....This is my fear.'

'But I mean, you've paid rent, yes?'

'Six months up–front, and I can't afford to lose that, and I've even looked at it from that angle, you know, whether if it comes to it they can legally evict me, but Jesus, it was just a kiss in a drunken moment, so in the end what the fuck, you know?'

'Sure, I understand that, but the other thing is that they don't have any track record with you, either. I mean had this happened six months down the road and if everyone was friends it could maybe have been looked at in a different light, but on a first night out I can sort of see it from her perspective.'

'Well, thanks for your encouraging words...'

'I'm just trying to think it through, and I know them even less well than you do, so it's hard, and impossible to know how she'll react when the heat dies down. It's probably just as well they're away, maybe he'll do the decent thing and take the blame.'

'Sure, and maybe he won't, and I'll be portrayed as the great seductress, ready to take advantage of his male weakness at any moment and jump into bed with him when her back's turned. I mean what's to lose, I'm nothing to him, and in my darkest moments I can imagine him simpering away and telling her that it was all me.'

'Well, if she's got any sense she won't believe that, but she might make herself believe it.'

'Exactly....Christ, I wish they'd just come back so we could have it out, I mean I'm happy to apologize for my part, but I have my angry moments, too, it was him kissing me as well, whichever way you look at it.'

'Which brings us back to the fact that you're all living under the same roof, and where does that leave me?'

'What do you mean?'

'I'm only here on your recommendation, and they don't know me, either.'

'Yes, but this has nothing to do with you, and we don't come as a set, do we?'

'No, but...'

'If he did it to me he could do it to you, too, and who would blame him, I mean look at you.'

'What do you mean?'

'Well, I'm not one to compare people, but from a purely animal perspective if I were him I wouldn't crawl over you to get to her, if you know what I mean.'

They laughed gently at this; it was a heavy conversation and it needed a moment of laughter.

'What about the beauty of the inner person?'

'I don't think he was thinking about the beauty of the inner person when he grabbed my tit, do you?'

'He did that, in five seconds? Christ, he wasn't standing on ceremony, was he?'

'Shocking, isn't it, I mean putting the boot on the other foot, I could ask myself whether I actually want to live here, maybe I should go live in a separatist house, there's a few of those around here, and the trouble with that is that I do want to live here that is. I mean it's a great house in a great location, and you're here, and all of the good accommodation will be long gone by now, and anyway when I'm in angry woman mode I think why the hell should I move out, just because the man of the house has a go at me in a moment of drunken sincerity?'

'Oh dear, it's complicated, isn't it?'

'These things are seldom anything else, I don't suppose.'

Rosemary inhaled deeply and exhaled slowly, which gave her a further moment of contemplation.

'Well, maybe it won't come to any of that. Maybe we're overthinking it and making more of it than there is. Maybe they've just gone away and will come back and everything will be okay, and it will all be put down to a moment of instinctive or hormonal weakness.'

'There's a lot of *'maybes'* there, but yeah, maybe you're right, and I'm prepared to forgive and forget, and it'll never happen again, so really it's all down to Toni, isn't it?'

'Yes, I suppose it is.'

'Anyway, sorry, you know, to have got you into all of this, not that you're in it, but you know what I mean.'

'It's okay, but I've just bought stuff and got settled in, and paid rent up front, and I want to live here, too, and I certainly don't want you to leave. I'll do what I can to pour oil on any troubled waters when they get back.'

'I know, and thanks, and whatever happens I won't let them kick you out as well, this is none of your doing. So, anyway, what's the plan?'

'What do you mean?'

'I mean what are you doing whilst you're here?'

'Oh, I don't know, I'll try to get Quentin down when his shifts allow, but otherwise no plans.'

'So shall we eat together later then?'

'Sure, of course.'

'Good, that'll cheer me up. I've got some things to do this afternoon, so shall we reconvene at about six?'

'Okay, see you then.'

During the latter part of their conversation, an idea had been forming in Rosie's mind, and as Grace left the room, she did not quite let her leave.

'Grace....'

'What?'

'If it does come to the big showdown, try to make sure I'm included, okay?'

'Are you sure?'

'Yes, I'm sure, I mean I get that it's a personal thing, but if you can work it, it might be for the best.'

'Okay...Okay, I'll try.'

'Good...See you later then.'

Sharon needed more time. She had left the apartment above the bookstore with only that which she could carry, she was too exposed, there, and must live elsewhere. Megan had gone; the woman that she had loved and her only ally, and the one person with whom Sharon had seen any shared future. She it was who had helped her through the early stages of her recovery, and Sharon had no sense of how her life would have been without her, but she was gone, now, and could not be found, because she would choose not to be found. She had turned away from the coven, this time forever, if Sharon was any judge of such things, and now Sharon was the last of them, and she needed more time. She had taken a train to Wales, and had spent several days walking in wild, mountainous places, in search of the perfect place, and had found it, or somewhere which would serve well enough; an old disused outbuilding, perhaps once a shearing room or storehouse, close enough to a small village, where every few days she could buy such provision as she needed, but otherwise she would live in isolation from the world. Each morning at dawn she ran, short distances at first, but slowly and by degrees her body became stronger, and her injured leg gave her less pain, and the distance became longer. She would drink from and bathe in the clear water of the brook which ran close to her living place, and from here she would collect water for her cooking pot, which she boiled over her fire, which once lit she kept alight with small logs from a nearby abandoned log store. She would live as the witches had lived of old, cast out from society, and at one with the natural world around her, and here she would meditate in her isolation, and do her exercise, until one day, soon, she would be strong enough in mind and body. This would be no place to live in the winter, but for now she had shelter from the rain, and she slept well enough, whenever sleep took her. Yes, this place would serve, until she was at last ready.

Chapter 11. The White House

The journey from Middlewapping village Green to the intended destination was uneventful. Breakfast was taken at a motorway service station about mid-way, and conversation when it happened was mostly mundane, pertaining as it did to the more mundane aspects of life, since the less mundane could not sensibly be discussed until the other end of this day, when both had spoken to the white witch, or at least hoped that they would have done so. She it was who held the key which would unlock the unknown and as yet unknowable, and so it was without significant prior event that Percival and Rebecca drove the track through the wooded land which was the final part of their journey, and pulled up beside the white house, which seemed to Percival to have become still more shabby and dilapidated since last he was here. He knew, of course, that this was a coven of witches, but had he not known, this was the sort of place that one might expect to find one, and this is what one might very well look like.

'Right, here we go, then.'

These words had barely died in the air-conditioned comfort of the vehicle before the front door was opened, and Charlotte appeared, bearing an expression of unreadable neutrality. They alighted from the hired car, Rebecca took Florence from her seat, and they walked the short distance to the foot of the steps.

'Hello Charlotte,' said Rebecca.

'Please, come in,' said Charlotte.

They walked to the lounge, but then;

'Actually, it's such a nice day, shall we take our drinks in the garden?'

They followed her through the kitchen to the back door of the property, Percival noting that the inside of the house tended to echo the dilapidation of the outside, and the 'garden' was more or less a small, roughly grassed clearing in the woodland which surrounded it on all sides, and threatened to soon engulf it entirely. There was, however, a wooden table and chair set, which was in passably serviceable condition, so the two guests sat whilst their host, who had shown no surprise at their unheralded arrival, fetched coffee and tea, and Florence looked for daisies. The coffee was awful, but Percival had remembered this from his last visit; whatever uncommon abilities this woman may possess, making anywhere near decent coffee did not apparently count amongst them.

'So, I'm glad to see you both, and that you've come together.'

'Well,' said Percival, 'I think there's a saying about troubles coming not singly but in battalions.'

'Indeed, and I assumed that you would both come, in time, and of course I know why you're here, but please tell me why you're here.'

Rebecca said nothing, so Percival continued; apparently he was to go first.

'Well, for my part, I'd quite like to know a bit more about the day that I was abducted, tied up, questioned, dosed with horse tranquiliser or whatever was the drug of choice, and left in the back end of nowhere. You were there, weren't you, with the chicken stranglers, or I've got something very badly wrong, and I'd also like to know why and indeed how that happened.'

'Yes, I apologise for your ordeal, and yes, I was there, and I had considerable influence over the cult's treatment of you, but I was unable to prevent that which happened from happening. It could have been worse, Percival….Much worse, in fact.'

'Yes, well that much I've worked out for myself, so if I read this right, you have somehow managed to convince them that I am no longer a person of interest, is that it?'

'I wouldn't put it quite like that, they are still interested in you, Percival, but they no longer see your death as a thing of advantage to them, in that at least I was successful, but my influence has its limitations. Let me tell you why I did what I did.'

Here there was a pause; Charlotte had spent the last days in preparation for this moment, but now she searched for the words with which to begin, whilst Percival lit a cigarette.

'The cult has been a thing of mystery to us for a long time. Ever since you, Rebecca, escaped from the Convent School and became, let's say, involved with them, we have known precious little about them, their philosophy, aims and motivations, and this was ever a thing of vexation for my predecessor, may her soul rest in peace. So, given all that has happened since, which I need not dwell upon, I took it upon myself, against the better judgement of others, to try to find these things out.'

'So, what did you discover?'

'Some of that I will tell you, and some I will not, not yet, and perhaps never, but I will say that they do not belong to or affiliate themselves with any religion with which we are familiar, or as the word is commonly used, and they are not Satanists. Indeed, and these are hard words for me to say, Rebecca, but however you claim to have been mistreated at their hands, they are not as a whole or by intent intrinsically '*evil*', and some might say that the opposite is true. So, understanding being my prime motivation, it was also my hope that henceforth they would no longer regard either of you as their enemy, and in this I was only partly successful.'

'So, I was the successful part, is that it?'

'Yes, you might say that. They don't know all that you have done, Percival, they have always seen your role as that of protector and defender of Rebecca, and nothing more. You did not burn their temple, and as far as they know or believe it isn't you who has caused the death of any of them, but in the matter of you, Rebecca, my influence failed. I cannot undo all that you have done, nor could I convince them that you are or were insane, or that your vengeance against them was in any way justified. They wish for nothing more than to continue practising their creed, but you they cannot forgive, your death is still their intent, and you will understand that I was unable to press your case further for fear of raising suspicion against myself. I was able to use my craft, but as I have said, I have my limitations, which I in any case pushed to their limits, and I could do no more. You are of our coven, and I will do all that I can to protect you, as did Helen before me, but I will not die for you, and my death was certainly a possibility had I tried to do more.'

All were again silent for a moment, Charlotte waited, and it was Percival who next spoke.

'Okay, so that's the *'why'*, but do I take it that the *'how'* is something you're also keeping to yourself?'

'Yes, you may take that as a given, Percival. You are not a witch, and you do not know our craft, something which many of us take many years to learn, and I cannot teach you, even if I so wished. You are an intelligent, perceptive and sensitive person, capable of deep love, and devotion to those who you love, however you may wish to portray yourself, but there are some things which you will never understand, and that is no fault of yours, but it is the case nonetheless.'

'Yeah, well, you witches can keep your secrets and welcome to them, but just for the record, have I you to thank for the water and painkillers? Had I woken up without them my ordeal would have been far worse.'

'Yes, I managed to gain that concession, and also to leave you with your cigarettes. The intent was that you be taught a lesson, so to speak, and that nevertheless you survive that lesson, and once again I apologise that you had to undergo that particular ordeal, and for the *'cloak and dagger'* means by which I made contact with you before the fact, I had no other choice.'

'Sure…Sure, I get that, and since it seems that I owe you my life, all other sins pale rather into insignificance, you might say.'

'Well then, I'm glad we understand one another, at least in these respects, but actually, can you tell me what happened, and how you found your way back to civilisation?'

'I woke up in a wood, walked for a mile or two, spent the night in some kind of a shack, and early the next morning I met someone walking a dog. I used their 'phone, and Keith came to get me.'

'I see, well...'

'Indeed, but as you say and as I told myself at the time, it could have been worse, and things got better once I'd had breakfast and bought cigarettes, so no hard feelings.'

Charlotte smiled, now, which was the first softening of her expression since their arrival; how many people, she wondered, would have regarded such an ordeal with such stoicism? Percival she had always regarded as someone whom she could respect, and even admire, and as she had predicted or hoped, that part of the meeting had been easy, but hard things still awaited the conversation, and it was Rebecca who continued.

'So, you now feel yourself to be at one with the cult, is that it?'

'Literally, yes, and I could return to Headwater if I so wished, and philosophically I am not against their beliefs, although I would not go so far as to say that I share them, or that I am at one with them. I think any form of extremism is in the end inappropriate and unsustainable in a wider context.'

'You're a fairly extreme witch,' said Percival

'That is a craft, not a belief or creed, and how we use our abilities is the important thing, and I realise, Rebecca, that I may be saying things which you don't wish to hear, but in all of this I have tried to reach a point of understanding, and that I think can only be reached from a position of neutrality. To overcome emotional prejudice and see all things from all sides is a hard thing to do, but that has been my aim, and I believe that I am as close to that as I can be. Had I listened to my '*heart*', Rebecca, and been influenced by those around me, you would long ago have been expelled from the coven, and would perhaps have suffered the same fate as your mother, who turned from our ways and from her ancestry, or birth right if such it can be called, but I have always tried to understand your actions, as did Helen before me.'

'And do you, understand my actions?'

'Yes, I believe I do, although that does not mean that I condone them, but you were young, and I think not as wise as you are now, and I have no wish to take away your sense of self-justification, for on that I think you depend. What's done is done, and for all of our sakes we must only now think of the future, and how we can best avoid further death and suffering, and I have long believed that this is also your wish.'

She looked now at Florence, who was playing contentedly at the edge of the wood, and again she smiled.

'We all of us want her to have a happy life, do we not, and a happier one than yours has been, Rebecca, and for that to happen we must all put away our hatred, of ourselves and others, and find a more peaceful way to be.'

All were silent for a moment, whilst the words of the head of her order found their place, and in the absence of any response from Rebecca, it was Percival who broke the contemplative silence.

'So the way you now see it, it's like two friends of yours who are having a bit of a spat, with you in the middle, yes?'

'If that is how you wish to describe it, and to simplify it.'

'Well, I'm all for simplification, and everyone wants peace, right, but...'

'Do they though, Percival? Has the pursuit of peace and simplicity been your prime motivator in all of this, or has your love for Rebecca and your wish for adventure coloured your actions, would you say?'

'I saw it as someone who needed to be rescued, and then the whole thing turned on me, and now it seems to me that all of the hatred emanates from your hooded friends, whatever their *'philosophy'*, and I get that there is some kind of natural justice to be had, here, and that neither of us are angels, but we're still at war with them, no matter how I might personally be off the hook. The burning of the temple was no small thing, I get that, too, but the fact remains that even if you've found your neutral place, the same isn't true of them, is it?'

'No, it isn't, and as I have said before, as long as I am head of our order and as long as Rebecca is one of us, she will have such protection as we can offer her.'

'Yeah, but that's just witch stuff, isn't it, exclusive to any who aren't witches. So if Rebecca left the coven of her own volition, she'd be left to whatever fate awaited her, is that what you're saying? See I don't get all this *'who's in who's out'* business, no one signs any forms, right, so who makes the decisions?'

'These are matters for the inner circle to decide, of which I am head.'

'Sure, okay, but Rebecca is still Rebecca, whether she's in or out, and so what happened to common humanity? Protecting someone who needs protection against people who abused her and are still out to get her? And sure, you'll say that the sisterhood has its own rules and history, and I can buy that, but what happened at Howard's Bench was nothing to do with saving witches, that was all about Rebecca having her revenge against her alleged abusers, a happy by-product of which was that my life was saved, so I'm not complaining, but I think if we're looking for simplicity in any of this we look in vain.'

'You speak of common humanity, which is enshrined in common law, is it not?'

'Of course, but what's been happening is so far beyond common law that it barely registers as being an influence.'

'Indeed, that is my point, and that is our way, since historically common law has seen to our persecution, and so many of us have died as a result. Things may be different now, of course, but witches have a long memory, Percival. Do you think that common law or common humanity saved you at Howard's Bench? Events at Howard's Bench happened under my predecessor, who also in her way loved Rebecca, so of course we are none of us immune from our own feelings, and since we are speaking frankly, it could be said that Rebecca used you for her own ends, and yet her love for you even then would not have seen her let you die. I understand the complexity, Percival, better perhaps than you think I do, and better perhaps than do you. I have not said that things are simple. I have thought long and hard about all that has happened, and since we are discussing motivations, I could have bowed to the will of the inner circle and let things be, but I did not, and that very nearly saw my expulsion from our order, quite apart from putting my own life in danger, but my motivations were otherwise. For me this strikes at the very heart of the reason for the coven's existence, and we stand at a unique place in our history, and I could not stand by in ignorance, for that should not be how history is written. The coven is my life, Percival, as it has been for others before me, and I do not take my decisions or act upon them lightly. As head of our order I have to find my own way, and am doing so, in difficult times, and the fact that you are here at all bears witness to that. You are not one of us, and yet I am revealing things about us which nobody before you has known who was not one of us, and for this I may yet face consequences, but I have let you in because I fully understand your importance and your role in all that has happened. I wish no harm to come to you, and have acted accordingly to the best of my judgement and ability, so do not speak of exclusion, or you will test my patience too far.'

Another moment of silence followed; another breath, whilst all present decided how the next breath should be, and again it was Percival who spoke.

'Okay....Okay I get that we are all friends, here, regardless of our motivations, and since conciliation with the chicken stranglers, who you say don't actually strangle chickens, isn't an option, and since none of us are of a mind any more to take the battle to them, we have to address the best way to keep us all safe, don't you agree?'

'Yes, in this we are of one mind.'

'Good, well let's start from there then, shall we? If I might speak about Rebecca's situation, since she seems reluctant to speak for herself, she's decided to hide out in the village, above Meadow's shop, and the *'It's the last place they'd look, who'd be daft enough to hide there.'* thing only holds so much water, in my opinion.'

'I see....Well, perhaps Rebecca would like to share her thoughts on that.'

Florence brought a small twig upon which grew some white flowers, and perhaps in an act of infantile and unspoken support, gave it to her mother, before once again going about her business as her mother spoke.

'In all of this,' she said 'the safety of Florence is paramount in my thoughts, and she will be safe, I've seen to that, but as I've told you, Percival, I will not hide forever, or deny myself the possibility of a life which I one day hope to have. Call it foolish if you will, but you don't know everything, and I too have my secrets. You will not condemn the sect, Charlotte, but you can only see them from your perspective, and not from mine. I appreciate the enormity of what you have done, which I believe only you could have done, and I understand your motivations, but I don't have the luxury of being able to view any of this with calm philosophy or neutrality, since it's me they will kill, if they can. I do not hate them, as I once did, in large part because of my beautiful daughter, there is no hatred left in me for past actions or events. Most of those responsible are dead, now, because I have killed them, and that is a matter between me and my conscience, but I will let no harm come to Florence, and for her I will kill again, if I must, and if it should come to that.'

Throughout her short monologue, Rebecca had made no eye contact with the others, but had rather studied the twig which she had been turning around in her fingers, as if she had the while been studying small white flowers, and not speaking her so significant words. Percival had watched her, and considered that she had gone 'witchy', and withdrawn into herself as he had seen her do so many times. Of course, she had secrets, and he now felt rather foolish himself, having viewed her situation and decision in such a superficial way; whatever else Rebecca may be, she was nobody's fool. So here he sat, in the quiet of an English garden, such an ordinary place, with two women who called themselves witches, and who possessed ancient and learned abilities of which he could only guess. And yet, quite possibly, Rebecca was only alive because of him, and he was only alive because Charlotte, the biggest white witch of them all, who made lousy coffee, had acted as she had, against the advice and wishes of other witches. For a moment, the whole situation struck him as quite absurd, and his instinctive reaction was to laugh, gently, and light another cigarette as he did so. The others looked at him, but said nothing; perhaps they understood well enough what he was laughing at, indeed perhaps they understood better than he.

'Where the hell is everyone?'

Anna Merchant had arrived in the morning at the Manor, and was not in good spirits. She and Roger Altman had walked the house, he demonstrating the work which he had thus far done to turn a partially modernised abode back to near its time of construction, which in accordance with his abilities, he had done well. He had been assisted in this by the fact that, in common with their predecessors, the current Lord and Lady had been keen to preserve as many of the house's original features as had been practical, so the house had largely retained its period charm, its character and its essence. This, however, was only the backdrop, a canvas upon which Anna would paint her passion play, and otherwise things were not going according to her wishes.

'So what's the problem, dear thing?'

'The problem is that I've got two of my main actors down with flu, so rehearsals are running behind, costumes are taking their sweet time, so even if I had actors they've got nothing to wear, the lighting and sound crews are supposed to be arriving this morning, and where the hell are the accommodation units? We're supposed to start filming any day now, and there's nowhere for anyone to sleep. Apart from that everything's just fine, and where the hell is May Thomas, I was supposed to be meeting her here this morning.'

'She's been here every day until now, punctual as you like.'

'Well *now* is what I care about.'

'Isn't David supposed to be directing?'

'David's had his hands full with the legal and financial stuff, that's why we made May co-producer, she knew I was here this morning, and she's not answering her 'phone. Christ, we haven't even started filming yet and things have already gone to hell in a bloody handcart.'

Rosemary was lying on her bed in the mid-morning when she heard the sound of the front door being opened and closed below her, and of two people talking as they entered the house. So, Mal and Toni had returned, then, and Grace she knew was in residence, and she considered what might be best to do. She should go and see them, if only out of courtesy, but under the circumstances she quickly decided to continue reading her magazine, at least for a few moments, to see what if anything would develop. Soon enough she heard sounds from the kitchen, and voices, one of which was Grace, and within moments a message appeared on her 'phone, and it was from Grace, who must have found a moment.

'*It's happening....Help!*'

She stood up, straightened her clothing, and descended the stairs. They were all three seated at the kitchen table, which was in fact the only table in the house which could be sat around; Grace was on one side, which was the near side, and Mal and Toni were facing her, nobody spoke as she entered, and a knife would have been a useful tool with which to cut the atmosphere and make her way to the electric kettle.

'I'm sorry, Rosie,' said Toni 'but this is a private conversation.'

So, there was to be no forgiveness, then, and the matter of a kiss was to be made much of.

'Oh, don't mind me, I'll be tea-lady, and I know what happened anyway.'

'You do?'

'Yes, I do, so please carry on, since you'll have to tell me what happens in any case, and I'm a part of the household, after all.'

'Well, then, Mal and I have decided that we have to ask Grace to move out.'

The kettle was in fact already boiled, and as Rosemary poured tea onto teabags, she exchanged the briefest of looks with Grace, who bore a look which looked like resignation.

'We'll refund her deposit and rental paid, of course, once we have a new tenant.'

Rosemary passed cups around the table, and now she sat down on the only vacant chair, which was next to Grace.

'Can you do that, legally I mean?'

'The agent is a family friend of my parents, which is how we have the house in the first place. Mal and I can choose who lives here, and who doesn't.'

'That doesn't sound very legal.'

'Nevertheless it's the case.'

'I see....Well, that's a shame.'

'I don't think we have any choice, under the circumstances.'

Rosie looked now from Mal to Toni. Mal had said nothing, and was avoiding eye contact, particularly with Grace; this was all coming from Toni, as she would have expected, and it was Toni with whom she now locked eyes.

'Of course you have a choice, and Grace isn't '*your tenant*' is she?'

'What do you mean?'

'Well, any financial arrangements are between Grace and the landlord, we're all equal, here, in the eyes of the law, or whatever, no matter who's friends with whom.'

'We were here first.'

'Yes, but it's not your house, is it, and if we're going to be democratic about it, I'm sure Grace doesn't want to move out, and I don't want her to, so it's a split vote, assuming that Mal agrees with you.'

'That isn't how it works, the situation as it stands is untenable, and we have made up our minds.'

Toni now looked at Mal, who was still studying his cup with intense interest. Rosie's intervention was not a turn of events which she would have anticipated, although she perhaps should have done; she had forgiven Mal, but their relationship was not so well established that she felt overly confident in her forgiveness, and whoever had been responsible for their encounter, and whatever the circumstances, she had quite made up her mind that Grace must go.

'Look at me, Toni.'

It was Rosie who had again spoken, and Toni looked, and saw in the eyes that studied her a depth that she had not noticed or been aware of before, and she was at that moment lost for words; words, however, soon came to fill the void as the eyes spoke to her.

'I think this is all rather silly, don't you? It was only a kiss, after all, and nobody was making Mal kiss anybody. It was just a moment between two people, and everyone was drunk, it seems, and I'm sure it won't happen again. Just forget the whole thing, Toni, and let's get back to where we were before, shall we?'

Such reasonable words, and any resolve which Toni had had seemed to her now to be rapidly dissolving into the air between her and those so beautiful eyes.

'I...That isn't how I see it...'

'Of course it is, nobody's hurt anybody else here, have they, and you really are making too much of this. Mal's prepared to forget it, aren't you Mal, and Grace is quite prepared I'm sure to forgive Mal for making a pass at her. It was just a moment, Toni, and we're all friends, here, so put the whole thing behind you, and change your mind.'

'*Change your mind....*' Yes, of course, that is what she should do. Those words now seemed to resonate or echo in her head; something wasn't right, but now she was having some difficulty focusing her thoughts on what that might be, and why she had thought there was a problem. She had had feelings of insecurity and doubt in her relationship with Mal, but now she began to realise that these feelings were quite without foundation or reason, and Rosie had of a sudden made everything clear, through those clear, deep eyes, which still held her in their gaze.

'So, what have you to say, I think you owe Grace an apology, don't you?'

'I...Well, I suppose....'

'You see, it's far better to forgive and forget, so let's all kiss and make up, only perhaps without the kissing part, since that appears to cause so many problems.'

The eyes still held her, as Grace looked on the proceedings with something approaching bewilderment, but said nothing, and Toni was the next to speak.

'I suppose….I suppose you're right then, Rosie.'

'Of course I'm right, aren't I, Mal? I'm sure Grace will forgive you, for her part, and I'm sure that she is prepared to forget the whole unfortunate incident as well, so nobody actually need apologise, so let's just enjoy one another's company. This will be a happy and harmonious household from now onwards, and let that be an end to the matter.'

A moment of confusion followed as the eyes let her go, and by the time Toni had fully gathered her thoughts, they were very different thoughts from those with which she had entered the house but a few moments before. Of course, Rosie was right, and of course, there was nothing more to be said. Grace and Rosie had by now departed, although she had not seen them depart, and indeed during her reverie she seemed to have lost a few moments of her life. Mal watched her carefully, and waited for whatever might happen next, but nothing happened, until Toni spoke.

'Let's get the bags unpacked, shall we?'

'What…? Oh sure…'

'I think I'll take a shower.'

'Right…Right, you do that. So are you okay, I mean is everything okay?'

'Yes…Yes, I'm fine, and yes, everything's okay.'

Mal gently shook his head, but said nothing; of a sudden everything had changed, he was off the hook, and something had just gone on that he felt quite unable to process, and which later he would put down to stuff that women do, which under the circumstances he didn't feel inclined to think too much about. Meanwhile Rosemary and Grace had made for Rosie's bedroom, and a different conversation.

'How the hell did you do that? I mean Christ, before you arrived I was packing my bags and looking for somewhere else to live.'

'Well, it's bloody silly, isn't it? All okay now though.'

'So it would seem...But, I don't get it.'

'There's nothing to get, people can always be reasonable if you talk to them in the right way.'

'Sure, I suppose...But it seems like something weird just happened...Was that weird?'

'Nothing weird, don't worry about it, everything's fine again.'

'Yes...Well, anyway, thanks, I owe you for that, whatever it was.'

'Forget it, and be careful who you kiss in future.'

'I will...'

Grace departed, still somewhat in a state of relief, and uncertainty and confusion as to that which had just happened. Rosie lay back on her bed, and continued to read her magazine; she didn't do that sort of thing very often, but sometimes she did, when she felt that the occasion called for it, and this, she felt, had been such an occasion. She and Grace had not been close at school, but they were becoming friends, and nobody in any case from those days knew certain things about her; Grace would not understand, of course, but it was no matter, and she would never explain.

May Thomas was at this moment still several minutes away from her destination. She had hitherto stayed with Barrington in the village every night, and had indeed arrived punctually in the mornings, until this morning. Yesterday afternoon she had made the decision to attend rehearsals of a quite different kind at the home of Ashley Spears, where the band were making their final amendments to the music before taking the album to the recording studio, where it would be heard in its true, amplified and balanced form for the first time. 'Keith's songs' would be finalised and recorded first, he was the only one of them to have a day job, to which he was keen to return as soon as may be, and so she had gone to witness and film the final session at the house, on the same evening that she had received a call from Anna Merchant to say that she would be on site in the morning. The evening had gone well, and she had some good footage of the band playing and talking together, and all would still have gone according to plan had she not accepted an invitation to drink Vodka with the others, and partake of marijuana, which had kept her awake until the small hours, and made driving back inadvisable. So, she had found floor-space and slept over, fully clothed apart from her shoes, and even then all would have been well enough had she not slept through the alarm on her telephone, and awoken better than an hour later than had been her intent.

So now she drove, somewhat hung-over and without the benefit of coffee, for which there had been no time, swearing quietly to herself as she ignored speed limits and watched for speed cameras. She kept water and painkillers in her car, and hoped that the effects of the latter would kick in before her arrival at the Manor. She badly needed to pee, but that would have to wait, and she had turned off her telephone; better not be available until just before her arrival. This would be the first time that Anna would be at the Manor House since work had begun there, the production team had worked well, on the whole, and she and David had thus far developed a good working relationship, but to be late on this day of all days was a minor disaster, and would get the on-location direction-production axis off to a bad start.

She turned on her 'phone and checked the time as she drove through the gates; she had made up some time but was still as good as an hour late, which was only an hour, but it was an important hour, and Anna was waiting for her as she pulled her car to a stop at the Manor House steps.

She alighted from the vehicle, prepared to make excuses if necessary, when there were no excuses, really, but just then at so fortuitous a moment, her blushes were spared somewhat by the appearance of his Lordship at the front door of the Manor, collecting his morning paper from the mail box. The expression on Anna Merchant's face changed seamlessly from a scowl into a smile; everyone involved in the production, Anna included, would have much preferred the family to move out for the duration, but there was no budget for providing them with suitable alternative accommodation, and their staying in residence had been a part of the agreement, so good relations must be maintained.

'Good morning, everyone...'

'Good morning, your Lordship.'

'I trust all is well in the cinematic world this morning?'

'Yes....Yes it's all fine, thank you.'

'Jolly good.'

Anna ascended the first steps, and took an opportunity whilst it presented itself.

'I in turn hope that we're not causing you too much inconvenience so far?'

'Oh well, you know, one must endure for the greater good, and I'm sure far more pressing and momentous matters await my attention in the pages which I am about to read. One must try to keep a sense of perspective, just as one must be careful not to be wandering abroad about the house in one's dressing gown and slippers, as is one's more general habit of a morning nowadays.'

Both smiled now; Anna had only met his Lordship once, and had taken to him on that occasion, which would make the family's presence here easier, at least. Her own Lordship was currently down with flu, which had forced her to rethink the order of filming, and for the first time it occurred to her that the juxtaposition of the real world and the invented story which she was about to create was an interesting one. Her Lord would be a very different person to the one who now stood looking down upon her, and would live for the next weeks in a very different world.

'Anyway, I suppose I'd better let you get on, one would not wish to prevent the wheels of artistry from grinding on, so to speak, but when will filming start, do you suppose?'

'I'm hoping very soon now, we just have to get a few more of our ducks in a line, but we're getting there.'

'Good, well, to that we look forward, and I wish you well with your ducks. I have been in industry and commerce myself for many years, and I'm aware that they can be tiresome creatures.'

A final smile and he was gone, and Anna turned now and descended the steps, where her co-producer and artistic director were in conversation, the lighting crew were unloading equipment from their van, and the cameraman was making his final preparations. Anna was still in bad temper, but his Lordship's timely intervention had rather served to steal her thunder.

'Look, I'm sorry I wasn't here when you arrived.'

'What...? Oh, well, whatever, but let's get on now, shall we, as best we can, anyway. We need to get ready for the bedroom scene, so if you two wouldn't mind pretending to have sex, we can work on the sound and lighting.'

'Oh okay....You okay with that, Roger?'

'The pleasure will be all mine, I'm sure...'

Roger was exclusively gay, but had a sense of humour. May now immersed herself in her day's work, as she also worked off the last of her hangover. She would 'phone her brother later, and end her day in his house on the village Green, where a hot and aromatic bath would await her; a better place for the day to end than that at which it had begun.

As had been the case on the outward journey, little was spoken on the way back from the white house. There was some irony in this, since there should have been much now to discuss, but both driver and adult passenger had thoughts to process after their meeting, which had ended in the early afternoon, and both now retreated into their own, private and contemplative world. Conversation around the table had continued for an indefinite while, but nothing more of note or significance was said or learned by any in attendance. Charlotte had made a light lunch as best she could for her unexpected guests, and had offered refuge to Rebecca for as long as she may need it, but the offer was refused, and Rebecca it was who had instigated their departure. She had now to come to terms with the head of her coven having become a member of the cult with whom she had been in conflict for so long, a turn of events which she would not have anticipated before its occurrence, and whilst she understood Charlotte's motivation and intent, it was a strange thing, which must somehow find its way amidst all of the other strangeness which had been her still quite young life. She also must once more reassess her relationship with the man who sat beside her at the steering wheel; he who had once and more than once been her saviour, whom she had loved, and still loved, in a way, but who had a different life, now, and one in which she would likely from now on play a less significant part. She would that they stop somewhere, anywhere, in a hotel, or a field, wherein she would allow her body to give expression to her feelings, and give relief to her frustration, and what the hell, there was no harm in asking.

'So, should we find somewhere, do you think?'

This took the driver by surprise, he hadn't seen that one coming.

'I take it we're not talking about a snack-break?'

'No, I wasn't thinking about food.'

'That would be a bit seedy, don't you think, and what about the kid in the back?'

'It wouldn't have to be. Nobody would ever know, and she'd be fine, she's asleep anyway.'

The timeless and age-old conflict between instinct and common sense, which had raged in the soul of men since time immemorial for a moment raged once more, but in the end, which came quickly, there was no decision to be made.

'I think of all the bad ideas you've had so far today, that rates as about the worst, nothing personal you understand.'

She laughed at that, any relief was better than no relief.

'A woman might be forgiven for taking it very personally indeed.'

'Yeah, well, there's no easy way to say *no* is there? It's the wife, you know?'

'You're not married.'

'Look upon it as a metaphor. Anyway, I think a change of subject's called for, so I thought I might head for Brighton once I've dropped you off.'

'We'll come with you, Florence has never been to Brighton. It's okay, we won't follow you around, and we'll make our own way home. I don't feel like going back yet.'

'Brighton it is, then.'

They parted company on the seafront, on a sunny and blustery afternoon, and it was a parting which asked for ceremony after such a day, but neither quite knew how the ceremony should go, so there would be little or none of it.

'So, I'll see you around, then.'

'Well, you know where to find us these days.'

'Sure, I'll call in for coffee and biscuits sometime, we can talk the day through.'

'Is there anything to talk about, do you think?'

'I don't know, seems like there ought to be, but it also seems like you know what you're doing, so maybe not.'

'You'll still call in, though? I'll buy some biscuits for the occasion.'

'Then you have me....'

'It seems not, but I'll buy the biscuits anyway.'

A parting smile, and they parted, she and her infant to the town centre, and he eastwards along the front. He took out his 'phone and spoke a message.

'Yeah, it's me, I'm in Brighton, call me when you're done.'

Decent coffee was needed, and he stopped at a café which had tables outside and a view over the shingle beach. The coffee was in fact of dubious quality, it had not been a good day for coffee, but the time alone for contemplation was the important thing. So, the witches were about their business, and Rebecca still had a death-warrant hanging over her. There had been no mention of the other witch who was also out for her blood, but that also was witch business, and none of his, and now at least he had chapter and verse on the day that he had been rendered unconscious and left in a wood. Charlotte had somehow cleared his name with the chicken stranglers, and he still had no idea how that had been done, but it was no matter, let her keep her secrets, and he owed her one for that. He checked the time on his 'phone; Louise would likely be another hour or two yet, so he finished his coffee, and walked on, a gentle breeze blowing through his always unkempt hair; the worst of the day was done, and all things considered, it could have been a worse day.

Chapter 12. One More Secret

During the time spent at the residence of Ashley Spears, an informal, largely unstructured evolutionary process had been undertaken, with each of the musicians contributing their creative input and musical output to each of the songs which would eventually and soon now become the third *'Tara'* album. As yet the album had no title, although several options had been discussed, and this would soon have to be decided, but the songs themselves had been reduced to fourteen in number, others having been rejected by popular consensus, and ultimately by agreement between Ash and Tara. Lyrics, melodies and harmonies had been changed, marijuana had been smoked, and on occasion musical sessions had degenerated into a party atmosphere as alcohol had been introduced to the mix. Aside from Ash, Rick Talbert and Samantha Rodriguez were the two people who represented the band which had been Dead Man's Wealth, and these three remembered well enough how that band had gone about its business, before the death of Mickey Martin had changed the emotional dynamics completely, and brought the band to its timely end. Al Talbert had instigated its resurrection, and played lead guitar during the last world tour that the band would make, but he was gone, now, and now different influences had come to bear on the eclectic group of people who had stayed together to give the voice of Tara its musical accompaniment. Aiko, the beautiful, enigmatic and technically proficient base guitarist, who avoided all forms of intoxication and spent a part of each day in solitude and meditation, had become increasingly integral and essential to the creative process, and everyone had collectively or individually decided that she was probably homosexual, although as with so much about Aiko, nobody was quite sure. Keith, who could not entirely abandon his primary responsibilities of converting a church and renovating a period property, and who each day spoke to Mike and Will respectively, nevertheless immersed himself in this so different activity, and by dint of his particular musical contribution would now play his acoustic guitar on four of the songs to be recorded. It was a thing of constant satisfaction to Keith to see his eldest daughter at the centre of such creativity, and he would speak to Meadow every day, where each would be kept abreast of the everyday occurrences in the life of the other; Keith was a builder, but for now he was a musician, and this temporary change in his life, which he would never have foreseen, was for him an entirely positive thing.

Now, however, the time of evolution and for informality was over, and sobriety was the order of the day. A van was hired, and for now each day Keith would drive the others to the outskirts of London, and to Studio Three, where the serious business of making music would take place. Creativity would from now on be replaced by technical proficiency; the songs were by now learned, and each note and each drumbeat must be delivered with care and professionalism, and the sounds mixed and balanced by technicians, on the way to final takes. Here would be Tara's presentation to the world of Ash's compositions, born of his intent to express his work and his world through the voice of a young woman, as an expression of their mutual respect and admiration, one for the other.

'Hi, it's me...'

'Hi, you, how's it going?'

Ross was in his bedroom in the early evening when the call had come in, and he was pleased to hear the voice.

'It's okay, it's a lovely house, of course, and the little ones are settling in well, so, yeah, all's well so far. I get a small room to myself here, well, it's more like a cupboard, really, but it's quite cosy.'

'Good, well, I'm glad it's working out, I think, although don't get too settled in down there, will you?'

'It wasn't my idea to come here in the first place, and I'll try not to. So how are things at the Manor?'

'Chaotic, you might say, although I'm literally an outside observer, of course, but people have started to arrive, you know? I'm still trying to turn a fairly modern garden back a few hundred years in time.'

'And how's that going?'

'As well as can be expected, I suppose you could say, but another couple of days should do it, then at least I'll have the consultant off my back.'

'Sure....So, any famous actors there yet...?'

'Haven't seen any, I think we're still at the preparation stage inside as well. So does Glebe House have a big garden?'

'Well yes, if it can be called that. I mean the grounds are quite big, and it must have been beautiful once, I suppose, but it's all kind of overgrown, and still looks a bit like a builder's yard at the moment. I was talking to Damien, one of the builders from the village, who's actually a landscape gardener. He's going to be prime-mover in its modernisation, eventually. Someone called Fifi Fielding's drawn up the plans, apparently.'

'Fifi Fielding? Well, she's a lass that gets about a bit then, she's the consultant at the Manor, too.'

'Is she....? Well that makes sense, I suppose, family connections and all.'

'Yeah, I suppose....'

'I, ummm...I miss my walks in the garden, I mean we walk around the garden here too, but it's not the same.'

'I miss your walks in the garden, too, especially if they're all like the last one.'

'Hmmm, well mostly I'll have the children with me, so don't bank on that happening again anytime soon.'

'I can wait, sort of, but I really want to see you.'

'Yes, I bet you do.'

'So when can I come down?'

'Soon, I hope, I mean I have to get the wee ones bedded in, and I'm not sure yet what the arrangements will be for Mike and Elin having them for my time off, which I suppose I'm bound to get at some juncture, but we'll see. As soon as I have news of that I'll let you know.'

'Well, whenever, I can come at the drop of a hat, so it's down to you. The timing's all off here, isn't it, you disappearing just when we're, you know....'

'I know, but it can't be helped, and I'm working on getting back as soon as I can get away with it. I've told Michael I want to be around for some of the time when the filming starts, so we'll see. Anyway, look, I'd better go, Nathaniel's on the move, I need to get them to bed, I'll call you in a bit.'

'Better not keep his future Lordship waiting, then....'

'We'll talk later....'

'Sure, okay....What will you be wearing?'

'I hope, sir, that you are not suggesting a lewd and improper telephone conversation?'

'Perish the thought, although now you come to mention it...'

'It wasn't me who mentioned it, now go...'

'I'm gone....'

The call was ended, and after the distraction of her telephone conversation, Abigail turned her mind to her charges. There was, however, something else which was distracting her thoughts on this particular day, but of this she would not tell Ross; not yet, anyway, and in any case, she had made a promise.

Ross was at this moment feeling equally distracted, and as may happen to a young man, an image appeared in his imagination of the young lady with whom he had just been conversing, and in his mind's eye, and in his slightly intoxicated state, she was wearing nothing at all. His thoughts were interrupted, however, by a gentle knock on his door.

'Enter....'

The door was opened, and another young lady stood before him, dressed in slippers and dressing gown, the latter of which was emblazoned with various images of teddy bears; Ruby was on her way to her evening ablutions.

'I'm just off for a shower, do you need the bathroom?'

'No, I'm good. Have a toke on this before you go…..'

'I'm okay….'

'Go on, it'll enhance the whole showering experience.'

'Oh, go on then…'

She sat down on the bed, whilst Ross, who was seated on the bedroom chair, lit an already half-smoked marijuana cigarette, and passed it to her.

'So, you okay? We haven't talked much since the party.'

'I'm fine, just been bloody busy with work, loads of overtime, you know?'

'Yeah, Steph said you were working late at the office.'

'Well, it's just a summer contract, so I'm making hay, you know? So how's the great love affair going?'

'Can't complain….Well, I could complain, she's living away at the moment whilst the film gets made. I told you about that, didn't I?'

'Yes you did mention it. Oh well, such things are sent to try us, so they say.'

'Ay, and so they do…So talking of making hay, how are things between you and Don since your brief encounter..?'

'Mostly he's been ignoring me, or talking nineteen to the dozen about nothing when he sees me, so I can't get a word in.'

'That'll be a nervous reaction, then, trying to pretend it didn't happen. So he hasn't done the decent thing and suggested marriage, then?'

'Oddly enough, no, but Christ, we only spent a night together, and it was consenting adults, you know? Why do boys make such a big deal of everything?'

'Because he probably thinks it's a big deal for you, women's sensibilities and all, and he's clearly feeling guilty as hell. Either that or he wants to do it again, and doesn't quite know how to ask. I mean it does change things, doesn't it?'

'I don't know, does it? Has he said anything to you about it?'

'Not a word, but we've not spoken much either, so no, no man to man stuff.'

'Oh well, I suppose it'll be consigned to history eventually, and the sooner the better as far as I'm concerned. So when are you and Abi meeting up again?'

'No idea, she needs to get some time off, but that hasn't happened yet. So she and I are too far away and you and Don are too close, seems like we can't win.'

'Look, Don and I aren't in a bloody relationship or anything, we got pissed and slept together, that's all.'

'Sure, sorry....'

'Anyway, time for my shower and an early night, and good luck, you know, with your Abigail.'

'Thanks....'

'You really like her, don't you...'

'Ay, I do. It's just a pity she doesn't, like, have a normal job or whatever.'

'Yeah, that is a shame. Do they know at the Manor House that you two are together?'

'No, not yet, I mean I don't mind either way, and I don't see what the big secret is, but she's closer to it all than I am, so I'm leaving that to her.'

'Well, like I say, good luck...'

She stood up, adjusted her dressing gown, and left, leaving Ross to consider all that she had said. He liked Steph and Don well enough, but it was Ruby to whom he had come to be closest since moving in, and he hoped that the emotional dynamics of the household would return to normal soon. His thoughts, however, were interrupted by a message on his 'phone.

'Hi, sorry I couldn't talk, I'll call back at bedtime, and I may not be wearing very much at all.'

He smiled, and it was somewhat ironic, whatever Ruby might say; a thin brick wall was all that separated her from Don at night in their respective beds, and Don would be doing his best, Ross was sure, to reign in his hormones after the fact, and the fact would not be repeated. And here were he and his significant other, who were separated by miles, and wanting nothing more than to be together.

Still, she was calling back, and that was somewhere to start, was it not?

'I think you and I should talk about something.'

'Oh, okay, sure....'

Tara was sitting alone in Ash's garden in the cool of the quite late evening, beside a quite large, reed-fringed ornamental pool in which swam several ornamental fishes. She had left her father inside, discussing Eastern philosophy with Aiko, whilst Rick watched a film on TV and Samantha went about some domestic activities, and it was Ashley who had found her.

'It's a nice pool.'

'Yeah, it was here when I came, and the fishes are kind of cool, although the heron gets a few of them.'

'You have herons here?'

'Sure, all manner of avian life, I sometimes think I should buy a bird book and some binoculars, you know?'

She smiled at the thought of this, and knew it would never happen.

'We get squirrels, too, and foxes.'

'Yes, I've seen the squirrels, and heard the foxes at night. Anyway, what should we talk about?'

She was sitting on a large, ornamental stone, and he sat down beside her and rolled a cigarette.

'How do you think the recording's going so far?'

'I think it's going well, don't you?'

'Yeah, it's going to be a good album, you should think about the title sometime.'

'Yes, I know….'

'Keith should finish his part in another couple of sessions, then he can go home if he wants.'

'I think my dad's enjoying his alternative career, but he'll probably go home.'

'Thing is, I know how it goes from here, as soon as the album goes into production the promoters are going to be on our case to take it out on tour.'

'Oh, right….'

'So we need to think about that, is all, and you're the main lady, now, so it'll be your decision.'

She smiled again.

'I think I'm still coming down from the last tour, it was such an amazing experience.'

'That was DMW, this will be you, it'll be different.'

'Yes, I know…So what do you think?'

'Well, it'll sell some albums, so from a commercial angle it makes sense.'

'So what are the other angles?'

'It's how you feel about it, you know? Whether you want to stand up in front of your adoring thousands and sing to them, there's no contractual obligation, so we have to control, and it's not just about the money.'

'No, of course not, I already have more money than I ever even imagined that I would have, so you know, I understand what you're saying. What do the others think, or what do you think they'll think?'

Ashley lit his cigarette, as the last rays of the sun turned the western sky a golden red.

'Aiko's probably already got her bags packed, and Rick was born to tour, so you'll meet no resistance from that quarter.'

'What about Samantha?'

'Yeah, Sam...She'll do it, of course, in her usual pragmatic kind of way. It isn't like the old days, touring's easy, now, compared to then.'

'You mean in terms of accommodation.'

'That, and the way we used to be with each other. I don't mean Sam, I mean when it was Al, me and Mickey. That was always complex karma, by the time we got back from a tour we were about ready to kill each other, and we sometimes didn't speak for weeks. The whole thing was held together with opiates and a love of the music, but we're all friends here now, and Al won't be around this time, so it's easy, you know?'

'And what about you, are you ready to go back on the road?'

'Sure….I mean you and I have created something, so I'll run with it. There's life in the old dog yet, you feel me?'

Again she smiled.

'So, no more doubts, then?'

'What do you mean?'

'When you disappeared, I mean I know you and dad were trying to protect me from something, but I think I know what that was all about.'

'No, no more doubts, and that was me, not the music, and certainly not about you, so it's all cool.'

'Good….Well, let me think about it, the tour, I mean. I mean of course I want to sing the songs, but right now I can't think beyond the recording. What about dad, I mean would we need a second guitar?'

'Yeah, I've thought about that. Keith won't want to tour, and we can get by. There's an option to bring in a session musician, there're plenty of guitarists out there who would jump down our throats for the chance, and I know some people, but I'm inclined not to do that, Sam can work some magic on keyboards, and we can cover for it. I've never thought that album tracks should be reproduced exactly as they're recorded.'

'Sure, I know, and that's your department. But I mean if we did tour, how would that work, I mean I'm not going to fill stadiums, am I?'

'I think we'd start small, and I'm not sure about a world tour, I don't think we're there yet, so maybe Europe, and see how we go from there. It's just stuff to think about, you know?'

'Well, as always I'll be guided by you, but I think I can cope. I mean I love the idea of touring as *'Tara'*, but at the same time the idea scares me to death, so you know….'

'Sure, and that's the point, you have to be ready for it, and I don't mean musically, this has to come from you, it's your time, now, and your life, and nobody's going to put you somewhere you don't want to be.'

'Of course, I know, and I appreciate that. You've always looked after me, haven't you?'

'I've seen what fame and fortune can do to people, it can fuck with your head, you know, and I've experienced some of that myself, and I lost my best friend that way, so maybe I'm getting cautious in my old age. Sam's got your back, too, she won't let me screw things up for you, but it's the music that matters in the end, and the music can speak for itself, if that's how we want to play it.'

'You mean just record the album, put it out there in the world and everyone goes home?'

'Something like that.'

'Okay…Okay, well let me dwell on it, will you?'

'Sure…Meantime we should get some sleep, we've got some recording to do in the morning.'

'Indeed…I think I'll just sit here for a bit longer, it's such a beautiful evening.'

They smiled, he stood up, and walked a few paces, but she was not quite done.

'*Contemplations…*'

He turned.

'What…?'

'That's what I think we should call the album. It's kind of a contemplative album, anyway, don't you think?'

'Yeah, good title, let's run with that...'

He left, and Tarragon watched her world until the darkness fell, and the foxes were barking as she walked to the house.

It had been earlier in Abigail's day that the conversation had happened. This would be her first full day at Glebe House with little Henry and Nathaniel, although little Henry wasn't so little anymore and was so far outgrowing his cousin. This was a working day and Elin had left for work, and so had Michael, but he had returned to his makeshift office in the late morning, from whence for now he ran his property business. She had given the children their breakfast, walked the grounds in order to familiarise herself with the entirety of the new working environment, introduced herself and her charges to any builders whom she came across, and Michael had been in the kitchen when she had returned there from her brief walk, and was making himself coffee.

'Hi….'

'Hi, so how's everything going?'

'All good so far, they both slept well last night, anyway, so that's a good start.'

'And how about you, you settling in okay..?'

'It's all fine, thanks, I think I'll enjoy being here, for short periods anyway, and Nathaniel in particular is fascinated by what's going on.'

'You mean the building, yes, well, the noise levels vary from day to day, but I hope it won't be too disruptive to your day, and we're getting somewhere near the end, now.'

'It'll be fine, I'm sure.'

'Well, jolly good then....Anyway, I'm glad we've got these few moments to ourselves, there was something which I've been wanting to talk with you about.'

'Oh yes...?'

'Yes...Thing is...Would you like some coffee?'

'I'm okay, thanks.'

'Right...Well the thing is...'

So what was this? Whatever it was, Mike was struggling with it as he poured hot water into a mug.

'I mean I was going to, you know, tell you it was the child of a friend, or something, which it is, really, I suppose, although *'friend'* is hardy an accurate description, at least from my perspective, but then that would be rather silly, wouldn't it?'

'I'm sorry, you've lost me.'

'Yes, yes of course...The point is, Abigail, are you able to keep a secret?'

'Yes...Yes, I can do that.'

Still there was hesitation; clearly her employer was undergoing some sort of internal dispute, and the dispute was not yet quite resolved.

'Let me put it like this, I mean you do a wonderful job with Nathaniel and Henry...As you know Victoria and I both, well, you know, we both think a lot of you, as it were.'

'Thank you.'

'Yes, we both see you as part of the family, now, and so, we, that is I, was wondering how you would feel if, just sometimes, you know, you had a third child in your charge.'

'A third child....?'

'Yes...A girl, actually, about the same age as Nathaniel and Henry, give or take. I mean I know it would be asking a lot, and we, that is I would of course pay you in addition to your normal salary, and as I say, it would only be here, and likely only to be for short periods of time, if at all.'

'I see…Well, actually I don't see, I mean I have no objection in principle, or from a practical point of view, I mean Nathaniel and Henry are both incredibly easy children, mostly anyway, so I'm sure I could cope, and perhaps I'll have that coffee after all.'

'Yes, yes of course…'

Michael poured more hot water, as Abigail wondered. Whatever this was, the layers which led to the truth of it were being unpeeled only slowly. Michael passed her the mug, she made space and sat at the kitchen table, and waited, and Michael smiled, perhaps ironically.

'You know, it's a funny thing. It's because I see you as a part of the family that I hesitate. If you were merely a nanny I wouldn't have any issue with telling you what I'm about to tell you, but well there it is, and I hope you understand.'

'Well, that depends, I suppose, on what you are about to tell me.'

'Indeed, well then, to get to the point of it…'

'Yes, please do.'

'To get to the point of it, I have a daughter.'

'Oh, I see…'

'Yes, so there it is, and I cannot I'm afraid tell you who her mother is. That is, I know who her mother is, of course, but you don't know her, and that part I would rather not tell you, not yet, anyhow.'

'Well, that's your prerogative, of course, and I suppose it makes no material difference, but does your daughter have a name?'

'Yes, forgive me, her name is Florence.'

'Florence, well it's a pretty name, anyway.'

'And she is a very handsome child…Takes after her mother, you know.'

'Whoever she may be....Well, this is all a bit of a surprise, of course.'

'Yes, of course, and I'm sorry to rather spring this on you, so to speak, but there's no easy way sometimes, is there?'

'No, I suppose not...Do you have a picture of, umm, of your daughter, on your 'phone or anything?'

'No...No, I'm afraid I don't believe I do.'

'Oh well, never mind.'

'The other point, and this is another reason for my hesitation, is that not everyone knows of her existence, Florence, that is.'

'Right....So might I know who does know?'

'Elin knows, of course, and Victoria, but the knowledge does not extend beyond that, within the family, that is.'

'I see. And just to be clear, are both of them allowed to know that I know?'

'Oh yes, that would be quite alright.'

'Right, well, you need have no fear of my telling anybody, I can give you my word on that, and thank you for being honest with me, as far as you are willing to be, anyway.'

'Yes, well I've discussed the matter with Victoria, but in the end my telling you was my decision, and I'm sure I won't live to regret it.'

'I'll give you no reason to regret it, I promise you. So, when might I expect to meet my extra charge?'

'Of that I really have no idea, and as I say, it may not happen. All I'm doing is laying a foundation, so to speak, in the event of its occurrence, and it would of course only be here, and not at the Manor House.'

'No, well, I can see how that would be the case.'

'I'm looking at the worst possible scenario, Abi, that her mother may ask me at short notice to provide childcare, in which case....'

'In which case you'll ask me here at short notice, with Nathaniel and Henry...'

'Yes, precisely...'

'Well then, consider me prepared for such a scenario, but can you tell me anything else about her, her temperament and so on?'

'Well, she's...She's a mostly quiet, thoughtful child, I would say, although she can talk when she has a mind so to do, and she's...Well, she's very clever, I would say. I wouldn't land you with a monster, that in turn is my promise.'

Both parties to this so particular conversation now smiled for the first time, as Abigail absorbed such extraordinary intelligence, and Michael felt a great sense of relief at its telling. He had had no idea how the conversation might go, and now he berated himself at his lack of faith in the young woman who now sat, thoughtfully drinking her coffee. He had ofttimes wondered how such a clearly intelligent young woman was content in the occupation of looking after other people's children, but he and Victoria were both pleased that this was the case, and now she knew, and it was testament to how she had become so much a part of his life that he was pleased that she knew, whatever might happen from now on. Nathaniel and Henry had the while been playing quietly about the kitchen, under the ever-watchful eye of their nanny, and it was she who now spoke, and brought the conversation back to the everyday.

'Well, I suppose it's time for their lunch, unless you have anything else you'd like to tell me, any more bombshells you'd like to throw in my direction?'

'No...No, I think that will about do it, and thank you, Abi, for your understanding and forbearance.'

'Oh, that's okay, to be honest nothing much surprises me about your family anymore, Michael, and for my part I'm glad to be considered a part of that family.'

They smiled again.

'Well, I'd better let you get on, and I've got a pile of paperwork awaiting me, mostly bills, unfortunately. No doubt we'll catch up again later.'

'No doubt we will.'

'Anyway, there it is, then.'

'Indeed, there it is.'

Michael left, and he left Abigail with a head full of thoughts which would need to be processed when she had her quiet time. For now though as she saw to her two charges, she attempted a quick summary of her understanding of the situation, a situation which now included three children. Henry had no father that anyone had ever spoken of, Nathaniel was as good as certainly not Michael's child, but was she now assumed child to the man called Percival, so Victoria and Rose both it seemed held their secrets, and now there was Florence, whose parentage at least was she assumed in no doubt, but who her mother was also remained a secret, at least from her. Michael had a daughter, and a daughter of whom the Lord and Lady were apparently quite unaware, so what deep shame lay behind her conception, and who was the mysterious mother, and if it were someone quite unknown to Abigail then why the mystery? There might be some connection, somehow, with the family or the local community, but Abigail had not seen anyone about with a daughter of that age, and she had not been shown a photograph, or any other image which might have given her some semblance of a clue. Michael had been rather defensive about that, so perhaps no image of Florence existed which did not also show her mother, so who was she, and what would happen, if she was of a sudden summoned to Glebe House; she assumed that in that case the child would be here, but the mother would have gone on her mysterious way, so what was to be made of it all? She smiled to herself as she scrambled eggs and kept a watchful eye on the two boys. This was a building site, and builders tended at any time to leave tools, chemicals and materials lying around, which could be dangerous in infantile hands, and she must be ever vigilant. Her smile, though was at the thought of her own little secret; that she was having romantic dalliance with the Manor House gardener, which seemed to her now to pale into insignificance in the face of so much secrecy. She would 'phone Ross in the evening, and to that she looked forward; he would want to know when he could meet with her, and here was a question which she too would very much like to know the answer, but they would have to wait, at least for now. For now, Michael had entrusted her with a secret, and he had been right in his first, rather confused approach to the subject; he could have told her that Florence was a child to a friend, or something similar, and she would have been none the wiser, but he had chosen to take her into his confidence regarding such an important thing, in a similar way to her having been a part of the conspiracy against the Lord and Lady in bringing the two boys to Glebe House in the first place.

As the day went on, more questions than answers entered the arena of Abigail's thoughts. Some were questions which she had asked herself before, such as whether Michael knew the identity of Henry's father, or whether this was something which Victoria kept even from her brother, and did the Lord and Lady know who was father to their grandchild? Who was Percival, and how had he and Rose come to conceive a child, and what had been the nature of their relationship, other than the apparently obvious? Rose had died giving birth to Nathaniel, who would likely be sole heir to the Lordship, so much was invested in the so far still assumed knowledge of his illegitimacy not entering the public arena, since that, she assumed, would see an end to the historic entitlement. Now, however, there were new questions, and a new and mysterious woman had entered the already complex thing which was the Tillington legacy; mother to Michael's secret daughter, who was called Florence, so who was she?

At the day's end Abigail saw the children to bed, showered in her nearly completed bathroom, put on her nightdress and climbed into bed. Her nightdress was a modest, comfortable affair, but as she reached for her telephone and made toward a conversation with her beau, she thought it best to keep one more secret, and keep the nature of her apparel to herself; it would not, after all, be quite the thing for the conversation which might follow.

Chapter 13. A Homecoming, a Guilty Secret, and an Uncertain Future

The news that their elder brother, Tarquin, was about to honour his two younger siblings with a visit so soon after the last, had in truth been received with mixed feelings by Quentin and Tristan. Quentin had hopes of soon being invited to an excavation in Kenya, which would further establish his place in the small, highly specialised and competitive world of archaic human discovery, but was awaiting confirmation, and in the meantime continued his employment at the warehouse, and Tristan had made little progress with his life plans, since he didn't in reality have any since returning from India. Tarquin's visit would come in the wake of the funds from the sale of the Clandon house having been distributed between the three brothers, so each now had their share of the parental legacy, which Tarquin had organized remotely, and now he was about to visit. They would take pleasure in seeing their brother, but although relative age differences lessened with age, he was and would always be their elder brother, and each would likely be subject to his judgement, and he could be a harsh judge. It would be quite possible now for Tristan to find his own accommodation, prior to deciding what to do with his newly acquired wealth, but for now he was content to sleep on Quentin's settee, and for now Quentin was content to allow him to do so. It was generally accepted that each of them would buy property, but neither had made any firm plans as to what and where that property might be, and they were company for one another, in which for now both found comfort, although nothing was said. Both were handsome of face, well-educated and eligible, and as regards the latter had just become more so, and whilst Tristan would have been pleased to become romantically and sexually involved with an as yet unspecified other, and would in theory have little difficulty in this regard, he had as little idea as to how to go about it in his present circumstances. He also knew well enough that in matters of the heart, success achieved may at times be inversely proportional to the effort expended in the attempt at its achievement; it was quite possible to try too hard, and so presently he did not try at all, and the matter remained theoretical. He was in a sense caught in a loop; he could not see a change in his circumstances without his being in a relationship, and he could equally well not see a relationship occurring unless he changed his circumstances. Chance, it seemed, was the only element which would undo this particular bind, but chance was a fickle and unreliable friend, and at times needed encouragement to play its part.

Quentin, on the other hand, had Rosie, and he had every intention of visiting her in her new accommodation in Brighton, when his shifts allowed and she had become more settled, but she was about to embark on a new phase of her life, and he had thought it best to allow her space in which to do so. He would go when he was invited, wait for news of the possible Kenya trip, and see in general how the land of his life lay before seeking to move from his rented accommodation, or encouraging his brother to vacate his sitting room.

In any event against this backdrop did Quentin and Tristan await the arrival of Tarquin, who would be flying in later this day; Tarquin needed no excuse or reason to visit, but rarely visited unless he had either, or both, and there was a certain yet uncertain unspoken and underlying anticipation about the matter.

In a general sense, events were by now moving ever closer toward the eventual beginning of filming at Middlewapping Manor. The mobile accommodation units at least had arrived, as had a mobile kitchen and water container, cables were being laid to provide an electricity supply, and

May Thomas had seen to the finer points of life such as bedding, towels and basic toiletries. The accommodation would not be luxurious, but it would provide all that was needed by the main players for the duration of the filming, and they would awaken each morning to the sights and sounds of an English woodland, which constituted a part of the Manor Estate, and would perhaps compensate in part for the lessening of their domestic circumstance. The resident chef would arrive shortly, to properly set up his place of work and buy provisions, the Manor itself would very soon now be in a state of preparedness, and May was in a general sense pleased enough with how things were progressing. There were, however, two things which were a preoccupation for her, and which she had yet to address, one of which related to the film, and one of which did not, and during one evening she approached the subject of the former with her brother, with whom she was currently staying. They were mid-way through their evening repast, and were discussing the day's progress, which seemed like an apt and appropriate moment to broach the subject, and so she broached it.

'The thing is, Bas, I was wondering whether you would mind giving your house over for a bit.'

'What do you mean?'

'Well, we need somewhere to shoot a small scene in a peasant's house, well two scenes, actually.'

'Oh, I see…Well it's good to know I'm living like a peasant.'

'Well okay, a tradesperson or whatever. I mean the kitchen's far too modern, of course, but we just need a sort of living space, and one bedroom scene, which I think we can get away with, with some careful camerawork.'

'Right…Well, I've no objection in principle, but what would it involve?'

'Not much, really, just changing some furniture, I would think, I mean the curtains will have to go, but the house and windows are made for it, it would only take a couple of days, and you'd be paid for the inconvenience, of course. I mean not very much, but you'd get something, so what do you say?'

'Well, I suppose there's some kudos attached to having one's house feature in a movie. I wouldn't have to move out or anything, would I?'

'Oh no, nothing like that, just change bedrooms for a night or two, and most of the filming would happen during the day anyway, so you'll hardly know we're here. There's one night time scene, which is the bedroom scene, but that's only a few minutes.'

'Right…Well in that case I see no reasonable objection. I mean I'll have to seek the permission of Percival, of course, since it's his house, but I don't imagine he'll object. So, which actors would be involved?'

'Maurine O'Connell, essentially, she has to have sex with someone in the village.'

'I see….Don't suppose they're looking for someone to play the other part, are they, I could do peasant if the need arose.'

'Sorry, that's covered. Anyway it won't be real sex.'

'Oh, pity….Still, even pretend sex with Maurine O'Connell would be something worth having, I would think. If I were the other actor I'd insist on several takes, as it were. I'd probably make a complete hash of things just to prolong the business. Anyway, that aside, having her in my house is sufficient incentive.'

'Good, well there you are, then.'

The decision to allow the use of his house had been taken quickly, because his sister had asked for it, and the possibility of meeting Maurine O'Connell had been an afterthought, but now he had a further afterthought.

'What will she be wearing?'

'What…?'

'Maurine O'Connell, in the sex scene…'

'I've no idea, not much, I wouldn't have thought, most of the time, anyway.'

'This gets better by the moment…'

'My dear brother, these are professional actors, behaving in an entirely professional manner.'

'Of course, I never thought of it in any other way.'

'Yes you did.'

'Okay, yes I did. Anyway as far as I'm concerned you may use my house, so as long as my landlord gives the all-clear you may do your worst, dear sister.'

'Thanks, Bas, it won't be for a while yet, probably, so I'll let you know, and there'll be legal papers for everyone to sign in due course.'

'Sure, whatever…'

So, there was one of her issues resolved, as May had assumed it would be. The other matter, however, was somewhat less easy to deal with, and there would be no easy resolution, but deal with it she must, whilst there was still time. In a matter of a few days' time, it would be too late, and she could not be too late.

Tarquin arrived in town in the early evening, and 'phoned to say that he was checked in at the White Horse Hotel, and would meet them there. The bar of the White Horse Hotel, however, was a sterile and soulless place, so the Red Lion public house was agreed upon as an alternative venue, and it was here that Quentin and Tristan found their brother, supping his ale, and here did they join him at table. There would be no standing on ceremony, but Tristan spoke anyway.

'So, bro, always a pleasure of course, but what brings you to our door? Making sure we haven't already gambled away our inheritance?'

'Something like that…I don't suppose you've made any life-changing decisions yet.'

'Then you suppose right.'

'I've got a chance of Kenya for a dig,' said Quentin 'just waiting for news.'

'Kenya….'

'Yeah, Kenya, why..?'

'Nothing…So where's Rosemary now?'

'Brighton, she's moved into a shared house, which I've not been to, yet. How long are you over for, anyway?'

'Couple of nights, probably, I'll have to see…'

'Right….'

Something was amiss. There need be no reason, but insufficient reason had so far been given, and some words awaited the conversation.

'So,' said Quentin 'everything okay with you?'

'Yeah, all good, getting married, actually…'

Here were the words, which hung in the air for a moment, whilst Quentin and Tristan wondered whether they had heard them correctly.

'Fuck off…' Said Tristan

Tarquin did not react, or smile, so the words remained, and must be dealt with, and Tristan saw to the continuation of the interrogation.

'Look, Freddo, to get married you have to be in a relationship, which means, you know, being nice to someone over a prolonged period of time.'

Still there was no reaction; so it was true, then.

'So like, who is she? I assume it's a she?'

'Her name's Adimu, which is Kenyan, as it happens.'

'So she's African?'

'Fifth generation, although her grandfather was French, and so's her father, but yeah, she's essentially African. Mum thought she'd go ethnic, hence the name. French is her first language, but she's fluent English, of course.'

'Well, fuck me....'

Quentin had been listening to the brief exchange, and watching his elder brother, who was clearly pleased to be imparting such significant news, whilst trying to appear not to be, and it was Quentin who next spoke.

'You've been keeping this one quiet, bro, so how long?'

'It all been quite quick, to be honest, well, a few months, you know? It's suddenly all got serious so we're getting married, that's why I'm over, to sort out the legal stuff.'

'Apart, of course, from telling us, your brothers, that you're about to be married, or even that you're in a relationship at all, for that matter.'

'Yeah, that too, I suppose... She's coming with me next time to sort out a venue for the reception, and before you jump to any conclusions, she isn't pregnant.'

'So you're getting married in England?'

'She wants that, she lived in England for a while, so we'll be moving back. I start at Kent Uni next term.'

'You're coming back to England to live?'

'Looks that way...'

'Well, aren't you the dark horse...You've been keeping a lot to yourself, man.'

'Nothing's been certain, not about the lectureship, anyway, so there's been no point, really.'

'This is big, Fred. So, more information, please, like how old is she..?'

'She's twenty-eight, only child, both parents dead, one to cancer and one in a car crash, and she lectures in French history. We've both got places at Kent, she'll be lecturing in Medieval and Modern History. Thing is, it makes sense for me to buy a place in England, she's an anglophile, even knows the rules of cricket, as much as any layperson knows the rules of cricket, so you two should get along anyway.'

'I like the lady already.'

'Anyway, I don't want to buy to rent, so we'll be looking at Canterbury or thereabouts, and with the money coming through it all kind of dovetails together, and we were lucky to both get jobs at the same university.'

'Kent's a bit of a downgrade though, isn't it?'

'I can live with it.'

'And you're getting married...'

Here was a statement which, if said often enough, would better find its way into the realms of reality, and it was almost there.

'Neither of you two fuck-heads are being invited, though.'

'I want best man,' said Quentin.

'Fuck off...'

'Come on, man, it's the least you can do, after all I've done for you.'

'You haven't done anything for me.'

'That's not the point, anyway I had your back when we were kids.'

'I'm talking about adulthood.'

'That's too specific. So do I get the job or not?'

'Well who the fuck else am I going to ask?'

'Good man...'

'So what am I going to do?' Said Tristan

'I don't know, chief usher, or whatever. We haven't worked out the finer points of it, yet.'

'Fair enough....You got a photo?'

Tarquin took out his telephone and found an image, which he showed to them.

'Fuck me,' said Tristan 'she's beautiful, bro, how'd you pull that one off?'

'Just lucky, I guess.'

'So, she's got no immediate family,' said Quentin.

'The rest of her clan's in Nairobi, upper echelons of society, you know, so the wedding will have an African influence, and she visits sometimes, but she's not really close to any of them...'

'Well then,' said Tristan 'we'll have to be her family.'

'That's what worries me. I told her about you guys, of course, I lied and said you were good people.'

'We'll soon put her straight, then.'

'She wants to meet you, so behave, okay?'

'Of course, you'll be proud to call us your brothers.'

'That would be a first...'

'Funny thing though, Quen, that you should be going to Kenya...'

'Yeah,' said Tarquin 'what's that about?'

'Cradle of humanity, we were all Africans once, and it's where I've always wanted to work, so I'm not getting my hopes up. I know someone who knows someone, so it should come off if the funding works out. I should know for sure in a week or so.'

'I'll tell Adimu, she'll be interested.'

'Well,' said Tristan 'I think more ale is called for, tonight we celebrate.'

'Yeah, but not too hard, I've got stuff to attend to in the morning.'

'So you've booked into the White Horse, last time you didn't even sleep there.'

'This time I'll sleep there, I'll go straight there from here and miss out the dope.'

'Come on, Fred, it's not every day you tell us you're getting spliced. The first of us to go....'

'Forget it,' said Tarquin, 'it's not going to happen. So how's it going with Rosemary, Quen?'

'Well, like I say, she's settling into Brighton so I thought I'd give her some head-space, and wait to be invited down.'

'She might think you don't love her anymore,' said Tristan.

'We talk most days.'

'We should go see her, why don't we all go down tomorrow night? We could get pissed and Fred and I could book into some sleazy Brighton hotel.'

'Let me think about that one.'

'You up for that, Fred..? That way you stay sober tonight, we celebrate in style tomorrow and Quen gets his rocks off, it's a win–win situation.'

'Yeah,' said Tarquin. 'I suppose that could work, I could stay an extra day or so.'

'I'll speak to Rosie.'

'No, man,' said Tristan, 'let's just do it, surprise her. You do still love her, don't you?'

'Sure, of course.'

'Well then, you got to stamp your authority on the situation, I mean Brighton isn't that far, you know, and she probably needs you around right now. You're being over-sensitive about it, wouldn't you say, Freddy? There's such a thing as being too considerate.'

'I don't know the dynamics of the relationship that well,' said Tarquin, 'but it seems to me that if there's any doubt about its continuation under the new circumstances, you should sort it out one way or the other, and as soon as possible.'

'There,' said Tristan, 'your big brother has spoken, and he knows about relationships and such, he's a married man, now, well, as good as.'

Quentin was thoughtful for a moment. It was true that he wanted very much to see Rosie, and was by no means sure that his quite deliberate lack of involvement in her first days away from home was the right thing to do, and how she would react to his absence, which he had always seen as being temporary.

'I'll talk to her later.'

'Yeah, you do that. Let's take her out and celebrate in style, behave badly in some swanky restaurant. After all, we have much to celebrate, and we're all rich now, richer than we were, anyway, and I need to let some steam off. My life's in neutral right now and I need to go do something, so talk to her.'

'I will, and meantime go get the beers in, will you?'

Tristan left, and left Tarquin and Quentin with a few moments alone together.

'So, is he okay?'

'Yeah, he's okay, mostly. He can stay at mine as long as he wants, but he needs to get some purpose or direction in his life, and I've told him so.'

'So have I, and I'm worried about him.'

'I know you are, but there's only so much we can do, bro, in the end it's up to him. Anyway, congratulations, I'm, well, you know…'

'Sure, and thanks. She's lovely, you know, and not just on the outside.'

'Of course, I would expect nothing less, well done.'

The evening ended at a quite early and sober time; Tarquin retired to his hotel and Quentin had a 'phone call to make. The evening had in a way been a catalyst for his wanting to know about his own future. If Kenya happened then that would see the fulfilment of a long and deeply-held ambition, and would for the duration be his focus, but he would have to come back, and he very much wanted Rosie to be there when he did so. She also was his future, or she was not, and Freddy had been right, he needed to know, one way or the other.

The dilemma facing May Thomas had been simple enough. She should be on the film set, the wardrobe department was due to make a delivery at any time, there were still some issues to resolve regarding the accommodation, and in any case this close to filming her place was at the Manor House. On the other hand, the recording of the 'Tara' album had moved to the studio. A process which had begun with just a guitar and a voice in the ancient church, and had then found its way to the lounge of Ashley Spears, was now in its full and final stage, and without this, her documentary would be rendered as good as pointless. She already had better than four hours of footage, which would, she supposed, eventually have to be condensed to one hour, but she needed the studio. And so, she had left her place of work, an hour before the two-hour session at Studio Three was due to begin, and had arrived in timely manner; this was the last day that Keith would be playing his acoustic guitar, so she would capture the entire ensemble, the final banter between all of the players, and the final take on at least a few of the songs. This, she considered, was in fact less interesting than the process had been during its embryonic and developmental stages, where tempos, chords and words had been changed, but it was completion, and she drove back to the Manor House with something on her passenger seat which would in time be her documentary, and the first piece of work which she could truly claim as her own. The ever-modest and self-effacing Tara was now finding her own place in the ever-competitive and nowadays more transient world of popular music, and anyone less like a rock-goddess May would be hard put to it to imagine, but the girl could sing, she looked great on stage, and she had the great Ashley Spears on her side. This would be her third album, captured from its infancy and one day soon to be shown to the world from its first day to its last, and May felt a lifting of her spirit at the thought of that. She had received no significant news from the Manor House during her absence, from now on the film would be her life, and as she drove through the gates of the Manor, she breathed an audible sigh of relief, and smiled silently to herself.

Meadow was making ready for her bed when she heard a sound outside the bus which she had not expected to hear. She quickly put on her summer dressing gown over her nightdress and walked to the door, where her supposition was confirmed, and there was Keith, in the semi-darkness, illuminated only by light from the bus, removing his safety helmet and removing the key from his motorcycle.

He walked to the door, carrying his overnight bag, and now she could see that he wore a broad grin, a smile which was returned, if a little uncertainly.

'Hello sweetheart, I wasn't expecting you....'

'Yeah, well, I'm done at the studio, last session today, so I thought I'd surprise you.'

'I see, well it's a lovely surprise.'

'Yeah, that and I forgot to charge my 'phone, I mean I could have used Tara's, but anyway, it was a lovely evening so I took the spontaneous decision to ride back through the sunset. I should speak to Mike anyway, and this way I can start back at Glebe House tomorrow.'

'Right, so have you eaten?'

'Yeah, well no, not really, but I'm okay.'

He entered the bus, took off his biker's jacket and put down his bag, bringing the cool evening air and the smell of motor oil with him as he did so.

'So, how did it all go?'

'Great...I mean Ash seems pleased enough in the end, so I'm an officially recorded rock musician again.'

'So there were no more moments of doubt.'

'I think that was just a glitch, anyway all's well now.'

'Well done....And how's my baby girl?'

'She's good, singing her heart out, of course, and sounding good.'

'So she's okay then...'

'Yeah, she's okay, recording isn't like touring, it's a lot more relaxed, in a way, so she's not gone back on the coke or anything, there's just some weed about, that's all.'

'Right....So, tea, then..?'

'Yup....'

Meadow set the kettle to boil.

'So how many more days will they be recording?'

'Hard to say, but not much longer I wouldn't have thought. Ash said he'd bring Tara home, he wants to see how the church is coming along. Christ, I'm looking forward to sleeping in a bed again, I'm getting too old for sleeping on floors, I mean a night's okay but after that, you know?'

'Yes, I'm sure.'

'So any news of our Rosie..?'

'Not since yesterday, but she's fine. Settling in okay, it seems, and looking forward to the beginning of term, now.'

'And how's our witch in residence?'

'No news, really.... I told you she'd had her wheel delivered.'

'So that was a spinning wheel, was it?'

Meadow smiled; Meadow had no fear of sleeping alone on the bus, and Basil had been staying in the trailer to make sure all was well, but she was pleased indeed to see her man return.

'I daresay from now on she'll be about her work, and I've hardly seen her.'

She poured them both tea.

'Right....'

He came up behind her and held her, in a way that was not entirely gentlemanly.

'Sir, you take liberties.'

'Well, here am I, fresh home from the open road, and here you are, barefoot and looking all maiden-like.'

'I've got my dressing-gown on.'

'That can be seen to.'

'I daresay.'
'Rock stars expect this kind of thing, you know?'
'Do they indeed….What about your tea?'
'We can take it to bed, rock stars don't really need tea, anyway.'

She turned to face him, their eyes met, and this was a happy homecoming, and a happy moment for both parties to the reunion.

'Hi….'
'Hi….'
'Everything okay..?'
'Yes, thanks, you..?'

We now intrude upon a conversation between Quentin and Rosemary, who was in her bedroom when the call came in. Her intervention in the matter of Grace's brief, unplanned and unfortunate dalliance with Mal had seen to it that the business had apparently been forgotten, and normal relations had resumed within the household, or at least as well as normal could be ascertained after such a still short time.

'I'm fine. Freddy's here, well, we had a couple of beers and he's at the hotel.'
'Oh, you weren't expecting him, were you?'
'No, he came with news, though, he's getting married.'
'What…? I didn't think he was even in a relationship.'
'Nor did anyone, but he's in one now.'
'So who is she?'
'Her name's Adimu, she's African, well part African, anyway, although there's some Caucasian thrown into the genetic mix now, but she still looks African. She's not here but I've seen a picture. They both lecture, and they're moving back to England, lecturing at Kent University from next term.'
'Really…? This is out of nowhere, isn't it?'

'Yes, it is. Anyway, they suggested that we all come to Brighton tomorrow evening, and stop over, you know?'

'Who's 'all'?'

'Fred, Tristan and I. They both want to see you, as do I, of course, and we thought we'd celebrate, go to some posh restaurant or whatever, then get a hotel for the night.'

'I see…Well, that would be great…I mean, sure.'

'Good…So, can you recommend anywhere, I mean what are the hotels like near you?'

'I've no idea, but I can look into it if you want.'

'Could you…? Thanks, something middle to lower end and close by would be the main criteria.'

'Okay, I'll try. So where would we eat?'

'Don't know, could you look into that as well, and book a table somewhere.'

'Yes, I suppose…I don't want to book the wrong sort of place, though.'

'Don't worry, I trust your judgement.'

'Oh, okay…What about Tarquin, though, he's the fuss-pot isn't he?'

'Tris and I can handle Freddy, anyway he's riding high on a cloud of romance at present, so I doubt if he'll mind that much, just somewhere half-decent and close to yours, if you can.'

'Well, again I'll try, I mean I've passed a few places, so I'll take a wander in the morning, as long as I can get somewhere at short notice.'

'Thanks….How are you settling in, anyway?'

'It's fine, I mean I love the house and the people are okay, so far.'

'Good….'

Here, then, were of a sudden things for Rosemary to consider, and now she had a further thought.

'Listen, do you think I could bring Grace tomorrow night?'

'She's your friend from school, isn't she?'

'Yes, well sort of, and she's at a bit of a loose end at the moment until term starts, and we start meeting some more people.'

'Sure, of course, it'll even out the boy-girl numbers a bit anyway.'

'I don't need that, Quentin.'

'No...No of course not, I was just...Anyway it'll be good to meet her.'

'Okay, I'll see if she's up for it, which I'm sure she will be. So what else is news?'

'Not much, really, still waiting to hear about Kenya, but otherwise it's just me and the warehouse. I'm looking forward to seeing your place.'

'Well it's not much, but it's becoming home, you know?'

'Sure....I'm looking forward to seeing you, too, Rosie.'

'Yes, well, good....So shall we say see you tomorrow, then?'

'Yes, let's do that.'

'Okay...I'll let you know if I have trouble finding somewhere, or a hotel or whatever.'

'Sure, otherwise shall we see you at your place around seven? Book the table for eight o'clock.'

'Okay, night then...'

'Goodnight.'

The call ended, and Rosemary found herself left with mixed feelings. She very much wanted to see Quentin, but as yet he was not a part of her new life, and how much he wished to be so was for now a matter for conjecture. They had been together for some time, now, and settled into a kind of life at home, but now things had changed, and she was uncertain. He had not come to see her of his own volition, it had taken his brother's appearance to act as the catalyst for his coming, and now they would have no time alone together; he was coming under cover of his brothers, so she would see. She went online in search of reviews of restaurants in Kemptown, which was a little restrictive, and they may have to take a taxi to or at least home from the town centre, but she would see. And then there was the hotel; she assumed that one twin room would suffice, on the assumption that Quentin would stay with her, and therefore that they would sleep together, and she assumed that this would also be his assumption, but her moving had created a schism between them which would have to be negotiated before anything was certain. Anyway, he could always sleep on the floor if things didn't work out between them. Grace was in the house somewhere, but she sent a message. *'You doing anything tomorrow night?'*

Chapter 14. Of Idiocy and Irony

The three brothers had travelled by rail to Brighton, and were by prior arrangement to meet the two girls at the appointed restaurant, which was a mid-level affair somewhat away from the town centre, a quite easy walk from the small hotel which Rosemary had booked for the night, and a short taxi ride from her rented house. The menu was fairly cosmopolitan, and looked to cater for all tastes, the hotel she was less certain about, but she considered that she had done the best she could, given the shortness of the notice and her still limited knowledge of the town. Both girls had dressed up and made up for the occasion, Rosie quite modestly so and Grace, in Rosie's opinion, less modestly so, and the brothers were already at the bar by the time they arrived. Drinks were bought, introductions were made, and Grace decided that an evening spent in the company of such fine young masculinity was a fine thing indeed to which to look forward. Quentin and Rosie smiled, and kissed, and exchanged brief words; there was an agenda between them which would have to be addressed, but not yet, and not in company. In large part the purpose of the evening was a celebration of Tarquin's forthcoming marriage, and as the small gathering took their seats at table and began to peruse menus, Rosie saw fit to raise the subject. She was still unsure as to how best to address Tarquin, knowing how he disliked his name, so she opted for the more familiar address.

'So, Freddy, I understand congratulations are in order.'
'Yeah, thanks.'
'And Quentin tells me he's to be best man.'
'There's always a downside.'
'I'm going to make you proud of me, bro.'
'I suppose there's a first time for everything.'
'I hope we'll get to meet the lady soon.'

'Yes, well I suppose she'll have to meet these two sooner or later.'

'Maybe better wait 'til the wedding day,' said Tristan 'then it'll be too late for her to change her mind.'

'The thought had occurred to me.'

Tarquin headed the small table, Quentin and Rosemary were on one side, which put Grace beside Tristan on the other. Champagne was ordered, and glasses were raised to toast the forthcoming happy event, and thereafter red and dry white wine flowed freely, as did the conversation; food was ordered, and the assembled party settled for the evening. As the only stranger amongst them, Grace watched the interactions between all others present with initially detached interest, before giving brief account of herself, her life and her future plans, which was her initiation into the group. There was one amongst them, however, who in particular held her interest, and as can be the way between people, she became aware that the interest was returned, although nothing in particular was said, because nothing in particular need be said, in such situations. In any event, if there was a spirit to be entered into here, the young lady was in all respects set fair to enter into it.

He was in truth and at first unsure what, on this particular day, had made him stop. He was perhaps ten minutes from hearth and home, and although on such a beautiful summer's day as this, a hearth was furthermost from his needs, he was always glad to be home, but still he stopped. In preparation for autumn's chill and winter cold, the central heating engineers were almost done at Glebe House, installing modern slim-line radiators, but he had had Keith carry out some essential renovation to the inglenook fireplace, which would once have provided the house with its only heat, and would now provide an occasional cosy ambience on cold winter's evenings. In any case, there was a place, which he had driven past many times, where one could pull off this minor road onto an unkempt, gravel layby, which afforded scenic, pastoral views over the countryside, and today, for reasons for which he was unsure, Michael Tillington, next in line to the Tillington lordship, pulled his car to a stop, and turned off his engine. He rarely smoked if he was on his own, but today he reached in his glove compartment for his cigarettes and lighter, and lit a cigarette. Something was troubling him, which for now on this day made him delay his homecoming, in favour of a few moments of quiet contemplation.

The night was still quite young by the time the quite adequately prepared meal was over, and the bill had been split equally between the three brothers. In fact Tarquin paid, the others would pay him their due in due course, or more likely they would not, so the split was perhaps more theoretical than actual; more likely the matter would be absorbed into the brotherhood and reparation would follow by other means, but in any case it was done. By now Tristan was apparently and actually the most drunk of the brothers; Tarquin had at some point slowed his alcohol consumption, as had Quentin, and both had reasons for so doing, but all had enjoyed the evening. For certain parties to the gathering, however, the evening had not yet run its course, and it was Tristan who had a proposition.

'Okay so what say everyone that we find a club somewhere, there must be clubs in Brighton.'

'Think I'll give that one a miss,' said Tarquin 'I'm on a flight late-morning.'

'How about you, Quen..?'

Within the confines of the place and company, Quentin had likely enjoyed himself as well as anyone, but beyond here there were other matters which awaited him, and although tempted by the idea of the evening's continuation, he equally well knew that they would be better dealt with in a state of relative sobriety, and that the evening should better continue in a different way. He looked at Rosie.

'It's up to you, I don't mind.'

So, the decision was his, then, and after a further moment of anyway quite drunken consideration, he decided.

'Think I'll give it a miss, too....'

'Oh, come on, you guys, we're celebrating, remember?'

'So go celebrate.'

Which was an end to the matter, as both brothers knew, and in any case the person whose life was to be celebrated would be absent from here onwards.

'Well then, fuck it, I'll go alone, unless you'll do me the honour of joining me?'

The last enquiry was directed toward Grace, who took somewhat less time to decide, but a young lady should not be seen to be too keen, so she did not commit, or respond.

'I need a chaperone in this strange town, someone who knows their way around the place.'

'I don't really know any clubs....'

This statement was not entirely true, since a certain small event in a certain club had recently led to controversy within her place of residence, which had for a time threatened her continued occupancy therein. It was not however a club to which she particularly wished to return, but it would suffice, if all else failed.

'Well then let's go find one, shall we?'

A swift glance toward Rosie, whose expression remained neutral, before;

'Okay....'

And so with little further ado, the party dispersed, Tarquin went in search of his hotel, Quentin ordered a taxi, and Tristan and Grace were for now last seen making toward the seafront, which seemed to them like a good place to make in their quest for further entertainment, and a continuation of their time together, which was their first.

That which currently begged the occupation of the thoughts of Michael Tillington was something to which he had in truth hitherto given little serious consideration, in large part perhaps because he had no wish to consider it. It was rather something which underlay his otherwise busy life, and even now it lay somewhere beneath other, more immediate matters and concerns. He was, after all, on his way home from the office of his solicitor, where contracts had just been exchanged on the sale of one of his renovated properties, which would shortly release funds with which he could for the most part pay off his bank loan. His two other properties were also in the final stages of renovation, and once both of these were sold his business would finally and once again be on a sound financial footing, which had been roundly undermined by his not selling Glebe House, formerly Orchard House, but rather keeping it as a place in which to live. The work at Glebe house was also nearing its final stages, the major expenditure in any case was done, now, and eventually the garage would be built, and the gardens landscaped, but these were not essential projects, and would be undertaken as and when funds allowed. Keith had done a good job, broadly within budget, if there could be said to have been such a thing, and he and his beloved wife, Elin, would quite soon now be living in the autumnal peace and quiet of their domicile, and all in this regard would be well.

A taxi ride later, Rosemary and Quentin arrived at her rented house, and entered there into, where all was quiet; Mal and Toni were either out or already abed.

'So, this is the kitchen…'

'It's a nice house.'

'Yes, I think so. Coffee…?'

'Sure…'

Both were a little drunk, but the sobriety of the new situation and circumstances had seen to it that the point at which the alcohol had reduced inhibition and created a sense of wellbeing had passed, and now began the early stages of hangover. Rosemary in any case seldom drank alcohol, preferring to keep her senses keen and her emotions reliable, but on this night she had made the exception, and allowed her emotions free reign. Quentin sat down at the kitchen table whilst his beloved prepared coffee for him and herbal tea for herself, and wished that he was still more sober. She took the seat opposite his, and spoke.

'Well, that was a nice evening.'

'Yes, I think even Fred enjoyed himself.'

'He's not how he seems though, is he, or how he wishes to appear, I mean he's a big old softie, really, and he clearly loves you both very much.'

'We love him, too, but nobody will admit any of that, it's always been our way.'

'This I have noticed….So, what's happening with us, Quentin?'

So here was the conversation which had been awaiting its moment all evening, and some time prior to it, and now its moment was here, but still somehow it caught Quentin unawares.

'What do you mean?'

'Well, let's start with the easy one, why haven't you been here?'

'I've been working shifts, you know?'

'Yes, I know you have, but that isn't it, is it?'
'No, that isn't it, not entirely.'
'So, what is it, then?'
'I mean…I just wanted to give you some time, to settle in and whatever.'
'What made you think I'd needed or wanted time to settle in?'
'I don't know….New life, you know?'
'I've changed where I am, not who I am, so again, why haven't you been here? I mean it would have been easy, you know, for you to ask me whether I wanted some time, I'd have said no, and that would have been the end of it, and I wanted you here.'
'And I wanted to be here.'
'So what went wrong?'
'Okay….Okay, so maybe I was feeling insecure, you know, about what might happen, when you met new people and so on.'
'I haven't met any new people yet, apart from the people who live here, and do you really think I'm that shallow? Did you think everything was going to change, that my feelings for you were going to change, just because I'm about to start at uni, and there'll be other people around?'
'No, well, I suppose…I mean I don't think you're shallow, of course not, you're about the deepest person I've ever met, it's not you.'
'So it must be you, then.'
'It's not me, either, I mean try to understand,'
'I am trying to understand.'
'I just…I don't know, I can't seem to put it into words, but I think I've been so afraid of losing you, that's all.'
'So because of that you're doing your best to lose me, is that it? This is sounding like a self-fulfilling prophecy.'
'If you see it like that…'

'Well, I don't know how else to see it. So this is a personal survival thing, is it?'

'I suppose so, but whatever it is I'm getting it wrong, and I'm sorry.'

They were silent for a moment as their respective words made their way into each other's respective thoughts, and it was Rosie who next spoke.

'You know it's a funny thing, I have certain, let's say abilities, you know this. I can sometimes control peoples' thoughts, and actions, and I do think I understand people quite well, but you've lost me completely.'

'Well maybe we're both in a new place, I mean I've never been in love before, so I'm still finding my way, I suppose.'

'Neither have I, and don't you think we should be finding our way together? Don't you think I want you to be here as I start my *'new life'*? People say, or at least used to say that I'm a cold person, unfeeling, and perhaps they were right, but I'm not that anymore, whatever else I am. I mean I don't make friends easily, or at least I don't seem to make the same emotional connections that people make with other people, but I've given myself to you, Quentin, and I don't mean just in a physical sense, and I suppose that's what love is, isn't it? Giving your soul to another person, or however you might define it?'

'Yes, I suppose it is.'

'So I don't understand how you have so little faith, you know? In me, in us....'

'Well like I say, I'm sorry, I got it wrong, and my not being here has nothing to do with my not wanting to be here, or to see you. I mean you haven't been here that long, Rosie, and the shift thing has been an issue, you know?'

'Yes, I know it has, but at the same time Brighton isn't that far, is it, and I wonder how long you would have stayed away had Tristan not suggested that you all come down.'

'Well, that I can't say, I hadn't planned anything, it was just, I don't know....I suppose I just didn't want to crowd you, to impose myself upon you, it was nothing more than that.'

'Wasn't it?'

'No, it really wasn't.'

'So since when has our being together been an imposition? Two isn't a crowd, two's company, and I wanted your company.'

'Yes, well I get that, and I should have got it sooner, and all I can do now is apologise, and hope that you'll forgive me.'

Another moment of silence and assessment; a process was underway which both now saw as ending in a better place than it had begun, but the process had not yet run its course, the alcohol was not helping either party, and the male element to the process smiled to himself.

'Tristan was right...I mean Tris has less experience than just about anyone when it comes to matters of the heart, but he was right this time.'

'What do you mean?'

'He said...Well, he said that you might think I don't love you anymore.'

'So you've discussed it, then?'

'Not really, it was just in passing, but anyway, the point is that I do still love you, I really do, and right now I feel like a complete idiot. I've heard it said that love makes fools of us all, but I'm the only fool here, I know that.'

He placed his hand at the centre of the table, and after a moment of hesitation, she took it.

'Well, I suppose I should forgive you, then.'

'I'd like that.'

'So anyway, you're here, now, and I suppose we'll sleep together, and I want us to be close, but...But I want us to get the love thing working again first, if you understand me?'

'Of course, I'm here with no expectations....'

She withdrew her hand and stood up, and he followed her upstairs to her room, where they undressed and got into bed, and held one another, which was the last memory of the day which either would take with them into the next.

So, then, it was not his marriage or domestic circumstances which gave Michael pause; he and Elin had found their way to a life together in which both had found contentment, and fulfilment, and Michael was content to allow his now beloved wife to give free reign to her sexual preferences, which were various, often premeditated and sometimes unusual. Relations with his parents were better, now that he saw them less often, and he now rather looked forward to his infrequent visits to his ancestral home, which would one day be his home, and he would go there again soon. During his last conversation with Victoria, she had informed him that filming was very shortly now to begin, and he would make time to see the matter in progress, and perhaps to meet actors whom hitherto he had only seen via his television screen. His father's health was for the most part stable, and at least gave no immediate cause for concern, and despite her initial resistance to the idea, his mother was apparently coping well enough with the disruption to her life and routines which were an inevitable and expected part of the making of the film. So, it was none of these things which had made him stop, and light his cigarette, and by degrees, as he looked over at cattle which were contentedly grazing the meadow below him, he was coming to the point of it, and the point of it was his son, Nathaniel.

Quentin awoke with sense that he was somewhere that he did not expect to be, or indeed recognise. At least, he was looking at a different ceiling, and a still semi-conscious glance around the small room told him that he had not awoken here before. There was a pile of clothes on the floor beside him; women's clothes, or girl's clothes, anyway, but they were not his clothes. The next thing to register was that there was daylight penetrating through and around the somewhat shabby curtains of the single window, so it must be morning, and he had a headache, and was thirsty. In the normal run of things he would have a glass of water on his bedside table, but today there was no glass of water, nor yet any bedside table upon which one might be put. So, not his bedroom, then; of course, he was in Rosie's house, and this was Rosie's sleeping place, but as he now glanced beside him, it was at least clear that aside from himself the bed was otherwise unoccupied. He sat up, as memories of the night which had just ended began to return, and just as the door was opened, and there stood Rosie, dressed only in his shirt and carrying two cups.

'Good morning.'

'Hi...Sorry, I borrowed your shirt, I haven't really got my clothes organised yet.'

'Borrow away, and as long as that's tea or coffee you carry, all is forgiven.'

'It's tea....'

She handed him a cup, and still wearing his shirt she got into bed beside him as he drank.

'How's the head?'

'Moderate to poor, yours...?'

'About the same, I'll look for tablets in a minute. By the way, your brother's here.'

'What....? What brother?'

'Tristan, I saw him coming out of the bathroom.'

This was not right, what was Tristan doing here?

'What time is it?'

'About seven-thirty...'

That was too early...Too early for Tristan to have made it here from the hotel, and he didn't even have the address, so what was going on? His last memory of Tristan was the sight of him walking away from the restaurant, and then he remembered with whom he had been walking.

'Oh....'

'Oh, indeed...'

'Where was he going when he left the bathroom?'

'Into Grace's room...'

'Right...'

'He didn't see me.'

'Fuck...'

'Yes, probably...I mean I'm not entirely surprised, she was all over him in the restaurant.'

'Was she, I didn't pick up on that....'

'No, well, that's because you're a man, and the way you have described Tristan's current state of being...'

'Yeah, he wouldn't have been trying very hard to resist her charms, that's for sure. I mean I'm not really thinking straight yet, but how does this stand, politically?'

'Well, they're both free agents, I suppose, so I suppose it doesn't stand anywhere, as far as I'm concerned anyway. I mean I told Toni, that's the other girl who lives here, that you'd probably be staying the night, but now there are two strange men in the house, so it's a bit, you know, one man too many, but they can't really object, can they?'

'No, I suppose not...'

'So how do you see it, politically?'

'Fucking hell, Tris....'

'That bad, is it?'

'What...? Well, I suppose you're right, what can anyone say, but even so...'

'Even so, what..?'

'I mean it's not quite decent, is it?'

Rosie laughed, gently.

'What do you mean?'

'Well, they'd only just met.'

'I don't think you and I had known each other very long.'

'Yes, but this is hours...'

'Well, if the girl was willing...I mean we are making assumptions, here, I suppose he could have slept on the floor.'

'No, Tristan doesn't do sleeping on floors. Anyway what would be the point, he had a bed in a hotel room much closer. And this would mean that Freddy would have been alone last night.'

'Yes, it would seem so, and there we were celebrating his forthcoming marriage, poor Freddy, seems like both of his brothers deserted him.'

'I was never meant to sleep at the hotel.'

'True...So what do you think big brother will make of it all, when he finds out?'

'God knows...I suppose we should go and see him, or I should, anyway.'

'He's flying out this morning, isn't he, which means that he'll be leaving the hotel quite early, I would have thought.'

'Yeah, I suppose...I mean I don't know what to make of all of this, really.'

'Well then don't make anything of it, at least until you've woken up a bit.'

'And dealt with the headache...So do you think this was a one-night stand, or what?'

'How on earth would I know?'

'Yeah, true...Christ, you let him out for one night and this happens...'

Rosemary was finding this conversation mildly amusing, despite her headache, which would indeed have to be dealt with soon. Grace had been drinking as hard as anyone, and she would be suffering this morning, and would likely also in due course have to deal with Toni, whose opinion of her was in any case not currently standing in a high place. There was no moral high ground upon which Toni could stand, she and Mal were not married, so there should not really be a problem, but all remained to be seen.

'So, anyway, shall I find us some medication, and I suppose you'd like your shirt back.'

'When you've finished with it...'

'You didn't bring an overnight bag, then.'

'No, it sort of felt like I would have been tempting fate.'

'I see...So you thought you might have been catching the last train home, is that it?'

'I wasn't really thinking anything. Look, we've had this conversation.'

'Yes, I'm sorry...'

'I did bring a toothbrush.'

'Where on earth did you carry a toothbrush?'

'Inside jacket-pocket, never leave home without a toothbrush...'

'So you were tempting fate to that extent, then.'

'It was more of a general preparedness.'

'You could have borrowed mine.'

'Well, now I won't have to, and look, as a final word on all of this, I know I've been a bloody idiot, so let's not dwell on my past stupidity, shall we?'

'Okay...Let's look to a bright new future instead then, shall we, once we've lost the hangovers?'

'Yes, let's do that, and meantime I need the bathroom, then I have a brother to deal with, so, shirt, please...'

'I'll go ahead and see how the land lies downstairs.'

She undressed, and then dressed again in her own clothes, and for a moment the man considered that the future might begin in a quite different way; the love, after all, had at least as far as he was concerned been roundly re-established, and whilst it was true that he had come here with no expectations, expectations may change. For now, however, she left the room, he had a headache as did she, and so he let the moment pass, but it was a moment which might be revisited at a later time this day, if he had any influence upon the matter.

    Abigail had it seemed settled herself and her charges well into their new and occasional place of abode, and by all appearances they were set fair to live at Glebe House from time to time. Thus had all concerned contrived to allow Elin her desire for she and he to have time with Nathaniel, and by default, with little Henry, without having to separate the two cousins, and Victoria, Michael knew, was by now quite in favour of the arrangement. Both children were growing strong and healthy, which had not been a given, given the traumatic entry into the world which had been Nathaniel's lot, and which had killed his mother, Rose. Rose, the thought of whom made Michael light another cigarette; she seemed now to belong to another life, and another love, which he would carry always, and even now, with so much that had happened, a sudden and unexpected memory or thought of her could tighten the pit of his stomach, and it would take a moment for the moment to pass. They had been so careful, once she had been told that she should not attempt to have children, and yet by some twist of fortune she had fallen pregnant, and her loss had given him a son, who would one day be a Lord himself, and would himself inherit the Manor, with all that all of that entailed. His son, Nathaniel, who had beautiful dark, wavy hair and a complexion which darkened, it seemed, at the very hint of sunshine. Indeed in appearance he had nothing of his mother or father in him, and it was a strange thing to Michael that he should rather resemble in so many respects a man who Michael nowadays saw on occasion on the village Green, when he found the time and inclination to play for the village cricket team. The man was Percival, who was the team's best batsman, and had, he knew, been a close friend to Rose. So, what then, was to be made of this? Had she been unfaithful to him, even whilst they had been married, and would he in time have to think the unthinkable, that Nathaniel was not his son at all? In his darkest moments, in the darkest hours of the night, such things had entered the realms of Michael's thoughts on more than one occasion, now, and thus far he had dismissed them as demonic aberrations of the night, which had no place in the real, waking world, but this was where, sooner or later, they would have to find their place, and be dismissed, if indeed and in the end he could dismiss them. So, just for a moment then, consider. If he were to allow himself this possibility, then Nathaniel was illegitimate, and would have no legal claim to the entitlement which would no longer be his birth right. There would perhaps be no more Lordship, and Michael would be the last of them, the last Lord Tillington, the last of a lineage which could be traced back to the eighth King Henry. And what of Percival, who had made no claim to the child; could he be aware that he was or at least could be father to Nathaniel, and indeed how could he not be? Had he and Rose kept their secret, a secret which Rose had taken to her grave; could the eyes which he had looked upon so often in her painted image which hung in the hallway of the Manor House, which had always seemed to him to hold so much mystery, really be saying something else? Whose child had she in truth been carrying when the portrait was painted? And continuing this thought process further, what of Victoria, his sister, who was he knew a friend to Percival? How could she not have noticed and noted the marked similarities between her friend and Nathaniel, and yet she had never spoken of it, which perhaps spoke more than if she had. Thus did the thoughts of Michael Tillington run; thoughts that he had consciously and perhaps unconsciously kept hidden from himself under a busy and otherwise mostly happy and contented life; perhaps after all he was being paranoid, and thinking himself into dark and dangerous places where he need not go, but the thoughts had of late it seemed to him found a life of their own, and would not let him be quite at peace.

We now enter the kitchen of the rented house, where Toni was about her first morning business of preparing a hot beverage for herself and Mal, and here did Rosemary encounter her.

'Good morning Toni.'

'Is it?'

'I don't know, isn't it?'

'Not if it's measured by the amount of sleep which preceded it.'

'Oh…'

'I thought it was you, coming in with someone at about two o'clock.'

'Not me, we were home just before midnight and quiet as church mice.'

'Yes, we gathered it wasn't you, and that you weren't the only one to bring someone back with you.'

'I brought Quentin back with me.'

'I mean the racket they made coming in was nothing compared to what happened after that, some people should learn how to have sex quietly, when there's only a thin wall separating them from other people who are trying to sleep.'

'Oh dear, well I didn't hear anything, but then not much wakes me up once I'm asleep.'

'She could have woken the dead. You want tea?'

'It's okay, I'll make it.'

'Well the kettle's hot. So who is he, do you know?'

'He's Tristan, Quentin's brother, we spent the evening together.'

'Christ, nothing like keeping it in the family, is there?'

'Quentin and I have been together for months, Toni, he's my beau, you know?'

'Yes, I know.'

'And I told you he'd be staying over.'

'I know you did, and that's not the issue. So did Grace know Tristan?'

'Not before last night, if you must know.'

'Well, she should try to learn to live up to her name, there was nothing particularly graceful about her behaviour last night.'

'I think she was drunk.'

'I would hope so, I don't know anyone who behaves like that when they're sober.'

'Well, I'm sorry, you know?'

'Not your fault, I'm just saying. Anyway I should get these drinks upstairs, I think we'll be having a lie-in, I'll see you later.'

'Sure....'

Enter Quentin into the room, bringing his handsome, masculine presence to bear on the situation, which had the effect of diffusing that which was in danger of becoming a somewhat tense atmosphere. Toni cast her quick, female eyes over the new arrival, and found him wanting in no regard, and a smile completed the diffusion.

'Good morning.'

'Quentin, this is Toni, my housemate, Toni, meet Quentin.'

'Pleased to meet you, I'm sure.'

'Likewise, Rosie's told me all about you.'

'Oh, has she?'

'Yeah, like how glad she is to be living here, and what a good person you are.'

'Is that so?'

'Absolutely....Although maybe I shouldn't have spoken out of turn.'

'Speak away...Well, he's a charmer, isn't he?'

'Charmed me, anyway....'

The two girls exchanged a look, Rosemary smiled, and Toni did not, but the expression had changed.

'Anyway, I'll see you two later, you're not rushing off, are you Quentin?'

'Not unless I'm evicted for bad behaviour.'

'Well, I can't see that happening.'

'What, the eviction or the bad behaviour?'

Which received no reply, but the implication was clear enough; Toni left the kitchen, and Rosie whispered her next words.

'"*Good person*"...? I never said that, did I?'

'Just pouring some oil...'

'Well, it worked.'

'Also covering my own back, I want to be invited back here, you know? Anyway, did you find some tablets, I've still got the head.'

'There's usually some in the kitchen cupboard, I think.'

'Right, well after that, how about we find somewhere local for breakfast..?'

'Oh, okay...What about the Tristan and Grace situation?'

'What about it? He's Grace's problem I would have thought, anyway he'll be asleep for hours, and by the sounds of it if she's got any sense she'll sneak him out before anyone else sees him.'

'You heard what Toni was saying, then.'

'Some of it...'

'So you don't want to see him, then?'

'Look, I don't care whether I see him now or later, we live in the same flat, remember, and if it comes to it he can make his own way home. He can always 'phone me.'

'So are you going to 'phone Freddy, let him know the situation?'

'I thought of that, then I thought better of it, I'm not my brother's keeper. I'll let Tris deal with Freddy.'

'Fair enough...'

All of this Quentin had been considering since he had news of his brother's presence, but now he had another thought.

'Is there a florist nearby?'

'What for...? I mean flowers, obviously, but what for?'

'Thought I might buy some for the house, like a sort of *"thank you for having me..."'*

'You can carry charm offensives too far, you know, but sure, Toni would love some flowers, I'm certain. We'll look out for a florist, then.'

They took tablets, did final preparations for their departure, and departed, and as they walked the streets of Kemptown in the direction of the city centre, further thoughts began to gain the forefront of Quentin's still awakening consciousness. It had been a good evening, on the whole, Freddy he thought had enjoyed the event, and any doubt regarding the love and trust between himself and Rosie had been dealt with, as had any misunderstanding, and all was now once again well between them. Tristan had met an attractive young woman, who could he was sure have been any attractive young woman, and had fulfilled his recently pending male instincts, and he could well imagine how that could have happened; Tristan could charm with the best of them given sufficient ulterior motive, and on this occasion the ulterior motive had been more than sufficient. Quentin's own primal instincts, however, within the context of a loving and caring relationship, had not been fulfilled, and he could not help but see an irony in this. He would not as things transpired see Tristan this day; they would speak by telephone and agree to make their own different ways home. Quentin himself would head homeward in the early afternoon, having made love with Rosie in the late morning, and he would sleep for a while in his own bed prior to the nightshift at the warehouse. By the time he awoke from his sleep, Tristan was no longer in residence, although he had clearly been there, and so whether by accident or design on Tristan's part they did not meet, and there was a conversation which would be had in due course. For now, though, we leave Quentin and Rosemary to their walk, as he took her hand and smiled.

'What are you smiling about?'

'I don't know, life, I suppose. Tell me I'm an idiot one more time.'

'You're an idiot.'

'There, that's done then.'

It was perhaps a thing of irony to Michael, that at odd times when his thoughts had turned to his beloved son, Nathaniel, and specifically to the doubts regarding the manner of his conception, that it was to another thought and another child to which and whom he turned for comfort, and solace; his beautiful daughter, Florence, about whom there was now no doubt regarding her parentage, and who had been conceived quite without his knowledge. The possibility existed, if he was correct in his darkest musings, that she was in fact his only child, in the genetic and biological sense, and it was the witch Rebecca, best friend and sometimes lover to his sister, and not Rose, with whom he shared parentage. He had been in love with Rose, and in truth was still in love with the memory of her, and he had never loved Rebecca, and yet, if he was indeed right, it was Rebecca with whom he shared this so particular bond, so here indeed would lay an irony.

Michael was uncertain for how long he had sat in the layby, but the sun was long into its descent into the western sky before he put away his pack of cigarettes and reached for the ignition key of his vehicle. Another question had by now entered the realms of his contemplations on this beautiful late summer's late afternoon; the question was simple enough, but the answering of it was far less simple. If he allowed himself the thought that Nathaniel, heir apparent to all that would one day be his, was not his son, then where did all of that implication go from here, and what, if anything, should he do about it?

Chapter 15. Sex and Furniture

Our tale now takes us to the early evening, and to a quiet, corner table of the Dog and Bottle public house, where two men have just arrived and are in earnest conversation over their beers, regarding a matter of great import to them both; they speak in hushed, conspiratorial tones, as seems fitting to them for that which they will discuss. For however else life may be, for a few hours on certain summer weekends, all else is put aside in favour of the cricket game on the village Green, or elsewhere on another village Green. The two men are Ron, local mechanic and captain of the cricket team, and Keith, second opening batsman, builder and sometimes musician, and these two are now joined by a third, who is Percival, former banker and number three batsman, who has still quite recently returned to the village after a period in self-imposed exile. Even during his time away, Percival would arrive as if from nowhere on the appointed day for most games, and then disappear again shortly after stumps, and no one asked where he had been, or where he was going, but he now basked in the comfort of a life at home, and an ale or two in his local pub. He was here by appointment, albeit loose appointment, and there was only one subject which the three had met to discuss, and without ado, Percival took his seat, supped his first ale of the evening, and asked the question.

'So, where are we, then, have we got Mike Tillington?'

All games were important, but this game held a special significance, the opponents being the village of Weybridge, against whom Middlewapping had won only one of their last three encounters, and these three were to say the least of it keen that the scores be levelled at the next and upcoming game. It was ofttimes the case, as now, that in terms of catchment and population, their opponents had a considerable advantage, and each member of the Middlewapping team was significant in terms of a positive result being achieved.

'Yeah,' said Ron, 'I spoke to him earlier, and he's up for it. He's coming back to the Manor for the weekend.'

'Good, we're going to need him. How about Quentin, Keith..?'

'Yep, he'll be here. He's working nights this week but I persuaded him to sleep for a bit and make it here by first ball. I said if he wasn't here he could forget about future relations with my daughter, that swung it our way.'

'That's also good news, so we'll be fielding a full team at least, even if we don't have a twelfth man.'

'Looks that way...' Said Ron 'So, if we put Mike in at number four, Quentin at number five, Reginald at six, Peter at seven, Will at eight, then Andy, Nigel and Don...'

'You still want to keep Will that far down the order, then,' said Percival.

'He's a better batsman than that,' said Keith.

'Of course he is,' said Ron 'he's been one of our top scorers this season, and last for that matter, but that's the point, nobody expects a number eight to bat that well, it's a bit of psychology, kind of a secret weapon. He holds the tail-enders together, and he doesn't care where he bats, I spoke to him about it last game.'

'Fair enough,' said Keith 'so as usual we're long on batsmen and short on bowlers, we'll need to put some runs on the board to stand any chance.'

'And their bowlers are good, we know that.'

'So are their batsmen,' said Percival 'although they seem to field a different team every game.'

'They have that luxury,' said Ron 'I mean Weybridge is practically a town, they can select their best players, we have eleven players from which to select eleven players. We're really missing the surgeon this season.'

'Quentin put in some good overs last game,' said Percival.

'Yeah, his bowling's really come on, he's becoming a central element to the team, better make sure he doesn't break up with Rosemary, Keith.'

'He's just been down to Brighton to see her, so as far as I know all's well there.'

'That's just as well….Anyway we beat them once, so I daresay we can do it again, but we need everyone to be at their best. So, Rosie's in Brighton, now.'

'Starts at uni next term, she's got a room in a shared house. I've got some stuff to drop down to her, but she put me off for now in favour of lover-boy.'

'And Tara's still off making music, is that right?'

'Yep, her third album...'

'She's doing well, and Barb tells me you're playing guitar on the album, is that right?'

'Yeah, I'm on a few tracks, but my bit's done now.'

'Al Talbut's a hell of a pair of shoes to be stepping into.'

'They would be, but it's not like that, Al played lead guitar, I'm just second acoustic guitar where it's needed. I mean Ash is an amazing guy, you know, despite past success he's got no side to him at all, and it just feels like a group of friends getting together and making an album. Anyway, I didn't know you were so well informed about matters musical, Ron.'

'Barb keeps me up to speed, she talks to Meadow at the deli. And talking of the deli, who's living upstairs, now that the old man's passed away? Barb said that Meadow was a bit reticent about it, so what's going on there?'

A look was now exchanged between Keith and Percival, who shrugged his shoulders; Ron was okay.

'Yeah, well this is about the world's worst kept secret, but Rebecca's back in town, but nobody is supposed to know that, so keep it under your hat, okay?'

'So what's the big secret, the chicken-stranglers still after her, or what?'

'Looks that way…'

'So, our resident witch is back in residence then…Well, at least we won't have to go so far to rescue her this time.'

'I suppose, but hopefully it won't come to that.'

'Well, if you need an extra pair of hands, you know where I am.'

'Sure, of course, if it comes to a fight you'll be the first to know. Anyway, I think more ales are called for.'

'It's my shout,' said Ron. 'So are we all okay with everything for the match on Sunday..?'

'Looks like we're good to go…'

Ron stood up and made for the bar. Ron and Barbara were for the most part peripheral to events pertaining to cults and witches, and knew nothing of Keith's recently rescuing Percival after his last encounter with the former, and despite their friendship, Meadow only imparted such information to Barbara as she thought appropriate. The mid-evening clientele had by now begun to patronise the establishment, but the next person to enter the room was someone that Keith had not seen for a long time, and Percival had not yet seen her.

'Well, well, look who's just arrived, an old flame of yours, Percival.'

Percival turned in his chair; she had seen him, and she waved and smiled on her way to the bar. She had not told him that she was coming.

'Better go buy the lady a drink, don't you think?'

'Yeah…Yeah, I suppose.'

'I wonder what she's doing back…'

'I've no idea.'

'Well, invite her to join us, we could do with some feminine company, and it doesn't get much more feminine than that, does it? Unless you two want to be alone..?'

'Fuck off, Keith.'

Keith smiled and Percival stood up; that which had begun as a meeting to discuss a cricket game was it seemed about to become something else; whatever else she had come with, and whatever the reason for her coming, Sally always nowadays came with an agenda.

Quentin, a player whom all so gathered at the Dog and Bottle who knew of such matters had agreed was now an integral part of the village cricket team, was during these moments at home in his rented flat, in conversation with his younger brother. Quentin's shift-work and Tristan's sometimes absence from the apartment had seen to it that these two had not met for conversation since their night spent in Brighton, and even now Quentin would be leaving for work shortly, but a conversation was needed, as both brothers knew. Having just awoken, therefore, Quentin brought his coffee into the lounge, where Tristan was distractedly watching an early evening television programme.

'So, Grace, what the fuck, Tris..?'
'What about her?'
'Turn this crap off.'

Tristan reached for the remote control, and duly turned off the television, as Quentin took an adjacent seat.

'Well, is this likely to become a relationship, or was it one night of wanton passion?'
'I don't know, to be honest, we've exchanged 'phone numbers, but we've not spoken since the morning after.'
'So are you going to 'phone her, or what?'
'Yeah, I guess, I mean what do you think?'
'Fuck should I know, I mean I'm sure you could fit her into your busy life right now, but how do you feel about seeing her again?'
'Yeah, I mean it was a great night, you know?'
'So I understand.'
'Meaning what?'

'Did you see anyone in the morning, I mean Toni, or what's his name, Mal, or whatever?'

'No, I think she was sort of keen to get me off-premises, but no, we didn't see anyone. So, who have you spoken to?'

'We saw Toni, who wasn't best pleased to have been kept awake most of the night by Grace's, shall we say, enthusiasm, for your love-making.'

'Shit…'

'Well, whatever, but how did you leave it with her?'

'We said we'd 'phone, you know, but I sort of wanted to speak to you first.'

'What, you forgotten how to do women, or something…? Need a bit of brotherly advice, do we?'

'Not that, really, but how does this all sit, with you and Rosie?'

'I don't think it sits anywhere, I mean it all feels a bit incestuous, but if it gets you off your arse and doing something then go for it, and I don't think Rosie has any particular issues.'

'Have you spoken to her about it?'

'Not in any great detail, but I guess us being together shouldn't present any encumbrance to your following through, as it were.'

'So has she spoken to Grace?'

'Look, I'm not going to act as your spy, Tris, this is down to you, you have to deal with your own stuff.'

'Sure…Sure, I know that, but this isn't how I saw my stuff going, you know?'

'What do you mean?'

'Well, I thought I'd like, get some gainful employment or whatever before I got involved with anyone, this feels a bit like putting the cart before the horse, if you see what I mean.'

'No I don't, not really, I mean I know you're on a low ebb right now, I get that, but man you have to start life again sometime, and this may be the beginning of the great reawakening. You've done some good things in your life, don't lose sight of that, and you've got some money, now, so you know, start looking seriously at buying somewhere, maybe get some income. I mean what were your last impressions, did you get the sense that she wants to see you again?'

'Yeah...I mean yeah, I think so, but it was easy the other night, I was pissed and so was she, and everything just happened, it was all very spontaneous, you know, and she was up for it, but this is the cold light of day, which is different.'

'Christ, and I always thought I was the sensitive one, you always used to take the piss out of me for it, so what happened to Tristan the confident?'

'I think I lost him, somewhere.'

'I mean, apart from the obvious, how did you relate to each other?'

'You mean, like, as human beings?'

'Yeah...'

'Well, I guess we didn't, really, I mean I didn't get around to exploring the innermost recesses of her soul, as it goes. We found a club, got more pissed, danced a bit, then we must have got a cab back to hers, you know, although I can't really remember how that was agreed upon, or much about that part of the night at all, really, and the rest is history. I couldn't tell you what she's studying at uni, or like, how many brothers and sisters she's got, if any. We sort of skipped the starter, you might say, and went straight to the main course, so I'm a bit hazy on the personal details.'

'Which once again feels a bit like putting your cart before the horse, is that it...?'

'Exactly, so now it's meeting sober, and like *'Hi, I forgot to ask last time we met, how many brothers and sisters do you have?'* '

'Yeah, I think I can see that, but you must have some kind of an impression, like how does your gut feel about her? I mean you were thinking with your balls, I get that, but was there any meeting of minds in the afterglow?'

'I think the afterglow mostly consisted of going for a piss and falling asleep, and in the morning I woke up with the mother of all hangovers, and as I say, she seemed keen that I leave the building, so we said our not particularly fond farewells, and that was us, really.'

'Yeah...Yeah okay, but I wouldn't read too much into the eviction, I mean she must have been aware of the kind of impression it would leave, and apparently relations between Grace and Toni are delicate at the moment anyway.'

'Any reason for that..?'

'Mal made a pass at her, or something, and she wasn't trying too hard to rebuff his advances, although she pleads innocence in the matter, but look, you really should contact her, don't you think, if only out of politeness?'

'Sure, of course, to do otherwise would not be gentlemanly, I'm not insensitive to that, although in the case in point it's a bit late to start being a gentleman.'

'Better late than never, man, stop beating yourself up, she was a willing participant in the whole deal, and she might be waiting for your call.'

'This sounds like me talking to you a few days ago.'

'That was different, Rosie and I had some stuff to work through, but that's done now.'

'I'm glad to hear it, Rosie's great, you know, and I guess it only happened with me and Grace because of you guys.'

'How do you come to that particular conclusion?'

'Well, you know, my being your brother maybe added a kind of respectability by association.'

'There was nothing respectable about it, as far as I can see. Maybe she thought you weren't the kind of guy who wouldn't call her, is that what you're saying, and here you are not calling her.'

'She could have 'phoned me.'

'That isn't how it works, you know that. Anyway you can't just hang out and wait for life and the world to come to you, this isn't India anymore, here you're just like everyone else, and it's tough sometimes, you know?'

'Sure, I know...I mean I'm finding that out, or better say remembering it. It's just such a reverse culture shock being back, India's a place of extremes, you know? The heat, the rain, the poverty, the riches, I mean it's hard, man, but you sort of get used to having it around, it's just a part of daily life, and the colours, and the art, and the food, you know, and just the way people have to live, and it's hard to make the adjustment back to all of this. Grey little England, where if the temperature hits thirty degrees everyone complains of the heat, and everyone worries about the price of vegetables and having the latest smartphone, and whether they're going to get a pay rise this year. It's just so fucking mundane, like everyone's lost sight of the big picture, you know?'

'I know, man, but it's where we live, and we're better off than most, and you didn't have to come back.'

'Sure, and there are days, you know, but I can't go back, not now, and yet I can't feel good about being back here, either, so I kind of belong nowhere.'

'You're a lost soul, I get that, and so does Freddie, and we're doing our best, you know?'

'Sure, I know that, bro, and don't think I don't appreciate it. I'm a thorn in everyone's side right now, and I suppose I could have seen this coming, but I'm working on it, and one day I'll come out the other side of all of this, but it's all taking longer than I'd expected.'

'Of course you will, but anyway, talking of things mundane, I'm to the fucking warehouse, so we'll talk later.'

'So no news of Kenya, then..?'

'Still waiting...Phone her, Tris, let her know what a good guy you really are underneath all the bullshit.'

'Good is as good does, man, but thanks, I needed to talk it through, even if it was only with you.'

'Go fuck yourself, and don't eat the pizza in the fridge, that's breakfast when I get home.'

'I hear you…I spoke to Freddo, by the way.'

'And…?'

'He was a bit pissed that I stood him up, but I told him the reason and we parted friends, as good as it gets, anyway.'

'So that just leaves the lady, so do what must be done, just don't bring her back here unless it's for tea and crumpets, if I find you've been using my bed we'll have an issue.'

'Wouldn't dream of it, brother…What do you take me for?'

'Same thing as you've always been…'

'Anyway from now on it's a courtship, I shall woo her, buy flowers and such, if she'll have me.'

'She'll have you, brother.'

'You have an inside line on that?'

'No, I just know you better than you know yourself right now, so trust me and make the call.'

'Okay, I'm on it….'

In fact Sally was at the table, drink in hand, before Percival had left it, so he retook his seat and Ron re-joined them. She had, as before, changed her attire and freshened up at the airport, and she brought with her her fragrance, her newly made-up face, and her legs, all of which brought a new and very different influence to bear upon the small, formerly all-male congregation.

'So, what are you three boys being so conspiratorial about?'

'Just enjoying some ales,' said Keith. 'What makes you think we're being conspiratorial?'

'I don't know, you just look conspiratorial…'

'Well, we did meet to discuss cricket, so I suppose you could call it that.'

'Cricket…How disappointing, I thought you were planning some kind of dastardly male intrigue or other.'

'Sorry, just cricket.'

'Well I'm afraid I can't help you with that, not knowing one end of a cricket ball from another, but please carry on.'

'Well, we've sort of done that, so we're open to changes of subject, like it's good to see you as always, Sally, but what brings you back from your broad, Nordic vistas to our humble village?'

'It's my tenants, or lack of them, since they seem to have completely vanished.'

'Yeah, I heard a rumour.'

'Well, I have to sort it out, and I did try to call you, Percival, but your 'phone's been off. I left a message.'

'I've not checked my 'phone lately. So what's the latest?'

'Well, the agents finally went in on my request, and found, well, you know what they found, the place has been empty for weeks, so now it's official, and if the rent isn't paid by the end of this week I'm within my rights to re-let, so I'm here over the weekend. I'm going to go in and do a first tidy-up, then I'll get cleaners in to do the rest, and now it's become a police matter.'

'How so..? I mean what's the process?'

'Well, the agents have reported them as missing persons, and I'll go to the local police to make a statement, and after that it's out of my hands, and I just assume they aren't coming back.'

'Maybe they've just moved on,' said Keith.

'Yes, perhaps, but….'

She now looked at Percival in enquiring manner.

'It's okay, you can tell Keith and Ron.'

'Well, Percival and I went in to check the place over, unofficially, and they seem to have just disappeared, half-eaten food on the table, unwashed dishes in the sink, that kind of thing, and they seem to have left all of their things there, clothes and so on.'

'Yeah, that's different, then…So will you stay at the house?'

'God, no, I mean it's still in the hands of the agents, really, and anyway I wouldn't stay there, not on my own, it'd freak me out.'

'Yeah, I can see that, so where will you stay?'

'I haven't got that far yet, but I'll find a hotel, or a friendly spare bed, I've still got friends around here.'

'We've got spare capacity at the bus at the moment, Tara's away, and Rosie's moved on, I mean it's not luxurious, but it's there if you need it….'

'Thanks, Keith, I'll bear it in mind.'

In fact Sally had made arrangements to stay with Polly, her long-time friend, but this she was keeping to herself, for now. She had assumed that Louise would be in residence, but she was aware that she sometimes stayed in Brighton, and that sometimes therefore Percival lived at the cottage alone, and so she was keeping her options open, just in case, but no invitation was as yet forthcoming.

'So,' said Keith 'do you miss the old place?'

'Of course, sometimes, I was very happy here for a while.'

The question had not been loaded, but the answer was, and there was a moment of awkwardness which Keith saw fit to diffuse, in a Keith kind of way, which often merely added fuel to the fire, and he was feeling slightly mischievous.

'Well, we can't always have everything we want in life, can we?'

'What do you mean?'

She should have let it go, but she did not.

'I mean things don't always work out like we want them to, do they, which is why I thought you left in the first place.'

'I left for my job, Keith, for the furtherance of my career.'

'Of course, that would be it, then. Anyway, I'm sure there are plenty of strapping, Viking types where you are now.'

'Well, I am in a relationship, if that's what you mean, although he's not particularly strapping, but that isn't why I left, either. Women do perfectly well without men, you know?'

This was old, well-trodden ground, upon which Sally could walk with confidence and could hold her own, but on this occasion she had met with Keith in his prevailing state of mind, and she should have let it go.

"Course they do, I mean Meadow's always saying she'd be better off without me, but then there's the whole sex thing, you know, and the furniture, of course.'

'What furniture?'

'I've made all of ours, and Meadow doesn't know one end of a chisel from another, a bit like you and cricket balls. With us it's all sex and furniture, that's the secret of our success.'

'You can buy furniture from shops, you know, and I'm sure there are plenty of women furniture-makers around, anyway.'

'And women to have sex with, I guess, but it's not the same, is it, as a woman, I mean, I mean it's missing one vital ingredient, you might say.'

'Women do perfectly well in that respect as well.'

'Sure, but how do you know when to stop?'

'I'm sorry...?'

'Well, with a man around, everything comes to a natural conclusion, as it were.'

'Rather too quickly, sometimes.'

'Be that as it may, everyone knows when it's time to put the kettle on, but women I assume can keep going 'til the cows come home, if that isn't an unfortunate analogy, so I've often wondered, you know?'

'Well you'll just have to keep on wondering, Keith, it's all a part of the mystery of womanhood.'

'Yeah, anyway how did we get onto this, I mean there we were talking about cricket, you arrive and suddenly we're talking about sex.'

'It wasn't me who started talking about sex.'

'No, but you put us in mind of it, as men.'

'How did I do that?'

'Well, you're not dressed to make furniture.'

'I'm not dressed f....Look, let's change the subject, shall we?'

'Yeah, I think I preferred it when we were talking about cricket,' said Ron.

Percival had listened without comment; he knew Keith well enough to know better than to try to intervene when he was in full flow, and he knew Sally well enough to know that she could look after herself, but even so he was glad when Keith continued in different vain.

'Okay, well since you'll be around for the weekend, you can come to the match on Sunday.'

'What, and be one of the little women who make the tea and sandwiches while you brave men do battle on the cricket pitch?'

'If you want to see it like that, although women's cricket's on the up these days...I'm all for a Middlewapping women's team, as it happens.'

'Well, I might come, I'll see what else is going on.'

'We might need all the support we can get.'

'Well like I say, I'll see what I can do, all those men dressed in white does have a certain appeal.'

'There you go...Anyway, your glass stands empty, so what's that?'

'Vodka and Tonic, although I really should be going, I only came here to...Well, anyway, I should be going.'

'One for the road then, Ron'll get beaten up if he doesn't get home for his supper, and Barb can pack a punch, you know, for a little woman, so none of us are hanging around.'

'Okay, if you're twisting my arm...'

The gathering dispersed shortly thereafter, and nothing more of note was said, until Percival and Sally said goodbye on the small forecourt, which at this time of year was patronised by people enjoying the balmy evening air.

'So, good luck with the tenants, let me know how it goes.'

'I will.'

'Oh, by the way, you left something behind when you stayed at the cottage.'

'Did I...?'

'Yeah, an item of underwear, Louise found it.'

'Oh Christ, I'm sorry, and I did wonder what the hell I'd done with them. Did it cause you any problems?'

'No, Louise took it for what it was, which was a mistake, right?'

'Of course, what else would it be?'

'Sure, well anyway, call 'round at the cottage before you leave, you can have them back.'

'Okay, I'll do that. Tell you what, I won't wear any knickers, then I'll be able to put them straight on, won't I?'

She smiled, and Percival watched her for a moment as she walked across the village Green, he assumed to the bus stop, and from thence to wherever she was going.

'So, any news of lover boy, then..?'

On the morning after her night of passion, Grace had nursed her way through the hangover and kept a low profile in the house, venturing forth only to buy such provision as she thought would aid her recovery, and she slept for a good part of the daylight hours. It was not until the next afternoon, therefore, that she and Rosemary met, which was in the kitchen. Mal and Toni were not in residence, and Rosie had made the enquiry.

'He hasn't 'phoned, but I suppose it's only been a day, and maybe he's not going to.'

'Do you want him to?'

'Yes, I do actually, I mean he's nice, you know?'

'I've always liked Tristan, and Freddy, for that matter, although Freddy takes a bit more getting to know.'

'He certainly takes his big-brother role seriously, doesn't he?'

'Yes, he does, bless him. It's funny, you know, I mean in all other respects Quentin is very much his own man, but he defers to Freddy, they both do.'

'Well, anyway, maybe I'll just put it down to a one-night stand, I've never had one of those before.'

'So how's it been with Toni?'

'Oh, you know, bad, really, I mean we've hardly spoken, and I've had a couple of black looks from that direction. She's definitely got me down as some kind of wanton hussy, first I try to steal her man, and now there's this, so we've not got off to a good start, really. Who bought the flowers, by the way?'

'That was Quentin, he wanted to say thanks for having me, it was his idea.'

'Well isn't he the perfect gentleman then, you stand in stark contrast to me at the moment.'

'Well, never mind, it'll all blow over, I'm sure, and I'd be surprised if Tristan doesn't call, to be honest.'

'Well, in all other respects you know him better than I do, so what can you tell me about him? I mean I know he's living with Quentin, but all I really know about him is what you've told me, which isn't much.'

'So you didn't talk much, then?'

'Hardly at all, I mean God, I've just slept with someone I know almost nothing about, maybe Toni's right about me. I wonder if I'd have done what I did had he not been Quentin's brother.'

'Well, we'll never know that, will we?'

'No, I suppose not...Anyway, tell me about him.'

'Well, I can tell you that he's recently returned from India, where he was doing some kind of unpaid voluntary work, a sort of meals and accommodation only kind of deal, and he's now looking for a new direction in life, and feeling a bit sorry for himself, apparently. I mean he's well educated, of course, but doesn't know quite where to put himself now he's back in England, sort of finding it hard to readjust, I think. They've just sold the family home in Clandon, which was a beautiful house, and the money's been split three ways, so he's got some money, quite a lot of money I would think, but otherwise I know about as much as you do. Quentin has said that he can stay living with him for now, but sooner or later he's going to have to move out and find his own way, and I think that's about where he is at the moment.'

'Right, well thanks for that, although it's probably all academic anyway, but I did like him. I mean what does Quentin think about the whole thing?'

'I don't know, I mean it's just boys being boys, I think, and he's not getting involved.'

'No, of course not, I wouldn't expect him to...I mean if it's just that, then I'm fine with it, one to put down to experience, you might say, all part of being a free, independent woman.'

'Indeed....'

'And I take it that you and Quentin have sorted out your differences?'

'Yes, we're fine now.'

'Well, that's one good thing, then. So what plans for the weekend?'

'Dad's coming down on Saturday with some shelves and stuff that he's made for me, and he wants me to go back with him, and Quentin's playing cricket for the village on Sunday, so I'll probably go back for a couple of days. Why don't you come with me?'

'What…?'

'Well, there's not much happening around here at the moment, is there, dad's borrowing a Land Rover, so there's room for you, and you could sleep in Tara's bed. I mean only if you want to, of course.'

'Sure, okay, why not? It'll give time for the smoke to clear in this place, and I don't fancy being here on my own at the moment, anyway. I've never seen where you lived, and I've never met your parents, so yes, I'd love to, thanks.'

'Good, that'd settled, then. I'll have to endure a game of cricket, and I'll probably be roped in to help with sandwiches, but that's optional for you.'

'Sounds great, I've never watched a whole cricket game, either, and I make a mean cheese and tomato, so it'll be a whole new experience. The idea has quite cheered me up, I must say.'

'Okay, well we'll probably leave sometime on Saturday afternoon.'

'I'll be here, packed up and ready.'

'Hi Vics, it's me.'

'Oh, hi Mike, everything okay?'

'Yes, I think so, although I'm not sure, to be honest. Are you around at the weekend?'

'Well, I'm working on Saturday, but I'll be here in the evening, and home on Sunday, why?'

'There's something I want to talk about, that's the thing.'

'Right…Nothing bad, I hope?'

'I don't know, probably not, but I won't know until we've spoken, really.'

'So are you coming to the Manor?'

'Yes, I'm playing cricket on Sunday, so I'll come up on Saturday sometime, and I'll be coming without Elin.'

'Okay, well I'll see you then. Are you okay?'

'Yes, yes I'm fine, and the children are fine too, it's not that...Anyway, see you on Saturday, tell mater and pater, will you?'

'Yes, of course, I'm sure we'll eat together, although it's all rather chaotic here at the moment as you may imagine.'

'Yes, I'm sure...Until Saturday, then.'

'Right you are...'

The call was ended, and it left Victoria wondering what could be amiss with her brother. It would have been an easy thing for Michael to wait for the right and appropriate moment to speak with his sister, but that moment may not arise for some time, and it was not a conversation to which he looked forward, and he could put the matter off no longer. And so, he had 'phoned her, not only to impart the fact of his coming, but now the conversation would happen, and there could and would be no further prevarication; now he could at last he hoped settle this so particular matter, one way or the other.

Chapter 16. A Possible Future

The morning of the cricket match dawned overcast, but with no real or apparent threat of rain, so the game would proceed. At least, there was no threat of its cancellation due to prevailing weather, but there was a problem for the home team, and as the players began to arrive and gather, Ron had an announcement to make.

'Okay, listen everyone, we have a problem. Don called late last night, he's turned his ankle badly and can't play.'

Keith was amongst those so far gathered, and one who knew as well as anyone the consequences of this.

'And since we have no twelfth man, we aren't fielding a full team...'

'Exactly, which means as things stand we forfeit the game.'

'Can't he just hobble out, hold a bat and be out first ball, and stand on the boundary when we're fielding?'

'Guy can hardly walk, apparently, he's going to the hospital for X-rays, thinks he may have cracked a bone.'

'Christ...And I've got new cricket whites. So what the hell do we do?'

'I've no idea, I don't know anyone from the village who'd be willing and able to step in at the eleventh hour, so if anyone has any ideas?'

By now all were assembled, the umpire, who had been provided by the opposing team, was setting up the stumps, and play would commence shortly, if play commenced at all. Percival, for reasons of his own, stayed clear of the discussions, and in any case Michael Tillington was amongst the group who had by now gathered, and there was a person who under the circumstances he had better not speak to. He had made up his mind not to deliberately avoid him, which might arouse suspicion of his having spoken with her, but nor would he encourage or instigate their meeting face-to-face, if that could be otherwise avoided.

'There must be somebody...' Said Keith.

'Well, we've only got a few minutes to find them, Keith, otherwise I'm going to have to find their captain and offer our apologies, and offer them the bloody game.'

'That can't happen, I mean I'd rope Bas in but he's not around, and I guess it has to be a man, does it?'

'Yeah, the days of mixed-gender cricket are not yet upon us. So, anyone....?'

Michael Tillington, who had all but not come to the game himself, was at this moment studying a certain house, to look for signs, but he was not hopeful.

'Ummm, well, I might know someone, but he's been away, and I'm not sure whether he's back, but it's worth a try.'

'Could be our last hope, so who is it?'

'Come with me, if he's there we may be able to persuade him, but I wouldn't bank on it.'

'I'm coming too,' said Keith 'in case we need to use threat of violence.'

The three men walked quickly, to the door of number seven, The Green, and Michael knocked at the door of the house, which was a house that he owned.

In the late afternoon of the day before the game, Michael had arrived at the Manor to find his ancestral home in a condition that he had not encountered it before. Several peasant folk of both genders were sitting in a rough circle on the lawn in front of the house, drinking coke and eating beefburgers with he who Michael assumed to be Lord of the Manor and others, the repast having been procured no doubt from the catering van which was parked nearby. The van would return to the woodland encampment at the end of the working day, but for now it provided sustenance to the various actors, technicians, make-up artists and so on who were involved in these early stages of filming. He pulled his car to a stop away from the general melee and throng of other vehicles, and walked to and ascended the steps of the Manor, where he encountered a rather austere and aggressive-looking gentleman who was on his descent, clutching a clipboard to his chest, and whom Michael assumed must be one of the production team.

'Who are you?'

'I'm Michael, son to his Lordship.'

'No you're not, we already have one of those, and he's not called Michael.'

'No, I mean I really am son to his Lordship, I mean his real Lordship, I live here, and one day this will be my house.'

'Oh, well, my apologies, then, but please be quick and quiet as you go, we're about to start filming in the library.'

'I'll bear that in mind.'

He found his parents in the small, paved area to the side of the kitchen, where they were passing an increasing amount of their waking time. His father was reading his daily newspaper, whilst his mother was about some embroidery, which was her occasional hobby.

'Hi Mater, Pater…Everything going okay here…?'

'Hello Michael, darling…' Said his mother.

'Yes, well,' said his father 'as well as one might have expected, I suppose.'

'Anyone famous turned up yet?'

'Well, we seem to have David Blake, who plays my namesake, in title at least, although he's Lord William Featherstone, I believe, and his wife, her Ladyship, AKA Ursula Franks is here somewhere, although they're having some issues with her costumes, as far as one can glean.'

'And Graham Dean plays me, is that right?'

'So I believe.'

'What's his stage-name, or film-name, or whatever?'

'That would be Thomas.'

'Thomas Featherstone...That has a certain ring, and what about Maurine O'Connell, she around yet...?'

'Of the daughter of the house we have had no sightings as yet, although we are rather kept in the dark and at a distance, of course.'

'Of course...'

'Still, one has befriended a rather charming young serving wench, who keeps us up to speed to an extent. So, to what do we owe the pleasure...?'

'Michael's playing cricket tomorrow, dear, I told you that.'

'Oh yes, so you did, and you're here without Elin?'

'Yes, she has some work to catch up with, and in any case we don't feel that we can leave Abi and the children at home alone overnight just yet.'

'No, perhaps not... So how's that all working out, anyway?'

'Very well, actually, everyone seems quite at home at Glebe House.'

'Well, that's all to the good under the circumstances, I suppose, this is scarce an ideal environment for children at the moment. So we'll be four for supper, then.'

'Yes dear, it's all been organised.'

'So' said Michael 'how does it work, then, are we told when we can go about the place and when we can't?'

'In no uncertain terms, and one would not wish to argue with Anna Merchant in full directional flow, so to speak. The worst of it is getting to my study, and even if one gains entry there's no guarantee of escape if they're filming around the main stairway, so I usually wait until everyone's gone home, which can it seems be at any time.'

Michael smiled to himself; his parents seemed to be coping well enough with the inconvenience of it all, and better than he and Victoria had feared might be the case, so far anyway, and he was pleased to see his parents, but they were not the main point or purpose of his being here. That would have to wait, until he and Victoria had time alone together, which would not he supposed be until the late evening.

It was a very sleepy and dishevelled-looking Horatio who opened the door to his home, wearing T-shirt and boxer-shorts, and clutching a mug of black coffee as if his life depended upon it. He offered a bewildered look to his unexpected visitors, only one of whom he knew, who was in fact his best friend, although he had seen the long-haired guy about the village.

'What the fuck, Tillers?'

'Thank goodness you're home.'

'Flew in from Rome last night, so, once again, what the fuck? Why is my being at home such a significant thing to three cricket players?'

'We've got a bit of an emergency, we're a man down and need you to step in.'

'What…? You mean you want me to play cricket?'

'It's a three-line whip, otherwise we lose by default.'

'Fuck off…I haven't held a cricket bat since school, and I've just woken up.'

'You made the second eleven as I recall.'

'That was then, for fucks' sake.'

'Look, the honour of the village is at stake here, this is Ron, our captain, and this is Keith, they're our opening batsmen, and we need you. Play's due to start in about fifteen minutes.'

'Well, sorry, gentlemen, but you can all….'

'Keith is sort of husband to Meadow at the deli, and you know how you rely on the deli.'

'Is that a threat, Tillers?'

'Call it an inducement, or emotional blackmail, or whatever you want to call it, and what better way to ingratiate yourself into the village, you'd be a local hero. Come on, no-trumps, this is cricket, you know?'

'I've got no whites, or bat for that matter.'

'I've got some old whites,' said Keith 'I'll wear those, you can have mine, and you can borrow my bat, it's a Gray-Nicolls.'

Horatio drank his coffee, and considered.

'Well, fuck off is still my holding position, but who's pulled out, batsman or bowler?'

'He's one of our bowlers, but we'll get by, and you can bat down the order, we don't expect anything from you, other than that you turn up and hold a bat.'

'Fuck that, if I'm playing I want to bowl.'

Michael looked at Ron.

'Sure, if you can bowl then bowl...'

'The fuck can I bowl, so who's the opposition?'

'Weybridge...'

'Lousy little middle-class place, we'll have to beat the crap out of them.'

'So, you're in, then?'

''Course I'm in, I'll need the cricket whites here.'

'I'll go change,' said Keith 'I'll be back in five minutes.'

Keith departed at pace, and passed Meadow on his way home.

'What's happening, Keith..?'

'Don't ask, but your inheritance and thus my new trousers may just have saved the day.'

'So the game's on, then?'

'Yep, looks like we're on, but I cannot tarry!'

Ron and Michael walked back onto the Green, where a coin was due to be tossed.

'If I win the toss we'll bat first, that'll give us more time, and give our new man a chance to get his eye in. Where the hell did you find him?'

'We were at school together, he can be a terrible snob, but underneath all of that his heart's in the right place.'

'I don't care where his heart is if he can play cricket. So what's *'no trumps'* all about?'

'It's a long story, but we used to be Bridge partners, we won the school competition a couple of years running, as it happens. Horatio's a very competitive person when he gets the bit between his teeth.'

'Sounds like just what we need.'

Ron lost the toss, but as luck would have it and somewhat to his relief, the opposing captain elected to field, and only a few minutes after the appointed time, play commenced, just as the sun broke through the cloud cover on this quintessentially rural English scene. Horatio arrived shortly thereafter, fully and appropriately dressed and now apparently fully awake, albeit that his somewhat weather-beaten brogues were not ideal footwear, and Michael took it upon himself to introduce him to the rest of the team, although Percival was not granted an introduction. The game was on, and there was indeed much at stake; the honour of the village now stood in the balance, but at least now the honour was there to be had, which but a few moments before had not been a given.

It was indeed the quite late evening before Michael and Victoria took coffee out onto the back terrace, their parents having retired for the night, which was a not unpleasant night, where bedroom windows would be left open to the cool, summer's air. There was no moon, and brother and sister sat opposite one another at table, in the semi-darkness of the borrowed light from the Manor House. Something was to be discussed, and Victoria had an unpleasant feeling that she knew what the something was, but nothing was certain, other than her wishing to get to the point of their private meeting as soon as may be.

'So, how's everything at Glebe House, are the children settled in okay?'

'Oh yes, that's working well, in all regards.'

'Good…..So, there's something you wanted to talk about?'

'Yes….In fact it relates to the children, well one of them, anyway.'

'I see….'

Here the unpleasant feeling had just increased in its intensity, and now she was almost sure.

'I have a question to ask you, well, perhaps several questions, actually, which would all relate to the first question, which is regarding…Got any fags on you?'

'She took a pack from the pocket of her frock, and they lit cigarettes.

'It's about…You know this all sounds rather silly, now, but something's been troubling me, for some time, if I'm honest. Please tell me if I'm being stupid, but I mean, there's no point in beating about the bush, is there?'

'So stop beating about the bush, what's the question?'

It was a question which he had no wish to ask, and which she had no wish to answer, for once done, there would be no way back to their present state of mutual, blissful ignorance.

'The question is, putting it frankly, do you think…Do you think that Nathaniel is my son?'

She took a moment. The question had lain out there, somewhere in the periphery of her thoughts and expectations, and now it had found its place, and it stood between them, in all of its long-considered implication and significance.

'You know what I'm speaking about, Vics, Nathaniel's....Well, his physical appearance cannot have escaped your notice, and well, frankly I'd hoped you might have been more surprised by the question, but I note that you're not.'

So, then, how to answer, but she knew and had known for a long time that there was but one answer.

'I don't know, Mike.'

'You don't know...'

'That's the only answer I have.'

'So, I mean, you're a friend to....You know who we're talking about.'

'Yes, Percival is my friend.'

And now the question had a name, and an identity.

'So have you discussed it with him, I mean does he know that...I mean is he aware of the situation?'

'He's aware of the possibilities, yes.'

'So the possibility does exist, then.'

'Yes, the possibility exists.'

'So he was with Rose, even when she and I were....'

'Yes, briefly...'

'And yet you didn't tell me, you didn't think to tell me any of this.'

'What was to tell, Mike? I can tell you that Percival had no idea of the danger that Rose may be in by becoming pregnant, and that the decision to keep the baby was hers, and hers alone, and that Percival makes no claim to fatherhood, and never will, I think. I mean, yes, they made love, or had sex, or whatever one may call it, and these things happen, Rose was, well, you know what she was, and the fact may have significance in itself, but beyond that, if Nathaniel didn't by some genetic misfortune look like Percival, then nobody would be any the wiser, would they? We can speculate, and draw conclusions, but the significant fact here is that nobody knows for certain, and that state of being could remain, and had perhaps better remain, for everyone's sake.'

'But this means that my son, heir to the Lordship, is illegitimate.'

'*May* be illegitimate, Mike, and that's the point, we don't know, and no one need know. To the outside world, he's your son, and ultimately what you do with all of this is up to you, you can either declare the possibility of his illegitimacy and have the tests done, in which case as things stand there may be no next Lord Tillington, at least not from our immediate family, or you can live with the possibility, and we keep it between us.'

'But who is '*us*', exactly? Who else is involved in this subterfuge?'

'Don't call it that, it makes it sound, I don't know, sordid, or something.'

'Well, it's hardly wholesome, is it? I mean my wife was unfaithful to me, for Christ's sake, and you've known about this for how long?'

'Look, don't put this on me, and you can make what you will of Rose's behaviour, but that really isn't the point, Mike, what's done is done, and when the dust settles on all of this, you will have to make the decision. As far as I'm aware, it's only yourself, Percival and I who know what went on, at least I've discussed it with no one else, and I trust Percival absolutely in this. As far as he is concerned, Nathaniel is and always will be your son, and he certainly has no wish to prove anything, one way or the other. This hasn't been easy for me, Mike, you are my brother, and I love you, and do you think I wanted to keep secrets from you? I've taken this whole thing upon myself, and I've thought about it 'til it's driven me crazy, and rightly or wrongly, for better or worse, I've said nothing, and you will judge me accordingly, but from now on none of that matters, does it? It's perfectly possible for the line and Lordship to continue, if that's what you want, or it can end with you, unless Elin gives you an heir, or some long-lost male cousin is found from somewhere, but I'm not aware of any other legitimate relation, are you? In any case, none of this is without precedence.'

'What do you mean?'

They both took cigarettes from the pack, and passed the lighter between them.

'I mean the line has been illegitimate almost since the beginning.'

'You're going to have to explain that one.'

'Well, the first Lord Tillington was clearly legitimate, as was his son, Edward, but the third Lord, who was the second Lord Edward, was not Edward's son, but was son to his sister. In all of this great history there have only been two legitimate holders of the title.'

'But…I mean how do you know all of that?'

'I studied it, Mike, looked into it, and there's no doubt, but I'm not going to explain everything now, it'll take a longer time than we now have. It was the portraits that made me wonder, or at least I wondered about them in retrospect, so you see, whatever you do, it doesn't really matter, in a way, and in an historical context. You will become the next Lord Tillington and nobody will ever dispute it, and the title will as things are pass to Nathaniel, but actually it's all pretence, whatever happens from now on. So, lots of secrets, you see, and I never told you because, well, what would have been the point? I wasn't going to be the one to take your future title away, but now it's come to this, and you must decide. I'm done with it, and done with keeping secrets. Yes, Percival and Rose were lovers, and the possibility exists that Nathaniel isn't your son, so you must decide what is important. Do you want your son, who is in all other respects your son, to be Lord Nathaniel, or do you want to bring the whole thing to an end? All I would say is that whatever you do, you wait, we can't tell father any of this, ever. He's not been well, he gets tired for days on end, and dizzy, sometimes, and he downplays everything, you know what he's like, but I'm worried for him, to be honest.'

'Well, wouldn't that be ironic, if the old boy pegged it just as I've got Glebe House into habitable condition, and I have to move back to this place anyway? I was hoping he'd give me a couple of years, at least.'

'Well, we'll see, but don't make this something which it isn't, Mike. I know it's hard, but don't decide now, and keep in mind that nothing is certain, and nothing need be certain, your son's future is in your hands, and nobody else's.'

They were silent for a moment, Victoria studied her brother as best she could in the dim light, and now he smiled, which was about the last thing that she had expected.

'Are you smiling?'

'An odd thought has just struck me, I'm supposed to be playing cricket tomorrow. How the hell am I supposed to play cricket with all of this going on?'

'Nothing's going on, Mike, not really, it's just nature, you know? People do what they do, and I've got a son of my own to prove that, and the world isn't going to end whether the Tillington Lordship continues or whether it doesn't. Rose died giving birth to little Nathaniel, when she knew the risks, and she didn't do that for Percival, about the last thing that Percival ever wanted was children. She had Nathaniel for you, Mike, because she knew it was her last chance, and because she knew that you so much wanted a son. All of this was an accident, and a tragic accident, but Nathaniel is here, now, and you must love him, no matter what else you do, because he deserves nothing else.'

She stood up.

'Where are you going?'

'I've nothing more to say, and I'm tired...I'm tired of being the only one who knows, and tired of keeping secrets, and you have a lot to think about, I know, but play your cricket game, dear brother, and go home to your wife, and your son.

Live your life, and you'll decide what's best to do, when the time comes to make that decision.'

'Well, thanks…I was hoping….I don't know what I was hoping, but it wasn't for this, and now you won't even talk about it.'

'I've said all I have to say, Mike.'

'At least leave me the cigarettes, will you?'

She left the cigarettes and lighter on the table, she had more in her bedroom, and he would need them.

'I don't know…'

'What don't you know, Mike?'

'I don't know what to make of it all, Vics.'

'Of course you don't, it's too soon, and I will talk to you about it again, of course I will, but not now, you need to collect your thoughts. All I would say is think long and hard before you do anything which you might later regret. Like I said, Mike, it's in your hands, now, and there are no words of comfort which I can offer you, other than to say that whatever you may one day decide, I'll understand, because frankly I don't know what I'd do in your situation either, and you will have my support, but in all of this the wellbeing of Nathaniel must come above all else. As far as he need ever know, you're his father, and you must trust me when I say that nobody wishes to take that away from either of you.'

She left, although Michael scarce noticed her leaving, and it would be a long and indefinite time before he himself stood, and walked the few paces to the Manor House, his ancestral home.

Percival watched from the boundary as Keith and Ron scored the opening runs in the middle of the pitch, and as he did so he became aware of a presence beside him, half a head shorter than he and somewhat slighter of build. He had been vaguely aware that a friend of Michael's was living at number seven, and it now struck him as odd that he had never come across him about the village, but such was the case, and here he now stood.

'So, you're Percival, then.'

'That'd be me.'

'Batter or bowler..?'

'I'm number three, my bowling leaves something to be desired.'

'The pitch has a short boundary, I don't know why I hadn't noticed that before, runs should be easy.'

'Yeah, for both sides, it's a high-scoring pitch.'

'You can toss a ball though, right?'

'Sure....'

'The guy bowling from the church end, he's quick and he's aiming down the offside, and there's a big gap between Deep Cover and Deep Point, there's some runs to be had there.'

'I gather you haven't played for a while.'

'Best part of a couple of decades.'

'You never forget though, right?'

'You don't forget the theory, but I need some off-pitch practice, if you wouldn't mind?'

'I'm next in, but I'll find someone. So how about you, batsman or bowler..?'

'Bit of an all - rounder on a good day, but bowler, I suppose you'd say, but I'll need to find line and length, it's been a while.'

'Of course...'

'Friend of Mike's, are you?'

'We rub along okay, on a good day, but he's not in the village much, and I'm a rare visitor to the Manor.'

'Never the twain, right...?'

'I'm more a friend of Victoria, to be honest. So you've known Mike a long time, then?'

'Yeah, Tillers and I go back. I was best man at his wedding, three times, as it happens, fucker's been unlucky in love, you might say.'

'Yes, you might say that.'

'So are you familiar with Elin, wife number three?'

'Can't say I am...'

'You were familiar with Rose though, yes?'

Percival was becoming a little uncertain about this conversation, but did not voice his uncertainty.

'Yeah, I knew Rose.'

'That's what I thought. Looks like you're in, our captain's just given his wicket away.'

'Shit...Okay, well look, see that young guy with the longish hair, his name's Will, he's not a bowler either but he'll throw a few balls at you.'

'Sure, thanks, and watch the bald-headed fucker, he's slower but more accurate, working off the seam.'

'I'll bear that in mind.'

Percival stepped over the boundary with the somewhat enigmatic part of the conversation in playback in his head, but now was not the time, he had a game to win, and Ron had given his wicket cheaply; the match had not got off to a good start for the home team.

Percival was seated on the step to the side door of his cottage, drinking Scotch, Lulu resting in the lane before him, when his telephone sounded. The hour was quite late, and Louise was upstairs taking her bedtime shower. He noted the caller and checked the time, which was a little before midnight; something was amiss, and his first thought was that this must concern Rebecca.

'Hello Victoria, to what do I owe the pleasure?'

'Hello, Percival, I'm sorry it's late, and I hope you weren't asleep, but something has happened this evening which I think you should know about.'

'I'm still awake, I'm a bit of a night bird these days. So what's our favourite witch been up to now then?'

'It's not her...It's Michael.'

'Oh, I see...'

'He knows, I mean he's worked it out, about Nathaniel, I mean.'

'Ah....'

'Indeed, he wanted a meeting with me, and well, he rather confronted me with it.'

'And what did you say?'

'Well, I could hardly deny any knowledge of the matter, could I, so I told him that you and Rose had, well, that you had been lovers, and therefore it was at least possible that Nathaniel was your child.'

'Shit...'

'I'm sorry, Percival, but I couldn't deny the blindingly obvious, and my line was that nobody knows for sure, and that it must be kept that way. I told him that you made no claim, of course, and that as far as anyone is concerned Nathaniel is his child, which was really the best I could do.'

'Sure...Sure, well, this is all very significant, isn't it, so how did he react, I mean do I now live with the threat of violence?'

'Mike's never been a violent man, but it's too soon yet to know how he'll react, or what he'll do, and frankly I didn't wait around to find out. He came to me with a question, which I answered as best I could, and I couldn't lie, and say that he was mistaken, and that everything was fine, because it so obviously isn't, but really it's down to him, now. I mean aside from the emotional aspect, this now brings into doubt the future of the Lordship, so everything has become uncertain, but we knew this might be coming, didn't we.'

'And now it's here…'

'I mean I might have waited to tell you, but you're both playing cricket tomorrow.'

'Of course…But will he play, do you think?'

'I told him that he should, that he should just live his life and let everything settle in his thoughts, which was the best I could do.'

'Yeah…Yeah it must have been tricky.'

'If only Nathaniel had been born with blond hair and blue eyes, none of this would have happened, but the older he gets, you know?'

'Sure, it's all very unfortunate, but Mike's a stoic, isn't he, and he's unlikely to act on impulse, I would have thought.'

'Yes, well I think you're right, and I hope you're right, but we'll see. I'm probably being a bit of a coward about this, but I really don't want to see him in the morning, and I daresay he'll go straight home after the game, so you'll probably see him before I do. I mean I tried to tell him not to make too much of it, and that life goes on, but it's weak, you know, in the face of the actual significance of it.'

'Sure…Well, look, there's nothing more we can say now, is there, so let's see how things go, and meet up if and when it proves necessary, but thanks, you know, for letting me know. I'll be on my guard, and of course I'll say nothing.'

'This conversation never happened. I can't and won't be seen to be in league with you over this, any further than I already am, he's my brother, and he's in a horrible place.'

'Of course, take it as read. My position in all of this hasn't changed and won't change, and should anything be said I'll plead ignorance, but I doubt if he'll confront me with it, at least not yet, and it may never come to that, but as you say, we'll see.'

'Indeed we will. Well, goodnight then, Percival.'

'You too, sleep well.'

'I'll try…'

The call was ended, and Percival drank his Scotch in one mouthful, and lit a cigarette.

'Well, what do you think, then? We humans get ourselves into some pickles, don't we?'

Lulu raised her head and looked at him, head cocked and trying to understand.

'It's okay, it's nothing you need to worry about. We call ourselves sophisticated, and advanced, and we think we're so clever, but really it's all the same shit that you guys go through, we just make more fuss about it.'

'Are you talking to your dog again?'

Louise had descended the stairs, and now stood behind him, dressed in bathrobe and slippers and brushing her hair.

'Who was on the 'phone?'

'Just Don, about the game tomorrow...'

'What, at this hour?'

'Takes his cricket seriously, does our Don.'

'Anyway, I'll make coffee, then I'm off to bed.'

'Sure, I'll be up shortly, leave mine in the kitchen.'

He would tell her. That had been their agreement, that there be no more secrets, but not now. She had no reason to see Nathaniel, and even more now, Percival would have to avoid situations in which he and his son would be together. He was not his son, after all, at least not in the eyes of the world, but now Michael Tillington knew, or at least suspected, which changed nothing, but changed everything, both at the same time.

By the end of the innings, which signalled the tea interval, the home team had scored a respectable but not exceptional total. Keith, ever a flamboyant batsman, and Percival, who better guarded his wicket, had between them compensated for Ron's early dismissal, but there had still been much for the other batsmen to do. Mike and Quentin between them consolidated the position, and Horatio gave good enough account of himself for a batsman so out of practise, and scored in excess of thirty valuable runs, which would in the end and in the context of the game prove to be invaluable. Reginald was his usual stoic self at the crease, and Peter Shortbody rose well enough to the occasion, but thereafter Will was the only reliable batsman, and as was often the case he scored well, and was the man not-out at the innings end, Andy and Nigel having capitulated quickly to the very good bowlers of the opposing team.

'So, what do you reckon then, Ron?'

Ron, who was feeling somewhat depressed by his own poor performance, was as was usual joined by Keith for a mid-game discussion, and neither were feeling confident.

'I don't think it's enough, and without Don our bowling's weaker than usual.'

'Yeah, I agree.'

Percival meanwhile had as was also usual found a quiet place for a cigarette, and he was now joined by Horatio.

'Got a spare fag, old chap?'

'Sure....'

'I get a general sense that the team feels we should have done better.'

'Yeah, we should, I mean it's not a complete disaster, but these guys can bat as well as bowl, so I can't see it, but there it is...'

'So do you have any influence on the bowling selection?'

'Not really, Ron calls the shots, but he'd better call it right today.'

'Well look, put in a word, will you, I'd like a crack at them from the pub end, the wicket's doing more at the other end, and I reckon I could make life difficult for the fuckers.'

'Why don't you ask him yourself, or get Mike to have a word?'

'I just see you as a man of influence.'

'We don't know each other.'

Horatio smoked his cigarette, although in truth he seldom smoked, and had used the cigarette as a way in to Percival, and he said nothing. Percival had for a short time been batting in partnership with Michael Tillington, and on the field of play nothing had been said between them, because in any context neither in truth yet had anything to say to the other, but this man had sought Percival out, and was saying something which he wasn't saying, and he was by all accounts Mike's best friend.

'Well, anyway, if things go bad, have a word, will you?'

'Sure, okay, I'll see what I can do.'

For the men of the village, match days were all about the cricket, but for certain of the village women they were a convenient excuse for gathering in numbers and exchanging news and opinions, whilst providing refreshment and sustenance for the players, and today their numbers included Rosemary, and Grace, who was herself in buoyant spirit, something about which Rosie saw fit to comment.

'You're cheerful, don't tell me you're actually enjoying this.'

'I think it's great, and I mean I'm having such a good time, and you're mum and dad are lovely, and I just love the way they live, and the way that you must have lived.'

'Well, it was different, anyway.'

'I mean look at your dad, all dressed up in his cricket stuff and looking like he's in the wrong decade by quite a long way.'

'Yes, he's always looked like that, whatever he's wearing.'

'Well I think it's great, and your mum's absolutely beautiful, isn't she, and I love that she doesn't wear shoes, and I mean you're beautiful, too, but you don't look like either of them, do you?'

'No, I don't. Basil looks more like his dad every day, and Tara looks like our parents, and then there's me.'

'Yes, I mean I've not met Tara, of course, but I've seen the album covers.'

'She's got their colouring, and she's tall, I ended up short and dark.'

It had not been in the nature of Rosemary during her school years to befriend her peers to the extent of inviting them to her home, a fact which had added an air of mystery to this otherwise in any case mysterious young lady, who unbeknownst to any of them had studied witchcraft, whilst others were about more conventional activities pursued by teenaged girls. All that they knew was that she had been born and raised on a bus, in a wood somewhere, but otherwise little was known of her, until now, and Grace, who had news to impart.

'Anyway there's another reason I'm feeling good, I had a 'phone call this morning...'

'Oh, do I take it that it was from a certain gentleman?'

'It was, and, well, I'm seeing him tonight, if that's okay.'

'Of course it's okay, why wouldn't it be?'

'Well, I'm here by your invitation, and here I am buggering off for the evening, but well, I'm here, you know, so it all sort of worked out, and I'm meeting him in town.'

'That's okay, I'll be with Quentin anyway, 'til he goes on nightshift, so go to it, and I'm glad he 'phoned.'

'So am I. I wonder if Quentin had anything to do with that.'

'I've no idea, but I daresay Tristan's big enough to make his own decisions, so, well done that girl.'

'Thanks, now I'm going to see him again I'm really glad I'm going to see him again, if you see what I mean. I mean I was cool with being the free, independent and sexually liberated woman, but this is better, potentially, anyway. I'll be back to sleep at the bus, of course.'

'Take a torch, then, otherwise you'll never find your way back, the cabs only work as far as the Green.'

'I'll have my 'phone with me.'

She as good as skipped away, and Rosie was left with mixed feelings, but on the whole she was glad for her still quite new-found friend.

By mid-way through the innings, it was clear that the visiting team were on course to take the game. Andy and Quentin between them had taken wickets and had stemmed the tide of runs, but Nigel was being hit all over the field, and as the afternoon wore on, the runs needed became ever less, until a point was reached where it was clear that the game was as good as lost unless something could be done. Thus it was that between overs, and whilst drinks were being taken, Percival approached Ron.

'Not looking good, is it?'

'No, the batsmen are looking too comfortable, and they clearly think they've won, they're just biding their time and picking off the odd loose ball, and they've got wickets in hand.'

'What about giving our new man a bowl?'

'Yeah, I wondered…Trouble is, if it turns out he can't bowl…I mean by his own admittance he hasn't played for years.'

'He did okay with the bat.'

'True, but if they put some quick runs on the board now we're dead in the water, it's a big risk.'

'I reckon a big risk's our only hope, and it was part of the deal, so Keith tells me. I understand he said he'd play if he could bowl a few balls.'

'Yes, but I was hoping things would be a bit less critical, right now I'm not sure we can afford the luxury.'

'I'm not sure that we can't afford the luxury, and even if we lose today, he's another player to call on, and we need that. My advice would be give him some match-practise, see what he can do, otherwise we might not see him again.'

'Yeah, there's that…'

'Up to you, of course, it's your call, but if you bowl him put him on from the pub end, I think he'd be more effective from there.'

Ron did take the chance on his new player, who after bowling a few loose deliveries, which were duly punished, took the next two vital wickets, knocking the stumps out of the ground on both occasions, and by the end of play he had added a third wicket to his tally. Buoyed no doubt by this sudden and unexpected change in the team's fortune, Quentin bowled the best session that anyone had seen him bowl, and at the death nine wickets had fallen, and the visitors were two runs adrift from the required total. One good shot or one more wicket would win the match, one way or the other, and Quentin had the bowling. First ball of the over, the batsmen took a quick single, the second was defended away, and the third ball saw a confident shout for leg-before-wicket from the home team, which was given. The game had been won, and the village honour restored, by the narrowest possible margin.

Nigel, who had not given good account of himself today on the cricket field, now returned to his day job as worthy landlord of the Dog and Bottle, beer was dispensed in plastic cups at the field's edge, and all sins of omission were forgiven. There was always at this time a melding of the players from both sides, and in the spirit of the game, the day became a social event, during which Keith and Ron found a moment for a quiet word.

'Christ, that was close…'

'Doesn't get any closer, and that was a brave decision, bringing what's his name into the attack, without him we'd have lost, I reckon.'

'We've got Percival to thank for that one, I wouldn't have done it without his suggestion, I didn't do well with the bat or as captain today, to be honest.'

'Never mind, man, we won, and it's all about the team, anyway, you can't always be the hero.'

'Quentin gets the accolades, too, he bowled superbly.'

'Yeah, on today's performance I reckon I might let him date my Rosie for a bit longer.'

'I would marry them off if I were you, for the good of the team, you know?'

Here we also find Michael Tillington in conversation with the new player.

'Well done, you played okay.'

'Should have got more runs, Tillers, it was a stupid ball to be out to, but I suppose not bad for a beginner.'

'So do you think you'll play again?'

'Already spoken to Ron, next game's in two weeks.'

'Funny, I was thinking of jacking it in, but if you're coming on board I might stay after all.'

'Why jack it in?'

'Let's call it personal reasons.'

'And am I not your best friend, always was, anyway, so what's the problem?'

'Not now, some other time…Now you're back we should get together more often.'

'Yeah, think I'll bed in for a while, 'til I get restless again, maybe find some food bank or charitable organisation that needs a hand.'

'Well, they say it begins at home, which is where I'll be going after this, but we'll catch up soon.'

Barbara had by now found Ron.

'Well done, captain, another fine victory.'

'No thanks to me, as it happens.'

'Don't be such a killjoy, your team won, which is what you wanted, isn't it?'

This last sentence was accompanied by a sharp dig in the ribs, which was witnessed from a distance by Horatio, who had by now sought out Percival.

'Fuck was that?'

'What...?'

'She's about half his size, and he puts up with that?'

'Oh, you mean Ron and Barbara, pay it no mind, it's her way of expressing her love for him, if she's not beating him up you know that something's wrong within the relationship.'

'That so....? Anyway, thanks for putting in a word, I understand it was you who talked Ron into giving me a bowl.'

'Turned out to be a good decision...'

'I knew you had influence, in more ways than one, it seems.'

Horatio walked on, but left his words behind; words which left Percival wondering as to which ways he was referring, but he would not find out, not on this day, anyway.

Later, Ron would exchange words with the opposing captain, who congratulated him on the victory.

'Tell me, how does a village as small as Middlewapping produce a team like this?'

'We almost didn't, as it happens, we're always living on the edge, you might say.'

'We've won most of our games this season, but today your lot surprised us.'

'Yeah, I mean I was surprised, to be honest, I thought we were dead in the water at one point.'

'So the guy with the dark hair, I don't remember him from the other games.'

'It's his first game for us, we found him at the last minute, he hasn't played since the playing fields of Eton, or Harrow, one of the two, anyway.'

'What, you mean we got beaten by a novice, that doesn't make me feel any better. Guy can bowl, though, I mean he's not that quick but he mixes it up well. I'd keep him in the team if I were you.'

'That's the intent, anyway.'

The afternoon was drawing to a close and giving way to the cooler evening air as the gathering slowly dispersed, and despite his personal disappointment in his own performance, Ron left for hearth and home with his beloved if ofttimes violent wife with a sense that cricket was indeed the finest of games, on such a fine day as this had been.

Grace and Tristan met in town, and visited a bistro which both had frequented before on occasion, and Tristan ordered tacos and a quite expensive bottle of wine. Given his current state of employment, which was non-existent, Tristan had become or had remained quite frugal by habit since his return to England, but tonight he decided to make exception. His inheritance was on deposit, but he could, he knew, organise a transfer of funds fairly quickly if need be, so he was no longer so concerned about matters financial, despite having been strongly advised by both of his brothers that the money should be kept for more substantial, longer-term projects such as the buying of property. But still, here he was with the young lady whom he had in certain respects come to know very quickly, but in other regards he knew hardly at all, and tonight he would try to put that to rights. Alcohol was once again needed to ease their way into easy conversation, and having been thus procured, the process could begin.

'So, tell me about yourself.'

She smiled, partly in understanding and partly because she was pleased to be here, and in his company.

'What would you like to know?'

'Well, let's start with, how many brothers and sisters to do you have?'

So did the evening begin, and thus did it proceed in decent and respectable manner, until the decency and respectability had been well enough established, and sufficient alcohol consumed to allow for their being put aside, potentially at least, in the interests of other, less decent and respectable activities. An invitation for coffee was accepted, and by around the stroke of midnight they had retired to Tristan's place of abode, she had quietly 'phoned Rosemary to say that she would likely be staying out after all, and he had found beer in the refrigerator.

'This is a nice flat, there's only one bedroom, though.'

'Yep, you see that pile of bedding in the corner, that's me, on the couch. It's surprisingly comfortable, actually.'

They kissed, and undressed one another, and he led her into the one bedroom, where they fell together, and the young lady had a question.

'So, this is Quentin's bed, then.'

'Yes, it is.'

'Won't he mind?'

'No, he'll be cool, we have an understanding.'

'Do you do this sort of thing a lot, then?'

'No, I mean Quen and I used to swap beds sometimes when we were kids, we've always taken the view that beds are for sharing.'

'Why did you do that?'

'Don't know, really, an act of defiance, maybe, and for the adventure of it. We just have to be out before he gets home, otherwise you'll have two of us to deal with.'

She smiled again, they kissed, and the night proceeded in less decent manner than perhaps had been planned, but in such situations plans may change, if both parties are in agreement as regards the changes.

Michael drove home from the game with so many thoughts and questions running through his head, which he was hard put to it to prioritise, so in the end he gave up trying. Hitherto he had taken his sister's advice, and allowed the game of cricket to provide distraction from that which must be addressed, but now the time had come for the addressing. Victoria had avoided him this morning, he was certain of that, and he knew and understood well enough the reason for the avoidance. She had known or guessed about Nathaniel's conception, and had not told him, and could he forgive her for that? As brother and sister they had been through much together, he had seen her through difficult times without question, and had always been there for her when she had needed him, but this most fundamental thing she had kept from him, and for how long had she known, or guessed? He tried to imagine conversations between her and Percival, perhaps they had agreed between them not to tell him, and she would have asked Percival whether or not he would make any claim to the child, and he would have said that he would not, but these thoughts were not useful thoughts, which led only to dark places. Rose had been unfaithful to him, so had she loved Percival? She would have known that the child that she carried when her portrait was painted was Percival's, and when she had made the decision to keep it, and yet she had put herself in mortal danger nonetheless. And then there was Percival, who had albeit indirectly, unconsciously and without deliberation killed his beloved wife, his beloved Rose, and yet without him there would be no Nathaniel, and no male heir; no son to whom he could pass on his title and the Manor House, should he now chose to do so. Nathaniel would now live his life with parents, neither of whom were in all probability actually his parents, and Elin's part in this he would understand well enough; he would one day see his mother's portrait, and understand that she had died bringing him into the world, but to be told that his father was not really his father, that would be a different matter entirely. Aside from the legality of the whole thing, he must guard his son, who he would still call his son, against such knowledge, must he not, and yet in doing so he would be lying to him, so what was to be made of that? And then there was the matter of the Lordship. In truth Michael did not care whether one day he would be Lord Tillington, which in any case if Victoria was right he now knew to be a false Lordship, to which he had no legitimate entitlement, and yet could he really end such a long and auspicious history by proving and declaring his son to be a bastard? Did he not owe something to his forebears, who would likely for the most part have been quite unaware of their illegitimacy, and to those who would come after; Nathaniel's son, if he were to have one, and his son, and so on into an indefinite and uncertain future. A Lordship, after all, was more than just one lifetime, and if its continuation was due entirely to an accidental conception in a moment of illegitimate passion, then had fate not played a part in all of this? He had replayed his conversation with Victoria in his head time and time again, and of all of it these words in particular kept coming back to him; *'Rose died giving birth to little Nathaniel when she knew the risks. She had Nathaniel for you, Mike, because she knew it was her last chance, and because she knew that you so much wanted a son.'* A son who would not otherwise have lived, and what, if he brought his almost certain knowledge into the public arena, would he tell Elin? That it was now beholden upon her to produce the son and heir? No, that would not happen, and Rose had given her life that Nathaniel might live, and although and perhaps indeed because the pain of her loss was something which would never entirely go away, did he not owe it to her to keep the secret knowledge, known only to the living few? And then there was the idea that perhaps there was someone out there who would by default become the next Lord, a Lordship after all existed in its own right, regardless of what he might do, but what would be the point of that, really?

Such were the thoughts of Michael Tillington, future Lord of the Manor, as he drove home to that which he now assumed was only to be his home for a quite short time, before history once again moved her inexorable and inevitable way, and it was a history which lay now in his hands. He drove home to a son whom he loved, as if he were certainly his own son, and to a wife who loved him, and somewhere there was a daughter, daughter to a witch, who was certainly his daughter, however that had come to be. History was bigger than him, and bigger than everyone, and he would keep the secret, for now at least, as his sister had said that he should do. One day was an insufficient time to decide the future of a dynasty, or to bring his thoughts to a place where he would know for sure what to do. Nathaniel could, after all, be his son, nobody knew for certain, and in that uncertainty lay a way for one possible future to follow its course.

Chapter 17. A History Rewritten

The arrival of Maurine O'Connell at the Manor House in a way heralded and in any case symbolised the true beginning of the production of the movie. The Lord and Lady, played respectively by David Blake and Ursula Franks, and their son, the future Lord, played by Graham Dean, were all significant players in the passion play which would one day be '*A Small Moment in English History*', which everyone now accepted would be the eventual title of the film. It was, however, the daughter of the house around whom the story would revolve; a notoriously beautiful young woman with an increasingly notorious rebellious streak, who would through her thoughts and eventual actions bring shame upon her family, and thus threaten their place in English high society. She had been to the Manor House once before, in contemporary dress and as Maurine O'Connell, but now she appeared in all of her Elizabethan splendour, in her first manifestation as Katherine Featherstone, and ready to play her part.

The prevailing weather was such that those not currently involved in the filming were able to pass the time between their periods of involvement outside in the Manor House grounds, and there was nowadays usually much activity around the steps and front lawn of the Manor, and thus it was that the actual daughter of the house, Victoria Tillington, came across her fictitious counterpart as she pulled her car to a stop at the end of her journey from London, and from her place of work. The young lady was sitting on a bright blue plastic chair, one of several which had been purchased by May Thomas, the cast and crew having complained that there was nowhere to sit, or rather nothing to sit upon, whilst waiting for their part in the production. Victoria and Maurine had met and spoken once before, and a certain familiarity had quickly formed between them at their first meeting, and here was their second.

'Hi….'

'Hello'

'You look rather splendid.'

'Thanks, I feel like a complete twit, I'm not quite used to this yet. I don't know how they used to wear all of this all the time, and I'm completely authentic today, right down to the bloomers.'

Victoria laughed.

'So you're not quite *'in role'* yet then, if that's the right expression.'

'Well, so far today I've been on set for about fifteen minutes, and said nothing, I've just had to give someone a seductive look.'

'Oh, how does that go?'

'I can't do it to order, well, I suppose I can, but not out here in real life.'

Victoria smiled, and the smile was returned, and a sense of rapport was quickly becoming re-established between them.

'So when are you on again?'

'Lord knows, I'm supposed to be having sex with a visiting dignitary at some point, if we ever get around to it, but we're on the mum and dad talking about their wayward daughter scene, which seems to be taking forever. There's a lot of sitting about at the moment, and it's bloody hot and uncomfortable, to be honest.'

'Can I get you a coffee or something?'

'It's okay, we're quite well catered for, and even having a wee in all of this is a major event, so I'm cutting down on the liquid intake. I'm not eating, either, got to look my most sylph-like for the sex, you know?'

'You're skinny as a rake anyway.'

'Have to stay that way for the cameras, and to fit into this bloody dress. Tell you what, though, you haven't got a fag on you, have you, I'm gasping.'

'Sure…'

They lit cigarettes.

'So, how's the accommodation, I mean what's it like living in the wood?'

'Oh, it's okay, I mean the woods are lovely, of course. Last night was my first night here, and I slept well enough, and they seem like a nice enough bunch, on the whole.'

'I've not been down there since you all moved in.'

'You should come down, have a drink with us. Actually I was thinking that you and I should have a chat, anyway.'

'Oh yes, what about?'

'Well, I mean I'm playing the daughter, but you're the real thing, aren't you, so I was wondering whether you could give me some pointers.'

'I don't suppose there's much similarity between my life and the way things were back in your day, as it were, but I'm happy to give it a go.'

'Good, well come down this evening then, I mean if you want to and you've got time, and assuming I ever manage to get this *'let's pretend to have sex'* thing out of the way. Not many lines to learn for this, either, just got to give it my best moan, I expect, and I might have to scream a bit if it's any good. I mean I don't even know how it's going to happen, it'll take about half an hour to get everyone undressed, the moment will have long gone by the time we actually get down to it. Mini-skirts and thongs work much better, I find.'

Victoria laughed again.

'So what's he like, your visiting dignitary?'

'Oh he's okay, nice enough chap, actually, the little time I've spent with him, I mean not screaming material I wouldn't have said, but it's all in a day's work, as they say.'

'Well, good luck with that.'

'Thanks….Anyway, men in general aren't necessarily my cup of tea, to be honest.'

This last statement was accompanied by the swiftest of looks, which could scarce have been described as seductive, but it had an enquiring nature about it, and Victoria had a sense that a light-hearted conversation had momentarily become something else. The moment was interrupted, however, by a group of people descending the steps of the Manor, who were the Lord and Lady, and several others in contemporary and period garb, and she who Victoria assumed was a make-up artist approached them.

'Oh shit, looks like this is me.'

'Well, as I say, good luck.'

'Don't forget to come down later and see us, if you want, it's an official invitation.'

'Okay, I may well do that.'

Maurine O'Connell passed her cigarette to a passing peasant for the continuance of its enjoyment, Victoria made for the side door, and coffee, and to the rest of her evening, which now promised to hold much more than she had been expecting when she arrived home from her day's work.

The next time that Percival would see Sally was on the afternoon following the cricket game, when she appeared unannounced at his side door, dressed to travel and wheeling her cabin baggage.

'Hi, any chance of coffee before I head north?'

'Sure, come in.'

There was usually coffee ready for consumption in Percival's percolator, and now was no exception; he poured two cups and they sat opposite one another at the dining table.

'So, how's everything with the cottage?'

'Well, it's cleaned up a bit now, anyway, so it's down to the agents to get the commercial cleaners in and find new tenants.'

'You shouldn't have any problems in that regard, period properties go like hotcakes.'

'Yes, so they tell me, and it's a buoyant rental market at the moment anyway.'

'So what of the disappearing duo, no news of them I suppose?'

'No, I've done my report to the police, who didn't seem very interested, so now it's just a matter of whether anything or anyone turns up. I've asked the agents to change the locks, so if you see a couple of people wandering around the village Green looking lost....'

'I'll keep an eye out.'

'Thanks for your help in all of this.'

'I didn't do much, and it was a pleasure. Where have you been staying, anyway?'

'I've been with Polly, you remember Polly?'

'Polly the florist, didn't like me very much as I recall...'

'That's the one. She's still in the house but she's finally getting around to divorcing George.'

'He didn't like me much, either. Remind me, who was he having an affair with?'

'Claudia, as in Claudia and Simon, although they aren't together any more, either...'

'Bit of a mess there, then.'

'There's a lot of it about, it seems, a lot of pain. Polly's taking it quite hard, actually.'

'Sorry to hear it.'

'Yes, the pain of separation, it can be quite horrible, you know? Or perhaps you wouldn't know about that.'

'Come on, Sal, let's not go over this again, we've both moved on, and Norway seems to be working out well for you.'

'Yes it does, lucky me...Are you okay, you seem a bit down, even by your standards.'

'I'm fine.'

'No you're not, I know you better than that, remember?'

'It's nothing you need be concerned about.'

'Okay, have it your own way.'

He had not yet told Louise, and here was someone who was now detached from everything, but with whom he still shared affection, and where would be the harm in telling her; it might be good practise for the main event.

'Thing is...'

'Come on, out with it.'

'You know Michael Tillington, and you know he has a son, right?'

'Yes, and Michael's wife, Rose, died giving birth, that's common knowledge.'

'Indeed...What isn't such common knowledge is that he isn't actually Mike's son, probably not, anyway.'

'Oh....Gosh, such scandal in the Tillington household...So how do you know, and whose son is he, probably?'

'Mine, as it happens.'

'What...? I mean why...?'

'I shouldn't have to explain the facts of life to you.'

'No, but, why is it only probably?'

'Yeah, thing is, Nathaniel, that's the son...'

'I know what his name is.'

'Right, well, as luck or rather ill-luck would have it he looks like me, practically a carbon copy only a bit younger, and I mean I'm cool with everything, I mean I don't want the kid, you know, but hitherto it's only been Victoria and I who have made the assumption, but now Mike's worked it out, so it's all hit the fan, you might say.'

'Jesus, Percival....'

'Indeed....'

'So has Mike confronted you with this?'

'It hasn't come up in conversation, not yet, anyway, and he doesn't know that I know that he knows. We actually played cricket together yesterday, which can't have been easy for him, but all of this has far-reaching implications, of course, regarding the Lordship apart from anything else.'

'Yes, of course…I mean he can't become a Lord, can he, Nathaniel I mean?'

'No, well not legally, anyway, but I suppose if no one proves anything one way or the other, then nobody would be any the wiser.'

'And how would you feel about that?'

'I don't care whether he becomes a Lord or not, I mean the title means precious little anyway since the hereditary peers were mostly kicked out of the Upper Chamber of our dear government. Frankly I'm more concerned that he learns to play cricket, and I daresay Mike will have that covered, I expect his name's already down for a good school, so I'm not concerned for his general wellbeing.'

'I see…So, you and Rose…'

'Yes, me and Rose, and she decided to keep the kid, I mean to keep Nathaniel, knowing that medically speaking it was high-risk, and as it turned out, well, she lost the gamble, and the rest is history. So okay, I mean I can live with all of that, but now that Mike's worked everything out it changes things, and in an odd way, well, Nathaniel's started to feel like my kid for the first time, and I can't really explain that. I mean Mike's a good guy, he'll make a good dad, you know, and Nathaniel will grow up in a better environment than I could have provided, and one day he could still be Lord of the Manor, so what's to worry about, but still, it's all just rather hit me, as it happens, and I hope Mike doesn't do anything stupid, like try to establish true parentage. Better that everyone stays ignorant, and everything goes on like before, but nothing's certain anymore, and it's just become a fucking mess, really, and it's hard to predict the outcome.'

'Oh, poor you…'

'No, that isn't it, Sal, I mean I'm not feeling sorry for myself, I just want what's best for everyone, you know, given the circumstances.'

'And what you mean by that is that you want what's best for your son, yes?'

'Yeah, I guess that's it.'

'Well....Fucking hell....'

'My sentiments exactly...'

He lit a cigarette and offered her one, which she declined, he drew once on his and she reached over and took it from him anyway; it was a quite well-established habit of hers whilst they had been together, and for a moment this could have been them, when they were together. He took another from the packet, and was the next to speak as she contemplated implications.

'Anyway, things are as they are, so to speak, so I'll just have to see what happens from here.'

'So what does Louise say about all of this?'

'Nothing, yet, she doesn't know, this is all new, and I've been mulling it over. I mean I'll tell her, of course, and I'm not concerned about that in the long-run, but I'm sort of waiting until the full story unfolds, or maybe reaches some sort of conclusion. She'll no doubt react in a Louise-type way, but in the end it's not a hanging offence, she's put up with worse than this from me, after all.'

'Yes, she has. And Victoria...?'

'Yeah, well that also remains to be seen, but the all but certain fact of it is well established between us, and she also takes the view that nothing must be proved, one way or the other. We'd both hoped that Mike wouldn't work it out, but that of course was wishful thinking. Last time I spoke to her was when she 'phoned to warn me that Mike knew.'

'So he must also have found out that she knew, and had said nothing to him, that must have been an interesting conversation between them, I would think.'

'I'm presently trying to put myself in Mike's place, trying to imagine what he must be feeling and thinking right now.'

'So do you think it'll eventually come to a confrontation between you two?'

'I've no idea, I mean what's to say, really? He could call me a cad, and I could apologise for having had intimate relations with his now-deceased wife, and that she died as a consequence, but I think we've moved beyond that now, and he may take the view that the least said the better, which is certainly my view. I mean sure, we could lock horns, but what in the end would be the point?'

'Well, well, here's a to do then….Nothing's ever simple with you, is it, Mister Percival?'

'I do seem to attract controversy.'

She laughed at that.

'And you do seem to be the master of understatement, but then you were always that, too.'

'Well, anyway, that's the current state of play, which could account for why I'm not my usual cheerful self right now, so we'll see. Anyway, don't you have a 'plane to catch?'

'I've got time, but yes, I suppose I should be going, I just called by to check the cottage, and to see you, of course, and I think you have something of mine.'

'Oh, sure, I'll go fetch.'

He went upstairs, and returned with a small plastic carrier bag, as she stood up to leave.

'There you go…'

A small plastic carrier bag which enwrapped minimalist and exotic underwear, and the symbolism as he passed it to her was not lost on either of them.

'Thanks, and thanks for looking after them for me…'

'You're welcome.'

'I'll have to be more careful where I leave my underwear in future.'

'That might be wise.'

'I'll think of you every time I wear them. So anyway, I don't suppose I'll be coming back for a while, so can I 'phone you sometimes?'

'Sure, if you want.'

'I mean apart from anything else I want to know how this scandal develops.'

'Well, as I say, I'm not expecting pistols at dawn, but we'll see.'

'You have a son, Percival, with a woman that you loved, and who loved you, I'm sure, and even you aren't immune from all of that, and I could help you through it, and I'd like to, but it's not my place anymore, is it, so all I'll say is care of yourself, although I know you won't, but well, take care of yourself.'

'Do my best...'

'You might start by examining the real reason why you don't want everything confirmed beyond all possible doubt.'

To which Percival could find no immediate reply, so instead he opened the door; she kissed him on the side of the mouth before departing with her cabin baggage, back to her other life, and the other man that she loved, in so different a way. Percival closed the door and sat down, and worked on his immunity.

'I don't think I can do this, Vics.'

It is now the mid-evening of the day, and Victoria was in her room, preparing for her planned excursion to the actors' encampment, when her 'phone sounded its tone, and she had no time to speak before her brother had spoken. She believed that she knew well enough to what he referred, but she had to ask.

'Hi, Mike, what can't you do?'

'I've been tying myself up in knots all day about it, and I hardly slept last night, but I've decided that, well...I mean okay, Rose and...Rose had a lover, that I can accept, because what else is there to do, and I'm working on forgiving you for not telling me that you knew, and for avoiding me the next morning, although that's taking a bit of doing, to be honest. So anyway I now have a son who probably isn't my son, and I'm prepared to love him and raise him as if he were, if only for his own sake, and I don't intend to prove anything, one way or the other, because at the moment and so far I agree with you, that things are best left as they are.'

'Okay, well, I'm glad about all of that, of course.'

'Yes, but the thing is, what I won't do is make him a Lord, Vics. Regardless of what you say happened in the past, or perhaps even because of it, I won't do it. I won't be party to something which is to all intents and purposes illegal, I couldn't live with myself knowing that, and knowing that....Well, that someone else's son will take the title. The blood ties are broken, and the Lordship will end with me.'

Victoria was silent for a moment, in part to give herself time for contemplation, and in part to allow Michael time to continue, but there was no continuation.

'That's a big decision, Mike.'

'Yes, it is, and it's not been an easy one, but none of this is my doing, and to be honest I feel poorly treated in the whole matter, by everyone concerned, but that isn't the point. I can at least take control from here on, and so I will. We can keep it between ourselves, there will be no need to tell father, who will die in ignorance, but on this I will not be moved. Nathaniel will have all of the benefits of my position and title during my lifetime, such as they are, but he won't inherit, no matter what it one day takes for that to happen.'

'You're angry, Mike, I can see and understand that, and decisions taken in anger are not always the best decisions, but okay, if that is your position now, then of course and as I said I will support you, but don't close the door in your mind just yet. Let everything settle, let Nathaniel grow up, and as you say, let's keep this between ourselves. You may feel differently in ten or twenty years' time.'

'No, Vics, I won't. If I don't decide now then this uncertainty will just go on and fester, and I'm not prepared to see that happen. My mind is quite made up, there will be no Lord Nathaniel, and that is final.'

'Very well, then, and so be it.'

'Well then, that's all I have to say, except that...Well, will you be coming to Glebe House any time soon? You also have a son here, you know?'

'Yes, of course, and I want to see you, and see the house again anyway. I've got a couple of days off this week so I'll come then, and we can talk this through face to face, and I'm sorry, Mike, for any part I have played in this which was ill-judged.'

'Well, we all must make judgements, ill or otherwise, and I have made mine, so, goodnight then.'

'Goodnight, Mike.'

The call ended, and Victoria leaned out of her bedroom window onto an already discernably darkening evening before lighting her cigarette; magic hour was fast approaching. Her brother was right, of course, he had been ill-treated, and ill-used, and her wisdom after the event told her that she should not have kept her knowledge or assumption from him, and indeed she now began to even regret telling him about Edward, the second Lord, and his sister, and their ancient subterfuge. Had she predicted that he would so react? Well, perhaps not, but there it was, and despite her brother's generally pragmatic and easy-going nature, she knew that in matters of import he would ofttimes not be moved, and this, she knew, would be such a time. There were already lights on in some of the village houses, and a few cars still passed on the main road in the middle distance, something which she was aware caused problems for the sound technicians during the filming of outside scenes; the Manor must be made old in all regards, and there were no cars in Maurine O'Connell's day.

Her brother was angry, with her, but also and more deeply so with the situation in which he found himself, through no fault of his own, and she must think more on all of this, but for now she had other business to attend to, and someone else to see. She changed quickly, and walked the long, gravel driveway which led away from the Manor, and which was empty, now, save for some cinematic paraphernalia strewn about the place, and a few cheap, plastic chairs, stacked and ready for the next day.

The encampment, as Victoria had heard others refer to it, was a fairly well-organised affair, set in a clearing in the woodland. Accommodation units were set around its perimeter, thus forming a quite large central enclosure, with portable sanitary amenities set at the farthest point away, and a kitchen somewhat closer. The place was adequately lit by electric lights, and the natural light was fading fast as Victoria entered the enclosure, but people were still out and about their business. Some were learning or rehearsing lines, singly or in groups, a card game between four of the cast or crew was in progress around a small portable table, whilst others merely sat eating a repast or drinking beer or coffee, and enjoying the pleasant summer's evening. Two latter-day minstrels played a duet of stringed instruments, Lyres, perhaps, although Victoria was not sure, but anyway they were clearly rehearsing for their part in the Queen's court, and the gentle strains of the music added to the strange sense of juxtaposition, or perhaps better say melding together in time of the two so different times. Little notice was taken of her as she enquired as to the whereabouts of Maurine O'Connell, and was directed to the third cabin on the right, where she met her new found friend, sitting at the entrance of her temporary home, now dressed in jeans and sweatshirt. She had in any case brought Prince and

Bathsheba with her, who were now busy introducing themselves to everyone, and receiving a generally warm reception as they did so.

'Hi, you came, then, that's great.'

'Well, I was curious, you know, to see how everything was done, and as I say, I've not been here since people started arriving.'

'Well, it's not much, but it's home…Hang on, I'll find a couple of chairs from somewhere so we can at least have somewhere to sit, and I've got a kettle so coffee's possible, I've even got some wine if you'd rather?'

'Well, wine sounds nice, actually.'

'Does, doesn't it, I've only got some cheap white stuff out of plastic cups, and it won't be very cold, but one must suffer for one's art, you know?'

'Just as it comes will be fine, thanks.'

Maurine duly begged or borrowed two plastic chairs from somewhere, whilst Victoria looked about her, and took in that which to her seemed like a cosy and amiable scene. The cutting edge of the production was of course the Manor House, but here was the engine room, from whence everything began on each day of shooting, and to where everyone returned to be themselves once more. In any case within a few minutes the two women were seated beside and above an upturned wooden crate, which would serve well enough as a low table, and the two dogs had settled beside their mistress.

'There, home from home….Lovely dogs.'

'Yes, they are, they usually have free-run of the grounds, but we're having to kennel them a bit at the moment so they don't get in the way of things, so they appreciate a walk.'

'Yes, I'm sure…Oh, hang on here's Vern, he's a lowly servant, and he's been sent out on a fag run, you'd be surprised how many of this lot smoke, despite being out of work actors most of the time.'

Vern got off his motorbike and began distributing packs of cigarettes and small change around the enclosure, beginning with Maurine.

'Thank you, lowly servant.'

'Fuck off your ladyship.'

'Ha, I've been elevated....Anyway sorry, what were we saying?'

'We were talking about dogs.'

'Oh, yes…'

'So who decides, then, who lives here and who doesn't, I mean this can't be everyone.'

'No, not by a long way, and it's all a bit random, I think, although I'm new on the scene anyway, and I hardly know anyone, really. I'm lucky enough to have my own small bedroom, but some people are doubling up, and a lot of people are living off site, or staying with friends or relatives within daily commuting distance, or whatever. May Thomas, one of the producers, is staying in the village, I think.'

'Yes, I know May a little, it was she who first approached me about using the Manor.'

'I see, so this was all your idea then.'

'Well no, it wasn't my idea, and I had to gain parental approval, but somewhat to my surprise I obtained that, so here we are.'

'Well, well done anyway. So what's it like then, being daughter to a Lord and Lady?'

'I suppose it depends on the Lord and Lady, but it doesn't bring with it any particular benefits in the real world. It's a hangover, really, from an ancient lineage which was part of an aristocracy which ruled the country back in your time, but no more. It's now just history, you know?'

'History's important though, don't you think?'

'Yes, I do, as it happens, but that may be because I was born and raised into it.'

'So…You're not married then, is that right? No ring, anyway, so no kids or anything…?'

'No, I'm not married, and there's no significant male other in my life, but I do have a son, Henry, who's three this year.'

'Oh, I've not seen any children around.'

'You won't, he'll mostly be staying away during production. My brother, Michael's got him at his other home with his son, Nathaniel. Michael's married, with just the one son.'

'So are there just the two of you, then?'

'Yes, just the two of us…'

These were lies, for the most part, but Victoria preferred to see them as inaccuracies, necessary during conversations with anyone who didn't know, and didn't need to know.

'So Henry won't be *'Lord Henry'* one day then.'

'Everything goes down the male line.'

'That's beastly unfair, don't you think, especially in this day and age.'

'It's just the way things are, all part of the history, you know?'

'Of course…So there'll be Lord Michael, then Lord Nathaniel, is that right?'

'Yes…Yes, that's right.'

Which it was not, any more; lie upon lie, and a sudden and fleeting sadness entered the arena of Victoria's emotions, which for its duration caused her distraction, and she missed the next words which were spoken to her.

'I'm sorry, what did you say?'

'I was just saying that we seem to have some parallels here, with the film, I mean. One brother and sister, with the sister being a bit wayward and all…Oh fuck, I didn't mean that like it sounded.'

Victoria smiled, and drank her wine, and they lit cigarettes.

'It's okay, and you're right, there are parallels, in the real world as well.'

'What do you mean?'

'I mean that Henry has no father, none that he will ever meet, anyway.'

'Right...So was it a donor job, then?'

'No, it wasn't like that, but I didn't...I mean I never expected to have children, and men aren't necessarily my cup of tea, either, is my point, so I'm not in any kind of a relationship, not with a man, anyway.'

The conversation had quickly become more intense and far more personal than either might have expected, the two women scarce knew one another, after all, but Victoria was feeling somewhat burdened by her present life and circumstances, and the unburdening to this new person, with whom she felt uncommonly comfortable, felt like a comfort to her, at least as far as she was able to unburden. Certainly she felt sympathy, not only with Maurine O'Connell, but also with her manifestation as Katherine, the wayward daughter, as much as she knew of either of them, and the one person with whom she most wished to speak, and with whom she would soon speak, was currently in hiding in the village. The quickness to intimacy was something which had not escaped the notice of Maurine O'Connell, either, any more than had the implied sexuality of the person to whom she had become quickly quite intimate, and she felt emboldened to speak her mind.

'Well, we're certainly getting down to brass tacks, as they say.'

'Yes, we do seem to be, and talking of relations with men, how did your particular scene go, in the end?'

'Oh, God, well that was a bit of a disaster, to be honest, I mean I couldn't get my bloody bodice undone, for one thing, and Ray, that's my visiting dignitary, who's gay, by the way, in real life I mean, turned out to have a sense of humour a bit like mine, and we couldn't stop laughing, even during the act itself when we finally got around to it. One of us would hold it together then the other one would start, it was hopeless, and then we lost a couple of takes because a bloody fly kept buzzing around. I don't think Anna was very impressed, but I think we got there in the end, as it were, but bloody hell, it took about fifteen takes, and we had to try various positions, which ended up girls on top, which seemed to work the best. Anyway I've only got two sex scenes, the other one is with some chap in the village, so hopefully that will go better, then I can at least keep my clothes on and get down to some proper acting, with proper lines to speak. I mean I've got pretend multiple orgasms down to a fine art, I think, I've never had sex like that in real life, anyway, more's the pity, but I think I winged it okay. I mean this all sounds like it's a porno movie or something, but it's actually very tasteful and sophisticated, mostly, and the script's very good, once I actually get around to saying anything.'

Victoria stayed for the better part of two hours, enjoying the company of this young woman, which had in the end been a light distraction after the heaviness of her earlier day, but now her host brought their meeting to a close.

'Well look, I could chat all night, but I'd better get some beauty sleep, I suppose, got to try to look beautiful in the morning.'

'Of course, and I should be getting back anyway. Thanks for the wine and conversation, I've enjoyed it very much.'

'Well, come back soon, anytime, this'll be me for a few weeks, so, you know….'

'I'll be sure to do that.'

Victoria stood up to leave.

'Don't get lost in the dark going home.'

'I've got my 'phone and two dogs, and I've probably done the walk a few hundred times, so I'll be fine. See you soon, then.'

A parting smile and Victoria departed, but she did not go home immediately. Whether it was intuition, or some inner voice which was speaking to her, she turned away from her home and walked the narrow path further into the woodland, as far as the ruins of the old summer house. Here she sat on the stone seat, the only light coming from the beam of her torch, and waited, listening to the sounds of the night as she relived the history once again. Here it was that she had found the mortal remains of Anne Tillington, sister to Edward, and mother to his namesake, Edward, the third Lord, and the first pretender. Here she had found also the metal box, which had contained pages from Anne's diary, written in the year 1587, which Victoria kept hidden from the world, and carefully enwrapped and protected like the precious writings which they were, and which only she had read. Anne had had two children, Edward and Annabelle; twins, whose father had been a blacksmith from the village, who had been called Seth, yet only Annabelle was known of, and recorded for posterity in the family records. The other child, the son, she had given away to her brother, whose own son had been so cruelly slain by the first Lord in his insanity, and thus had the Tillington line continued, and so had Anne and Edward returned to the Manor House after Edward's time in exile as a carpenter. From thence they had raised and elevated the two children into the life of the nobility, and into the court of the first Queen Elizabeth, the Virgin Queen, who had ruled over the country during the golden age. The witches had known, the witches had always known, the knowledge having been passed down through their long and often tragic line, and they had told her where to look, else this knowledge would have remained unknown to all others, and likely would never have been discovered. Here also was the place where she and Rebecca had met again after their better than ten-year separation, a meeting which had begun so much, and that particular story had yet to play out. Her beloved Rebecca, who was herself a witch, and the direct descendant of Jane Mary, Edward's wife, whose remains had been found behind the wall of the Manor... So much history was here, recent and ancient, and now there was Florence, Rebecca's daughter and daughter to her beloved brother, Michael, and as Victoria sat in the darkness of the summerhouse, she understood, perhaps for the first time, why Rebecca had done as she had done, and seen to it that Michael would be father to her child. Yes, the witches had always known, and the history would live on through Florence, and Florence's daughter, if she had one, and now a silent but sure resolve grew in the mind of Victoria; that whatever else happened from now, Florence must be kept safe, for she was the last of them, and her brother's daughter, and it was through her that the memory and bloodline of Jane Mary would live on.

Victoria stood, and she and the two dogs made ready for their walk home. There was no sign, now, that anyone had been buried here. Keith had in-filled the grave and reset the ancient flagstones, and now no one would ever guess, or know, but the witches had known.

And now a quite different history was being enacted at the Manor House; a history invented by a script writer, a thing of fiction and imagination, and yet was real life so different, really? Within the context of that which was happening, her life and the lives of those around her felt for a moment like live theatre, with each player playing their part as best they could, none of them knowing how, when or where it would all end, for when does anything really end? It was almost as though, when the day's acting was done, everyone could go home, and go about their ordinary lives, but she had no home, other than the one where two dramas were currently being played out. There was always a connection, no matter how far back one chose to look, and now the great and often glorious history of the Tillington Lordship was about to be ended by her brother, or else given to someone who was unknown to them. Just one more generation, and yes, there was a significance and sadness to that, no matter how well she may understand his feelings and motivations.

Thus did the contemplations of Victoria Tillington run, as she walked home in the darkness of this dark night, and it was now, as though from nowhere, that the seed of an idea began to germinate in some quiet corner of her consciousness; something which as she tried to turn her thoughts toward it would disappear from sight, and yet it was there, if she could just allow herself to think a little harder. It was something which Maurine O'Connell had said, a part of their quite casual conversation which had by degrees now grown into a quite ridiculous notion, a passing fancy and no more, surely, but it was one which she would take with her to the Manor House, and to her bed, and which, for a while and during its time would keep her from sleep, and which would still be there when she awoke the next morning. After all, it had happened once before, and perhaps, just perhaps, this small moment in English history could yet be rewritten, before the players had acted out their parts, and before it was too late.

Chapter 18. Singing in the Shower

For Barrington Thomas these were heady days. His time spent as a monk, when he had tried through prayer and meditation and in the end had failed to find emotional connection to or belief in his inherited god, and then his addiction to opiates, were past lives, now, and he had found a place to live where he could better be at peace with himself, and with his life. His employment as a gardener with the Local Council did not place any demands upon him in any kind of intellectual sense, nor would it lead to significantly higher things in terms of any possible future career, but it was a job which he enjoyed, on the whole. Indeed the tending of lawns, shrubs and herbaceous plants in all of their variety in the public areas around the town could even be said to be therapeutic, and in a sense fulfilling, providing as it did green space and colour for the townsfolk, and the modest income he received was sufficient for his modest needs, if he was careful in matters financial. He loved his rented cottage, and its location on the village Green, and whilst Barrington had never been a person who generally or easily formed deep emotional ties with those around him, or who craved the collective company of others, living in this ancient village gave him sufficient sense of belonging to this small community to see to it that he did not feel lonely, when he went about his daily business. His daily business, however, and in any case, was currently dominated, in the domestic sense at least, by the presence of his younger sister, May, who was occupying his spare bedroom during her time working on the movie at the Manor House, a project which for the most part left her with precious little time for anything else, and on an average working day saw even her considerable reserves of energy taken to their limits. She would offer to buy food, occasionally, or at least offer to pay her share for their provision, but Barrington never pressed his acceptance of her offers, which in any case she would quickly forget the making of. Nor would he mention the considerable increase in his electricity consumption which could be directly attributed to her presence, or the amount of coffee required for the fuelling of her commercial endeavours, because she was his sister, and Barrington knew full well that without May his life would likely be a very different thing. She it was who had been the lone voice supporting him against their parents in his resistance to becoming a Catholic Priest, who had been quite and rightly set against his becoming a monk, and who had of her own volition flown to Thailand to rescue him from his life, when otherwise he may have turned to a life of crime to maintain his heroin addiction, or died somewhere on a palm-fringed tourist beach. So, he begrudged her nothing, and her presence was nothing but a joy to him, even though her presence was an ever-fluid and unpredictable thing.

  She would rise early, to try to prepare herself for the day's shooting, but there was little preparation to be made, it seemed, for the hundred or so things which could and so often did go wrong during the course of her working day, which, if they were shooting scenes after dark, would sometimes not end before midnight. Whatever time she arrived home, however, she would unburden herself, and he would without complaint accept the unburdening. She would arrive with such statements as *'You'll never bloody guess what they had me doing today...'* or *'Christ, remind me never to work with actors again, will you?'* Officially she was only a part of the production team, but David Bates, the main producer, was it seemed on site only occasionally, and the day-to-day running of the enterprise and the coordination between its various component parts was left to May, in that which she described as her *'Baptism by fire'* in this which all involved knew was a critical production for the media company. It was also the case that she was working within a strictly limited budget, and her complaint of having to try to *'make a silk purse out of a pig's ear'* seemed to Barrington at times to be fully justified. At the end of each working day, however, and regardless of the hour, she would come home to her brother, and his wine, and his bath, and a prepared meal, and all of this was something which her brother was more than happy to provide, for as long as the provision was needed. His cottage was to be used at some time in the near future as a setting for a brief scene in the production, but this had not yet come to pass, although he quite looked forward to its passing, whenever that may be.

The homecoming of Tarragon after the recording of her third album was a thing of little fanfare, which occurred one day in the quite late afternoon. She had travelled thence in the backseat of a car which had been hired by Samantha Rodriguez, who held a current Driver's License, and driven by Ashley Spears, who did not, this particular symbiosis having worked well enough for them on numerous occasions. These two had at various times considered buying a motor vehicle, money being no hindrance to their so doing, but Samantha did not enjoy driving, and Ashley could not legally do so, having had a somewhat chequered relationship with law enforcement authorities in this regard. They in any case had a sufficiency of friends with cars upon whom they could call at short notice, village shops within a quite easy walking distance of their home, which provided their daily needs, a housekeeper who would otherwise shop for them if asked, and vehicles could always be hired. In any event thus did the three musicians drive the lane to the bus, where Meadow had by pre-request of her daughter prepared a vegetarian meal of nut-loaf, with potatoes and vegetables freshly and respectively dug and picked from the allotment, which provided the family with most of its needs at this time of year. Tarragon had spent her recent days in the company of fine musicians, fulfilling her creative instincts to their limits, but she had eaten quite enough takeaway pizzas to last her a lifetime, and craved her mother's cooking. In any event, Meadow had heard the car, and was waiting at the door of her humble abode as they arrived, hugs were exchanged between all of the women, Meadow set the kettle to boil for herbal tea, and the four people sat outside, around the makeshift table and chairs which Keith had made.

'So, how did it all go, then?'

The question was general in its address, but it was Ashley who answered.

'Yeah, it's a good album, your daughter is in fine voice, and Keith's guitar worked well.'

'So how does it compare with the first two?'

'I don't think it helps to compare albums, or songs for that matter, I mean if I were to compile a *'greatest hits'* album so far there'd be three or four songs from this one, I guess, but that's personal taste. It's sort of mellow, I think, compared with the others, but beyond that it stands alone. People who listened to the first two will buy this one, and *'Tara's'* becoming a household name.'

'Is that a good thing, as far as you're concerned? I mean I believe you're quite cynical about commercialism in general.'

'It's what sells records. I mean the industry's different, now, everything's more transitory. The *'Rock Goddess'* is a thing of the past, people are looking for a quick fix, but we've found our audience, I think, and the point is that we've made something good, and contributed to the whole, so yeah, I think we should all be pleased. The other, like, important thing is that *'Tara'* has become a force unto herself, it's no longer DMW with a new female vocalist, which is what we've been trying to achieve, and I think three albums on we've achieved that transition. Now that Al's gone there's only Sam, Rick and I from the original line up, and *'Ashley Spears'* is no longer the main attraction, he's just some ex-rock band junkie who turns up and plays guitar.'

'And writes the songs...' Said Tara.

'No one cares who writes the songs, anyway from now on it's going to be jointly attributed.'

'You didn't tell me that.'

'It's all part of the process, and anyway it's no lie, you had more input into this album, so you should share the accreditation. '*Spears-Knightman*', has a certain ring, don't you agree?'

'Well, yes, but I don't think that's quite fair, but....If you really think so, then, well, thanks, you know?'

Ashley Spears rarely spoke of his musical philosophy, and compared to the usual light and occasional rain of the revelation of his inner thoughts, this was a deluge. Of the three women present, Samantha knew Ashley the best, and she said nothing, but merely exchanged smiles with Tarragon, and it was Meadow who continued her enquiry.

'So, what now then, Ash..?'

'Yeah, there's the thing…We're talking about touring on the back of the album, just Europe, maybe, but right now I think I want to kick back for a while, maybe tour in the autumn, I don't have the energy for this shit that I used to have, need some time out, if you feel me.'

All smiled at this, and so did the evening proceed. Any doubts which Ash had harboured regarding the album and its musical direction had it seemed run their course, which for all present and concerned came as a great relief. At some juncture Keith arrived in his builder's attire, all enjoyed the evening repast, and the conversation flowed amongst the four musicians who had indeed made something good, and Meadow, who basked in the glow of her daughter's achievement, and her man's contribution thereto. The evening was drawing in before a sixth person briefly joined the ensemble, who was in her own way a part of the band's recent history, and she was a person who had come with a particular and other agenda.

The underlying domestic and other stability which were nowadays Barrington's lot, allowed him to better invest sufficient reserves of mental and emotional energy into his relationship with she who had become the other significant woman in his life. Sandra Fox, the beautiful and clever young woman who had fought with her inner demons all of her life, lent Barrington's life its elements of excitement, unpredictability and, most significantly, love. She lived in Bath, ostensibly, a place to which he would travel some weekends, but increasingly Sandra would make the train and bus journey to Middlewapping, the place of her birth and of her not always happy childhood. She had left him, for a while, but then they had made their Balinese trip together, in a once and for all attempt to find a way that they could be together, and accept each other and their shortcomings; this was to be all or nothing, and in the end it would be all, and thus, in the end, had both found moments of happiness which neither had truly expected to find with another. They could be together, sometimes, and find fulfilment in one another, and then be apart for periods of time to live their own lives, and had learned to make no lesser or greater demands than this upon each other or their relationship.

Presently, however, it was his sister who for the most part required Barrington's attention, and he was surprised to arrive home from work on this day to find May already there, and having already begun to create the mess and general domestic chaos which it was Barrington's last job of an evening to try to quell. She was working at the coffee table on her laptop as he entered.

'Hi you, this is unusual.'

'Got some stuff to catch up with, and we've done filming for the day.'

'Dare one ask what sort of a day you've had?'

'Ask away, but don't expect a very positive response. Today we had David on site and he and Anna at loggerheads over various things.'

'Anything in particular..?'

'Well, I suppose chief amongst it all is the fact that we can't find anyone to do the film score, the guy we had lined up didn't work out, for contractual or financial reasons or what the hell ever, so it's suddenly become a serious issue.'

'Right....Yes, well I can see that that would be a problem.'

'It is, at the moment we have the makings of a film without music, so that sort of doesn't work, you know?'

Barrington entered the kitchen, where there was further evidence that his sister had been in residence without him.

'The kettle's hot. I was starving and made an omelette, I'll clear up in a bit.'

Barrington smiled a rueful smile to himself, made himself tea and re-joined his sister, taking the seat opposite her.

'So, I mean, that's not really your problem, is it, the film score I mean?'

'Not officially, but someone's problem sort of becomes everyone's problem, you know?'

'Yes, of course.'

'Anyway I'll be going out for a bit later, Tara's coming home today, with Ash, and I want to talk about the documentary.'

'So, how's that going?'

'Okay, thank God, I've got a friend working on the cutting, under my guidance, of course, so it shouldn't be long before we're done.'

'Well, that's good then.'

'I wish I had time to do it all myself, and we've still got to sell the thing, but that's another problem for another day. Anyway, I'm knackered, think I'll take a shower, freshen up a bit, then I'll make us some supper, shall I, it's about time I did some cooking around here.'

'I'll do it if you want.'

'Let's do it together.'

'Okay, whatever…'

So they showered, and cooked together, and it was during this process that an idea was thrown into the arena of May's already over-occupied thoughts; it was Barrington's idea, and a long-shot, certainly, but it was one which caused May to love her brother even more, and which came to occupy her thoughts during the eating of their meal. She berated herself for not thinking of it herself, and sooner, it was so obvious, if she could pull it off; she had it seemed become by necessity so engrossed in the finer points of the film production that she had lost sight of the bigger picture, and the bigger ideas, and at such times, brothers can indeed have their uses.

The next time that Quentin and Tristan were in residence together and awake simultaneously was of a morning, which was two days subsequent to Tristan's evening and night spent with Grace. This was at the point of Quentin's shift change at the warehouse; for the next two weeks he would be on the day shift, and in the meantime had two clear days off to which to look forward. Quentin awoke and arose to find Tristan in his small kitchen, making his morning beverage.

'Hey, bro, you want coffee?'

'Sure…'

'You at home today..?'

'No plans, although I'll probably head for Brighton this evening, and we need groceries…'

'Yeah, coffee's in short supply for one thing. We could hit the supermarket together,'

'Wouldn't that be romantic...So when are you seeing Grace again?'

'At the weekend, probably, although we haven't made firm plans yet. This is a kind of weird situation, don't you think, I mean if we're in Kemptown at the same time we could meet in various kitchens in the morning.'

'Yeah, we're real close these days, we even sleep in the same bed.'

'Ah, yeah, sorry about that, it just kind of happened...I made the bed, didn't think you'd notice.'

'She and I don't use the same perfume, you were always crap at covering your tracks.'

'Well, like I say, it was a kind of spontaneous event.'

'So you spontaneously brought her back here, and then instead of watching TV as you'd planned, you both came over all hormonal and just had to spend the night in my bed, is that it?'

'Yeah, it's weak, isn't it?'

'It's verging on pathetic.'

'Tell you what, I'll change your bedding today, straight after coffee.'

'I don't have any spare bedding, on account of you're using it.'

'Yeah, we do seem to have a crisis situation when it comes to sheets, and whatever. I'll buy some today, two sets, then we're both covered for all eventualities.'

'Yeah, do that.'

'I'll even buy matching pillow cases, just to show you what a good brother I really am. You see, some good will come out of all of this. You have any colour preference?'

'Just buy whatever, no floral patterns.'

'There won't be a flower in sight. While I'm in the sheet shop I'll pick up some towels, we never seem to have enough of those.'

'Yeah, towels would be good.'

'Then towels it shall be, and I'm sorry, man, for the bed, but you know how it is.'

'Yeah, I know how it is, and don't overdo it, you've always been a fuck-head and I guess you always will be. Shall we take our coffee in the lounge?'

They moved through, Quentin took the only available easy chair, and Tristan sat on the settee, which was presently still covered by his borrowed bedding from the previous night.

'So what's new, bro, you heard about Kenya yet?'

'Actually yes, I got a message last night, we leave in three weeks, and we'll be there for about a month.'

'Oh well done, that's brilliant news, right?'

'Yeah, it's the best. I mean Kenya, Tris, it's every paleontologist's dream ticket, you know?'

'Sure, the birthplace of humanity, or whatever, I'm pleased for you, man. I'll look after this place while you're away, if I can have the bed.'

'Take it…So what's new on your horizon?'

'I've started seriously looking for a place, in fact what I was thinking of doing was buying two flats, maybe in the same block, or whatever, one to live in and one to rent out.'

'That could work.'

'The location's the thing, though, I mean there's here, but maybe I need a change of scenery, so I was thinking about Brighton. Property's expensive there, but there're always students looking for somewhere, so it's an option.'

'Sure, sounds like a plan.'

'I mean I'd need to find gainful employment, and I'm still no further with that, but I'll make some enquiries today, once I've bought the sheets.'

The two brothers smiled, an incident had occurred in their long history, which had now become a small part of the history. The future now held promise for both of them in the romantic sense, Quentin had reached a state of greater understanding with Rosemary, and he was keen to know how his brother was faring.

'So how is it with Grace, I mean clearly certain aspects of the relationship are working well, but how's it going otherwise?'

'It's good, you know, I mean I found out all kinds of stuff about her, like her family and such, so we're catching up with ourselves, and I like her, you know?'

'Well that's good.'

'Yeah, for the first time since India I feel like I can maybe handle stuff again, my renaissance may be starting from here, which is a good feeling. I know I've been a pain, bro, so thanks for staying with it.'

'Fuck off, you're making me want to forgive you for the bed, and you haven't bought the sheets yet.'

'Sheets are coming, man, trust me.'

They drank their coffee, and began their day, which for both felt as though it would be a good day.

The evening was darkening quickly by the time May Thomas walked down the lane and stood beside the assembled party, who greeted her in a general way before Tara made it more personal, and specific.

'Hi, May, how are you, and how's the documentary coming along?'

'I'm knackered, generally speaking, but the documentary's going fine, I should have something to show you within a few days. I've got a question, though.'

'Sure, fire away....'

Keith stood and offered May his seat.

'It's okay, I don't want to disturb everyone.'

'I insist, I'll pull up a crate or something. Can we offer you an ale?'

'Sure, okay then, why not, thanks.'

May took her seat whilst Keith fetched cold beers from the refrigerator. She was struck for a moment as she sat by an overriding sense of charisma and something like power which emanated from this gathering of people. Here was Ashley Spears, of course, who came with all of his musical prowess and his history, Tara, his young protégé, and Samantha, the quiet, unassuming but clearly quite brilliant pianist, who had stayed loyal to the band, the music and her now husband through all of the many and she was sure often difficult years. Here also were Keith, the tall, handsome guitar player, who had always been the perfect gentleman towards her, and Meadow, mother to Tara, the beautiful, enigmatic woman who had served her at the delicatessen, but who in this context turned into something else. May spent her working days amongst actors, famous and otherwise, but these were different people, this was all about the creation of music, and for a moment she allowed the sense of them to find its place within her before she spoke.

'So it's about the opening number, what to use as an intro. I thought I'd use *'A Woman's Time'* for the closing credits, that seems to fit, apart from being my favourite song on the album, I think, but I don't want to use any of the new songs for the intro, so I was thinking about *'All that I will ever be'*, which sort of defines the second album, but I'm open to other ideas.'

'Sound fine to me,' said Tara.

'Good, well okay then, so just to let you know where we are with it. So the album's done now, yes?'

'Yes, it's done, for us anyway, so now we just wait for a release date.'

'Right, well we'll try to coordinate with the documentary, get it out there as soon after the release as we can.'

'Yes, that seems to make sense. So how's the filming going, anyway?'

'Well, it's going. One of our main actors is still off sick, so we're having to adapt and shoot things out of sequence, but I daresay it'll all come together in the end.'

'Yes, I'm sure.'

Keith returned with beers, which were passed around the table, as May collected herself for that which had become for her the main event of the evening.

'There was, umm, there was something else though.'

'Oh yes, and what would that be?'

'Well, this is for Ash, really, but I was wondering…How would you feel about composing and making a score for the movie?'

This was met with silence, and with looks exchanged amongst the party, but in the end all eyes were on Ashley, and only Samantha knew at once what his answer would be.

'No, man, I mean no, thanks for the offer but I've never composed a film score before, it's a specialised art.'

'You'd never composed a symphony, either, until you composed a symphony.'

'You raise a salient point, but a film score's a different animal.'

'So's a symphony, but okay, it was just an idea.'

The silence returned briefly in all of its pregnancy, and for its duration a quite odd sense of disappointment pervaded the gathering. It was broken by May, who finished her beer quickly, and was by some measure the most disappointed of them.

'Anyway, that's all I came to say, and now I need sleep, so I'll be in touch when I have news of the documentary. So that's your final answer, then.'

'Yeah, that's it, I need a break after the album, you know?'

May stood, Tara offered a sympathetic smile, and Samantha waited for Ash, who had rarely if ever disappointed her.

'What kind of a film is it, anyway, just out of interest?'

May re-took her seat, Ash rolled a cigarette, and Samantha kept her smile to herself. May had indeed been feeling tired, but now hope rekindled anew gave her renewed energy, for as long as the hope endured.

'It's an Elizabethan drama, based around the daughter of the household, whose wayward spirit threatens to bring the family to ruin. It's going to be a high-end production, not for the masses, you know, the script's brilliant, and we've got Maurine O'Connell in the lead, with David Blake, Ursula Franks and Graham Dean if he ever turns up, he's the one who's sick. David Bates is producer and Anna Merchant's directing, although you probably won't have heard of either of them. So we're a small, independent company, making our first feature movie, so we're working within tight financial confines, you might say, and there won't be a huge budget for the music, but, well, there's money there, of course.'

Samantha looked on. It was a good sales pitch, emphasising the smallness and independence of the project, which would appeal to Ash's general dislike of large corporations, and he wouldn't care about the money.

'So what's your role, exactly?'

'Officially I'm co-producer, which in reality means I'm the general dogsbody. It was my idea to make the film at the Manor, actually, which seems to be working okay. I mean the thing is, the final decision won't be mine, but I can let you have a script, of course, and you'd be welcome at the Manor anytime, if you just wanted to get the feel of things before making any final decision.'

Ashley smoked, and considered.

'Fuck...I don't know.'

She was working well. May already had traction via the making of the documentary, which gave her kudos and emotional connection, and she had played her little woman in distress card, which was probably the truth of it, but this would have appealed to Ash's sense of male chivalry.

'And there's one other thing, which actually only occurred to me as I was walking over here. It would be great, I think, if…Well, if Tara could sing, you know? If you could compose a song specifically for the movie, she could sing us out through the credits, that's worked really well with other films, but, you know, that's just something else for you both to think about, maybe.'

So now Tara's career could perhaps be embellished, which was ever a thing of import to Ashley; good shot, and it was time for him to respond, one way or the other.

'So it would be mostly light orchestral, with maybe some period instrumentals thrown in…'

'Yes, I suppose so, but if everything could be agreed you'd have complete artistic license.'

'So who's musical director?'

'We haven't really got one, a guy called Roger Altman is our artistic director, but he's not really music, he's more aesthetics, and sets. I daresay everything would go through Anna, ultimately, and I suppose you and I would be working closely together. It's all a bit ad-hoc, but in a way that's the beauty of it, don't you think? I mean I really believe it's going to be a great movie in the end, otherwise I wouldn't even have brought this to you. It's important that the film succeeds, for all of us, and despite my moans everyone's working really hard, you know? We're all trying to do about three peoples' jobs, to be honest, but none of us has any choice, we're just hell-bent on making the piece of work, and making it work.'

Ashley Spears was a rock musician, but he was also now a classical composer, and had always been keenly interested in all manifestations of musical expression, ancient and modern. He had made his money, and had been blessed, it seemed, with a limitless reserve of creativity and energy when it came to the matter of music, but he needed reassurance, and now turned to the woman that he loved.

'Come on, Sam, help me out here, I mean is this a crap idea to even be considering?'

'You could do it, Ash, you know you could.'

'What the fuck instruments did they used to play in those days?'

'I don't know, flutes, violins, harps, I think they even had the harpsichord. I wouldn't mind having a go at that. You could get Evie involved, I'm sure your sister could adapt to a period instrument.'

'Yeah, she's come back for that...So what do you think, Tara, would you want to sing a movie theme tune?'

'If you compose it, I'll sing it, you know that, and yes, I'm really into the idea, actually, I mean if the film's as good as May says it is.'

'For that we'll have to take her word, for now.'

'Well, if it's good enough for the likes of David Blake and Ursula Franks, we're not talking 'B' movies here, are we? And don't forget how we two first got together, I was singing '*The Ballad of Seth and Sarah*', just over there, actually, so we know we can do old, history is how we started.'

'Okay, so no dissenting voices, then. Look, let me sleep on it, okay, I mean I'm not saying I'll do it, I'm a long way from that, but give me twenty-four hours, I owe you that much. It's a big thing to take on, you dig?'

'You don't owe me anything, Ash, but I do, dig, and I'll talk to David and Anna, just to sound them out on the idea, but they'll say yes, I'm certain of it, so it's up to you.'

'Yeah, well like I say, I need some time to get my head around the idea, which may not happen, so you know...'

'Of course, I'll wait for your answer, and take as long as you need, I mean within reason, we have to find someone fairly quickly now. So, now I go, I've intruded enough on your evening, and I'll see you all soon in any case, and thanks for the beer, but please give it your best consideration, I mean it would be…I don't know, just promise you'll think about it.'

'Sure, I'll do that.'

May stood again and walked away, which in the event signalled an end to the gathering, the longest days were over, and the evenings were beginning to draw in, and becoming chilly. After little further ado, therefore, Tara retired to her bed in the trailer, her mother and father to their bed, and Ash and Samantha took their place on the floor of the bus, which was a familiar place for them. They lay still for a few moments, and then Ashley spoke.

'I don't think I'll do this.'

'What…?'

Samantha always fell quickly into sleep when it was time, and she had almost been there when Ashley had spoken.

'You know, the film score, I don't think I can take it on right now, even if I was sure I could do it, I mean the idea's insane, right?'

'If you say so…'

'I mean I said that I'd, like, sleep on it, but it's just too far out there, it's a whole new genre, so I'm going to say no, I've decided.'

'Well, whatever you think…'

Her inner smile returned; this was a process, at the other end of which she knew what he would decide, but then, she had known from the beginning.

'Hi, it's me….'

'Hi….'

At some juncture during the time that the musical ensemble was gathered at the bus, Victoria had 'phoned Michael.

'So, how are you, Mike?'

'Okay, as far as it goes.'

'Good…Well, look, we need to meet, and I said I'd come to Glebe House, so how about Thursday, I'm off work then until Saturday.'

'Thursday's fine then.'

'The thing is, we need some time alone together, quite a lot of time perhaps, so when are you free?'

'Thursday….There's nothing that can't be changed, so when should I expect you?'

'I'll be there late morning.'

'Okay, well, see you then.'

So, he was still angry, then, and who could blame him? She would leave after breakfast, and she would be taking an attaché case.

'Yes….! Yes, yes, bloody yes…!'

Barrington had waited up for his sister, who had returned home after her actually quite brief absence in apparently exuberant spirits.

'Well, you seem rejuvenated, when you left you looked done in.'

'Ah yes, genius brother, but that was before I'd spoken to Ash about doing the film score.'

'So I take it he said yes, then.'

'Well, he didn't actually say yes, in fact he said no, but that wasn't what he meant to say.'

'Oh, I see, I think….'

'Imagine it, Batty, *'Music by Ashley Spears, additional music or whatever it's called by Tara Knightman,'* it'll be brilliant, don't you think, and all because of a moment of inspiration by my brother.'

'So Tara's going to sing, is she?'

'Yes, well that was my idea, actually, and she said she would, if Ash writes the song.'

"*If* Ash writes the song..?'

'Well, it's not exactly in the bag, yet, but if I know anything at all about Ash Spears then he'll be all over it once he's had a bit of time to think, he's going to let me know tomorrow, and I'm sure Samantha wants him to do it, and she's always influential. I mean if he still prevaricates I'll have to get him to the Manor house, meet some people, like Maurine O'Connell, she's the kind of girl who any man would write a musical score for, don't you think?'

'Well, yes, I suppose, but won't this mean a lot more work for you?'

'Truckloads, I expect, but who cares, working with Ash again will be inspirational.'

'Well, you certainly seem inspired.'

'It'll be like, I don't know, the meeting of my two worlds, or something, and imagine the kudos when I bring Ashley Spears and Tara Knightman into the production, I mean it's not just the icing on the cake, it's the bloody cake. I mean it's not the whole cake, obviously, so maybe the cake analogy doesn't really work, but you know what I mean, it'll give the film the leg-over that it needs, and it can't do Tara's career any harm, can it? It's the perfect symbiosis.'

'I think you mean *'leg-up'* rather than *'leg-over'* but I take your point, I just hope he doesn't say no in the end, that would be disappointing for you.'

'It would be devastating, but one must remain positive, Bats, and I'll know for sure by this time tomorrow, probably.'

'Well, like our father used to say, hope for the best and prepare for the worst.'

'Did he used to say that?'

'Frequently, as I recall.'

'Yes, I suppose it's the sort of thing he would have said. Anyway I'm keeping you up, and I should try to get some sleep, but I'm kind of hyped-up now, so I might take another shower if that's okay, when you've finished in the bathroom.'

'I'm done, shower away…'

'If you hear me singing it'll be imaginary musical scores.'

'Well okay, just don't sing all night.'

They smiled, and in a rare expression of affection, May kissed her brother's cheek.

'You really are the best of brothers, Batty, I don't know what I've done to deserve you.'

'That sort of works both ways, you know?'

They parted, she to the kitchen and he to his bed, where his thoughts this night were leaning heavily toward the positive, and the hopeful for his sister. He drifted into sleep to the sound of the shower running, and the sound of her singing tunelessly; whatever her involvement in the music industry, she had always had a terrible singing voice, and he smiled. For Barrington Thomas, former drug addict and formerly Brother Barrington of a very different kind, these were heady days indeed.

Chapter 19. Unexpected Visitations

The woman stood before her, her expression unreadable but not unfriendly. She was perhaps late in her third decade or early into her fourth; an attractive woman, quite smartly but comfortably dressed in slacks and blouse, who had carried her doubtless youthful beauty into her middle years. There was no vehicle, so she had walked here; it happened sometimes that hikers lost their way and strayed onto the woodland paths, but she was not dressed for hiking. Charlotte had been about her studies when the door knocker had sounded, and she was expecting no one; none of the inner circle had informed her of their likely arrival, and she had spoken to all of them during the morning, which now grew late. She answered the door of the white house, and there she stood, a stranger, but she had found her way here and had come with purpose, this much was clear.

'Yes, can I help you?'

'Hello, Charlotte....Please forgive my coming unannounced, but this was the only way.'

And the woman knew her name.

'Well, here you are, so, once again, how can I help you?'

The woman smiled, now, but there was no mirth or happiness to the smile, it was a smile of sadness, or irony, perhaps.

'I don't know, perhaps you cannot, or perhaps I can help you, I'm not certain, but I would like to speak with you, if you will allow me to. You and I are not of the same coven, but we do perhaps have common purpose, but that remains to be seen.'

So, a witch, then, but how had she found the white house, and Charlotte was now on her guard.

'You will not have heard of me, but my name is Sabina, and I am here in a spirit of, well let's call it cooperation, and I mean you no harm.'

'I see...Well, you'd better come in, then.'

The woman walked across the threshold, and Charlotte led her into the lounge, where common courtesy took precedence, for now at least.

'Please sit down, may I offer you tea?'

'No, thank you, perhaps after I have explained myself and my presence here.'

'Well then, please do so, and you can begin by telling me how you found me, and how you know of me.'

'Yes, of course, you wish to know that, so let me say that I have been aware of you for a long time, as I was aware of your predecessor, Helen, and her daughter, Helena, who met her untimely end, as did her mother.'

'You know a good deal, it seems, but I still await your explanation.'

'My explanation begins by my telling you that my former coven no longer exists. It was destroyed, you see, burned to the ground, or at least beyond further use, and our ancient burial place was desecrated. In any case since its physical destruction, and the death of some of us in the burning, the coven has been broken, and now only one of us remains, although her whereabouts are currently unknown to me. I speak of it as my coven, although I have not been a part of it for many years, not since a certain something happened.'

The woman called Sabina took pause, as though that which happened still caused her pain for the thinking of it, and Charlotte waited.

'There was once a young witch, you see, who knew of and indeed was party to the witches' curse on the house of Tillington, after the first Lord of that name murdered Jane Mary, and of that you will no doubt be aware. You will also perhaps be aware that the youngest son of the present Lord, whose name was Alexander, also met his end alone and in a car accident, and as far as most of the world knows, that is the end of the story, but there's more to it than the world knows.'

Charlotte was aware that there had been a third child, and that he had died at a young age; Rebecca had spoken of him. She watched as the woman now fought to find the words to continue her story, or perhaps the words were there, and the saying of them was the difficulty.

'He was bewitched, you see, by the young witch, who was also foolish, and in her foolishness she fell in love with Alexander, who also loved her, and in the end she had no intent to kill him, but because of her bewitchment of him and his love for her he became, well, insane, and because of his insanity he died, there can be no other explanation. It is hard, perhaps to understand how all of that could have been, and even I now look back at my young, passionate years and wonder, but it is the truth, nonetheless. In any case the young witch thereafter hated herself and her coven, who had encouraged her in her endeavours, and she left the coven, and has in a way lived a life of solitude ever since, and now the young witch sits before you, older and perhaps wiser, now, but in truth never fully at peace with or to terms with her foolishness.'

Charlotte continued to wait in silence, as the woman called Sabina once more drew breath; there was as yet nothing she could say.

'So then, the curse continued, until Eve, the last descendent of the witch Edith, who in the year 1572 first placed the curse upon the household was also killed on the steps of the Manor House, and there the curse should have ended, and there should have been peace. But then came the burning of the coven, and the one witch who remains has the intent of killing she who caused the fire and still lives, the witch Rebecca, who is well known to you, I think.'

'Yes, I know Rebecca.'

'Indeed you do, and so you must also know that she is the last known direct descendent of Jane Mary, and so therefore is her daughter, Florence.'

'What I know is as yet my business, I cannot yet trust you, or your account, and I still don't understand your reason for coming here, or how you apparently know so much, or how you found me.'

'As to what and how and how much I know, that must remain my secret, at least for the most part, but if I may continue my story, which is almost done…'

'Please do.'

'I have been married, and have two children, although I'm divorced now, but my point is that to the outside world I have since leaving my coven lived an ordinary life, as far as I have been able. I once believed that I could leave my youthful years behind, and that time would allow me to forget, but once we learn the ways of witches such things cannot be unlearned, and I have watched, and waited, and I have spoken to people, who have told me things that they perhaps should not have told me. As to my reason for coming here, that is simple enough. The witch Rebecca is in danger, and although once I would have killed her myself for killing those of my coven, my love for Alexander changed everything, and since the very reason for the coven's existence was to avenge the death of Jane Mary, it is now my belief that above all else her descendants must be kept safe, and that the bloodline must remain. Such are the strange vagaries of our history, and our emotions, but my mind is now quite set. Rebecca must be protected, and I will do all within my power to see that she is. I come with warning as one who knows who of us is intent upon her death, that she is clever, and powerful, and will not I think stop until she has killed, or been killed herself.'

Charlotte had made a quick assessment of this so unexpected visitor, and concluded that she was probably speaking the truth, as far as her story went, for such a story was too unlikely to have been an invention. Her demeanour, the way she carried and expressed herself, had no lie to it that Charlotte could see, or perceive.

'Well then, I think tea, don't you?'

The smile was now more natural, and perhaps an expression of relief that the conversation had at least got this far.

'Tea would be very nice, thank you.'

During the early afternoon on this same day, Horatio had received a telephone call from his younger sister, Olivia, who had taken a few days leave from her work, and had the idea of coming to see her brother. Thus it was that she arrived in the village and at his cottage in the early evening, and he had prepared a meal for them of chicken, roasted in a single pan with lemons, potatoes, garlic and other vegetables, which he knew to be one of her favourite meals. She had come with an overnight bag, and with the intent of staying for as long as she saw fit, and it was for both of them a glad reunion.

'So, this is nice, old thing, but to what do I owe the pleasure?'

'I just needed to get away, you know, and what better place?'

'You look bloody awful.'

'Thanks, that makes me feel better already. I'm starving, too, and something smells good.'

'Yes, well you're lucky, I went shopping today, else 't would be beans on toast. Wine....? I bought some half-decent stuff from the supermarket, or do you want to freshen up first?'

'Wine would be good, please.'

He poured wine, and they sat at table whilst the supper was roasting.

'So dear old London getting the better of you is it?'

'Sometimes....'

'Still trying to keep the great unwashed off the streets...'

'And not always succeeding, people have an inexhaustible ability to screw things up for themselves, it seems.'

''twas ever thus, the Africans were good at that as well.'

'It looks like we're going to lose the Camden house, too, people are getting behind with the rent.'

'And you're not bailing them out again, is that it?'

'It has to end somewhere, I don't earn enough to support the community, and I'm not using the other money.'

'So you might find yourself homeless as well, then, just to add to your woes.'

'I'll find somewhere, I'm not worried about that, it's just, I don't know, it kind of never ends, you know?'

'Do I sense a chronic and continuing case of compassion fatigue?'

'Battle fatigue, anyway, things are just getting worse for people, it's like trying to stem an ever-rising tide of despair and grinding poverty, and it gets you down, sometimes, so I've taken time out, I'm owed a lot of leave now, anyway.'

'Well you're welcome as the lark in spring here, but you should get away somewhere, go meditate on some Caribbean beach or whatever.'

'I hate beaches, you know that, except maybe English beaches in wintertime.'

'So go climb a Tibetan mountain, it's not like you don't have the money, have you checked the investment accounts lately?'

'No, not lately...'

'Mater and Pater are selling the foreign properties like hot potatoes, mainland Europe isn't such a friendly place for Brits to invest or live these days, and our dear father continues in his unerring quest to throw money at us.'

'Yes, I knew they were selling.'

'In the end I think they just intend to keep France.'

'Yes, I can't imagine mum selling France. So you've spoken to them, then?'

'Called in for lunch and a bollocking on my way to somewhere else, as it happens...'

'Oh, and how are they?'

'As ever, dad's looking older, you know, and he's not been so well, lately, which is probably another reason for the sell-off. I think he wants to consolidate and simplify his assets and finances, and spend his dotage in dear old Blighty, be near the kids and such, and since we're both here now, that at least makes sense.'

'I see...'

'So have you spoken to them?'

'I had quite a long conversation with mum a few weeks back, but not since, really.'

'Well, anyway, the net result of the sale is more money for us, you're a multi-millionairess, dear thing, and not just on paper, one bank transfer and this becomes real, available cash. The rising tide of unearned wealth keeps rising, too, and I know you don't regard that as real money, but it exists, nonetheless, and it's got your name on it.'

'I know, and you know how I feel about that, too.'

'Going to have to let your principles go sometime, you know, fuck the world and take the money, the devil's going to take the hindmost anyway, and in the end there's nothing you can do about it. You can't change society until society wants to change itself. As long as the turkeys keep voting for Christmas, and until middle-England wakes up to the fact that it's being taken to the cleaners, nothing's going to happen.'

'I know, and you've said it before a hundred times.'

'It's always been true old thing, you're a lone voice in the wilderness, my dear Oli, which by definition is a lonely place to be. I mean you've got me, and I get it, but that is scant consolation, I'm sure.'

'It helps, sometimes….So, what's new in your life, anyway?'

'Just got back from my pan-European tour, actually, got as far as Croatia and covered…Seven countries, I think. I just turned up at airports and saw what flights were going where, found a hotel and a local prozzie and took it from there, did a bit of sight-seeing.'

'I see, so working girls are still a big part of your life, then.'

'Saves a lot of inconvenience, you know?'

'Like emotional engagement and the sharing of a warm, caring relationship, that kind of thing….'

'Yes, that's it…So how's your life in that regard then, you got your rocks off lately?'

'Not lately, no.'

'Still waiting for Mister Right, is that it?'

'Something like that, although not actively seeking, and I'm working up to the conclusion that he doesn't exist anyway.'

'You're probably correct in that regard, can't imagine anyone being good enough for you, to be honest, you're between the devil and the deep blue sea, old thing, they're either pricks without money or pricks with money, but either way they're pricks, are they not? You could search amongst the proletariat or go the other way and end up finding someone like me.'

'Perish the thought…'

'See that's the thing, I wouldn't wish myself on anybody, women are way too good for men, so keep it professional, that way everyone benefits.'

'That's one way of looking at it I suppose, but what about the longer term, don't you ever think you might get lonely one day?'

'Loneliness is a state of mind, and from what I've seen, most of your warm, caring relationships go cold anyway, and it just becomes a habit.'

'Having someone else always around isn't necessarily a bad habit, but I've never experienced that so who am I to talk? It's just...When you don't have the energy anymore, to travel the world or visit prostitutes or whatever, what happens then?'

'I don't know, I suppose one could always find somebody else of like mind and in a similar situation.'

'I don't think things work quite like that, but anyway, let's not dwell on the negative.'

'You started it.'

'I know...So what else have you been up to, apart from being a sex-tourist?'

'It wasn't sex tourism, I went for the cultural experience, the sex was just for the sex, something to do in the evenings, as it were.'

'Fair enough...I just wonder sometimes, is any cultural experience worth having unless you can share it with someone, you know? I mean London's awash with galleries and museums, concert halls, all the culture you could ever want, and I've probably been to all of them, but I rarely go anywhere, partly because I'm exhausted a lot of the time, but also because it's just me, you know? You can be the most cultured, informed person around, read all the right books and so on, but so what, unless you can share that?'

'You're moving in the wrong circles, I've said that before as well, and to use another maritime analogy, you're a fish out of water, you're not living the same life that you started with, and one isn't necessarily or entirely better than the other, but they're different. It's been said that we live in a classless society these days, but that's bullshit, and it's not just about the money, any working-class idiot who can kick a football around can make a fortune, and good luck to them, but it doesn't change what they are, any more than your dwelling amongst the poor will change you, you're dyed in the wool sticky-beak, same as I am, and you know that I have nothing but contempt for the rich and pretentious, in love with themselves and their money, but they're our tribe, warts and all, and that's where we belong, if we decide to belong anywhere.'

'Which is why we belong nowhere, which is depressing, sometimes, but that's not the whole thing either. I mean the people that you have to admire are the ones who actually paint the paintings or write the books, or do the science, I mean they may have had crap lives as far as anyone knows, and died in poverty or whatever, but they left something behind, some kind of lasting legacy or evidence of their existence.'

'They're dead, so they don't benefit from that, but I take your point, I suppose you might at least die feeling as if you've achieved something.'

'Exactly, I mean at the end of each working day what have I achieved? Someone might have food on the table, regardless of what kind of table that is, or somewhere to sleep, or have been prescribed the right medication to keep them from going completely off the rails, or whatever, and the next day I get up and do it all over again, but beyond that what's the point?'

'That could be said to be an achievement in itself, but I do know what you mean, the sustaining of humanity for its own sake, when we should all be searching for higher things, or aiming for higher achievements, and here's you and me who don't have to worry about the daily grind, and could do that, but instead we've devoted our working lives to dragging other people out of the mire of their fucked-up lives, dusting them off and putting them back on their feet until the next time, and that's where I lost it, you know? In the end I got to think, '*fuck them*', and having a gun pointed at your head for trying to help the wrong people does nothing to discourage that feeling, believe me. So then we live with the guilt, which is just as nullifying as not having the fucking money in the first place, so you can't win, Oli, you just have to accept things as they are, and either get on with it or make the conscious decision to change your life. I mean for me now it's all about self-indulgence, travelling wherever the wind takes me and high-grade sex on demand when I get there because I can pay for it, and it's not wholesome, or nice, I get that, but it's a way to live, and it's all I've got right now until I can work things out.'

Olivia poured herself more wine.

'Sounds like we've both got issues, doesn't it?'

'Same as it's ever been, sister, and we're getting down to it early this evening, maybe we should lighten things up.'

'Yes, perhaps we should, this is definitely second or third bottle material. So, tell me something light which has happened in your life lately, anything exciting happening in the village?'

'Not that I'm aware of, but I've not been around.'

'No, well, I doubt if you'd notice even if you had been.'

'That's a bit unfair old thing, I catch up with news at the deli sometimes. No one's moved into Tara's house yet, but she hasn't been around either, I believe she's been off recording another album. A single white male has moved into number three, that's the place where the last tenants mysteriously disappeared, at least there was a van there yesterday, but otherwise it's all quiet. I did play cricket for the village team, which I suppose counts as light.'

'You did what...?'

'I was kind of press-ganged into it, Tillers and a couple of others turned up on my doorstep, day after I got back from Europe, as it happened. They were a man short so I stepped in, and didn't do too badly for someone who hasn't played since they were just out of short trousers.'

'So will you play again or is this a one-off?'

'Reckon I'll give it a go as long as I'm around, they're an eclectic bunch, but not bad sorts on the whole. There's an air of amiable eccentricity about the whole thing.'

'That's high praise indeed coming from you. So you like living in the village, then?'

'There're worse places to live, whilst trying to sort one's life out, so I could be here for a while.'

'And how's Mike, do you see much of each other?'

'Not lately, he's living away, of course, and he's busy with his work, and having the place renovated, so he's not been around here very much. We talk by 'phone occasionally, he seems to be keeping his end up, new marriage and all.'

'I see...'

'Yes, there's something about that, though...'

'What do you mean?'

'I mean not about the marriage itself, and I probably shouldn't say anything...'

'Well you're going to have to, now.'

'Hang on, I just have to check dinner.'

He left Olivia to her wine and her observations as to how her brother was living. The house was sparsely appointed, and nothing had been added since she helped him move in and furnish his living place, but it looked comfortable enough, and her brother did not decorate; even when they were children his bedroom had lacked any embellishment beyond the essential. She herself lived in similar fashion, and she had wondered perhaps whether this was because they were moved so often as children, from one country and one expensive school to another, and never really settled anywhere. Her thoughts turned momentarily to cricket, and the thought of her brother playing for the village team, which was a pleasant thought. She had seen him play only once, in an inter-school competition during school holidays, when a flu virus had run through most of the first team and he had been temporarily promoted. She would have been in her early teens, and had gone with their parents to watch him play. He had played well enough, as far as she understood such things, and he had always maintained that it was schoolboy politics rather than his ability to play which had prevented his permanent inclusion in the first team. He had been a maverick even then, and had never suffered fools gladly, even when they were the sons of the well to do, which had led to his social isolation, and his leaving school with only one friend, who was Michael Tillington.

'Well that all seems to be in order, we can eat whenever you want.'

'Good, soon then, but you were about to say...?'

'Yes, well, it was cricket which brought it to mind, actually. There's this guy called Percival, never spoken to him before but he lives in the village, I've seen him a few times, on his way to the deli, I suppose, damned good batsman as it happens.'

'Right...So what about him?'

'Well, the thing is that he's the split image of someone else, or rather the someone else is the split image of him, I suppose one should say, since he was there first, as it were.'

'What are you talking about, and so what, a lot of people look like other people.'

'Yes, but this is more than mere similarity, and this is a particular person, he being only son to Michael Tillington, and therefore next but one in line for the Lordship.'

'What...? So what are you saying, that you think Mike's son isn't Mike's son?'

'In a nutshell, yes, I mean Rose, his second wife...'

'Yes, I know who Rose is.'

'Well, she was once a lady of the night, too, if you know what I mean.'

'I knew that as well, but what's that got to do with anything?'

'Nothing, I suppose, except she might not have been quite so careful as others where she put herself, you might say.'

'That doesn't follow, either, but the implication is that she and this Percival character had an affair, is that it?'

'Yes, which in a way makes sense, you know? I mean after her operation Rose wasn't supposed to get sprogged-up, that was to be the end of the line, so Mike was always careful in extremis, about contraception and what have you, and everyone was surprised when she conceived, Mike more than anyone, but if she was sowing some wild oats elsewhere, well, that could explain it.'

More wine was poured, whilst the thought and its implication found its place in Olivia's mind.

'Christ…So I mean…But does Mike know, I mean will he have guessed, and have you spoken to him about it?'

'As to the latter, no, and as to the former, I don't know, but you'd have to be blind not to notice it, and as you have pointed out many times I'm not the most observant of people, and I've only seen the boy Nathaniel a handful of times.'

'So, Rose wasn't supposed to have children, and if you're right, she died in childbirth giving birth to an illegitimate son, have I got that right?'

'On the button, dear thing, and maybe nothing will come of it, I don't know, but it's a thing, don't you think?'

'Yes, it certainly is….'

'So I sort of kept an eye out, at the match, and whilst nothing was said between them, and I wasn't aware that they were avoiding one another, well, they didn't speak, so perhaps they've come to some sort of gentleman's agreement. Mike said that he was thinking of giving up the cricket now he's living away, but I do wonder whether there's more to it than that. I mean I don't want to sound like some sort of village gossip, and I won't broadcast my thoughts about the place, but you're not in the village, and you're my sister, so there it is.'

'Yes, well, it is, isn't it, and if this goes any further then the Lordship will or should end with Michael, but do you think Percival is aware of the possibility?'

'Almost certainly, I would think, and he's pretty thick with Victoria, and it can't have escaped her notice, I'm sure.

Question is, of course, whether, assuming any of this is remotely true, he makes any claim to the child, and whether Tillers wants to confirm anything, one way or the other. Otherwise it could all go through on the nod, so to speak, but it's a rum do, whichever way you look at it. I mean it's not as though he's got heirs lined up for the title, it's our Nathaniel or it's nobody.'

'Of course…Well, well, such scandal in the English aristocracy. You're not going to mention anything to Mike, then?'

'Not my place, old thing, even with one's best pal. He'll come to me if and when he's ready. So, shall we eat?'

'Yes, let's…'

'We're going to have to do something about you though, aren't we?'

'What do you mean?'

'I mean you can't sustain this life forever, Oli, it'll be the undoing of you in the end, sooner or later you're going to have to stop mixing with the low-life and become yourself.'

'What else to do, that's the thing.'

'Why don't you take up painting again, you know, become a lady of leisure? Live off the fat until you're good enough to sell? As I recall you have an exceptional talent with the watercolours, Mater and Pater still have some of your work hanging in the English house, and there's your higher purpose on a plate.'

'I haven't held a paintbrush since school, or just after.'

'I haven't played cricket since school, either, but I can still wield a cricket bat. One does not forget, you have an innate ability which won't have gone away.'

'Fuck the world and pass the brushes, yes?'

'That's the idea…I mean, when was the last time you danced?'

'What…?'

'You used to love dancing, as a kid you could never keep still, you used to dance at the dining table, so, when was the last time?'

'I don't know, maybe at a New Year's party a couple of years ago.'

'You see, the life you lead is crushing the spirit out of you, anyone who knows you can see that. In the end it's about personal survival and happiness, even if the latter remains elusive. Give it up, Oli, while you can still dance, wear some make up and buy some new clothes, do stuff that young women do, embrace your natural feminine beauty, all you look these days is tired.'

'I must say you're being very profound this evening.'

'I'm worried about you, that's all, concerned for your wellbeing, I mean someone has to do it, since you have so little concern for yourself.'

'I'll have to go back, people are depending on me.'

'No one is indispensable, dear thing, the world of Social Services would get by without you, and you could work out your notice, make it a smooth transition at both ends.'

'My notice and leave due are running about even at the moment, I could probably walk out next week.'

'Well there you go, then, it's only your conscience which stands between you and a different life, and if you're about to lose your place of abode, what better time than now to make the change?'

'Okay, so where would I live?'

'Well, you could start here, there's a spare room, and plenty of stuff to paint in the locale, there's the lake for one thing, and the heath, vistas in abundance on your doorstep to get going on.'

'Do you really think we could live together?'

'I don't see why not, I'm not very demanding, and we always rubbed along okay in the family home, did we not?'

'I suppose so. From London to Middlewapping, it'd be a big change…'

'A big change is what you need right now, and you could sort out your fucked-up brother into the bargain, so there's your worthy cause. Compassion begins at home, after all, and Tillers wouldn't mind, I'm certain.'

'Are you paying him rent?'

'Yes, of course, well theoretically anyway, when we get around to it, so it wouldn't even cost you anything, since I'd be paying. You could come and watch me play cricket on Sundays, get involved in rural English life, and you'd have time to travel, your Tibetan mountain awaits. Once you got the hang of it again you could paint your way around the world, dear sister, call in at our parents on the way to places, they'd like that, and come home to this English idyll whenever you so wished.'

'You paint a tempting picture, brother.'

'Well then, give in to it, and become what you were destined to be. Meanwhile we should eat, otherwise we'll be destined to eat charcoal.'

Chicken, roasted with lemons and vegetables, and a young lady on her second bottle of wine, with a big question to ask about her life, and a big decision to make, which is where for now we will leave Olivia, and Horatio, who was right about the succession to the entitlement of his best friend, but as we will shortly learn, he could also be wrong.

Sabina left the white house in the early afternoon. At Charlotte's request she had embellished her history, especially that part which concerned a young witch and a young man who had fallen in love. It had been a part of her bewitchment to play upon the desires and emotions of her quarry; to drive the young man to distraction with promises of fulfilment, to dress in a certain way when they were together, and then to rebuff his advances, finally administering the poison in a last act of horrible vengeance upon the house of Tillington. In all of this was she encouraged by the others of her coven, and during their last meetings she had carried the vial of poison with her, in preparation for the moment. But then by degrees her own emotions and desires had entered the realms of their so unique relationship; twice had she almost carried out the final act, and twice had she waited, until in the end she knew that she could not kill him, but by now her power over him was such that he was not himself. Certain of her words to Charlotte were words that she would not forget, at least in their essence, but would live with her always.

'We did make love, once. It was in woodland which belongs to the Manor House, in the old summerhouse where we would meet sometimes. It was never my intent, but by then I was not entirely in control of the situation, one might say, because by then I was, as I have said, in love with him. Then the next day I heard news of the accident, and that he was dead, and for the first time I understood how a heart can be broken. I returned to the coven for a time, but was plagued by dark thoughts of my dark deeds. The others told me that I had done well, and that my task had been accomplished, but I knew in my soul that I could not stay there. I mean the coven and the others had been my young life until then, and I had nowhere else, my own parents having deserted me and I them, but one day I packed my things, such as they were, and left the next day before the others were awake, and I never returned. And then, shortly after that, I discovered that I was with child, and it was Alexander's child, so you see, it's not just me, it was the father to my child that I killed, or as good as killed. I called the child Alexander, and he has grown into a fine young man, and I have never told him why his father died, and I will never tell him the whole truth of it. After that I raised my son alone as best I could, which were hard times, but I eventually married, to a good man, and had another son, who lives in Italy with his father. Alexander has been schooled abroad, but I made the decision to come back after the divorce, at least for a while, and I have stayed, and I am alone, now, and content enough in my own way, but I still carry the bitterness, and Alex of course is a constant reminder of my former life, because I do not wish to forget, any more than I wish to remember. So you see, it was an act of courage or perhaps stupidity for me to come here, and to tell you all of this. I have for long years thought deeply about all that happened, and all that I did, and now, well, I will not see Florence lose her mother, if I can prevent that from happening, quite aside from her connection to the ancient line of witches, which I would not now see broken. I do not know you well, of course, but I know something of you, and I came here with no real intent to speak as I have spoken, and tell you as much as I have told you, but now we have met, and I see that you are a good person, and I see the power in you, so now you know a part of my story, and I am grateful to you for listening.'

After she had gone, Charlotte walked the woods to the old mill stream, and sat for a while in contemplation. So, she now knew something more of the history of the Tillington household; that there was another child of the next generation, that the Lord and Lady had a grandchild and Michael and Victoria a nephew, of whom they knew nothing, any more than he knew of them, who was cousin to Florence, Rebecca's child. She was unsure and had not asked how long ago Alexander had died, and therefore how old his son would be by now, but she assumed that he would be somewhere in his late teens; he who had grown up and would she assumed continue to grow in ignorance of his other family, and of who his father had really been. Charlotte had been sworn to secrecy, and she would hold to her promise, but the tangled web of relations within that family had just become more entangled, and the witches continued to have their influence, as they had done since the beginning, and the death of Jane Mary. She had fought hard with herself during their conversation as to how much she should in turn reveal to Sabina, and some things she had told her, and some things she had not, and she hoped now in the cold light of retrospection that her judgement had been sound in this regard. Rebecca had used her powers to conceive a child with Michael, although she had never loved him, and Sabina had loved Alexander, brother to Michael and Victoria, and had quite by happenstance born his child, which had not been her intent, so the web of emotion and intent was also complex, but the two children were related by blood, and would likely never know of each other. So, then there was the woman herself, and Charlotte found her primary sense toward her to be one of sympathy; the best part of her life had also been the worst, and her wish to forget, and yet not to forget, must be a hard thing to carry through life. She had mentioned her solitude, and Charlotte of all people could understand how that condition could prevail, even through marriage and the raising of children. She had described her former husband as a good man, and had made it clear enough that it was she rather than he who had caused their divorce, for how could such as she sustain an ordinary life, with ordinary love, when her first life had been so different; to be a witch is not an ordinary thing, as Charlotte knew well enough. Perhaps though, the most extraordinary aspect of the woman had been her knowledge of Charlotte's coven, and of Helen, and Helena, and she wondered how she had even known of the burning of her own former coven, and the death of the witches, and of who had been responsible for that, for if Charlotte had been careful as to how much she revealed, then Sabina had clearly been equally careful, and had not told her everything, she was sure. How could anyone acquire such knowledge and yet have remained hidden from the coven for so long, until she had decided that it was time to reveal herself?

Here then was much to be considered, and to be meditated upon, and in one thing at least Sabina had been right, regardless of her motivation; Rebecca and Florence must be protected, however that would be achieved, and to this did Charlotte once again turn her thoughts as she walked the woodland paths back to the white house, and closed the door to the ever so and it seemed ever more complex world behind her.

Chapter 20. Upon a Certain Day at Glebe House

When Victoria arrived at her brother's house, she was not met by her brother, who had been called away unexpectedly on matters pertaining to one of his properties, and had 'phoned her whilst she had been en-route to say that he would be an hour or so late for their meeting. It was Abigail, therefore, who greeted her on her arrival, and who made her tea, whilst Victoria spent time with Nathaniel and little Henry, who did indeed seem perfectly and contentedly at home here. This was the first time that she had seen Nathaniel since her definitive discussions with Michael regarding his paternal parentage, and his future, and the first time that she had seen her son since she had made her decision as to the agenda of this meeting with her brother. Her son, whom she loved, in a way, and yet in truth she felt no greater sense of love or emotional connection with him than she did her brother's son, and this realisation, which had in a way been a long time in the realising, merely reinforced her conviction that her thoughts were not so outlandish, and that she was at least perhaps attempting to do the right thing. She was in any case pleased to see Abi, whose presence around the Manor she had also missed since the filming began, but there was too much disruption at present for the children to sensibly live there.

Will she was also pleased to see; he who had gone with her to the temple, and to the place where Rebecca had once lived, which seemed such a long time ago now, but such was the significance and intensity of that day that she would never forget, and would ever be grateful to him, and for Will she had always since held affection.

It was Keith, however, who took it upon himself to give her a tour of inspection of the house in its newly and nearly renovated condition, and these two spent half an hour or so walking the rooms, which were by now in an almost finished state.

'You've done well, Keith.'

'Yeah, everyone seems pleased enough, anyway, and we're almost done, just the painting and final finishing, really. Damien's gone now, he's got his landscape gardening business to attend to, and a stack of work building up, so it's just me, Will and a couple of painters to see it through to the final end.'

'It's a beautiful house, isn't it?'

'Yes, it is.'

'So what for you after this..?'

'Well, I've got the village church to convert for Ash Spears, so I might lend a hand there for a bit, Mike's been there alone so far, and after that I'm not sure. I'm in the fortunate position these days of being able to decide what I do and where I work, I've been turning work away since I've been here, and I'm going to miss the old place, to be honest. I think I'll try to specialise in period properties from now on, I quite like having a sense of history around me when I'm mixing cement, you know? Still, whatever, Mike and Elin will be pleased to see the back of us, I'm sure.'

Letters had been found here, written by Jane, sister to William Tillington, the fifth Lord of that name, who together with his wife had died of the great plague of the 17th Century. The house had been built for Jane, who had on her brother's bidding hidden out here away from danger of infection, with William's son, John, who would become the sixth Lord, and his sister, Margaret. The letters had been heart breaking, and John had been of such a young age when they had returned to the Manor House, and he to his entitlement. The letters had never been sent, but rather Jane had hidden them beneath the old floorboards, perchance that one day they would be found, and Michael of all people had by some almost fantastic chance found them, and it was the letters which had finally persuaded him to keep the house, for he could not thereafter sell it. There was so much of their family history here, and so much of its future, and today would see the beginning of a process which would decide that future, one way or the other. Her brother would not agree at first, she was sure, but Victoria clung to the hope that in time he might be persuaded, and she waited now impatiently for his return.

Abigail had awoken on this morning with her own agenda. She and Ross had met only once since she had taken up residence in Michael's house, and whilst it was true that she was contented enough here, her life was different, now. No longer were the children her only focus, as they had been for so long; the missing part of her life had been found, now, and so a new state of being had entered her life, which was a sense of emptiness when she was not with him, or near him. She was realistic enough to know that their being together would for now be a sporadic and temporary thing in any case, and their relationship was still new and uncertain, but she missed seeing him around the grounds of the Manor, and the existence of the possibility of spending time with him during his working day. On the day that they had met, she had walked from the house to an agreed meeting place a short distance away; they had driven to some local woods, talked about their future and made love, and in the evening they had eaten in the gardens of a local public house, and it was late in the evening before she returned to the place which was for now both her home and her place of work. They would meet again, soon, but for both of them the day had been a thing of magic, and she wished now very much to return to the Manor as soon as that may be, so that they could more easily meet, however that meeting could be done, and for however long she could return. To this end she determined to speak to Victoria during her time at Glebe House, and so, not long after they had met, she had made enquiry as to how long she would be staying in her brother's home.

'I'm not sure, Abi, I've brought a change of clothes, but I may decide to go home this evening, it depends. I'll be sleeping on the settee if I stay, which is okay, but we'll see.'

'Okay, well I'm sure you're busy now, but I'd like to have a chat about something before you go.'

'Chat away, then, I'm waiting for Michael anyway.'

'Well, for a start I was wondering how much longer the filming was going to go on for at the Manor.'

'I think everyone's wondering that, including the people making the film, so who knows, why do you ask?'

'Well, I mean I know and understand that you need to keep little Henry and Nathaniel away, generally speaking, but it might be quite fun for them, don't you think, to be there when it's all going on, even if it's only for a day or so?'

'Yes, I suppose it might.'

'I'd keep them out of the way and everything, people would hardly know they're there, and there are some famous people there, aren't there, and I'd love to take some photos with the children, if that might be possible at some point.'

'I see, well, I'll talk to Michael, then, I hadn't really thought about that to be honest, but I'm sure it could be arranged. I expect you'd like to see some famous people as well, would you not?'

'Yes, I suppose…'

'And perhaps some not so famous people..?'

Victoria had been smiling as she had spoken the words, which had if anything emphasised their meaning, and for a moment Abi was unsure how to respond.

'I'm sorry?'

'Well, come on, Abi, I've no wish to pry, but coordinating your days off was a bit of a giveaway.'

'Oh, so you've spoken to Mike, then, I mean to Michael.'

'Yes, and as I say, I'm not spying on you, it came up in conversation, so if there's anything you want to tell me, please feel free, I'd far rather we were honest with one another.'

'I was going to tell you, that is, we were going to tell you, but I wasn't sure how you'd react, to be honest.'

'Well, now I'm reacting, and the sky hasn't fallen, and Ross is a nice young man, which is partly why he got the job in the first place, against more qualified opposition, so all power to you both. Just don't make any mistakes, I'll never find another nanny like you, and there are enough unwanted babies around.'

'No, well we've got that covered, but you really don't mind?'

'Why should I mind? It's your life, my dear girl, but you're part of the family, now, so let's not have secrets, shall we?'

'No, okay, let's not…What did you mean, though, about the unwanted babies?'

'Nothing, it was just a general observation. Anyway, who am I to talk about families having secrets?'

'I don't get that, either.'

'No, of course you don't, and ignore me, I'm just rambling on. I'm here to speak to Mike about something, apart from seeing the house, and the children, of course.'

'Oh well….So, ummm, since were talking frankly, what do you know about Florence?'

Now it was Victoria's turn to take pause, she had not expected that.

'What about Florence?'

'Well, Michael has asked me whether I'd mind looking after her sometimes, that's all.'

'That's all…'

'I'm sorry?'

'Okay…Okay, well, I know of Florence, of course, her mother is a friend of the family, she was….She was a friend of mine from school, actually, and we've been, ummm, we've been friends ever since, and Michael didn't…So how do you feel, about looking after Florence?'

'I don't mind at all, I mean I've not met her, of course, but I've no objection in principle, and a little girl will make a nice change, or a nice addition, anyway.'

'I see…Well, if that's what Mike wants, that's up to him, I suppose.'

'So, I mean he didn't tell me who the child's mother is, or anything much at all about her, actually.'

'So what did he tell you?'

'Well, he told me that….That Florence is his daughter, and that it would be okay if you knew that I know, but that nobody else knows about her, in the family, I mean.'

'I see…'

'Oh dear, have I said something wrong?'

'What…? No, no, not at all, but let's keep this conversation just between us, shall we..?'

'Sure…Mum's the word….I mean…Anyway, I think that's him arriving now, so I'll leave you to it and get back to doing my job. And you'll think about what I said, about going back to the Manor sometimes?'

'Yes, yes of course.'

'And you know, thanks for being so understanding, about Ross, I mean.'

Victoria smiled again.

'What's funny…?'

'You speak of my understanding, dear Abi, but sometimes I wonder whether I understand anything, but anyway, it's been good to talk, has it not?'

'Yes, it has. Well, see you later, then.'

She departed, and each was left momentarily to their own thoughts. So, Victoria had known, then, or guessed at least, about her and Ross, and Abi wondered for how long she had known. She would 'phone him later, but here was the end of their secret, about which Abi had mixed feelings; on the one hand it had been strangely exciting, both keeping their relationship from the knowledge of their employer, but this was better, was it not, in the long run. So, what then, of the child Florence, the identity of whose mother she was not supposed to know, according to Michael, but now Victoria had told her, or she had at least hinted at her identity; a friend of the family, she had said, and yet not so much a friend that the family were allowed to know that she and Michael had a child, so what intrigue lay behind this particular story, and Victoria had clearly been surprised that Michael had discussed the child with her at all, and what was the big secret, anyway? As she went about her work, Abigail considered that she could be forgiven for wondering whether any of the children in her care actually belonged to the right people, and how many more illegitimate children might come crawling out of the ancient woodwork before she was allowed to know everything. She would look after whatever child was presented to her, she was in the end merely a paid nanny, after all, and she was well paid, with generous benefits when she asked for them, which would pay for her silence when it was asked for. She lived and worked in beautiful houses, and a child was a child, but she wondered now as she had wondered before, how such educated, intelligent, rich and aristocratic people as were Michael and Victoria had managed to make such a hash of things, in the parental sense. But still, she would do as she was told, know what she was permitted to know, keep her head down, and see to her own affairs of the heart whilst she awaited further developments within that which was the ever-unpredictable Tillington family, which had suddenly grown a daughter.

As she briefly prepared herself for the meeting with her brother, Victoria knew that she must put away any thoughts of Florence, and Rebecca, for now, that was not what she had come here for, and there were matters of still greater weight to attend to, but if Florence and little Henry and Nathaniel were to be together, and perhaps become friends, then what different dimension would that add to the already complex entanglement of the people that she loved? Michael had said nothing to her of the matter, that he would reveal the existence of Florence to Abigail, so what was he doing? Of course he and Rebecca would have spoken many times, she was sure, and she and Michael were not on good speaking terms at present. It still at times gave Victoria pause to think of her brother and the woman that she loved being parents to the same child; try as she may, she could never quite come to terms with that, and now perhaps their child would meet her child, and Rose's child, who was Percival's child, she assumed on Rebecca's instigation, which seemed to Victoria to be a very significant coming together of the next generation, and that must be thought about, but not now. Now other matters pertaining to the next generation were that which she must focus upon, and Michael was here, so here it would begin.

'Hi Mike.'

'Hello, sorry about that, had a minor crisis to deal with on the Stoughton property.'

They met in the kitchen, which now, within certain tolerances and the application of some imagination, looked like a completed kitchen, and now at least all white goods were in their rightful place and properly functioning.

'It's okay, Keith gave me the tour, the house is looking lovely, Mike.'

'Yes, it's coming along, isn't it, if I had a Keith at all of my properties I'd be a happier man.'

She smiled, but there was no reciprocation, and Victoria doubted whether she would induce a smile from her brother, today of all days. He was still angry with her, of course, and with the world as he currently perceived it, and his anger would likely increase with that which she was about to do, but it had to be done, it being an integral part of the process, and

Victoria now had an abiding sense that she should have done it long ago.

'So, coffee....?'

'I'll make it. The children are both looking bonny.'

'Yes, they like it here, it seems, which is all to the good.'

The children, their children, at least to the eyes of the world, and neither would now be a Lord, unless she could persuade him. She made coffee, and let him settle into general conversation, such as that currently was between them, before she began, but it was time.

'So, are you all done for the day, work-wise?'

'Yes, well I can be, a couple of 'phone calls notwithstanding.'

'Good, because I need your undivided attention...Let's go to your office.'

Michael's office was a small anteroom off the lounge, which would likely once have been a storeroom, but it was set up now with a desk, lamp and workstation, and he had had a small window put in place, affording views over the garden to the side of the property. As everywhere within the house, the air was pervaded with the smell of new paint and wet cement, smells which would linger for a while, until the essence of the old house would once again take its rightful place.

'What's all this, Vics, and what's in the case?'

'Something you should see, Mike, and you'll say that you should have seen it a long time ago.'

He sat down, she opened the attaché case, and found to her surprise that her hands were shaking as she did so; in a sense the future of their family was contained within it. She pulled out photocopies of several sheets of ancient writing, and placed them carefully upon his desk, with the same care as if they had been the original manuscripts.

'What are these?'

'A journal...Well, all that remains of a journal, anyway. You remember that I discovered the remains of Anne

Tillington, under the old summerhouse, and that we buried her in the family plot.'

'Yes, of course.'

'You will also remember that we found a metal box, containing a lock of hair, perhaps her daughter's hair, and some items of jewellery. Well, also within that box were these, pages from her journal, begun in the year 1587 and ended in 1595, at the time of her death.'

Michael looked at the papers without speaking, but now he spoke.

'So…So you've had these since…Why the hell haven't you shown them to me before?'

'Because, my dear Michael, they are proof positive that your legitimate line was broken. That the third Lord Tillington was not his father's son, but the son of the second Lord's sister, and until now, well, I decided not to tell you, but things are different, now. Aside from me you are the first person to read these in our lifetime. There are twenty entries in total, the first was written at the time that she and Edward, the second Lord, returned to the Manor after their years in exile, when they had lived as commoners. This was at the time of the death of the first Lord, who was also Lord Edward. They tell of the deception which Anne and her brother perpetrated in order that Edward, Anne's son, and her daughter, Annabelle should enter the court of Queen Elizabeth, and that Edward would become the third Lord. So you see, the male line was broken, but the bloodline was not, and only in law is your title falsely given, but anyway, I'll leave you alone so that you can read them for yourself.'

'But I mean hang on, where have you been keeping these?'

'At the bottom of my knicker-draw, actually, the safest place I could think of, although these are only copies, of course. Read them, Mike, then we can talk again, come and find me when you're done. Do you have cigarettes?'

'In the glove compartment, I don't generally smoke in the house.'

'Well you might want to now, take mine, I'll get yours.'

Victoria left, and Michael picked up the topmost page, and read.

'The 1st of May 1587

It is perhaps a thing of irony that as I begin this journal of my life, at and from the age of thirty one, I at once find myself all but lost for words.'

'Hi...'

Ross was in his garden shed when his telephone ringtone sounded. He and Abi would often exchange messages during the working day, but here was the young lady herself, and this was unusual.

'Hi, you okay?'

'I'm fine, are you busy?'

'Nope, unless you count sitting here drinking a cup of tea and eating a cheese and cucumber sandwich as busy...'

'This isn't your normal lunch break, is it? I tried to 'phone earlier but got caught up with the kids.'

'No, well, it's a nice day so they've sent the drone up to take the aerial shots of the Manor for the film, so everything post Elizabethan had to be removed from the gardens, which included me, and we're under instruction not to be seen, so I thought I'd retire to the shed for the duration.'

'How long will that be?'

'Don't know, about an hour so far, and it's still buzzing around up there. I thought about donning 16th Century gardener's garb and carrying on, but I came unprepared as it happens.'

'Twit....Anyway, I've got news.'

'Oh yes?'

'Our secret is out, Victoria knows about us.'

'How, did you tell her?'

'No, she must have worked it out.'

'So what did she say?'

'Nothing, really, I mean she seems quite okay with the idea, just told me not to get pregnant.'

'What, she said that? That was real woman-to-woman stuff, wasn't it?'

'More employer to employee, I think, she doesn't want me to leave and have kids, or have a kid and have to leave.'

'Well there's no danger of that, but I wonder how she knew, I thought we were being careful.'

'We were, but not careful enough, apparently. Anyway we can talk later, but I thought I'd let you know.'

'Right…Okay well thanks for that, so she's cool about it, then?'

'Completely, I mean she seems a bit weird today, I think something's going on with her and Michael, but yes, she's cool.'

'Well the day she's not weird will be weird, but we're glad, aren't we?'

'Yes, we're glad, I think…Our clandestine affair is no longer clandestine.'

'You'll still be able to come and see me in the shed, though, yes?'

'I don't see why not, I just won't have to sneak about anymore. I don't think I'm very good at sneaking about anyway.'

'So it would seem….Well, this is news to brighten my imposed internment. Don't suppose you want to get naked and do this on video, do you?'

'No, I'm working and there are children present.'

'I'd settle for half naked, the kids won't know the difference.'

'Forget it, it's not going to happen.'

'Okay, just an idea, looks like it's me and the cheese and cucumber sandwich, then…So did you talk about you coming back here?'

'Yes, and she said she'd think about it. I played the "kids should meet the actors" card, so we'll see. Anyway I'd better go, got children to look after, we'll talk this evening.'

'Sure, and thanks for the update.'

'Bye, then.'

Ross continued his light repast, and considered implications, but decided that there probably weren't any of any significance, and concluded that all things considered this would be a far better way of going about things. Despite finding himself in charge of the whole estate, which he had not expected, the job was working out well, and now he had fallen in love with the nanny, and she apparently with him, which was sort of corny, and probably more the stuff of novels than real life, but he wasn't complaining.

It was better than an hour later that Michael emerged from his small study, and found his sister sitting upon a low wall in a quiet part of the garden, bearing a half-drunk cup of coffee and a neutral expression. Michael sat down beside her, neither looked at the other, and at such times an author may be tempted to intervene in their conversation, which would clearly not be an easy thing, but in the end the matter is best left to find its own way. Michael took a cigarette from her borrowed pack, and lit it with her lighter.

'Last one, sorry, there were only four left, and I've been smoking, you know?'

'It's okay, I'll smoke yours.'

The garden had for the most part still not been attended to in any way since its purchase, and they sat amongst over-mature shrubs, which would be heavily pruned or removed when the time came, but which for now provided a private place for them to be.

'Christ, Vics....'

'Indeed...'

'And you kept that from me for all of this time.'

'I kept it from everyone, Mike, and it wasn't an easy decision, or an easy thing to keep, and the longer I kept it, well the harder it was to un-keep it, if you understand me.'

'Yes, well, you've been keeping quite a lot from me lately, haven't you?'

'None of this is my fault, Mike, and what was I supposed to say, that you're future Lordship is illegal and that your son probably isn't your son? How was any of that going to be an easy thing to do?'

'So why now?'

'You know very well why now, as I said before, everything's different now, isn't it? Now you know about the Lordship, and about the other matter, which are two separate things, of course, but in a way it's all connected.'

'You mean there are now two reasons why Nathaniel can't be the next Lord Tillington after me, and even I in all conscience should revoke the title.'

'Well, that depends, doesn't it, on how you look at it? The bloodline wasn't entirely broken, Mike, she was his sister, and it's only the vagaries of ancient English law which say that a woman's son can't inherit, and we live in different times now.'

'Not according to the law of the land when it comes to such ancient entitlements, that hasn't changed as far as I'm aware.'

He took the coffee cup from her and drank from it, a simple gesture between brother and sister, which spoke of their deeper love and understanding for and of one another, even during this.

'I just....I wanted you to get some historical context, it isn't enough just to say *'he was her son, so he shouldn't have had the title'* is it? Consider what they went through, Mike, and the danger that they put themselves through in order to achieve the continuation of the line, how they took it upon themselves to educate both of the children, and make them ready for their new lives. They had lived in poverty together, and came back to a ruined Manor House and a dying father, and she gave up her son so that her brother...Well, so that her brother could claim him, there's far more to all of this than cold, calculated law, these were real people, Mike, with very real feelings, living in far more difficult times than do we, and the reason for *'why now'* is that I wanted you to see it for yourself. I haven't told you before, or shown you these before because how easy would it have been for you to live these past years knowing that you were not to be legally entitled, or that father isn't legally titled, I've kept all of this to myself for all of this time to keep you from the knowledge of that.'

'So it was an act of sisterly love then, was it?'

'Yes, it was, regardless of what you may think.'

They were silent for a moment, and both watched as a butterfly went about its business on the over-mature Buddleia.

'Well, anyway, it's academic now, isn't it, since I don't have a son to inherit the title after me.'

So then, here was the moment, and Victoria let the words pass her lips, and go where they may.

'Well, that depends.'

'No, it doesn't, my mind is quite made up on that, I mean I'm sure we agree to keep all of this from mum and dad, they must never know any of it.'

'Yes, on that we agree.'

'Well, there it is, then, Nathaniel doesn't get the title, and I'm willing to pretend for the duration, until both of our parents are no longer with us, but it ends with me, or else I give it away to some relative who none of us has met, if the law says that's what must happen.'

'Of course…'

She now took cigarettes from his pack and they lit them together, and shared the remains of the coffee.

'Nathaniel can't have the title, I understand that, but…There may be another way.'

'What are you talking about, Elin doesn't want children, and it's only fifty-fifty anyway even if she did, but that's not going to happen, and I'm not marrying again, not even for this, three times is enough.'

'No, of course you're not…'

'Well then, what other way are you talking about, there is no other way.'

'I've thought about this a lot, Mike, and I don't want it to end, for us I mean, there's too much history, and it isn't just the title, is it? If we lose the Lordship we also lose the estate, and the Manor, the two are inseparable as far as I'm aware, so where's everyone going to live, you know?'

'You mean where will you live if I peg it first.'

'I was more thinking about our children, I mean you have Glebe House and I have my house in the village, but the Manor would be gone, and can we really live with the thought of that?'

It was a thought which brought further momentary silence to the conversation; both had considered the wider implications, but this was the first time they had been spoken of, and it was Michael who broke their mutual contemplation.

'Well, whatever, if it goes it goes, and there's still nothing to be done, is there?'

'Well, perhaps there is…I have a proposition to put to you, Mike, which I want you to consider very carefully before you reject it, okay?'

'What proposition?'

'Just promise me that whatever I'm about to say, you'll give it your full consideration.'

'Whatever, yes, I promise.'

'It will all depend, of course, on whether, knowing all that you now know, you actually want to be sure that the Tillington Lordship will continue, through our immediate family.'

'It can't continue, not with my offspring anyway, that's the point...'

'Perhaps not with your offspring, but would you want the bloodline to continue, if it were possible...?'

'Yes, under different circumstance of course I would want it to, but it can't.'

'Yes, it can, actually, at least theoretically.'

'You've lost me...'

'Well, consider this. There's nothing....There's nothing in English law which says that siblings cannot adopt one another's children, nor is there anything in English law which states that adopted children can't inherit certain titles, and yours is one of them. I've looked into this very carefully, and well, I'm quite certain of it.'

That gave the conversation further brief pause, as she waited, and he began to understand.

'So what are you saying, that I adopt Henry, and that he becomes the next Lord, is that it?'

'Yes, that's exactly what I'm saying. Anne gave her child away to her brother, and I would be prepared to do the same. I'll give you Henry, Mike, if you want him, and if you really want our family line to carry on.'

The butterfly was still about its innocent business, as Victoria waited once again, and Michael took a step deeper into the abyss of his thoughts.

'Fucking hell, Vics, I mean you're not joking, are you?'

'Far from it...It would only be a legal adoption, I would of course pay for Henry's education, and anything and everything else that he needed, otherwise we would continue the way we are, sharing all other costs between us. In all other intents and purposes Henry would remain my son, but think about it, Mike, they live together as brothers anyway, so really, what difference would it make to their lives? They would of course continue to live at the Manor, Abi would care for them both, and they could come here sometimes, so nothing would change in any practical sense. Henry is the eldest of them, so in that sense it would be a natural line of succession, it need only involve the signing of legal papers and so on, and it could wait, if you wanted, until father and mother have both passed away, but we would need to set the idea of it in both of the children's heads from now on, whilst they're still young enough not to understand what we're doing. Nathaniel isn't going to be Lord Nathaniel anyway, so he'd be none the worse for it, and little Henry would become Lord Henry. None of it would be illegal, and the bloodline would continue, it would just be my blood instead of yours, just as happened before. I'd do it, Mike, for us, and for Anne, and Edward, and for Jane Mary, and everyone who came thereafter, but more importantly, I'd do it for those who come after us, for our grandchildren, if we have any, and for, I don't know, for the continuation of our history. You, and father, and all past and future Lords are just part of the continuum, and part of something far bigger than any of us, and I'm not looking to do this for the glorification of my son over yours, and I see no personal gain to it, but as things are, well, it's the only way that I can see that we can do it, and it could work, you know, if you could ever bring yourself to agree.'

Several butterflies had now joined in the feeding frenzy, giving credence to the shrub being commonly known as the 'butterfly bush', and Mike laughed as he exhaled his cigarette smoke, but it was a mirthless laugh.

'You know the thing which I think got to me most, about the journals?'

'No, tell me.'

'The fact that as it now seems, all of us in all of our former pomp and greatness, are all descended from a blacksmith called Seth. That's the break in the bloodline, isn't it? I mean sure, Edward and Anne were brother and sister, but there's other blood in there, isn't there?'

'Yes, there is, and if that can be overlooked, then what I'm proposing pales into insignificance. It's your choice, Mike, and I'll love you whatever you decide, and you'll need time, of course, to consider everything, and Elin will have to be a party to the decision-making, although we should make it clear to her that in fact it'll make no difference to her.'

'In any practical sense...'

'Indeed...I mean how much have you told her so far, about all of this?'

'Nothing, yet, but I will, of course.'

'Of course...'

'She's had a lot to put up with, you know? First she learns that I have a daughter, who is daughter to a witch, and now this, when I tell her that I probably don't actually have a son after all.'

'She's made of stern stuff, Mike, she'll come to terms with it all, I'm sure.'

A daughter, Florence, who might be coming here soon, but now was not the time for that conversation, as both of them knew. There was another conversation somewhere in the offing, about Alex and a witch, but that too would have to wait before finding safe harbour.

'Of course, we don't even know yet who Henry's father is, do we?'

'No, and that I still won't tell you, but it makes no material difference to the adoption, I'll see to that...'

'You talk as though it's actually going to happen.'

'I'm sorry, it was just a turn of phrase.'

The butterflies continued in their innocent oblivion, and it was time for the conversation to run its course.

'Well, I promised I'd think about it, and so I will, but beyond that there's nothing more to say, is there?'

'No, I'm done.'

'Yes, I think you've done enough. So, what now then, Vics..?'

'What do you mean?'

'I mean, do we just go indoors and do ordinary things, like prepare dinner, or what?'

'No, I suppose not.'

'I suppose not, too.'

'I'll leave, then. You need time to think.'

'Yes, you could say that.'

'I'll leave the copies with you, read them again.'

'I've read them twice already, but sure, leave them here.'

'I must have read them twenty times, and I've cried every time, and I say none of what I say lightly, Mike.'

'I know, and it's no light decision, there's a lot to consider, and I probably haven't thought of half of it yet, so don't press me for an answer, okay? I have to weigh up the implications before I say no, which I almost certainly will.'

'Of course...'

'Do you have any more cigarettes?'

'Yes, in my bag. I'll leave those as well, I can buy some more on the way back to the Manor.'

'The Manor...Do you ever wonder, Vics, how life would have been for us, if we'd just been born ordinary people?'

'Often, but we're not, are we? We can't have ordinary lives, Mike, so there's no point in wishing for them.'

'Like father, like son...'

'What do you mean?'

'Dad carries his Lordship like a burden, sometimes.'

'I know he does.'

'And what's the Manor, anyway, but a decaying pile, far too big for anyone to sensibly live in? Dad's been putting things off, but it's going to need some major work in the next decade, which falls on me. Better perhaps to let the whole thing end, don't you think, just give it away, if anyone could be found who wanted it?'

'Perhaps, but that's up to you, only you can decide, I'm just giving you another way, that's all.'

'Well thank you for that, I think....I had it all set in my mind, you know? I believe I was actually beginning to come to terms with it all.'

'Yes, I'm sure, but I've always been trouble, you know that.'

'Yeah, I know that. Well, go, then, I'll be in touch.'

'Okay...Just give me a few minutes with the children. There was one other thing, though.'

'Which is...?'

'Abi wants to take Nathaniel and Henry to the Manor sometime, to meet the actors and so on.'

'Sure, why not, I'll bring them over next time I come.'

'Thanks, Mike, and I'm sorry, you know, for everything, I really am. If I've made as big a cock-up of everything as I currently think I have, then you have every right to hate me, but don't hate me forever, and please don't let that cloud your greater and better judgement, okay?'

'I'll try, in both regards....It's as well that we understand one another, isn't it?'

'Yes, it is.'

'I'll think I'll wait here 'til you're gone.'

'Okay, well, I'll see you soon, then.'

'Yes I daresay, just...'

'Just what...?'

'Fuck did I ever end up with you as a sister?'

'Just bad luck, I suppose. Call me, Mike, I'll wait for your call.'

'Do that...'

She walked away, but her brother spoke again.

'Henry....'

She turned.

'What?'

'The first Lord was Lord Henry.'

'Yes, I know.'

She waited, briefly, but nothing more was said, so she spoke in his stead.

'It's just a name, Mike.'

'Yes, it's just a name.'

On the drive home, Victoria tried once again to consider and to piece together all of the various aspects of this so complex a web of love and hatred, in which her brother was entangled. He had loved Rose, and yet she had betrayed him, and only after her death had he found this out. Rose had loved Michael, but she had also loved Percival, and yet it was true, surely, that the keeping of Percival's child, which she must have known was his child, was not for Percival's sake, or for her own, but surely an act of love for Michael, to try to give him the son that he so badly wanted. Anne had given up her only son to Edward, her brother, as an act of love for him, born of the hatred which both must have felt for their father, the first Lord. She tried then to better understand and rationalise her own actions; she was willing to give up her own and only son, in a way, which she knew to be a far lesser sacrifice than Anne had made, for in truth and as she had come to realise, she held no great love for Henry, as a mother should for her child. Michael, her beloved brother, she knew wished so much for the Lordship to continue, yet she had come to him with this proposition not for his sake, not really, but for her own sense that she wished the line to carry on in a way which would mean anything to any of them, and for the sake of Anne, her so distant predecessor, who through the reading of her diaries she had also come to love. The centuries which separated them had become less with each time she read the writings of this so particular and special woman, without whom there would have been no Lordship for her own brother to continue, even if he chose so to do, and in the end time had come to mean nothing. She tried once again to imagine her, writing her diaries somewhere in the Manor House, seated by candlelight in all of her Elizabethan finery, and now once again the Manor had gone back in time, to Anne's time, and now Maurine O'Connell, a woman born of so different an age, wore similar garb, and complained of her discomfort. In any case, as she approached her ancestral home, she had a sense that she had now done all that she could, and that all now rested in the hands of her dear brother, and not for the first time her heart went out to him; he had had hard enough decisions to make, and now, he had perhaps the hardest of them all.

Chapter 21. Life After Death

His Lordship lay dying. His health had not been good of late, and of a sudden his condition had worsened, to the point where, two days previously, he had taken to his bed, and could scarce now speak. His wife and daughter were present at his bedside, and with a last and final effort, he beckoned his daughter to come closer. He gripped her hand as best he could, whilst he whispered in her ear, words which were barely audible even to her, before catching his last breath; his head rolled slightly to one side, his grip upon his daughter's hand loosened, his body became limp, and he stared, lifeless, at the ancient ceiling.

'Okay, and….Cut. That was better, we'll probably use that one, take a break everyone.'

Lord Featherstone, who in his real life persona was David Blake, sat up in bed.

'Thank Christ for that, I'm dying for a fag, and badly need to pee.'

Ursula Franks, who was Lady Featherstone, and Maurine O'Connell, their daughter, who alone had heard his dying words, save all who would one day watch the movie, left the room, and then left the Manor through the front door, and all assembled on the lawn below the steps, which had become the natural and general gathering place. Anna Merchant spoke encouraging words before departing to deal with some other matter, and David Blake joined the assembly, which now included Graham Dean, the son of the household. This was Graham's first day on location, and he was not yet dressed in Elizabethan garb, and was not yet in character, having been sick with or recovering from the flu for several days. Even now his voice had not fully returned, but he had come to be with his fellow actors and prepare himself for his return to work. He and David Blake had worked together before on a televised play, and had become friends, although neither had seen the other for several months.

'You look like death, David.'

'Well, that's the general idea, and I feel remarkably chipper for someone who just died five times.'

'Six, actually...' Said Ursula.

'Was it six, one loses count.'

Cigarettes were passed around amongst those who partook, and there was a general sense of relief that the death scene had probably been successfully accomplished.

'Of course I have to rise again now, I've got several scenes before I finally croak, but we've had to do everything arse about face because you haven't been around.'

'Yeah, sorry about that, but I should be back and fully functioning in a day or two.'

'Well, that's good to know.'

Maurine O'Connell had missed the brief conversation, her attention having been drawn to that which Anna Merchant was attending to.

'I recognise him, isn't that...?'

All eyes now followed hers, and it was David who replied.

'Christ yes, it has to be, he looks older but it's definitely him. What the devil's he doing here?'

A few moments prior to this, May Thomas had been speaking with sound technicians, when she had been interrupted by a voice at her side.

'Yeah, so, like, what's the deal here, then?'

She turned.

'Oh, hello Ash, I didn't see you arrive, I'm sorry, so, this is a surprise.'

'Well, you said come to the Manor, so here I am. I'm heading home later, so if we can get this done...'

'Yes, of course, great. I mean it's great to see you...Hang on, I'll get our director.'

Anna was duly summoned, and May made the introductions.

'Anna, this is Ashley Spears, Ash, this is Anna Merchant.'

'Hello Ashley, I understand from May that you may be interested in providing our sound track.'

'Interested in the idea, anyway, although I need to make it clear from the off that I've never composed a musical score before.'

'Yes, May mentioned that, but said that that shouldn't necessarily be an obstacle, given your prior and various musical experience, so have you thought further on the matter?'

'I mean, sure, you know, and I could do it, I guess, I mean I've got contacts in the industry, so the orchestra wouldn't be a problem, but I need to get the vibe, you know?'

May had noted with interest that in such situations, when meeting with new people, Ash would habitually revert to his somewhat spaced-out ex-drug-abusing rock star persona, perhaps as some kind of a defence strategy, or to cover the inherent shyness which was a part of his nature, she wasn't sure, but Ash could act with the best of them if he felt the occasion called for it, which apparently he now did.

'Of course from our perspective, we would usually be looking for someone with experience, so we all need to be sure what we're taking on.'

'Yeah, I feel that, so it's your call, but I'm into exploring the idea if you are.'

Before so much as a note had been written, these words were already music to the ears of May Thomas, whose instincts had been right all along. She had been certain that Ash would not turn down the challenge, and Anna Merchant would be insane to in the end turn down Ashley Spears.

'Well, we'll see how things develop, but I can set up a meeting with David Bates, our producer, perhaps at his London office, if that would be convenient.'

'Sure, do that.'

'Aside from anything else we need to discuss fees and such.'

'Yeah, I get that too, I mean the money's whatever it is, you know, but I'd need to cover the orchestra and such, so let's take it to the next stage and see where we go.'

'Yes, okay, let's do that. May has your number, so can I call you once I've spoken to David?'

'I'll wait for your call.'

'Good, well from a personal perspective I'd be very happy to work with you, Ashley, I mean I've always loved your music, so it would be great to have you on board.'

'Cool, so yeah, let's do it if we can.'

'Indeed….So can I leave May to show you around, so you get some idea of what's going on, at least, we've got a lot to try and get done today.'

'Sure, you press on, I'll just hang for a while, and maybe see you soon.'

'I very much hope so.'

Anna departed, and May smiled broadly to herself as she and her rock-star friend made for the steps which led to the front door, her intention being to at least show him the sets, but on the way they encountered Maurine O'Connell, whose curiosity had by far got the better of her.

'So, what's this, May, why do we have the great Ashley Spears walking amongst us?'

'Ash has volunteered his services to write our film score, if everything can be agreed.'

'Really….? I mean, none of us knew about this, did we?'

'First I've heard of it as well,' said Ashley 'until May here decided it would be a good thing.'

'Well, that's amazing….I mean, what a brilliant thing it is.'

'That remains to be seen, just trying to get my head around the whole deal, so we're not there yet, but I'm sort of warming to the idea.'

May wondered how much warmth the presence of this young and beautiful woman had added to the matter, but decided to work her into the equation in any case.

'This, by the way, is Maurine O'Connell, who's sort of our leading lady.'

'Delighted, I'm sure.'

'So how much of this kind of thing have you done before?'

'None whatsoever, so if it comes off I'll be learning on the job, as it were.'

'Oh, well, I've never done a full-length feature film, either, or done any period work earlier than the 1960s, so I suppose we're all learning together.'

'Yeah, seems that way.'

'I was just going to show Ashley around.'

'Sure, well I won't keep you, but I'm really pleased to have met you, a legend has come amongst us. I was in white socks and gymslip when you were making the albums, but my dad's got them all, I'm sure, so I grew up listening to you.'

'That's good to hear, I think.'

Maurine smiled her naturally beautiful smile and left, and May carried on. It was testament to the courage and imagination of David Bates and Anna Merchant that the production hung so roundly on the performance of such a relatively untried and inexperienced actress as Maurine O'Connell, and now the soundtrack would perhaps be in the hands of someone who had never written a soundtrack before. The leap of faith continued, and became an ever wider chasm, it seemed, and there was an underlying sense amongst the production team that the film would either be a resounding success or a catastrophic failure, but having Ashley Spears in the mix would surely mitigate against the latter; at least, this was May's hope as they mounted the steps.

'I'm really pleased, Ash, that you decided to take this on, or will at least consider taking it on.'

'Sure, well, challenges were made to be risen to, and one day I might thank you for asking me, but you'll forgive me for deferring that moment for now.'

'Of course, consider yourself forgiven.'

During these days, the emotional landscape of Ross Farrier was a complex and fluid thing, both in regard to his private and working lives, the two having in any case to an extent now become enmeshed, and the enmeshing was a part of the complexity, and of the fluidity. Having, under the largely unwanted guidance of Fifi Fielding, done all that could be done to backdate the Manor House grounds by several hundred years, his working day had largely returned to its former patterns, of tending borders and cutting lawns. There was, however, something new to factor into his working day, which was that there was now a film being made at the Manor. For perhaps an hour or two in the morning, therefore, he would as a general rule have the gardens to himself, and during this time he would cut the lawns and tend the borders immediately surrounding the Manor, whilst he had access, and a peaceful working environment. By mid-morning, however, the trucks, cars and catering van began to arrive, bearing equipment, people and provision for the day's shooting, and thereafter chaos would ensue. People in period costume would singly or in groups walk the long driveway from the encampment in the wood, and the gardens would from then on be awash with technicians, and famous and not-so-famous actors and actresses, dressed as would be appropriate to Elizabethan England, and Ross would as far as was possible retire to more remote and isolated parts of the garden. So there was an inconvenience to the matter, but Ross would nevertheless watch with interest from afar as the day's filming proceeded, the proceedings carrying on until and well after the time that he packed away his tools at the day's end, and he made his way home. So, there was some good to the matter, but Ross knew well enough that the presence of the film crews and actors kept Abigail and the children away from the Manor, which as far as Ross was concerned was only a bad thing, and his frustration in this regard grew with each passing day. He would speak to Abi every evening, and each would be kept abreast of each other's respective days, which mainly consisted of the mundane, he attending to gardens and she attending to children, but there was one particular conversation, which actually occurred during his lunch break, which during the course of the rest of the day set an idea in his head, which would add an entirely different dimension to this particular day, if he could pull it off.

'Hi, how's life with you?'

'Oh, you know, the usual rollercoaster, cheese and tomato sandwiches today.'

'Gosh, life must be exciting.'

'You've no idea. Everything okay your end?'

'About the same, really, although there's an atmosphere, I don't know, Mike's been a bit off since Victoria was here, he's hardly speaking to me, or to the kids, it's weird. I mean Victoria was supposed to stay the night, I think, and then she just left, so something's going on, and Mike and Elin are going out this evening, which is unusual in itself, mid-week.'

'Well, something must be afoot then. Oh well, I daresay all will be revealed in the fullness of time.'

'Yes, I daresay.'

At the end of the working day Ross drove home, but he had by now decided that this evening would be different. He showered, spoke briefly with Ruby, cooked himself a light meal, and then instead of settling to an evening at home, he got back into his car, and set off on his journey.

Michael Tillington had also come to a decision during this day. He had much to discuss with Elin, and needed to be somewhere other than the place that they lived in order to do so. He was not sure why; perhaps such a particular conversation should be had in a more auspicious environment, where a different and distanced perspective could be had, but in any case, he booked a table at a quite nearby and quite salubrious restaurant, and ordered a taxi. On her return from work, and once she had showered and settled, he showed Elin the copies of the extracts from the diaries of Anne Tillington, which she duly and quickly read, and he explained from whence they had come, and what was their implication. Thus it was that by nine o'clock in the evening, they had eaten their first and main courses, drunk their first bottle of wine, and he had given his wife chapter and verse on all that had recently happened, and the nature of his present dilemma. Elin listened attentively, and took a moment to collect her thoughts before replying.
'So, Michael, let me reiterate. We are now working with the assumption that Nathaniel is not in fact your son, but is the son of a man called Percival, who was lover to Rose, and who lives in the village.'
'Yes, th....'
She raised her hand.
'Please let me continue. You do have a daughter, but she cannot inherit any title, and you are now of a mind that Nathaniel cannot or should not inherit, as you are as good as certain of his fatherhood. Although I feel sadness for Nathaniel, this I agree with, since it would in any case be illegal.'

'Everything's already illegal, and has been almost since the beginning.'

'Yes, perhaps, but I think it is not your place to take historical matters into consideration in this, we have only ancient writings to rely upon, which may or may not be accurate and truthful, but nothing can be proved either way, so these I think should not be taken into account. We are, however, in a position to verify your assumption as to Nathaniel, so this should be done before any final decision can be made, but let us assume that your assumption is correct.'

Michael drank his wine, and said nothing; already cold and calculated analysis and perspective had brought some order into his chaotic thoughts. Elin was after all a lawyer, whose profession had taught her to apply cold and calculated reason, and he was keen now that she continue.

'So, given that assumption, you are content to raise Nathaniel as if he were your own son, and are content that Percival will make no claim upon the child. Victoria has suggested that you, in other words we, should adopt her son, Henry, in order that he may in due course inherit your title, and I agree with her that subject to verification in this particular case, there is nothing in general law which says that this cannot happen. She has given her word that she will support Henry whatever happens, and whilst there would be no legal obligation to do so if the adoption went ahead, you are content to trust her in this, and take her word as binding. So, what this comes down to is whether and how you think that your entitlement should continue after your death, however that may be done. There may of course be a relative who by law would have legitimate claim to the title, but this would not be your wish. You love your sister, and you have affection for Henry, so there is nothing that I can see from an emotional perspective to prevent its happening. This is the horn of your dilemma, as I see it.'

He waited, but Elin seemed to have stopped, just as she was getting to the nub of the matter.

'Yes, well all of that is true, I suppose, so what the hell should I do, do you think?'

'Well, I believe the first thing that you should do is to ask your wife whether she has any objections in principle to adopting your sister's child.'

'Yes, well I would have done that, of course....'

'Go on, then.'

'What...?'

'Ask me, Michael.'

'Oh, right...Umm, Elin, would you have any objections in principle to adopting my sister's child?'

'No, I would not, provided that Victoria reiterates to me her commitment to fund Henry's professional childcare, education and so on, so that better clears your way to making your decision, does it not?'

'Yes, I suppose it does.'

'Well, then, the only thing that remains is for you to make your decision. Either the Lordship will end with you, or be given to an as yet unknown other, or we formerly and legally adopt Henry, these are your only options as the situation stands, and given your current feelings on the matter.'

'My feelings aren't going to change, Elin.'

'So be it then.'

Again she had stopped; clarification and academic advice were all very well, but Michael had hoped that her help would extend somewhat beyond the academic. All that she now did, however, was to study *'Today's Specials'* on the chalkboard.

'Tiramisu....'

'What...?'

'I would like tiramisu for dessert, and then I think coffee, don't you?'

'Right...Yes, of course, but do you have an opinion, as to what I should do? I mean I know nothing about adoption, how it works or how long it takes.'

'Well, this is not my area of expertise, but my understanding is that it can take up to six months, the process being application, assessment and approval, and there must be an adoption agency involved. In your case, of course, the adopter and parent of the child to be adopted are known to each other, which may simplify the process, but this would have to be looked into at the point of application by Victoria, and there would be a cost, of course, which I assume Victoria would bear.'

'About how much..?'

'Again that depends, but it could I believe be upwards of twenty thousand pounds.'

'I see, well, the money wouldn't be an issue under the circumstances, and if this were ever to go ahead by joint agreement then I suppose Victoria and I would split the cost, but the point is, should I even be considering it?'

'Yes, you asked for my opinion, and in fact it is very clear to me what you should do, but ultimately the decision will be yours, and you are currently under the influence of alcohol, which reduces inhibition and clouds rational thought.'

'But that's just the thing, isn't it? I mean none of this is *'rational'*, is it, it's just a series of cock-ups. Victoria had no intention of having a child in the first instance, I'm sure that Rose didn't intend to get pregnant, and even Percival I'm certain had no intention that any of this would happen, or that Rose would die, so it's all just one big accident, really, and one could argue that so what if the Lordship ends, or someone else gets it, it's just a title, after all, and makes precious little difference in any practical sense.'

'Except that you will also lose the Manor House and Estate to unknown others, which is no small consideration in itself, is it?'

'No, of course not... I mean you and I will live there whatever happens, it's all about what happens after that, isn't it. I mean the possibility exists that we could sell it during my lifetime to some American or Chinese billionaire, or let the National Trust take over the running of it.'

'Yes, these things would be possible, but would you wish any of them to happen?'

'Well, no, in a perfect world of course not.'

'Indeed, which as far as I can see also makes your decision easier, and I believe you are now beginning to understand that from now on you in fact have only your emotions to guide you. Mistakes have been made, of course, for that is the nature of people, but you can only address the situation as it now stands, and use the opportunities which have been presented to you as you best see fit. If Rose had not died then we would not be married, and if Victoria had not become pregnant or had terminated her pregnancy then there would be no Henry, but all of that is history, now, and need not be considered. It's now only about how you feel, Michael, and as well as I know you, I cannot guide you in this respect. Would you like to go outside for a cigarette?'

'What...? Yes, I would, actually.'

'Come on, then. In fact forget the Tiramisu, I suddenly find this atmosphere oppressive and feel the need for fresh air. Let's pay and go, shall we?'

She placed her napkin on the table, and stood up.

Abigail was about her ablutions, having settled the children for the night, when her telephone ringtone sounded, and it was Ross.

'Hi...'

'*Hi...*'

'This is an unusual time for you to 'phone.'

'Ay, well it's an unusual evening, I'm not at home.'
'Where are you?'
'I'm outside your front door.'
'What...? What do you mean you're outside my front door?'
'Well, I don't know how else to put it, there's a pile of building materials and an ancient Wisteria up the wall, which badly needs a prune, by the way.'
'But...I mean you can't just turn up like this.'
'I just did, and there's no rule about not having visitors, is there?'
'Well, no, but you're not a visitor, are you, you're a young man, and I'm not sure I'm allowed to entertain young men, especially ones who just turn up out of nowhere in the dead of night with no prior notice.'
'I didn't come from nowhere, and it's...eight forty-five. Don't tell me I'm going to have to climb the Wisteria to your bedroom window.'
'I'm 'round the back, you'd end up in the wrong bedroom. Oh, bloody hell, hang on a minute.'

She dressed quickly in knickers and a long, baggy T-shirt which she wore for sleeping, and padded downstairs to the front door.

'You'd better come up.'

They ascended the stairs to her small lounge next to her bedroom, in which the children were sound asleep; she closed the door, and they spoke quietly.

'What are you doing, you mad fool?'
'I've come to see you, I miss you.'
'Yes, I get that, and I miss you, too, but....I mean, they're out for the evening.'
'I know, you said, what time did they go out?'
'About an hour ago, I think.'
'And they've gone for a meal, right, or whatever, so they won't be back before eleven, so that gives us a couple of hours, I'll be gone before they get home.'

'But why didn't you 'phone?'

'Because you'd have told me not to come...'

'Yes, well, there's a reason for that....Where did you park?'

'Down the road a bit, don't worry, I've covered my tracks.'

'Oh good grief....Just when I get us all sorted out at the Manor House, you do this to me, and I'm not even dressed.'

'Oh, yeah, you know I hadn't noticed.'

'Liar...I was just going to bed with a good book.'

'Don't let me stop you, I can read to you if you want.'

'We can't...I mean we can't go to bed, not with the children there.'

'No, of course we can't, I was kidding. Look, I don't care what we do, I just wanted to see you, that's all. We can drink tea and discuss the meaning of life if you want.'

'I just haven't had time to think all of this through. You can't be seen to have been here, I mean we can't go downstairs and act normal, like you, the Manor House gardener, just happened to turn up on the one night that they go out, and anyway Victoria knows about us, so maybe Michael does, too, and this isn't proper.'

'That's why I'll leave, even an hour with you will be worth it, and if we have to stay here that's fine with me. Look, I'll go now if you want, I came here to see you, so mission accomplished, and I don't want to get you into trouble, that was never my intention.'

'Who said I wanted you to go, we'll just have to be quiet, that's all.'

'Sure, okay, so what shall we do, then?'

'Well, for a start you can come here and give me a kiss, you wild and impetuous boy.'

'That might not be proper.'

'Who said I wanted proper, either. Christ, you get me into all sorts of trouble. I'm not pleased with you, and I don't condone your behaviour, so don't think that I do.'

'Fair enough, you can tell me off tomorrow.'

Earlier this day, Victoria had arrived home from London at about the usual time, and had negotiated her way through the now usual chaotic activity outside her home. Amongst those present was Maurine O'Connell, who was sitting on the steps of the Manor House, drinking coffee from a plastic cup, but otherwise looking fine indeed in her period costume.

'Hi, Victoria…'

Victoria smiled, and not just at the person herself, but what she was doing, or rather where she was doing it.

'Hello…That's funny, where you're sitting, that's my step.'

'What…?'

'It's where I sit, and have done since I was a child.'

'Oh, I'm sorry….'

'Don't be, you can keep it warm for me. So how's everything been going today?'

'Well, you know, we're making progress, I think. I'm done for the day, anyway, so I'll be heading home shortly, well as good as home gets at the moment, anyway.'

'Okay, well, I'll see you then.'

'Sure…'

Victoria had almost made the front door, but for some reason she turned her head, at the same time that Maurine did the same.

'It's a very nice step.'

They smiled.

'Yes, it is, isn't it…'

'Are you doing anything this evening?'

'Nothing in particular, why?'

'You could come and see me, if you wanted.'

'Oh, okay, I'll do that.'

'I don't recommend the food, but I'll be there, if you want.'

'I'll come after supper, then.'

'Good, I'll look forward to it, I could do with talking to someone who isn't an actor.'

A final parting smile, and Victoria was home, with new plans for the hours ahead.

Outside the air was cool as they awaited their taxi; Michael lit a cigarette, and both were silent for a moment. At this time of the night there was only occasional vehicular traffic on this minor road.

'You think I should do it, don't you?'

'What do I think you should do, Michael?'

'You think we should adopt Henry, and that I should somehow keep this bloody mess of a Lordship going.'

'Well, I know what a fuss you English people make of your Lordships, and Dukedoms, and so on. As a Norwegian I think the whole thing is ridiculous in any modern, democratic society, but we live in England, and you are an Englishman, and if you wish for my opinion, then what I think is this, that if you don't do it then you will live to regret not having done it.'

He exhaled, and a light pall of smoke drifted away on the cool, English air.

'Is that what you think?'

'Yes, that is what I think.'

'I don't know, Elin, I mean I wonder, you know, what my sister's motivations are in all of this. She says she isn't doing it for Henry, and I believe her, I think, but there's still a part of me which thinks I should just let the natural order of things be, and forget the whole thing. Just somehow explain one day to Nathaniel why he can't be Lord of the Manor and leave it at that.'

'Yes, that is one option, of course.'

'I mean who's to say that Henry will even want the bloody Lordship, he can hardly speak for himself, can he? And it could all end up in disaster, you know, if we do as Victoria says, I mean she's hardly got a good track record for making good decisions.'

'That may be true, but the decision is yours, not hers.'

'Yeah, I suppose. She says that she's doing it for me, but I wonder whether it's not the other way around, I just can't work that one out. I mean sure, as you say, I love my sister, and I know what she wants me to do, but it's not that straightforward, is it?'

'No, of course not...'

'Anyway, this is hardly an auspicious place to decide the future of my family, outside a restaurant having a fag, but there it is, such is the nature of things, and I suppose the world will keep turning, whatever I do.'

'Yes, I daresay it will.'

'And you're right, the whole thing is bloody ridiculous. I'll 'phone Victoria in the morning, I suppose. If I do, you know, go ahead with it, father and mother must never know.'

'If that's what you think best.'

'Dad's not been well lately, I mean it's nothing serious, I don't think, but he certainly doesn't need this, I'm sure he only agreed to have the film made to please Victoria. So many secrets....'

'Indeed....'

''twas ever thus, it seems, so why should I go against ancient family traditions, is one way to look at it. Christ, what a mess, really, but thank you, Elin, I really was in a dilemma, both horns, as it happens, and I suppose I still am, but I needed your input.'

'Yes, I know you did.'

'He'd be your son, too, to the outside world you'd be mother to a future Lord, or not, but you really are okay, whatever I decide?'

'Yes, Michael, I'm fine, and I will support you, either way. I've known your family for a long time, and have always held affection and respect for your parents, and now I love you, and you have always accepted without question that we will not have children, for which I am grateful, so I will not discourage you from continuing your family name, if that is in the end what you wish to do, and however that may be done, it would be wrong of me to do so.'

'None of this is of your making, Elin, I mean nobody blames you for not wanting to have our children, you understand that, don't you?'

'Of course...'

'Right, well then, so long as that's clear. I mean I haven't decided even now, or maybe I have, I don't know, but let's go home and get drunk, shall we?'

'We have work tomorrow.'

'Right now I don't care,to be honest.'

'Well, I suppose under the circumstances we could make an exception, just this once.'

Victoria walked to the encampment during the mid-evening; this time she did not take Prince and Bathsheba, and she did not return to the Manor House until early the following morning, in time to prepare herself for her day's work, and to catch her train. She had come with no expectations, but the expectations were there to be had, had she taken notice of them, and in her current state of distraction, when her mind was in truth quite elsewhere, her instinctive need to find comfort and perhaps a quite different kind of distraction with another had made the short journey with her. The fictitious daughter of the household and the actual daughter of the household had reached an understanding, and had by dawn of the next day given fulfilment to their understanding.

Ross and Abigail had agreed that Ross could stay until ten-thirty, which would leave a sufficient margin of safety for him to quietly disappear before her employers returned. Their well-laid plans, however, were undone by the cancellation of Tiramisu, and a few minutes before the appointed departure time, they heard the sound of the front door of Glebe House being opened and then closed, and now their hushed voices became whispers.

'Shit, their home early….Now what do we do?'

'Do they come and check on you or the kids?'

'Well no, I mean not usually, but this hasn't happened very often.'

For a moment the situation and the tension which it engendered got the better of Abigail, and she put her hand to her mouth in an attempt to repress irrepressible laughter, in which she was only partially successful, and she whispered through her laughter.

'Stop laughing, it isn't funny.'

'It's not me who's laughing. Looks like I'm stuck here 'til they go to bed. We'll have to find some quiet activities for a bit. Where do they sleep?'

'In the next room, unfortunately...'

A fact which only served to set the young lady off again, and laughter can at times be infectious, so now they both laughed quietly, which during its duration did not serve to aid their concealment. They listened as Michael and Elin used the bathroom, but Michael and Elin had much to discuss, and descended the stairs to the dining room for their discussion, and their alcohol, and it was well past the hour of midnight before Abigail and Ross heard sounds from the next room, which became sounds of people making love.

'Now might be a good time for me to leave, don't you think?'

'No, wait 'til they're asleep.'

'This could take ages.'

Try as she may, Abigail could not but see the situation as being extremely funny, and her ill-suppressed laughter commenced once again.

'I mean do they usually take a long time about it?'

'Sometimes, it depends...'

'And is she always this vocal?'

'Shhhh, shut up, or you'll get me going again.'

Going, however, she already was, and it was not until a little after two o'clock, following a decent span of time during which no further sound emanated from behind the ancient wall, that they kissed goodnight.

'Some of the stairs creek, and be quiet closing the door.'

Ross removed his shoes and walked quietly through the house, where fortunately a light was always left on downstairs at night. He successfully and quietly negotiated the front door, put his shoes on, and within a few more minutes he was in the car and on his way. Shortly thereafter messages began to appear on his 'phone.

'They didn't wake up. Don't ever do that again, I'm still cross with you.'

'I'm glad you came, though.'

'No I'm not, what am I saying, you'll get me hung one of these days.'

'You are a bad man.'

'Next time they go out I'm not telling you.'

'Well maybe I will.'

'I love you, even though you don't deserve it.'

'Drive safely.'

Ross smiled to himself as the miles melted away on the empty roads. He would get little sleep tonight, but of that he cared not in the least, he was in love, and the world was a good place to be.

Victoria's last thoughts as she fell into sleep in the arms of her new-found lover were of her brother. She had heard nothing from him since her departure from Glebe House, and she could have no idea as to what he was thinking, or doing. Victoria had died once, at her own hands, and it was only by pure chance that she was alive today. Had Reginald not chosen that moment to knock on her door, or had not looked through her window, she would have remained dead, a chance in thousands, millions, perhaps, had saved her. She was in a way literally living life after death, and since her reprieve she had held an underlying belief that nothing really mattered as it once had, not even the continuation of the Tillington dynasty, so she would let her brother decide as he may. In any case she could do or say no more, and the future of her family and of her son now rested in Michael's hands, and perhaps in the hands of Elin, who in her ever-practical way would no doubt have her own views on the matter. She knew her brother well, and Elin less well, and there was little point in speculating; the die had been cast, and at that moment she had no reliable sense or idea as to where it would fall.

Chapter 22. A Greater History

Gwendolyn awoke in the half-light of the early morning, a time when to switch on the bedside lamp was more a matter of habit than necessity, but she switched it on nonetheless. Reginald was not abed, but rather was looking outwards somewhat furtively between the bedroom curtains. He wore his dressing gown over his pyjamas, and as he now paced the room she noted that he was wearing his extremely shiny outdoor shoes over bare feet, the shoes catching the first rays of morning sun as he walked, and looking incongruous with the rest of his attire. It took a moment for her to register the incongruity, and to find her first words of the day, which entered the world through a yawn.

'Good morning Reginald, what are you doing…And where are your slippers?'

'Yes, good morning, my slippers are by the front door, where I left them.'

'I see…Well actually I don't see, and again, what are you doing?'

'The thing is, there's someone on the village Green.'

'Oh, well that's not so unusual, is it someone we know?'

'No, I don't believe I've ever seen the young lady before.'

'So is she walking a dog or something?'

'No, in fact she isn't walking anywhere, she's lying down.'

In her now somewhat increased state of awareness she noted that his shoes were in fact wet above the soles, indicating that the wetness had come from below rather than above, as if he had walked across dewy grass.

'Reginald, have you been out on the village Green dressed like that?'

'Yes.'

Gwendolyn was by now well accustomed to Reginald's sometimes eccentric behaviour, but here was something new, and she sat up in bed, the better to address the situation.

'So is she asleep, the young lady I mean, and how did you even know she was there?'

'I glanced through the curtains having visited the bathroom. It was almost dark but I saw something, and thought it better to investigate as quickly as possible, so I went out.'

She tried to assess his state of mind; he did not appear agitated, although something was surely amiss, and her general impression was that he was contemplative, and his next words were indeed thoughtful.

'I mean I wouldn't mind so much, but this is not the first time that this has happened.'

'The first time that what has happened..?'

'There was the young man in the stream, and Victoria Tillington, although Victoria Tillington is alive now, of course.'

'Reginald will you please stop talking in riddles and explain what has happened.'

'I gave her a gentle nudge, the young lady, I mean, and then a somewhat less gentle nudge, but there can be no doubt, the young lady is unfortunately dead.'

On the morning prior to Reginald's discovery, Victoria had been at the gallery when she had received a message on her telephone.

'Vics, 'phone me when you're free.'

She had half an hour before a group of French students were due to come under her tutelage, she knew her subject well and needed no preparation, so she 'phoned her brother immediately.

'Hello Mike.'

'Yes, hello Vics, you may as well know that I believe I have made my decision, with Elin, of course, at least I've reached a point where I'm prepared to discuss the matter further.'

'I see...'

'Yes, we have decided that all things being equal, we are willing to seriously consider going ahead with what we talked about. We will need a meeting, of course, and it had better be here, so let me know when you can next come to Glebe House.'

'Oh, right....Well I'm not working tomorrow, so I could come this evening if that suits.'

'Elin will need certain assurances, of course, so it's by no means cut and dried yet, but, well, we can discuss everything this evening.'

'Of course, I'll get there as soon as I can, and I expect I'll stay the night this time.'

'As you wish, we'll prepare supper for three in any case.'

'Thank you, Mike, for letting me know, and so quickly...'

'Yes, well, until tonight then.'

There was a place toward the back of the gallery, no more than a small, internal yard, really, where deliveries were taken and which was open to the sky, where she and others would go on occasion to smoke cigarettes during the working day, and she had time. She sat down on the sort of makeshift bench, lit her cigarette, and considered. So it was to be done, then, and the part of her which had wished or hoped that Michael would reject her proposal out of hand could be consigned to a part of this particular history. She would give her son away to her brother, which would be the first step in a process which might in time see Henry inherit a Lordship, with all that this would mean for his future, and the future of her family, and the question which she now asked herself for the hundredth time came to the forefront of her thoughts again. Were they doing the right thing? Was this some ill-conceived plan, which would go badly wrong somehow as the two boys grew into adolescence, or adulthood? How in the course of time would Nathaniel feel about having his rightful inheritance, which was in all probability not his rightful inheritance, taken from him by a brother with whom he shared no blood ties whatsoever, each having a different mother, and a different father. Henry had been born out of a single night of wanton passion, with a father who he would never know, because Victoria herself could not tell him who his father was, and Nathaniel was born of the love between his mother, Rose, and a man whom he would perhaps and even probably never meet, for how could such a meeting happen? How much of the truth of it all would they need to keep from both of them in order to see this done, and in order that they would not suffer in the end for the actions of their respective parents? Her brother would have his doubts too, she was certain, and now in the light of the likelihood that she and Michael would go ahead with the idea, which had been entirely and only her idea, Victoria felt again and more strongly the pangs of uncertainty, and guilt for things not yet done, with which she had been living these past days. She loved her brother, and knew that he loved her, and yet things had changed between them, now, perhaps forever, and anyway not for the better, however things may go from here. From now on they would be enveloped in matters legal, and cold, and calculated, Nathaniel's hair, or blood, or saliva would be tested as if he were some laboratory animal, to see if he had the right genes, or the wrong genes, and all feelings of warmth between brother and sister would be set aside in order to achieve their now apparently mutual ambition, the result of which neither could foretell. Perhaps in time they would find their way back to one another, and would laugh together about their current circumstances, and how they had made so much of such a thing, and of her dishonesty, but for now the thing which would likely unite them in common cause would at one and the same time cause a rift between them, which neither would be able to cross, at least for the foreseeable future.

There was an old, rusting tin can, which was used by all for butt-ends of cigarettes, and into which she placed her cigarette; such a small, dirty and uncouth thing in the midst of such great art; such a human, every day object, a thing of the absolute present, amongst so much history. All of the great artists whose works now hung in echoing halls were dead, now, and who now knew the sordid, vulgar, secret parts of their lives, hidden now forever behind canvasses upon which they had painted their lasting legacy? Who knew their dark thoughts, brushed away with oils and watercolours, and how much guilt they had felt for their actions when they had been a part of the unending mess which was humanity, a thing of which Victoria now felt so much a part? Perhaps, after all, the end to all of this would justify the means, if by such means the Lordship could continue, and her brother's legacy remain within their close family for future generations. At least this was Victoria's hope as she stood up, put all other thoughts aside, and made ready to impart such knowledge as she had of the paintings which were daily a part of her working life, even if in truth she knew so little of the painters. Aspects of their lives may be known and documented, and history may tell so much about their lives, but it was after all only so much.

On a more ordinary day, the folk who now lived in the houses which for so long had stood along two sides of the village Green, would awaken and rise at their various and natural times. Lights would perhaps be switched on, alarms turned off, clothes would be found and bathrooms visited, and a new day would begin. On this early morning, however, the process was interrupted by the presence of a police vehicle, which on Reginald's instigation had arrived on the main road, and which momentarily and sporadically sent a blue beam of light across ancient walls and leaded windows, and in the still dim light began an awakening process ahead of its usual time. People arose and peered from behind curtains, and thereafter some dressed quickly, the better to be prepared for this unusual event, and some saw fit to emerge from their houses to see what may be seen. That which they saw was a now quite visible human form, which lay about mid-way between the road and the cricket square, and which was now being cordoned off by two policemen with lurid, plastic tape, at a distance of about five metres on all sides, which was all that could be done for now. Closer inspection revealed that the form was without doubt female, who was slim of build with short, mid-brown hair, who lay face-down on the grass, and was wearing denim trousers and a casual, beige top, the only notable aspect of her attire being that she wore no shoes. Reginald, who was by now fully dressed, stood at a respectful distance from the clearly deceased, and he now became the focal point for those who had come to see.

'What's going on then, Reginald?'

This was Nigel Hollyman, landlord of the Dog and Bottle public house, who was next on the scene. The question was somewhat academic, since that which was going on was really quite obvious, but something had to be said, and conversation begun.

'I noticed that there was a dead lady on the Green, and called the police.'

'Christ...I don't recognise her, I don't think she's from the village, at least she's nobody I've ever seen, as far as I can tell from the back of her head.'

'No, I don't believe I know her, either.'

'Looks like she's been there for a few hours...'

'How can you tell?'

'You can see where the police have been walking by the footprints in the dew, and she was probably dragged or carried here, probably from the main road, and there are no drag-marks, or other footprints. She must have ended up here before the dew formed.'

'Yes, and it's unlikely that she would have walked here barefoot.'

'Indeed…Could be a hit and run road accident, but why move the body, or take her shoes off, and there are no obvious signs of injury.'

'Yes, apart from being dead she looks quite well.'

By now Peter Shortbody had joined them; he had care of Bronwyn and Elizabeth, and had left them at home to guard their young sensibilities against such a scene, and Alice Turner now stood beside him.

'Dear me, poor girl, whoever she is.'

'Yes, I left the girls at home.'

'Of course….'

Within a quite short space of time, and despite the endeavours of the two policemen to keep the scene clear, a small crowd had gathered around the cordoned-off area, and even a few inquisitive drivers and riders had interrupted their journeys to see what was happening. An ambulance now arrived, and the next person to break the cordon was a quite young lady, dressed in a full body-suit and hood, who everyone agreed was a pathologist, such as they had seen innumerable times on their television screens, but never in real life. Photographs were taken, a careful inspection of the body was undertaken where it lay, and pockets were searched, at which point it became clear that the young lady carried nothing about her person which would aid identification, nor any keys, or wallet. This process having been completed, the pathologist gave instruction that the body be removed, and two medics moved the young lady carefully onto a stretcher, covered her over in her entirety, and moved her to the ambulance. For a brief moment her face had been uncovered, and in her death-stare she was it seemed still a stranger to all; none of the assembled crowd recognised her. By degrees the crowd began to disperse, and in the end there was no trace of her, save a place of dry grass, where the dew had not formed in the early hours of this particular morning, when those who resided around the village Green had had their daily rituals untimely interrupted.

'Victoria, can you spare a few moments for your father?'

It is now the early evening, and Victoria had arrived home from London, and was preparing herself for a swift departure to Glebe House, when she had encountered her father in the downstairs hallway. This was therefore not a convenient time, far from it, but this was her father, and she had been summoned.

'Yes….Yes, of course, Papa.'

'Let's to my study, shall we?'

They walked to the small room below the stairs, which had long been her father's refuge from the world, and they took their accustomed seats, he behind his grand desk, which in truth took up most of the room, and she before it.

'So, to where are you off in such an apparent hurry?'

'I'm going to Glebe House for the evening, and probably the night.'

'I see, this is all rather spontaneous, is it not?'

'Yes, well, I should see Henry sometimes whilst he's away.'

'Indeed, but that does not really explain the spontaneity, I'm sure you will have been cooked for.'

'I told Mama I wouldn't be eating this evening.'

'Yes, I know, and it was this which alerted me to your imminent departure, and it's laudable, of course, that you should want to see your son, but the suddenness of the arrival of your maternal instinct is the thing, when he's here you barely see him.'

Which was true, and already this interview had become difficult.

'That isn't true, I see him every day.'

'Yes, well I'm sure it's difficult to avoid him entirely, and all things are relative, I suppose, but the point is made.'

'Yes, well, I decided that since I'm not working tomorrow, I should go, and I'm sorry if it's inconvenient.'

'The inconvenience of it isn't the point either, and you are of course free to come and go as you see fit, but your general demeanour of late has led me to believe that something beyond the usual is afoot, and your brother has been particularly accommodating on his visits here, which tends to raise one's suspicions.'

'Has he, I hadn't noticed.'

'No, well, take my word that it is the case. I believe you two are hatching something, as was the case when you contrived to have Henry and Nathaniel live together at Glebe House, but this I think is something different.'

'They're living at Glebe House because of the filming.'

'Oh come, Victoria, that may now be a convenient excuse, but it is by no means the whole thing, is it? I may not be as sharp as I once was, but I have not entirely lost my faculties.'

'No, of course you haven't, but....Well, do you think it's a bad thing that they are together?'

'No, I don't, but I don't understand why the subterfuge. I am not parent to either child, of course, so my influence is once removed, but these are family matters, and you are, after all, living under my roof, as it were, as are the two children as a general rule, so at least a more open dialogue would be appropriate, don't you think?'

Her father was cross with her, and his own general demeanour suggested that he was not happy in a more general sense. He had never complained about the filming, but Victoria was sure that it must be influential upon his state of being, and he had not been well lately; she had brought this upon him, and upon all of them, and as had so often been the case, when she had acted counter to his wishes, her heart went out to him. That Henry and Nathaniel should stay together was something which in her soul she had known that he would in the end accept, but matters had moved so far beyond that now, and the subterfuge gone so much deeper. The mere possibility that Henry, and not Nathaniel, would one day be Lord of the Manor was something he could not know, not yet, with so much more going on, and perhaps never, but the desire to tell him everything, that Nathaniel was not Michael's son, and that she had such plans now for Henry, her bastard child, for a moment threatened to get the better of her. When she had done stupid and thoughtless things during her younger years, and they had fought with each other, in the end her father's wisdom had always prevailed, and she had always in the end however grudgingly seen the error of her ways, and now she and Michael were about to embark upon something so uncertain in its eventual consequence, that her wish to now seek her father's wisdom prior to the embarkation was all but overwhelming. He would know what to do, and whether that which she and Michael would soon discuss was sheer, misguided folly, for in truth there was no guidance, and in an instant he could remove all doubt, one way or the other, but it was too late for that, now, for at one and the same time she knew that she could not betray her brother. In the end the decision as to whether and how the Tillington Lordship should continue beyond his lifetime must be Michael's, however uncertain that decision may be, and it was right that this was so. Her father would pass his legacy on to his son, he had done his part, and Michael's time was coming, and he must be the one to decide the future, knowing that which he now knew of the history of their family. Her musings had for a moment taken Victoria away from the here and now, and her momentary silence had been too long.

'Victoria, my dear, are you still with us?'

'What....? Yes, Papa, I'm sorry.'

'Good, for a moment there I thought we'd lost you entirely.'

No, she could not tell him, but she must allow him something, albeit a so much lesser thing.

'It's not you, Papa.'

'What do you mean?'

'It's true that Michael and I have decided that Henry and Nathaniel should stay together, and that they should live sometimes at Glebe House, everyone including Elin is agreed upon that, and Abi is happy it seems with whatever arrangements are made, but we were unsure how mother would react to the idea, that was all.'

'I see, well if that's all it is then we are making much out of not very much, and I thank you for finally letting me in on the secret.'

'We just didn't want there to be any awkwardness between you and mother.'

'Well then I also thank you for your consideration, but you should have told me.'

'Yes, of course, I know.'

'I have been married to your mother for a long time, Victoria, and there are ways that this could have been done which would have negated any need for secrecy.'

'Yes, I'm sorry.'

'Well then, let's say no more about it for now, and I will think on that which we have discussed. Anyway you should be on your way, but in future I'd be pleased if you would keep me in the loop, as the saying goes, pertaining to matters familial.'

'Okay, I'll try.'

'Good, off you go, then, but before you go, we missed you last night, and wondered about your absence. You were missing but your car was not, so you must have walked to and from wherever you went. Is anything amiss?'

'No...No, nothing's amiss. I have....I have become friendly with one of the actors, and stayed at the encampment for the night, that's all.'

'I see, and I had assumed as much, which is why we didn't send out a search party. May I know with which actor in particular you have become friendly?'

'It's Maurine O'Connell, actually.'

'Our leading lady, and daughter to his temporary Lordship....Well, one is glad that you have set your sights high, I would fight shy of approving any dalliance with such as a chambermaid, or anyone of otherwise lowly status.'

He smiled his wry smile, and the smile was returned.

'Thank you, father, for your understanding.'

'I have also been a father for a long time, Victoria, and have endeavoured to always understand my offspring, although I confess I have been hard put to it at times, but such are the trials of fatherhood. Anyway, you should be going, and I'm to a warm bath and bed, a weariness has of a sudden come upon me, which I confess has become a more frequent occurrence of late, and there appears to be no filming this evening, so one must make the most of the peace and quiet whilst one has it.'

'So...I mean, how are you feeling, generally speaking?'

'No worse, I suppose, although I also suppose that one instinctively tends to err on the positive side in such matters. The doctors issue me with ever-increasing amounts of tablets, and your mother feeds me ever-increasing amounts of lettuce, and all manner of that which she calls *'health foods'* so I suppose everyone is doing their best. One has perhaps eaten more salad and certainly taken more tablets in the past year than in the rest of one's years combined, so we shall see, but one is not overly hopeful that any changes from here on will be for the better.'

'Well, I for one will continue to hope.'

'I know you will, my dear, and for that I also thank you. Whether it be sooner or later, it will in time be Michael's turn to pick up the mantle and take over the running of this decaying edifice of a house, and I am at least glad that you and he are getting along, he will need you and your support when the time comes.'

'Yes, well he will have that....'

'And in the longer run of course there will be Nathaniel, so one must as always count one's blessings, and one will leave this world with the knowledge that all will be well, for two generations at least.'

Had his gentle and thoughtful words been designed to further unsettle Victoria's already unsettled soul, they could not have done so with greater effect, and it was as much as she could do now to prevent tears welling up in her eyes, and this meeting must end before her resolve lessened still further, and she gave in to her better instincts. Instead she gathered herself, stood up and walked around the table, and kissed her father's forehead.

'Bless you, dear father, I'll see you sometime tomorrow.'

'Indeed, go forth and hatch your plots, and give the little ones a hug from me. One may have skipped a generation in terms of showing very much affection for one's family, something which I have come to deeply regret in my dotage, but I do miss their presence about the place.'

'They'll be back soon, I'm sure, and I always knew that you loved me, really, at least since I was old enough to know and understand such things.'

A smile was again given and returned, and she had almost reached the door.

'You will have missed a bit of a to-do this early morning in the village, apparently the body of a recently deceased young woman was discovered on the Green.'

'A young woman....?'

'Yes, the police light was clearly visible from the Manor, but you would perhaps not have seen it from the woods or on your walk home.'

Victoria now felt an unpleasant heat rising from the pit of her stomach, and now she looked for words.

'Has she....Has the body been identified?'

'I don't know, such intelligence as Molly has been able to glean does not extend that far, but no doubt all will be revealed in time.'

'Yes…Yes, I'm sure. Well, goodnight then, Papa.'

'Goodnight Victoria, safe journeys…'

Victoria quickly collected some clothes and toiletries into an overnight bag, and left the Manor, glancing in the direction of the village as she descended the steps. A young woman, but it could not be, could it? Someone would have 'phoned her, Percival would have 'phoned her, surely, if he had been on the scene, but it had been in the early morning, so perhaps he had not. She was already running late, and had the drive ahead, but she could not leave until she had gleaned more information, and put her mind at rest. She sat in her car for a moment, and considered whether a detour to the village would be the best way, but that would make her still more late. She steadied her breathing, started her car, and reached for her telephone as she drove the driveway to the Manor House gates.

The first that either Keith or Meadow knew of the incident on the Green was via Will Tucker, who had passed by in his Land Rover on the way to picking Keith up for the day's work, as was now their daily custom. Will could offer nothing by way of information other than the fact that there was a police presence, that door-to-door enquiries were being made around the Green, and that a body had been found. The situation had not changed when a few minutes later they passed the Green together on their way to Glebe House and their day's work, but Meadow left the bus somewhat earlier than was usual. By now the ambulance had departed, and the congregation had largely dispersed, but there were now two police cars parked on the main road. She entered the premises of the delicatessen via the side passage and back door, and went in search of Rebecca, but of her and Florence she found no sign. She went to the workshop, Rebecca often set to work early, but the potting wheel stood silent and redundant, and the upstairs living and sleeping room was empty, there was nobody. For a moment her worst fears, that the body had been that of Rebecca, came to the fore again, but surely had it been her someone would have known, and Will had been quite clear that the body was unidentified, and where was Florence? It was not until she entered the delicatessen through the back door that she saw the note, which had been left on the counter; in Rebecca's all but illegible scrawl had been written;

'Meadow, we've gone away, perhaps for a few days, I apologise for lack of notice, I'll see you soon, R.'

So, what was the implication, then; a dead body on the village Green and Rebecca gone, and Meadow tried her best not to make a connection between the two. She had killed before, but surely not now, and not like this. Rebecca was in danger, but a single, female body did not fit somehow with those who were seeking her. Her musings were interrupted by the sight of a police officer at the front door, which she unlocked, and she invited entry, having first hidden the note under the counter, and the wind chimes sounded a note of caution as the quite young man crossed the threshold.

'Good morning, madam.'
'Good morning officer.'
'Do I take it that you are the proprietor?'
'Yes, I am.'

'I'm sure you are aware that the body of a deceased young woman was found on the village Green early this morning.'

'Yes, I'm aware of that.'

'We're just doing house to house, see if anyone saw anything.'

'Well, I can't help, I'm afraid, I've just arrived here.'

'Indeed, I saw you arrive….Does anyone else live here?'

'There's nobody else in residence at the moment.'

'I see, well, if you could give me your name and home address…'

'Of course...'

She complied, having to explain that the bus had no address as such, but she could be found and contacted here, and shortly thereafter the officer departed, having given her a somewhat uncertain look, the wind chimes sounding relieved as he left. She had lied, in a way, although there was no lie in her actual words; there was nobody here but her. The untruth, for such did she prefer to call it, had been instinctive, and without sound explanation, other than that she wished to speak with Rebecca before revealing the fact of her living here to anybody, even to and perhaps especially to a police officer. The fact of her leaving with her child at some uncertain time since yesterday afternoon, when Meadow had last seen her, and the death of the young woman was surely coincidence, but as with so much regarding the affairs of her extraordinary and secret tenant, nothing was certain, and nothing could be taken for granted. Meadow went about preparing her shop for the day's trading; she would 'phone Keith later in the day, although for now there was really nothing new to say. So, more death, however it might eventually be explained; a young woman had died, perhaps through something as innocent as natural causes, but she had worn no shoes, so what of that? A signature, surely, from her killer, to tell the world that this was no natural death, and in her most wild imaginings, Meadow imagined that a witch had this morning lain dead on the village Green.

Charlotte was about her morning exercise and meditation routine when the call came through on the 'phone of which only the inner circle knew the number, so she gathered herself, caught her breath and answered the call.

'Hi Sophia…'

'Yes, good morning Charlotte, I think you should be aware that something happened in the village this morning.'

'Oh yes, what was that?'

'The body of a young woman was found on the Green, she must have died sometime during the night. I mean it might be nothing to do with anything, of course, but anyway, there it is.'

'Has she been identified?'

'No, not as far as I know, and nobody from the village seems to have known her….I mean the obvious thought is that it could have been Rebecca, but I don't think so, somebody would surely have recognised her.'

'So you didn't see the body yourself?'

'No…Thing is, I know you put me in the village to keep an eye on things, but this morning of all mornings I overslept, the body was gone by the time I got my act together, and I didn't have long to find anything out. I'm on my way to work now, and I'm running late.'

'I see…Well, thanks for letting me know. So I assume you've not seen Rebecca recently?'

'No, well other than lights on over the delicatessen, and I'm sure they were on last evening, which is the last indication I have of her, but she wasn't on the Green this morning, not alive, anyway, and I really don't think it was her, the dead person I mean.'

'Okay…Okay, well thank you for letting me know.'

'Of course I'll….out as much as I….and keep you…to date.'

'You're breaking up, Sophia.'

The signal was lost, and the call ended. Charlotte cut short her exercise and made for the shower, after which she made tea, which she took into her back garden, where she sat in the quite pleasant morning, although the sky was becoming overcast, and rain threatened. At this time of year the garden looked particularly unkempt and out of control; Charlotte was no gardener, but the woodland threatened to take over completely, and she should get down to some quite heavy cutting back at the end of the growing season. So, a young woman had died, and nothing very much could be gleaned from this until Sophia was able to provide more intelligence, but it was something to consider. In terms of the village, Sophia was not even supposed to know that Rebecca was living there, and there had been no contact between them, but perhaps it was time now for that to change. Sophia was indeed the eyes and ears of the coven in the village, but Sophia was Sophia, and she had found the love of a good man, and a job which she enjoyed, and was less effective as a spy than Charlotte might have hoped, and less dedicated to the coven than she had once been. Perhaps it was time, therefore, for Charlotte to be more proactive in terms of Rebecca's situation; she had not seen or heard from her since her visit here with Percival, so perhaps she should go herself, and speak with Meadow, and Percival, and Rebecca, of course. The sect, of which Charlotte was now a member, were looking for Rebecca, but her instinct told her that this incident was unrelated to any of that. Had the young woman perhaps been a witch, for the witches of Farthing's Well were also after Rebecca's blood, but that did not ring true either; had Rebecca killed again she would not have left the body to incriminate herself, Rebecca was far more clever than that. And yet, unless this had been some accident or natural death, someone had killed the young woman, and such things did not happen without reason. Since the death of the mother, Charlotte had taken it upon herself to oversee this particular chapter in the long history of her coven, and one thing about which she was certain was that the chapter had not been written yet in its entirety, and likely not by a long way. She finished her tea, and went about the rest of her day, with an increasing sense that something had just occurred which would be written of, when the writer knew what to write.

Victoria arrived at Glebe House only a little later than she had anticipated, and found her brother and Elin seated on makeshift chairs in the garden, if such it could yet be called, to the front of the house, where Abigail was amusing her two charges with ballgames as best she could amongst the building materials and debris. This was all as she might have expected, but that which she did not expect was that here also was a third child, who stood at a distance next to Michael and looked upon the two boys and now at the newcomer with an air of detached interest; Florence was here, and whilst Abigail had warned her of such a possible eventuality, her presence took Victoria by surprise, and she took a moment to come to terms. She had 'phoned Percival on her way, who had largely missed the events on the village Green in the morning, but by dint of intelligence that he had later gleaned was able to reassure her that the body on the Green had not been Rebecca, so she had not driven to the village, but as time had been pressing had come straight here, and would see Rebecca as soon as may be. It was time that they met, and she would go to the delicatessen, and by no means for the first time she cursed Rebecca for not turning on her telephone, something which she seldom if ever did unless it was she who instigated a conversation. So that was something for later, but for now her attention must be and was focussed on the assembly which was now before her. Her son, Henry, barely acknowledged her arrival, but continued his game with Nathaniel, and she was struck once again by the similarity between Nathaniel and the man with whom she had spoken but an hour previously. Such similarity, a thing of genetics, which had they been differently configured might have prevented so much, but there it was, and here was Florence, who as she grew into her childhood bore a striking similarity to her own mother. Victoria had met Rebecca when they had been teenagers at school, and as far as she knew only one photograph existed of Rebecca as a child, but that same child could have been standing before her now, studying her with studied intensity; such a beautiful child, who like her mother would doubtless grow into a beautiful woman, but how and why was she here? Abigail smiled somewhat wanly and knowingly at her employer, Elin's expression was hard to read, but maintained its accustomed Nordic neutrality, and it was Michael who first spoke.

'Hello Vics, we're just catching the last bit of sunshine, the evenings are getting colder, don't you think?'

Indeed they were, and the coldness was not confined to the weather, was it, Michael? An explanation was needed, as brother and sister both knew; Rebecca was not here, that was clear, but she had been here, and here was Florence, so how and why had that come to be? Victoria had come to discuss the future of their family; a thing of coldness and calculation, which seemed to Victoria to have little to do with the two boys who played ballgames together, and whose future was perhaps about to be decided, but also into the equation had now come Michael's daughter, born of the woman that she loved, and an explanation was needed before any of that could happen. She looked at her brother, who at last responded to her unspoken question.

'Let's go inside, shall we?'

Elin remained seated as Michael stood, and he and Victoria entered the house where such a significant moment in their family history had long ago been played out, when a once future Lord had been kept safe from the plague by his father's younger sister. Lord William, the fifth Lord Tillington, had died of the sickness in 1665, but here had his son, John, and John's sister, Margaret, been kept in isolation by Jane Tillington until the plague had abated, and they could more safely return to the Manor. The letters written by Jane to her brother, which she had written but had never been sent, were found here, hidden beneath the now warped and twisted floorboards for hundreds of years, until Michael had found them, and had decided to keep the house. Commercially this had been a near disaster for her brother, and had set his business back perhaps by years, but once the letters had been found there had been no choice in the matter; the history of the Tillington family was written into the walls of the old house, as clearly as if Jane herself still walked its rooms in all of her hunger, worry and uncertainty, and now her descendants, brother and sister, had their own part to play in the ancient and ever it seemed complex thing which was the Tillington dynasty. It was a history which was so much bigger than both of them, as both of them perhaps understood now more clearly than ever before, and they both felt the weight of it, but together they must decide how the history would be written by generations to come, but that, for now, was not the thing. For there was a more recent history to be discussed; an illegitimate daughter to the next Lord, who would no doubt make her own contribution to future history as she grew into womanhood, and who had today entered Glebe House for the first time.

'What's going on, Mike, why is Florence here?'

'Rebecca brought her here earlier today.'

'Yes, well I assumed that much, but did you know she was coming?'

'Yes, at least I knew it was likely to happen, although to be honest I received little warning.'

'So how long is she here for?'

'I don't know, a few days I would think, although Rebecca could not be certain.'

'So is Abigail okay with it?'

'Oh yes, she at least had fair warning that this might happen, and she's fine with having care of a third child, Nathaniel and Henry will have to double-up for the duration, but we've explained everything to them, and everyone's fine with the idea.'

'But, I mean, did Rebecca explain why now in particular?'

'No, and she has no need to. I mean the timing isn't perfect what with everything else that's going on, but such are the joys of parenthood, I suppose.'

'But what about Elin, is she fine with it, too?'

'She understands, Victoria. She and Rebecca don't exactly get on as you may imagine, but Rebecca wasn't here for long, and she understands that I have a daughter, however that came to be, which is no fault of Florence, and as such I have responsibilities, and to be honest I'm rather looking forward to having her about the place.'

'I see…'

'Well, then.'

Victoria took a moment to process this situation, and its implication. She was aware that Michael had by degrees and over time come to terms with the fact of Florence, and that whereas she assumed that many people would have wanted nothing to do with her, her brother had in the end embraced the idea of having a daughter, although in the strangest way imaginable he had had nothing to do with her conception, in any sense other than the purely biological. And now, for the first time, he and Rebecca were sharing the responsibilities of parenthood in more ways than the purely financial; Michael was being a parent to Florence, she was becoming a part of his life, and in her turn Victoria should embrace this, should she not, but such a coming together, of which she had had no prior intelligence, was something else which for now she was having some difficulty coming to terms, and why now, in particular?

There had been the dead body of a young woman on the village Green, and on the same day Rebecca had come to Glebe House, and left her daughter, and for now Victoria was being hard put to it not to connect the two unusual things, and where was Rebecca now? She had not come for this, she had come to decide the fate of her own offspring, and she must not allow it to distract her thoughts from her main purpose, but she allowed herself a moment of contemplation, before;

'So, anyway, I suppose we should get on with it, don't you think?'

'Yes, we should, I'll ask Abi to make tea, and we may as well go to the dining room, I think we've had the best of the day. Elin has some questions, of course, and seeks some reassurances, so as I mentioned, it's not cut and dried yet.'

'No, of course, but there's a big question, Mike, which you and I must decide, which is whether we're doing the right thing at all.'

'This was your idea, Vics, not getting cold feet, are we?'

'Well, no, but the point is, Mike, that you and I must be completely together on this. I need to be certain that you're doing this because you think it's the right thing to do, and not just because I came to you with the idea.'

'Yes, well, who knows what the right thing is to do, and I've thought about it a lot, but I'm no closer to answering that particular question, so I suppose we'll just have to sally forth and see where it all ends up, will we not? By the end of the evening we'll know, one way or the other.'

'Will we?'

'No, probably not, and a lot of water will have to flow under the proverbial bridge before we do, I'm sure, but that's life, don't you think? I mean I know what you mean, Vics, and it's not too late to change our minds and stop everything. We think we're in control, but perhaps we delude ourselves, and perhaps it's already too late. History may get the better of us all, and land us all in the shit, if you'll excuse the expression, but who knows, really?'

'Indeed, who knows, but what's also important to me, Mike, is that you and I don't fall out over this, now or in the future. I haven't always been the easiest or nicest of sisters, I know that, but I need you, Mike, and always have, and the thought that this could come between us is an unbearable thing for me.'

'Well, we've made it this far, have we not? Your lover has had my child, and I know you're wondering why she's here, and I can't really answer that, either, but the mere fact of it would have rent most people asunder, I daresay, but we've always been different, Vics. We are son and daughter to the aristocracy, and as much focus and conclusion as I'm able to bring to this tells me that we're going to do it, if we can, our own happiness or otherwise notwithstanding, and regardless of the rightness or otherwise of it. I mean look at this place, Vics, and just think of Jane, sister to Lord William, who had the house built for her, and how she suffered in this very room to keep John alive, and keep this whole bloody mess going, so maybe you're right, at least about that, maybe we should do it for her, if for nothing else. Fate may yet make fools of us all, but let's at least get the first hurdle over with, shall we?'

'Okay, Mike, let's do that, but first I need a cigarette, and I don't suppose we can smoke in the house, can we?'

'No, not really, although it has been known, but you're right, let's to the garden, and then let's begin, and hope that the Gods are with us.'

They walked out together, and there would be a meeting, but that now was mere formality; window dressing to convince all present, and particularly themselves, that they were being clever, and knowing, but neither of these would in the end be a given.

Three children, now all playing ballgames together with their nanny as best they could; the future, which would be their future, over which they would one day have control, but for now that future was being decided for them, for better or worse, and no one present could, if they searched deeply enough into their souls, say which of these it would be. So perhaps Michael was right; better not to search too deeply; best just to carry on, and hope that in the end, all would be well.

The by now well-established infamy of the village of Middlewapping had begun with the arrival one summer's night of a meteorite, which had landed on the cricket square, proof positive that events in the vastness of space and nature herself are no respecters of ballgames. Since this time, however, this formerly quiet backwater of southern England, which had for centuries gone about its quiet business, had gained quite other reputation. There was talk nowadays of witches, and curses, and of satanic sects. The dead body of a woman had after all been found here, an event which had never been explained, nor any cause of death verified, and now, another young woman had died under equally as yet unexplained circumstances, and with the advent of increased social media, news of this latest mystery quickly spread far and wide, adding yet more fuel to the fire of reputation and speculation. It was said by many that an ill wind indeed must blow through this place, and as metaphor would have it, someone would surely benefit, and one such beneficiary was a certain Mister Nigel Hollyman, worthy proprietor of the Dog and Bottle public house, who by dint of the village's repute and consequential increase in trade, had seen off attempts by the bigger breweries to take over his business. Instead he had remained staunchly independent, where other such establishments had failed in the face of social and economic change; Nigel Hollyman served fine ales, and wholesome fare, in a place which looked out over this now most infamous village Green, and as people will tend to gather at the scene of strange or macabre events, so once again did Nigel and his good wife, Susan, find themselves having to order extra barrels of ale, and Susan found herself hard at it to keep up with demand for the few choices of food on offer.

Nothing was said, or arranged, but on the evening following the discovery of the body, when, unbeknownst to him, Victoria was in discussion with Michael and Elin regarding the future of his son, Percival availed himself of said fine ale. He had come with Louise, she with whom he was by degrees finding a way to be at peace, as was she with him, their love for one another finding its way to the resolution of their differences, and their different expectations. Here also and without arrangement Keith had come, with Meadow, and these four now sat together at a corner table, because it was something which should be done. Of sects and witches, Louise knew only that which Percival had told her, and on his insistence she had stayed away from the village when Percival had considered it too dangerous for either of them to live at the cottage. Percival, Keith and Meadow, however, knew perhaps as much as anyone about such matters, and more in truth than any of them wished to know, and now there had been another body on the Green, so what of that?

'I mean it's weird, whichever way you look at it.'

This was Keith, who had bought drinks for everyone, and Percival replied.

'Yeah, you might say that.'

'I mean at least we know where Rebecca went after the event.'

'What do you mean?'

'She turned up at Glebe House today, complete with infant child.'

'What....? What the hell's Rebecca doing at Glebe House?'

'No idea, but there she was, large as life.'

'Was Victoria there?'

'Nope, just her and the little one...'

'What time was she there?'

'I don't know, we hadn't long started work so I suppose about nine o'clock.'

'Did you speak to her?'

'No, I kept away, I had some re-pointing to do so I kept out of it, Will said hello, but that was about it, and we left without seeing them. She wasn't there for long, anyway.'

'Christ...I don't get that. I mean I didn't even know they knew each other that well.'

'Rebecca's been a friend of the family for decades,' said Meadow.

'Yes, but even so, why go to Glebe House on her own?'

Percival took a moment to absorb this new intelligence, and Meadow in particular had been considering its implication since Keith had told her, for it was news which was worth the consideration.

'Nathaniel was already there, and what's his name, Henry, they're staying there while the filming's going on at the Manor, so now Abigail the nanny has three kids to look after.'

'What do you mean?'

'I mean Rebecca left quite quickly, but the little one stayed, whatever her name is.'

'Florence,' said Meadow.

'Yeah, that's her, nice looking kid, looks like her mum.'

'What,' said Percival 'so now Michael's providing childcare for Rebecca's child, what the hell's that about?'

'No idea, but that's the way it looked.'

'That makes no sense to me at all.'

'Yeah, I thought that, unless of course....'

'Keith...' Meadow had been ahead of her man's thought processes, and thought it better that nobody express them, but Keith apparently thought otherwise.

'What…? I perceive that something is going on here, or maybe better say has already gone on. I mean what other explanation is there? Looks like our Michael's been sowing his wild oats, and as ye sow….'

'We can't know anything for certain, Keith, and we mustn't start unsubstantiated rumours.'

'Who's doing that, there are only the four of us, and I'm not saying anything. Anyway what's her name, Florence, looks fairly substantial…I mean nobody has ever known who her father is, have they?'

'No, but still, you're making wild guesses.'

'Yeah, well, maybe, and who cares anyway, but it's a thought to conjure with, isn't it? I mean a dead person turns up on the Green, with no apparent injuries but which looks like foul play, Rebecca choses the next morning to disappear without warning, turns up at Mike's place and leaves her kid as though it's the most natural thing in the world. Like I said, weird stuff's happening.'

'All of that's true,' said Meadow 'but to have an affair with your sister's best friend is surely not in Mike's nature.'

'Yeah,' said Keith 'there's that, I mean Mike does come across as being the perfect gentleman, but even gentlemen have their moments of weakness, and if Rebecca dropped her knickers at the wrong time, or the right time, who knows what a man might all of a sudden find himself doing? Men can't always control stuff like that, speaking as a man.'

'You did…' said Meadow, who regretted the words as soon as they had left her mouth.

'What do you mean?' Said Percival.

'The lady tried it on with me, once, but I resisted manfully, I said *"Get thee gone, woman, for…."'*

'Yes, alright Keith, I think we get the general idea.'

The evening proceeded, the Dog and Bottle continued its brisk trade, and it was near to closing time before the four friends decided to head homeward. The two ladies retired briefly to the restroom, Percival went outside to light a cigarette, and for a moment he and Keith found themselves alone, and looking out over the Green, which was this evening bathed in gentle moonlight.

'So, what do you reckon, Keith, is this going to come back to bite us?'

'I don't know, man, but someone's going to pay for it, somewhere down the line. If Rebecca didn't kill her, whoever she was, then someone else did.'

'Who the hell was she?'

'That's the question, and probably the only person who knows isn't around to tell anyone. This is going to run, don't you think?'

'Yes, I believe it is.'

The small party walked together until their ways parted, as the last customers left the public house, leaving the village to the night. The last of the lights were turned off in upstairs windows, the moonlight faded as the moon continued on her celestial journey, and as all became dark, a brooding and uneasy silence fell upon the village Green.

END OF PART XV